In Freedom's Cause
A Story of Wallace and Bruce

A Meeting of Wallace and Bruce

G.A. Henty

Revised and Edited by Michael J. McHugh

Printed by
Christian Liberty Press
502 West Euclid Avenue
Arlington Heights, Illinois 60004
www.christianlibertypress.com

Cover Images by N. C. Wyeth

Cover design and graphics by Christopher D. Kou
Maps created by Timothy B. Kou
imagineering studios, inc.

Layout by Edward J. Shewan

ISBN 1-930092-20-2

Set in Trump Mediaeval

Printed in the United States of America

Preface

My Dear Lads,

There are few figures in history who have individually exercised so great an influence upon events as William Wallace and Robert Bruce. It was to the extraordinary personal courage, indomitable perseverance, and immense energy of these two men that Scotland owed her freedom from English domination. So surprising were the traditions of the feats performed by these heroes that it was at one time the fashion to treat them as belonging as purely to legend as the feats of St. George or King Arthur. Careful investigation, however, has shown that so far from this being the case, almost every deed reported to have been performed by them is verified by contemporary historians. Most of the information regarding the character of Sir William Wallace has, regrettably, come down to us principally by the writings of his bitter enemies, and even modern historians, who should have taken a fairer view of his life, repeated the cry of the old English writers that he was a blood-thirsty robber. Mr. W. Burns, however, in his masterly and exhaustive work, *The Scottish War of Independence*, has torn these accusations to shreds, and has displayed Wallace as he was, a high-minded and noble patriot. While consulting other writers, especially those who wrote at the time of or but shortly after the events they record, I have for the most part followed Burns in all the historical portions of the narrative. Throughout the story, therefore, wherein it at all relates to Wallace, Bruce, and the other historical characters, the circumstances and events can be relied upon as strictly accurate. The only exception concerns the earlier events of the career of Wallace, of which the details that have come down to us are somewhat conflicting, although the main features are now settled past question.

Yours sincerely,
G.A. Henty

Archie Forbes Defies Sir John Kerr

Contents

Introduction

In recent times, there has been a renewed interest in the study of Scottish history in general and in particular the lives of Sir William Wallace and Robert the Bruce. Major motion pictures and popular novels have featured one aspect or another of the titanic struggle that took place between England and Scotland during the late 1200s and early 1300s. The novel that follows provides readers with a stirring account of the exploits of Wallace and Bruce during the climactic days that preceded Scottish independence. This true adventure story clearly portrays how two men were instrumental in giving the land of Scotland its own national identity and political freedom.

The author, G. A. Henty (1832–1902), was one of the most respected historians and writers of his day. He wrote over 144 books of historical fiction covering a wide range of history topics from the fall of Jerusalem to the American War Between the States. Most of his historical narratives revolve around the adventures of some young boy who is caught up in a particular event of history. This writing technique helps younger readers to more easily relate to the study of history without getting lost in a sea of dry and impersonal details. The enduring popularity and esteem of Henty's writings is a fitting testimony to the quality of his work as a master storyteller.

Michael J. McHugh
Arlington Heights, Illinois
1998

The following novel, *In Freedom's Cause*, was revised and edited by Michael J. McHugh. He has worked in the field of Christian education for over twenty-five years with the Christian Liberty Academy of Arlington Heights, Illinois. During his time with the academy, Mr. McHugh has worked as a teacher, administrator, curriculum director, and textbook author.

As a father of seven children, Michael lives in the Chicago area where he is active as an elder in an independent Reformed Church by the name of Church of Christian Liberty.

No one wins when freedom fails,
Good men rot in filthy jails,
And those who cry, "Appease! Appease!"
Are hung by those they tried to please.

Scots Who Have

Scots, who have with Wallace bled,
Scots, whom Bruce has often led,
Welcome to your gory bed,
Or to victorie!

Now's the day, and now's the hour:
See the front o' battle lour,
See approach proud Edward's power—
Chains and slaverie!

Who will be a traitor knave?
Who can fill a coward's grave?
Who so base as be a slave?—
Let him turn, and flee!

Who for Scotland's King and Law
Freedom's sword will strongly draw,
Freeman stand or freeman fa',
Let him follow me!

By Oppression's woes and pain,
By your sons in servile chains,
We will drain our dearest veins
But they shall be free!

Lay the proud usurpers low!
Tyrants fall in every foe!
Liberty's in every blow!
Let us do, or die!

ROBERT BURNS, 1759–96

Chapter 1

Glen Cairn

T he village of Glen Cairn was situated in a valley lying to the west of the Pentland Hills, some fifteen miles north of the town of Lanark, Scotland. The country around it was wild and picturesque. The villagers for the most part knew little of the world beyond their own valley, although a few had occasionally paid visits to Glasgow, which lay as far to the west as Lanark was distant to the south. On a spur jutting out from the side of the hill stood Glen Cairn Castle, whose master the villagers had for generations regarded as their lord.

The glory of the little fortalice had now departed. Sir William Forbes had been killed on his own hearthstone, and the castle had been sacked in a raid by the Kerrs, whose lands lay to the southwest, and who had a long-standing feud with the Forbes clan.

The royal power was feeble, and the Kerrs had many friends, and were accordingly granted the lands they had seized; only it was specified that Dame Forbes, the widow of Sir William, should be allowed to reside in the fortalice free from all hindrance, so long as she meddled not, nor sought to stir up enmity among the late vassals of her lord against their new masters.

The castle, although a small one, was strongly situated. The spur of the hill ran some two hundred yards into the valley, rising sharply some thirty or forty feet above it. The little river which meandered down the valley swept completely round the foot of the spur, forming a natural moat to it, and had in some time past been damned back, so that, whereas in other parts it ran brightly over a pebbly bottom, here it was deep and still. The fortalice itself stood at the extremity of the spur, and a strong wall with a fortified gateway extended across the other end of the neck, touching the water on both sides. From the gateway of the hold itself, and between these walls and the water every level foot of ground was cultivated; this garden was now the sole remains of the lands of the Forbes clan.

It was a meager inheritance for Archie, the only son of Dame Forbes. His lady mother had hard work to keep up a respectable state and to make ends meet. Sandy Grahame, who had fought under her husband's banner and was now her sole retainer, made the most of the garden patches. Here he grew vegetables on the best bits of ground and oats on the remainder; these crushed between flat stones, furnished a coarse bread. From the stream an abundance of fish could always be obtained, and the traps and nets therefore furnished a meal when all else failed. In the stream, too, swam a score and more of ducks, while as many chickens walked about the castle yard, or scratched for insects among the vegetables. A dozen goats browsed on the hillside, for this was common ground to the village, and Dame Forbes had not therefore to ask for leave from her enemies, the Kerrs. The goats furnished milk and cheese, which was deftly made by Elspie, Sandy's wife, who did all the work indoors as her husband did without. Meat they seldom touched. Occasionally the resources of the small estate were enriched by the present of a little hill sheep, or a joint of prime meat, from one or other of her old vassals, for these, in spite of the mastership of the Kerrs, still at heart regarded Dame Mary Forbes as their lawful mistress, and her son Archie as their future chief.

Dame Mary Forbes was careful in no way to encourage this feeling, for she feared above all things to draw the attention of the Kerrs to her son. She was sure that did Sir John Kerr entertain but a suspicion that trouble might ever come from the rivalry of this boy, he would not hesitate a moment in commissioning his death. Sir John was a rough and violent man who was known to hesitate at nothing which might lead to his aggrandizement. Therefore she seldom moved beyond the outer wall of the hold, except to go down to visit the sick in the village. She herself had been a Seaton, and had been educated at the nunnery of Dunfermline, and she now taught Archie to read and write, accomplishments by no means common even among the better class in those days. Archie loved not books; but as it pleased his mother, and time often hung heavy on his hands, he did not mind devoting two or three hours a day to the tasks she gave him. At other times he fished in the stream, wandered over the hills and brought in the herbs from which Dame Forbes distilled the potions which she distributed to the villagers when sick.

Often he joined the lads of the village in their games. They all regarded him as their leader; but his mother had pressed upon him over and over again that on no account was he to assume any superiority over the others, but to treat them strictly as equals. Doubtless the Kerrs would from time to time have news of what was happening in Glen Cairn; and while they would be content to see him joining in the sports of the village lads, with seemingly no wish beyond that station, they would at once resent it did they see any sign on his part of his regarding himself as a chief among the others.

No inconsiderable portion of Archie's time was occupied in acquiring the use of arms from Sandy Grahame. His mother, quiet and seemingly resigned as she was, yet burned with the ambition that he should some day avenge his father's death, and win back his father's lands. She said little to him of her hopes; but she roused his spirit by telling him stories of the brave deeds of the Forbeses and Seatons, and she encouraged him from his childhood to practice in arms with Sandy Grahame.

In this respect, indeed, Archie needed no stimulant. From Sandy even more than from his mother he had heard of his brave father's deeds in arms; and although, from the way in which she repressed any such utterances, he said but little to his mother, he was resolved as much as she could wish him to be, that he would some day win back his patrimony, and honor his father's memory.

Consequently, upon every opportunity when Sandy Grahame could spare time from his varied responsibilities, Archie practiced with him, with sword and pike. At first he had but a wooden sword. Then, as his limbs grew stronger, he practiced with a blunted sword; and now Sandy Grahame had as much as he could do to hold his own with his pupil who was fifteen years of age.

At the time the story opens, in the springtime of the year 1293, he was playing at ball with some of the village lads on the green, when a party of horsemen was seen approaching.

At their head rode two men perhaps forty years old, while a lad of some eighteen years of age rode beside them. In one of the elder men Archie recognized Sir John Kerr. The lad beside him was his son Allan. The other leader was Sir John Hazelrig, governor of Lanark; behind them rode a troop of armed men, twenty in number. Some of the lads would have ceased from their play; but Archie exclaimed:

"Heed them not; make as if you did not notice them. You need not be in such a hurry to tip your caps to the Kerr."

"Look at the young dogs," Sir John Kerr said to his companion. "They know that their chief is passing, and yet they pretend that they see us not."

"It would do them good," his son exclaimed, "did you give your troopers orders to tie them up and give them a taste of our stirrup leathers."

"It would not be worth while, Allan," his father said. "They will all make stout men-at-arms some day and will have to fight under my banner. I care as little as any man what my vassals think of me, seeing that whatsoever they think they have to do mine orders. But it needs not to set them against one needlessly; so let the varlets go on with their play undisturbed."

That evening Archie said to his mother, "How is it, mother, that the English knight whom I today saw ride past with the Kerr is governor of our Scottish town of Lanark?"

"You may well wonder, Archie, for there are many in Scotland of older years than you who marvel that Scotsmen, who have always been free, should tolerate so strange a thing. It is a long story, and a tangled one; but tomorrow morning I will draw out for you a genealogy of the various claimants to the Scottish throne, and you will see how the thing has come about, and under what pretense Edward of England has planted his garrisons in this free Scotland of ours."

The next morning Archie did not forget to remind his mother of her promise.

"You must know," she began, "that our good King Alexander had three children—David, who died when a boy; Alexander, who married a daughter of the Count of Flanders, and died childless; and a daughter, Margaret, who married Eric, the young King of Norway. Three years ago the Queen of Norway died, leaving an only daughter, also named Margaret, who was called among us the 'Maid of Norway,' and who, at her mother's death, became heir-presumptive to the throne, and as such was recognized by an assembly of the estates at Scone. But we all hoped that the king would have male heirs, for early last year, while still in the prime of life, he married Joleta, daughter of the Count of Drew. Unhappily, on the nineteenth of March, he attended a council in the castle of Edinburgh, and on his way back to his wife at Kinghorn, on a stormy night, he fell over a precipice and was killed.

"The hopes of the country now rested on the 'Maid of Norway,' who alone stood between the throne and a number of claimants, most of whom would be prepared to support their claims by arms, and thus bring unnumbered woes upon Scotland. Most unhappily for the country, the maid died on her voyage to Scotland, and the succession therefore became open.

"You will see on this chart, which I have drawn out, the lines by which the principal competitors—for there were nigh upon a score of them—claimed the throne.

"Before the death of the maid, King Edward had proposed a marriage between her and his young son, and his ambassadors met the Scottish commissioners at Brigham, near Kelso, and on the eighteenth of July, 1290, the treaty was concluded. It contained, besides the provisions for marriage, clauses for the personal freedom of Margaret should she survive her husband; for the reversion of the crown failing her issue; for protection of the rights, laws, and liberties of Scotland; the freedom of the church; the privileges of crown vassals; the independence of the courts; the preservation of all characters and natural muniments;[1] and the holding of parliaments only within Scotland. It also provided that no vassal should be compelled to go forth of Scotland for the purpose of performing homage or fealty; and that no native of Scotland should for nay cause whatever be compelled to answer, for any breach of covenant or for a crime committed, out of the kingdom.

"Thus you see, my boy, that King Edward at this time fully recognized the perfect independence of Scotland, and raised no claim to any jurisdiction over it. Indeed, by Article I it was stipulated that the rights, laws, liberties, and customs of Scotland should remain forever entire and inviolable throughout the whole realm; and by Article V that the kingdom of Scotland shall

---

1. A means of protection or defense.

remain separate and divided from England, free in itself, and without subjection, according to its right boundaries, as heretofore.

"King Edward, however, artfully inserted a salvo, 'saving the rights of the king of England and of all others which before the date of this treaty belong to him or any of them in the marches or elsewhere.' The Scottish lords raised no objection to the insertion of this salvo, seeing that it was of general purport, and that Edward possessed no rights in Scotland, nor had any ever been asserted by his predecessors—Scotland being a kingdom in itself equal to its neighbor—and that neither William the Norman nor any of his successors attempted to set forward any claims to authority beyond the border.

"No sooner was the treaty signed than Edward, without warrant or excuse, appointed Anthony Beck the warlike Bishop of Durham, Lieutenant of Scotland, in the name of the yet unmarried pair; and finding that this was not resented, he demanded that all the places of strength in the kingdom should be delivered to him. This demand was not, however, complied with, and the matter was still pending when the Maid of Norway died. The three principal competitors—Bruce, Baliol, and Comyn—and their friends, at once began to arm; but William Frazer, Bishop of St. Andrews, a friend of Baliol, wrote to King Edward suggesting that he could act as arbitrator, and more than hinting that if he chose Baliol he would find him submissive in all things to his wishes. Edward jumped at the proposal, and thereupon issued summonses to the barons of the northern counties to meet him at Norham on the third of June; and a mandate was issued to the sheriffs of Northumberland, Cumberland, Westmoreland, York, and Lancaster, to assemble the feudal array at the same rendezvous.

"Now, you know, my son, that, owing to the marriages between royal families of England and Scotland, there has been a close connection between the countries. Many Scottish barons have married English heiresses and hold lands in both countries, while Scottish maidens have married English knights. Thus it happens that a great number of the Scottish nobility are as much Englishmen as Scotsmen, and are vassals to England for lands held there. Because four of the competitors—John Baliol, Robert

Bruce, John Comyn, and William Ross—are all barons of England as well as Scotland and their lands lying in the north, they were, of course, included in the invitation. In May, Edward issued an invitation to the Bishops of St. Andrews, Glasgow, and other Scottish nobles to come to Norham, remain there, and return, specially saying that their presence there was not to be regarded as a custom through which the laws of Scotland might in any future time be prejudiced. Hither then came the whole power of the north of England and many of the Scottish nobles.

"When the court opened, Roger Brabazon, the king's justiciary,[2] delivered an address, in which he stated that Edward, as lord-paramount of Scotland, had come there to administer justice between the competitors for the crown, and concluded with the request that all present should acknowledge his claim as lord-paramount. The Scottish nobles present, with the exception of those who were privy of the true motive behind this pretension, declared their ignorance of any claim of superiority of the King of England over Scotland.

"'By holy Edward, whose crown I wear, I will vindicate my just rights, or perish in the attempt,' insisted Roger Brabazon.

"However, he saw that nothing could be done at that hour, and adjourned the meeting for three weeks, at the end of which time the prelates, nobles, and community of Scotland were invited to bring forward whatever they could in opposition to his claim to supremacy.

"At the time fixed, the Scottish nobles again met, but this time on the Scottish side of the border, for Edward had gathered together the whole of the force of the northern counties.

"Besides the four claimants, whose names I have told you, were Sir John Hastings, Patrick Dunbar, Earl of March, William de Vesci, Robert de Pinkeny, Nicholas de Soulis, Patrick Galythly, Roger de Mandeville, Florence, Count of Holland, and Eric, King of Norway. With the exception of Eric, the Count of Holland, Dunbar, and Galythly, all of those were of Norman extraction, and held possession in England. When the meeting was opened the prelates and nobles present advanced nothing to

---

2. The chief political and judicial officer of the king; a judge of a superior court.

disprove Edward's claim, for which, indeed, my son, as every man in Scotland knows, there was not a shadow of foundation.

"The king's chancellor declared that there was nothing in these objections to Edward's claim, and therefore he resolved, as lord-paramount, to determine the question of succession. The various competitors were asked whether they acknowledged Edward as lord-paramount, and were willing to receive his judgment as supreme. In a moment of folly, these wretched traitors proceeded to barter their country for their hopes of a crown, acknowledged Edward as lord-paramount, and left the judgment in his hands.

"Bruce and Baliol received handsome presents for thus tamely yielding the rights of Scotland. All present at once agreed that the castles and strongholds of Scotland should be surrendered into the hands of English commanders and garrisons. This was immediately done; and thus it is, Archie, that you see an English officer lording it over the Scottish town of Lanark.

"Then every Scotsman was called upon to do homage to the English king as his lord-paramount, and all who refused to do so were seized and arrested. Finally, on the seventeenth of November last, 1292—the date will long be remembered in Scotland—Edward's judgment was given at Berwick, and by it John Baliol was declared King of Scotland.

"Thus for eighteen months Scotland was kept in doubt; and this was done, no doubt, to enable the English to rivet their yoke upon our shoulders, and to intimidate and coerce all who might oppose it."

"There were some that did oppose it, mother, were there not?—some true Scottish patriots who refused to own the supremacy of the King of England?"

"Very few, Archie. One Sir Malcolm Wallace, a knight of but small estate, refused to do so, and was, together with his eldest son, slain in an encounter with an English detachment under a leader named Fenwick at Loudon Hill."

"And was he the father of that William Wallace of whom the talk was lately that he had slain young Selbye, son of the English governor of Dundee?"

"The same, Archie."

"Men say, mother that although but eighteen years of age he is of great stature and strength, of very handsome presence, and courteous and gentle; and that he was going quietly through the streets when insulted by young Selbye, and that he and his companions being set upon by the English soldiers, slew several and made their escape."

"So they say, Archie. He appears from all description of him to be a remarkable young man, and I trust that he will escape the vengeance of the English, and that some day he may again strike some blows for our poor Scotland, which, though nominally under the rule of Baliol, is now but a province of England."

"But surely, mother, Scottish clans will never remain in such a state of shameful servitude!"

"I trust not, my son; but I fear that it will be long before we shake off the English yoke. Our nobles are for the most part of Norman blood; very many are barons of England; and so great are the jealousies among them that no general effort against England will be possible. No, if Scotland is ever to be freed it will be by a mighty rising of the common people, and even then the struggle between the commons of Scotland and the whole force of England aided by the feudal power of all the great Scottish nobles, would be will-nigh hopeless."

This conversation sank deeply into Archie's mind; day and night he thought of nothing but the lost freedom of Scotland, and vowed that even the hope of regaining his father's lands should be secondary to that of freeing his country. All sorts of wild dreams did the boy turn over in his mind; he was no longer carefree and light-hearted, but walked about moody and thoughtful. He redoubled his assiduity in the practice of arms; and sometimes when fighting with Sandy he would think that he had an English man-at-arms before him, and would strike so hotly and fiercely that Sandy had the greatest difficulty in parrying his blows, and was forced to shout lustily to recall him from the clouds. He no longer played at ball with the village lads; but, taking the elder of them aside, he swore them to secrecy, and then formed them into a band, which he called the Scottish Avengers. With them he would retire into valleys far away from the village, where none would mark what they were doing, and there they practiced with club and stake instead of broadsword and pike, defended narrow passes against an imaginary enemy, and, divided into two parties, did battle with each other.

The lads entered into the new diversion with spirit. Among the lower class throughout Scotland the feeling of indignation at the manner in which their nobles had sold their country to England was deep and passionate. They knew the woes which English domination had brought upon Wales and Ireland; and though as yet without a leader, and at present hopeless of a successful rising, every true Scottish patriot was looking forward to the time when an attempt might be made to throw off the English yoke.

Therefore the lads of Glen Cairn entered heart and soul into the projects of their "young chief," for so they regarded Archie, and strove their best to acquire some of the knowledge of the use of sword and pike which he possessed. The younger lads were not permitted to know what was going on—none younger than Archie himself being admitted into the band, while some of the elders were youths approaching manhood. Even to his mother Archie did not breathe a word of what he was doing, for he feared that she might be forced to reveal his plans. The good lady was often surprised at the cuts and bruises with which he returned home; but he always turned off her questions by muttering something about how hard country life can be, and so for some months the existence of the Scottish Avengers remained unsuspected.

Chapter 2

Leaving Home

O ne day when the "Avengers" were engaged in mock battle in a glen some two miles from the village they were startled with a loud shout of "How now, what is this uproar?" Bows were lowered and hedge-stakes dropped; on the hillside stood Red Boy, the henchman of Sir John Kerr, with another of the retainers. They had been crossing the hills, and had been attracted by the sound of shouting. All the lads were aware of the fact that Archie needed to avoid the notice of the Kerrs, and Andrew Macpherson, one of the eldest of the lads, at once stepped forward.

"We are playing," he said, "at fighting Picts against Scots."

This was the case, for the English were so hated that Archie had found that none would even in sport take that name, and the sides were accordingly dubbed Scots and Picts, the latter title not being so repugnant, and the companies changing sides each day.

"It looks as if you were fighting in earnest," Roy said grimly, "for the blood is streaming down your face."

"Oh, we don't mind a hard knock now and again," Andrew said carelessly. "I suppose, one of these days, we shall have to go out under Sir John's banner, and the more hard knocks we have now the less we shall care for them then."

"That is so," Roy said; "and some of you will soon be able to handle arms in earnest. Who are your leaders?" he asked sharply, as his eye fixed on Archie, who had seated himself carelessly on a rock at some little distance.

"William Orr generally heads one side, and I the other."

"And what does that young Forbes do?" Red Roy asked.

"Well, he generally looks on," Andrew replied in a confidential tone; "he is not much good with the bow, and his lady mother does not like it if he goes home with a crack across the face, and I don't think he likes it himself; he is but a poor creature when it comes to a tussle."

"And it is well for him that he is," Red Roy muttered to himself; "for if he had been likely to turn out a lad of spirit, Sir John would have said the word to me before now; but, seeing what he is, he may as well be left alone for the present. He will never cause trouble." So saying, Red Roy strolled away with his companion, and left the lads to continue their pretend fight.

News traveled slowly to Glen Cairn; indeed, it was only when a traveling chapman or peddler passed through, or when one of the villagers went over to Lanark or Glasgow, carrying the fowls and other produce of the community to market, that the news came from without.

Baliol was not king long before he discovered that his monarchy was but a nominal one. The first quarrel which arose between him and his imperious master was concerning the action of the courts. King Edward directed that there should be an appeal to the courts at Westminster from all judgments in the Scottish courts. Baliol protested that it was specifically agreed by the treaty of Brigham that no Scottish subject was liable to be called upon to plead outside the kingdom. Edward, nevertheless, openly declared, "Notwithstanding any concessions made before Baliol became king, I consider myself at liberty to judge in any case brought before me from Scotland, and would, if necessary, summon the King of Scots himself to appear in my presence." He then compelled Baliol formally to renounce and cancel not only the treaty of Brigham, but every stipulation of the kind "known to exist, or which might be thereafter discovered." Another appeal followed, and Baliol was cited to appear personally, but refused; he was thereupon declared contumacious by the English parliament, and a resolution was passed that three of the principal towns of Scotland should be "seized," until he gave satisfaction. All this was a manifest usurpation, even allowing Edward's claims to supremacy to be well founded.

At this moment Edward became involved in a quarrel with his own lord-superior Phillip, King of France, by whom he was in turn summoned to appear under the charge of rebellion. Edward met this demand by a renunciation of allegiance to Phillip and a declaration of war, and called upon Baliol for aid as his vassal; but Baliol was also a vassal of the French king, and had estates in France liable to seizure. He therefore hesitated. Edward further ordered him to lay an embargo upon all vessels in the ports of Scotland, and required the attendance of many of the Scottish barons in his expedition to France. Finding his orders disobeyed, on the 16th of October, Edward issued a writ to the sheriff of Northampton, "to seize all lands, goods, and chattels of John Baliol and other Scots."

The Scots leaders held a parliament at Scone. All Englishmen holding office were summarily dismissed. A committee of the estates was appointed to act as guardian of the kingdom, and Baliol himself was deprived of all active power; but an instrument was prepared in his name, reciting the injuries that he and his subjects had sustained at the hands of the English king, and renouncing all further allegiance. Following this up, a league was formed, offensive and defensive, between the French king and Scotland, represented by the prelates, nobles, and community. Edward Baliol, the king's son, was contracted to marry the French king's niece. Phillip bound himself to assist Scotland against any invasion of England, and the Scots agreed to cross the border in case Edward invaded France.

In making this alliance the Scots took the only step possible; for they had no choice between fighting England with France as their ally, or fighting France as the subjects of King Edward. The contest which was approaching seemed all but hopeless. The population of England was six times as large as that of Scotland, and Edward could draw from Ireland and Wales great numbers of troops. The English were trained to war by constant fighting in France, Ireland, and Wales; while the Scots had, for a very long period, enjoyed a profound peace, and were for the most part wholly ignorant of warfare.

Edward at once prepared to invade Scotland; in January he seized the lands owned by Comyn in Northumberland and sold them, directing the money to be applied to the raising and maintenance of one thousand men-at-arms and sixty thousand foot-soldiers, and in February issued a writ for the preparation of a fleet of one hundred vessels.

On the 25th of March, he crossed the Tweed with five thousand horse and thirty thousand footmen. The Scottish leaders were, of course, aware of the gathering storm and collecting their forces, attempted a diversion by crossing the border to the west and making a raid into Cumberland. King Edward, however, marched north and besieged Berwick, the richest and most flourishing of the towns of Scotland. With the exception of the castle, it was weakly fortified. The attack was commenced by the fleet, who were however repulsed and driven off. A land assault, led by the king in person, was then made; the walls were captured and the town completely sacked. The inhabitants were butchered without distinction of age, sex, or condition, and even those who fled to the churches were slain within the sanctuary. Contemporary accounts differ as to the numbers who perished on this occasion. Langtoff says four thousand; Hemingford, eight thousand; Knighton, another English writer, says seventeen thousand; and Matthew of Westminster, sixty thousand. Whichever of these writers is correct, it is certain that almost the whole of the men, women, and children of the largest and most populous Scottish town were butchered by the orders of the English king, who issued direct orders that none should be spared. From this terrible visitation Berwick, which was before called the Alexandria of the West, never recovered. The castle, which was held by Sir William Douglas, surrendered immediately; and Sir William, having sworn loyalty to the English king, was permitted to depart.

The English army now marched north. Patrick, Earl of Dunbar, was with King Edward; but his wife, a noble and patriotic woman, surrendered the castle to the Scots. The Earl of Surrey, with a powerful army, began a siege of the castle. The Scottish nobles and people marched in great numbers to defend the castle, but with little order and discipline. They were met by the troops under Surrey, whose forceful attack easily routed the Scottish gathering; no fewer than ten thousand being killed in the conflict and retreat. The English army was joined by fifteen thousand Welsh and thirty thousand from Ireland, and marched through Scotland. Many of the castles and towns opened their gates to Edward as he came, and the nobles, headed by James the Stewart, coming in and doing homage to him. Baliol was forced to appear in the churchyard of Strath-Cathro, near Montrose, arrayed in regal robes, and to resign his kingdom to the Bishop of Durham as Edward's representative, and to repeat the act a few days afterwards at Brechin in the presence of Edward himself. He was then, with his son, sent as prisoners to London, where they were con-

fined in the Tower for several years. From Brechin Edward
marched through the whole of Scotland, the country being considered as virtually part of England. Garrisons were placed in
every stronghold in the country, and many new castles were built
to dominate the people. The public documents were all carried
away to England, the great seal broken in pieces, and the stone of
Scone—upon which, for five hundred years, every Scottish monarch had been crowned—was carried away to Westminster,
where it has ever since formed the seat of the thrones upon which
English monarchs have been crowned.

The tide of war had not passed near Glen Cairn; but the excitement, as from time to time the news came of stirring events, was
very great. The tidings of the massacre of Berwick filled all with
consternation and grief. Some of the men left their homes and
fought at Dunbar, and fully half of these never returned; but great
as was the humiliation and grief at the reverses which had
befallen Scottish patriots, the feeling was even deeper and more
bitter at the readiness with which the Scottish nobles flocked in
to make their peace with King Edward.

It seemed so incredible that Scotland, which had so long suc-
cessfully resisted all invaders, should now tamely yield without
a struggle, that the people could scarce believe it possible that
their boasted freedom was gone, that the kingdom of Scotland
was no more, and that their country had become a mere portion
of England. Thus, while the nobles with their Norman blood and
connections accepted the new state of things contentedly
enough, well satisfied to have retained rank and land, a deep and
sullen discontent reigned among the people; they had been
betrayed rather than conquered, and were determined that some
day there should be an uprising, and that Scotland would make a
great effort yet for freedom. But for this a leader was needed, and
until such a one appeared the people rested quiet and bided their
time.

From time to time there came to Glen Cairn tales of the doings
of that William Wallace who had, when the English first garrisoned the Scottish castles, while Edward was choosing between
the competitors for her throne, killed young Selbye at Dundee,
and had been outlawed for the deed. After that he went and
resided with his uncle, Sir Ronald Crawford, and then with

another uncle, Sir Richard Wallace of Riccarton. Here he gathered a party of young men, eager spirits like himself, and swore perpetual hostility to the English.

One day Wallace was fishing in the Irvine when Earl Percy, the governor of Ayr, rode past with several soldiers. Five of them remained behind and asked Wallace for the fish he had taken. He replied that they were welcome to half of them. Not satisfied with this, they seized the basket and prepared to carry it off. Wallace resisted, and one of them drew his sword. Wallace grabbed the staff of his net and struck his opponent's sword from his hand; this he snatched up and stood on guard, while the other four rushed upon him. Wallace smote the first so terrible a blow that his head was cloven from skull to collar-bone; with the next blow he severed the right arm of another, and then disabled a third. The other two fled, and overtaking the earl, called on him for help; "for," they said, "Three of our number who stayed behind with us to take some fish from the Scot who was fishing are killed or disabled."

"How many were your assailants?" asked the earl.

"But the man himself," they answered; "a desperate fellow whom we could not withstand."

"I have a brave company of followers!" the earl said with scorn. "You allow one Scot to outmatch five of you! I shall not try to go after your adversary; for were I to find him I should respect him too much to do him harm!"

Fearing that after this adventure he could no longer remain in safety with his uncle, Wallace left him and took up his abode in Lag Lane Wood, where his friends joining him, they lived a wild life together, hunting game and making many expeditions through the country. On one occasion he entered Ayr in disguise; in the middle of a crowd he saw some English soldiers, who were boasting that they were superior to the Scots in strength and feats of arms. One of them, a strong fellow, was declaring that he could lift a greater weight than any two Scots. He carried a pole, with which he offered, to let any Scot strike him on the back as hard as he pleased, saying that no mere Scot could strike hard enough to hurt him.

Wallace offered him three groats for a blow. The soldier eagerly accepted the money, and Wallace struck him so mighty a blow that his back was broken and he fell dead on the ground. His comrades drew their swords and rushed at Wallace, who slew two with the pole, and when it broke drew the long sword which was hidden in his garments, and cut his way through them.

On another occasion he again had a fracas with the English in Ayr, and after killing many was taken prisoner. Earl Percy was away, and his lieutenant did not venture to execute him until his return. A messenger was sent to the Earl, but returned with strict orders that nothing should be done to the prisoner until he came back. The bad diet and foul air of the dungeon suited him so ill, after his free life in the woods, that he fell ill, and was reduced to so weak a state that he lay like one dead; the jailer indeed thought that he was so, and he was carried out to be cast into the prison burial-ground, when a woman who had been his nurse, begged his body. She had it carried to her house, and then discovered that life yet remained, and by great care and good nursing succeeded in restoring him. In order to prevent suspicion that he was still alive a fictitious funeral was performed. On recovering, Wallace had other frays with the English, all of which greatly increased his reputation throughout that part of the country, so that more adherents came to him and his band began to be formidable. He gradually introduced an organization among those who were found to be friendly to the cause, and by bugle notes taken up and repeated from spot to spot orders could be despatched over a wide extent of country, by which the members of his band knew whether to assembly or disperse, to prepare to attack an enemy, or to retire to their dwellings.

The first enterprise of real importance performed by the band was an attack by Wallace and fifty of his associates on a party of soldiers, two hundred strong, conveying provisions from Carlisle to the garrison of Ayr. They were under the command of John Fenwick, the same officer who had been at the head of the troop by which Wallace's father had been killed. Fenwick left twenty of his men to defend the wagons, and with the rest rode forward against the Scots. A stone wall checked their progress, and the Scots, taking advantage of the momentary confusion, made a furious charge upon them with their spears, cutting their way into the midst of them and making a great slaughter of men and horses. The English rode round and round them, but the Scots defending themselves with spear and sword, stood so staunchly together that the English could not break through.

The battle was long and desperate, but Wallace killed Fenwick with his own hand, and after losing almost a hundred of their number the English fled in confusion. The whole convoy fell into the hands of the victors, who obtained several wagons, two hundred carriage horses, flour, wine, and other stores in great abundance; with these they retired into the forest of Clydesdale.

The fame of this exploit greatly increased the number of Wallace's followers. So formidable did the gathering become that convoys by land to Ayr were entirely interrupted, and Earl Percy held a council of the nobility at Glasgow and consulted them as to what had best be done.

Finally, Sir Ronald Crawford was summoned and told that unless he induced his nephew to desist from hostilities they should hold him responsible and waste his lands. Sir Ronald visited the band in Clydesdale forest, and rather than harm should come upon him, Wallace and his friends agreed to a truce for two months. Their plunder was stowed away in places of safety, and a portion of the band being left to guard it, the rest dispersed to their homes.

Wallace returned to his uncle's but was unable long to remain inactive, and taking fifteen followers he went with them in disguise to Ayr. Wallace, as usual, was not long before he got into a quarrel. An English fencing-master, armed with sword and buckler, was in an open place in the city, challenging any one to encounter him. Several Scots tried their fortune and were defeated, and then seeing Wallace towering above the crowd he challenged him. Wallace at once accepted, and after guarding himself for some time, with a mighty sweep of his sword he cleft through the buckler, arm, headpiece, and skull. The English soldiers who were watching the duel at once attacked him; his friends rallied round him, and after hard fighting they made their way to the spot where they had left their horses and rode to Lag Lane Wood.

When Earl Percy heard that Wallace had been the leader in this fray, and found on inquiry that he had slain the sword-player in fair fight after having been challenged by him, he refused to regard him as having broken the truce, for he said the soldiers had done wrong in attacking him. Earl Percy was himself a most gallant soldier, and the extraordinary personal prowess of Wallace excited in him the warmest admiration, and he would gladly, if it had been possible, have attached him to the service of England. As soon as the truce was over Wallace again attacked the English. For a time he abode with the Earl of Lennox, who was one of the few who had refused to take the oath of allegiance, and having recruited his force, he stormed the stronghold called the Peel of Gargunnock, near Stirling. Then he entered Perth, leaving his followers in Methven Wood. Wallace soon learned that an English reinforcement was upon the march, so he formed an ambush and fell upon them and defeated them; and pressing hotly upon them entered so close to their heels into Kincleven Castle, that the garrison had not time to close the gate, and the place was captured. Great stores and booty were found here; these were carried to the woods, and the castle was burned to the ground, as that of Gargunnock had been, as Wallace's force was too small to enable him to hold these strongholds. Indignant at this enterprise so close to their walls the English moved out the whole garrison, one thousand strong, against Wallace, who had with him but fifty men in all. After a desperate defense in which Sir John Butler and Sir William de Loraine, the two officers in command, were killed by Wallace himself, the latter succeeded in drawing off his men; one hundred and twenty of the English were killed in the struggle, of whom more than twenty are said to have fallen at the hands of Wallace alone. Many other similar deeds did Wallace perform; his fame grew more and more, as did the feeling among the Scottish peasantry that in him they had found their champion and leader.

Archie eagerly drank in the tale of Wallace's exploits, and his soul was fired by the desire to follow so valiant a leader. He was now sixteen, his frame was set and vigorous, and exercise and constant practice with arms had hardened his muscles. He became restless with his life of inactivity; and his mother, seeing that her quiet and secluded existence was no longer suitable for him, resolved to send him to her sister's husband, Sir Robert Gordon, who dwelt near Lanark. Upon the night before he started she had a long talk with him.

"I have long observed, my boy," she said, "the eagerness with which you constantly practice at arms; and Sandy tells me he can no longer defend himself against you. Sandy, indeed, is not a young man, but he is still hale and stout, and has lost but little of his strength. Therefore it seems that though but a boy, you may be considered to have a man's strength, for your father regarded Sandy as one of the most stout and skillful of his men-at-arms. I know what is in your thoughts; that you long to follow in your father's footsteps, and to win back the possessions of which you have been despoiled by the Kerrs. But beware, my boy; you are yet but young; you have no friends or protectors, save Sir Robert Gordon, who is a peaceable man, and goes with the times, while the Kerrs are a powerful family, able to put a strong body in the field, and having many powerful friends and connections throughout the country. It is our obscurity which has so far saved you, for Sir John Kerr would crush you without mercy did he dream that you could ever become formidable; and he is surrounded by ruthless retainers, who would at a word from him take your life; therefore think not for years to come to match yourself against the Kerrs. You must gain a name and a following and powerful friends before you move a step in that direction; but I firmly believe that the time will come when you will become lord of Glen Cairn and the hills around it. Next, my boy, I see that your thoughts are ever running upon the state of servitude to which Scotland is reduced, and have marked how eagerly you listen to the deeds of that gallant young champion, Sir William Wallace. When the time comes I would hold you back from no enterprise in the cause of our country; but at present it is hopeless. Valiant as may be the deeds which Wallace and his band perform, they are as vain as the strokes of reeds upon armor against the power of England.

"But, mother, his following may swell to an army," insisted Archie.

"Even so Archie; but even as an army it would be but as chaff before the wind against an English array. What can a crowd of peasants, however valiant, do against the trained and disciplined soldiers from England. You saw how at Dunbar the Earl of Surrey scattered them like sheep, and then many of the Scottish nobles were present. So far there is no sign of any of the Scottish nobles giving aid or countenance to Wallace, and even should he gather

an army, fear for the loss of their estates, a jealousy of this young
leader, and the Norman blood in their veins, will bind them to
England, and the Scottish would have to face not only the army
of the invader, but the feudal forces of our own nobles. I say not
that exploits like those of Wallace do not aid the cause, for they
do so greatly by exciting the spirit and enthusiasm of the people
at large, as they have done in your case. They show them that the
English are not invincible, and that even when in greatly superior
numbers they may be defeated by Scots who love their country.
They keep alive the spirit of resistance and of hope, and prepare
the time when the country shall make a general effort. Until that
time comes, my son, resistance against the English power is vain.
Even were it not so, you are too young to take part in such strife,
but when you attain the age of manhood, if you should still wish
to join the bands of Wallace—that is, if he be still able to make
head against the English—I will not say nay. Here, my son, is
your father's sword. Sandy picked it up as he lay slain on the
hearthstone and hid it away; but now I can trust it with you. May
it be drawn some day in the cause of Scotland! And now, my boy,
the hour is late and you had best bed down, for you need to make
an early start for Lanark."

The next morning Archie started soon after daybreak. On his
back he carried a pack, in which was a new suit of clothes suitable for one of the rank of a gentleman, which his mother had
with great difficulty procured for him. He strode briskly along,
proud of the possession of a sword for the first time. It was in
itself a badge of manhood, for at that time all men went armed.

As he neared the gates of Lanark, he saw a party issue out and
ride toward him, and recognized in their leader Sir John Kerr.
Pulling his cap down over his eyes, he strode forward, keeping by
the side of the road that the horsemen might pass freely, but pay-
ing no heed to them otherwise.

"Hello, sirrah!" Sir John exclaimed, reining in his horse, "who
are you who pass a knight and a gentleman on the highway without tipping his cap in respect?"

"I am a gentleman and the son of a knight," Archie said, looking fearlessly up into the face of his questioner.

"I am Archie Forbes, and I tip my cap to no man living save
those whom I respect and honor."

So saying, without another word he strode forward to the town. Sir John looked darkly after him.

"Red Roy," he said sternly, turning to one who rode behind him, "you have failed in your trust. I told you to watch the boy, and from time to time you brought me news that he was growing up but a village runt. He is no runt, and unless I am mistaken he will some day be dangerous. Let me know when he next returns to the village; we must then take speedy steps for preventing him from becoming troublesome."

Chapter 3

Sir William Wallace

Archie's coming had been expected by Sir Robert Gordon, and he was warmly welcomed. He had once or twice a year paid short visits to the house, but his mother could not bring herself to part with him for more than a few days at a time. In his youth, Archie would be expected to focus on the rudiments of learning as were deemed useful at the time, but now that the time had come when it was needful that he should be perfected in the use of arms, Archie's mother felt it necessary to relinquish him.

Sir Robert Gordon had no children of his own, and regarded his nephew as his heir, and had readily undertaken to provide him with the best instruction which could be obtained in Lanark. There was resident in the town a man who had served for many years in the army of the King of France, and had been master of arms in his regiment. His skill with his sword was considered marvelous by his countrymen at Lanark, for the scientific use of weapons was as yet but little known in Scotland. This master swordsman had also, in several trials of skill, easily bettered the best swordsmen in the English garrison.

Sir Robert Gordon at once engaged this man as instructor to Archie. As his residence was three miles from the town, and the lad urged that two or three hours a day of practice would by no means satisfy him, a room was provided and his instructor took up his abode in the castle. Here, from early morning until night, Archie practiced, with only such intervals for rest as were demanded by his master himself. The latter, pleased with so eager a pupil, astonished at first at the skill and strength which he already possessed, and seeing in him one who would do more than justice to all the pains that he could bestow upon him, grudged no labor in bringing him forward and in teaching him all he knew.

"He is already an excellent swordsman," he said at the end of the first week's work to Sir Robert Gordon; "he is well-nigh as strong as a man, with all the quickness and activity of a boy. In straightforward fighting he needs but little teaching. Of the finer strokes he as yet knows nothing; but such a pupil will learn as much in a week as the ordinary slow-blooded learner will acquire in a year. In three months I warrant I will teach him all I know, and will be surprised if he is not a match for any Englishman north of the Tweed, save in the matter of downright strength; that he will get in time, for he promises to grow out into a tall and stalwart man. It will take a skilled champion to hold his own against him when he comes to his full growth."

In the intervals of pike and sword-play, Sir Robert Gordon himself instructed him in equitation; but the lad did not take to this so kindly as he did to his other exercises, saying that he hoped he should always have to fight on foot. Still, as his uncle pointed out that assuredly would not be the case, since in battle knights and squires always fought on horseback. Archie strove hard to acquire a firm and steady command of his horse. During the evening hours, Archie sat with his uncle and aunt, the latter reading, the former relating stories of Scottish history and of the doings and genealogies of great families. Sometimes there were friends staying in the castle; for Sir Robert Gordon, although by no means a wealthy knight, was greatly liked, and, being of an hospitable nature, was glad to have guests in the house.

Their nearest neighbor was Mistress Marion Bradfute of Lamington, near Ellerslie. She was a young lady of great beauty. Her father had been for some time dead, and she had but lately lost her mother, who had been a great friend of Lady Gordon. With her lived as companion and guardian an aunt, the sister of her mother.

Mistress Bradfute, besides her estate of Lamington, possessed a house in Lanark; and she was frequently at Sir Robert's castle, he having been named one of her guardians under her father's will. Often in the evening the conversation turned upon the situation of Scotland, the cruelty and oppression of the English, and the chances of Scotland some day ridding herself of the domination.

Sir Robert ever spoke guardedly, for he was one who loved not strife, and the enthusiasm of Archie caused him much anxiety;

he often, therefore, pointed out to him the madness of efforts of isolated parties like those of Wallace, which, he maintained, advanced in no way the freedom of the country, while they enraged the English and caused them to redouble the harshness and oppression of their rule. Wallace's name was frequently mentioned, and Archie always spoke with enthusiasm of his hero; and he could see that, although Mistress Bradfute said but little, she fully shared his views. It was but natural that Wallace's name should come so often forward, for his deeds, his hairbreadth escapes, his marvelous personal strength and courage, were the theme of talk in every Scottish home. The people near Lanark were particularly interested in talking about Wallace, for with his band he had taken up his abode in a wild and broken country known as Cart Lane Craigs, and more than once he had entered Lanark and had fights with the English soldiers there.

It was almost a year since the defeat of Dunbar; and although the feats of Wallace in storming small fortalices and cutting off English convoys had brought hope among the Scots and anger in the English, the hold of the latter on the conquered country appeared more settled than ever. Wallace's adherents had indeed gained in strength; but they were still regarded as a mere band of outlaws who might be troublesome, but were in no degree formidable.

Every great town and hold throughout Scotland was garrisoned by English with a force deemed sufficient to repress any trouble which might arise, while behind them was the whole power of England ready to march north in case it should be needful. It seemed, indeed, that Scotland was completely and forever subjugated.

One afternoon, when Archie had escorted Mistress Bradfute to Lamington, she said to him as he bade her farewell:

"I think you can keep a secret, Master Forbes."

"I trust so," Archie replied.

"I know how much you admire and reverence Sir William Wallace. If you will come hither this evening at eight o'clock you shall see him."

Archie uttered an exclamation of delight and surprise.

"Mind, Archie, I am telling you a secret which is known only to Sir William himself and a few of his chosen followers; but I have obtained his permission to divulge it to you, assuring him that you can be fully trusted."

"I would lay down my life for him," the lad said.

"I think you would, Archie; and so would I, for Sir William Wallace is my husband!"

Archie gave a gasp of astonishment and surprise.

"Yes," she repeated, "he is my husband. And now ride back to your uncle's. I left the piece of embroidery upon which I was working on your aunt's table. It will be a good excuse for you to ride over with it this evening." So saying she sprang lightly from the pillion on which she had been riding behind Archie. The lad rode back in wild excitement at the thought that before night he was to see the hero whose deeds had, for the last three years, excited his admiration and wonder.

At eight o'clock exactly he drew rein again at Lamington. He was at once admitted, and was conducted to a room where the mistress of the house was sitting, and where beside her stood a very tall and powerfully-built young man, with a singularly handsome face and courteous and gentle manner which seemed altogether out of character with the desperate adventures in which he was constantly engaged.

In Scotland the laws of chivalry, as they were strictly observed in the courts of England and France, did not prevail. Sir William Wallace had not received the order of knighthood; but in Scottish families the prefix of "sir" descended from father to eldest son, as it does in the present day with the title of "Baronet." Thus William Wallace, when his father and elder brother were killed, succeeded to the title. Knighthoods, or, as we should call them, baronetcies,[3] were bestowed in Scotland, as in England, for bravery in the field and distinguished services. The English, with their stricter laws of chivalry, did not recognize these hereditary titles; and Sir William Wallace and many of his adherents who bear the prefix of "Sir" in all Scottish histories, are spoken of without that title in contemporary English documents. Archie himself had inherited the title from his father; and the prefix was,

---

3. The title, rank, or status of a baronet who is a man who holds the lowest hereditary title in Britain—below a baron but above a knight.

indeed, applied to the heads of almost all families of gentle blood in Scotland.

"This, Sir William," Marion said, "is Sir Archibald Forbes, of whom I have often spoken to you as one of your most fervent admirers. He is a true Scotsman, and he yearns for the time when he may draw his sword in the cause of his country."

"He is over young yet," Sir William said, smiling; "but time will cure that defect. It is upon the young blood of Scotland that our hopes rest. The elders are for the most part but half Scots, and do not feel shame for their country lying at the feet of England; but from their sons I hope for better things. The example of my dear friend, Sir John Grahame, is being followed; and I trust that many young men of good family will soon join them."

"I would that the time had come when I too could do so, sir," Archie said warmly. "I hope that it will not be long before you may think me capable of being admitted to the honor of fighting beside you. Do you not remember that you yourself were but eighteen when you slew young Selbye?"

"I am a bad example to be followed," Sir William replied with a smile; "besides, God made an exception in my case and brought me to my full strength and stature a full four years before the time. Mistress Marion tells me, however, that you too are strong beyond your years."

"I have practiced unceasingly, sir, with my weapons for the last two years; and deem me not boastful when I say that my instructor, Duncan Macleod of Lanark, who is a famous swordsman, says that I could hold my own and more against any English soldier in the garrison."

"I know Duncan by report," Sir William replied, "and that he is a famous swordsman, having learned the art in France, where they are more skilled by far than we are in Scotland. As for myself, I must own that it is my strength rather than my skill which gives me an advantage in a conflict; for I put my trust in a downright blow, and find that the skill of my antagonist matters but little, seeing that my blow will always cleave through sword as well as helm. Nevertheless I do not decry skill, seeing that between two who are in any way equally matched in strength and courage the most skillful swordsman must assuredly conquer. Well, since that be the report of you by Master Duncan, I should think you might even take to arms at the age that I did myself; and when that time comes, should your intentions hold the same, and the English not have made an end of me, I shall be right glad to have you by my side. Should you, in any of your visits to Lanark—whither, Marion tells me, you ride frequently with Sir Robert Gordon—hear ought of intended movements of English troops, or gather any news which it may concern me to know, I pray you to ride hither at once. Marion has always messengers whom she may despatch to me, seeing that I need great care in visiting her here, lest I might be surprised by the English, who are ever upon the lookout for me. And now farewell! Remember that you have always a friend in William Wallace."

Winter was now at hand, and a week or two later Mistress Marion moved into her house in Lanark, where Archie, when he rode in, often visited her. In one of her conversations she told him that she had been married to Sir William nigh upon two years, and that a daughter had been born to her who was at present kept by an old nurse of her own in a cottage hard by Lamington. "I tell you this, Archie," she said, "for there is no saying at what time calamity may fall upon us. Sir William is so daring and careless that I live in constant dread of his death or capture. If it should ever become known that I am his wife, doubtless my estate would be forfeited and myself taken prisoner; and in that case it were well that my little daughter should find friends."

"I wonder that you do not stay at Lamington," Archie said; "for Sir William's visits to you here may well be discovered, and both he and you be put in peril."

"I would gladly do so," she said; "but as you may have heard, young Hazelrig, the governor's son, persecutes me with his attentions; he is moved thereto methinks rather by a desire for my possessions than any love for myself. He frequently rode over to Lamington to see me, and as there are necessarily many there who suspect, if they do not know, my secret, my husband would be more likely to be surprised in a lonely house there than he would be in the city, where he can always leave or enter our abode by the passage into a back street unseen by any."

A few days later Archie rode into Lanark bearing a message from his uncle; he had put up his horse, and was walking along the principal street when he heard a tumult and the clashing of swords. Archie naturally hurried up to see what was the cause of the fight, and he saw Sir William Wallace and a young companion defending themselves with difficulty against a number of English soldiers led by young Hazelrig, the son of the governor, and Sir Robert Thorne, one of his officers. Archie stood for a few moments irresolute; but soon the number of assailants increased as fresh soldiers responding to the sound of the fighting came running down the street. Sir William and his friend, although they had slain several, were greatly overmatched, and this fact caused Archie to hesitate no longer, but, drawing his sword, he rushed through the soldiers, and placed himself by the side of Wallace. As the fighting continued, Wallace recognized him with a nod.

"It is sooner than I bargained for, Sir Archie; but you are very welcome. Ah! that was well smitten, and Duncan did not overpraise your skill," he exclaimed, as Archie cut down one soldier, and wounded another who pressed upon him.

"They are gathering in force, Sir William," the knight's companion said, "and if we do not cut our way through them we shall assuredly be taken." Keeping near the wall they retreated down the street, Archie and Sir John Grahame, for it was he, clearing the way, and Wallace defending the rear. So terrific were the blows he dealt that the English soldiers shrank back from attacking him.

At this moment two horsemen rode up and reined in their horses to witness the fray. They were father and son, and the instant the eyes of the elder fell upon Archie he exclaimed to his son:

"This is good fortune. That is young Forbes fighting by the side of the outlaw Wallace. I will finish our dispute at once."

So saying he drew his sword, and urged his horse through the soldiers toward Archie; the latter equally recognized the enemy of his family. Sir John aimed a sweeping blow at him. The lad parried it, and, leaping back, struck at the horse's leg. The animal fell instantly, and as he did so Archie struck full on the helm of Sir John Kerr, stretching him on the ground beside his horse.

By this time the little party had retreated down the street until they were passing the house of Marion Bradfute. The door opened, and Marion herself cried to them to enter. So hemmed in were they, indeed, that further retreat was now impossible, and there being no time for hesitation, Wallace and his companions sprang in before their assailants could hinder them and shut the door behind them.

"Marion," Wallace exclaimed, "why did you do this? It mattered not were I killed or taken; but now you have brought danger upon yourself."

"But it mattered much to me. What would life be worth were you killed? Think not of danger to me. Angry as they may be, they will hardly touch a woman. But waste no time in talking, for the door will soon yield to their blows. Fly by the back entrance while there is time."

So saying, she hurried them to the back of the house, and without allowing them to pause for another word, almost pushed them out and closed the door behind them. The lane was deserted; but the shouts and clamor of the English soldiers beyond the houses rose loud in the air.

"Quick, Sir William," Sir John Grahame said, "or we shall be cut off! They will bethink them of the back way, and send soldiers down to intercept us."

Such indeed, was the case, for as they ran they heard shouts behind, and saw some English soldiers entering the other end of the lane. In front, however, all was clear, and running on they turned into another street, and then down to the gate. The guard, hearing the tumult, had turned out, and seeing them running, strove to bar their way. Wallace, however, cleared their path with sweeping blows of his sword, and dashed through the gates into the open country where they were safe. For some distance they ran without checking their speed, and then as they neared a wood, where they no longer feared pursuits, they broke into a walk.

"My best thanks to you," Wallace said to Archie. "You have indeed proved yourself a staunch and skillful swordsman, and Duncan's opinion is well founded. Indeed I could wish for no stouter sword beside me in a fight; but what will you do now? If you think that you were not recognized you can return to your uncle; but if any there knew you, you must even then take to the woods with me."

"I was recognized," Archie said in a tone of satisfaction. "The armed knight whom you saw attack me was Sir John Kerr, the slayer of my father and the enemy of my house. Assuredly he will bring the news of my share in the fight to the ears of the governor."

"I do not think that he will carry any news for some time," Sir William replied; "for that blow you gave him on the head must have well-nigh brought your quarrel to an end. It is a pity that your arm had not a little more weight, for then assuredly you would have slain him."

"But the one with him was his son," Archie said, "and would know me too; so that I shall not be safe for an hour at my uncle's."

"In that case, Sir Archie, you must needs go with me, there being no other way for it, and truly, now that it is proved a matter of necessity, I am glad that it has so chanced, since I see that your youth is indeed no drawback; and Sir John Grahame will agree with me that there is no better sword in my company."

"Yes, indeed," the young knight said. "I could scarce believe my eyes when I saw one so young bear himself so stoutly. Without his aid I could assuredly have made no way through the soldiers who barred our retreat; and truly his sword did more execution than mine, although I fought my best. If you will accept my friendship, young sir, henceforth we will be brothers in arms." Responding with pleasure, Archie grasped the hand which the young knight held out to him.

"That is well said, Sir John," Wallace assented. "Hitherto you and I have been like brothers; henceforth there will be three of us, and I foresee that the only difficulty we shall have with this our youngest relation will be to curb his courage and ardor. Who knows," he went on sadly, "but that save you two I am now alone in the world! My heart misgives me sorely as to the fate of Marion; and were it not for the sake of Scotland, to whom my life is sworn, I would that I had stopped and died outside her door before I entered and brought danger upon her head. Had I had time to reflect, methinks I would have done so; but I heard her call, I saw the open door, and without time for thought or reflection I leaped in."

"You must not blame yourself, Sir William," Grahame said, "for, indeed, there was no time for thought; nor will I that it could have been otherwise, even should harm befall Mistress Marion.

It is on you that the hopes of Scotland now rest. You have awakened her spirit and taught the lesson of resistance. Soon I hope that the fire now smoldering in the breast of every true Scotsman will burst into flame, and that Scotland will make a great effort for freedom; but were you to fall now, despair would seize on all and all hope of a general rising would be at an end."

Wallace made no reply, but strode silently forward. A short distance further they came to the spot where three of Wallace's followers were holding horses, for he had on his entry into Lanark, been accompanied by another of his party, who had been slain at the commencement of the fight. Wallace directed Archie to mount the spare horse, and they then rode to Cart Lane Craigs, barely a word being spoken on their journey.

Wallace's headquarters were upon a narrow shelf of rock on the face of a steep and craggy hill. It was well chosen against surprise, and could be held against sudden attack even by a large force, since both behind and in front the face of the hill was too steep to be climbed, and the only approach was by a steep and winding path which two men could hold against a host. The ledge was some fifty feet long by twelve wide. At the back a natural depression in the crags had been deepened so as to form a shallow cave just deep enough to afford a defense against the weather; here a pile of heather served as a bed for Wallace, Grahame, and one or two others of the leaders of his company, and here Wallace told Archie that his place was to be. On the ledge without were some low arbors of heather in which lay ten of Wallace's bravest companions; the rest of his band were scattered among the surrounding hills, or in the woods, and a bugle note repeated from place to place would call all together in a short space of time.

Of stores and provisions there was no lack, these having been obtained in very large quantities from the convoys of supplies and the castles that had been captured. Money, too, was not lacking, considerable amounts having fallen into their hands, and the peasantry through all the country round were glad in every way to assist the band, whom they regarded as their champions.

Archie sat down by Sir John Grahame, who gave him particulars regarding the strength of the various bands, their position, and rules which had been laid down by Wallace for their order, the system of signals and other particulars; while Wallace paced

"I have done with weeping"

restlessly up and down the narrow shelf, a prey to the keenest anxiety. Toward nightfall two of the men were despatched toward Lanark to endeavor to find out what had taken place there; but in an hour they returned with a woman, whom both Sir William and Archie recognized as one of the female attendants of Marion. A single glance sufficed to tell her tale. Her face was swollen with crying, and wore a look of horror as well as of grief.

"She is dead!" Wallace exclaimed in a low voice.

"Alas!" the woman sobbed, "that I should have to tell it. Yes, my dear mistress is dead; she was slain by the orders of the governor himself, for having aided your escape."

A groan burst from Wallace, a cry of horror and indignation from his followers. The former turned, and without a word strode away and threw himself upon the heather. The others, heart-struck at the cruel blow which had befallen their chief, and burning with indignation and rage, could only utter oaths of vengeance and curses on the English tyrants.

After a time Grahame went to the cave, and putting his hand on Wallace's shoulder strove to address a few words of consolation to him.

Sir William rose: "I have done with weeping, Grahame, or rather I will put off my weeping until I have time for it. The first thing to think of is vengeance, and vengeance I swear that I will have. This night I will strike the first blow in earnest toward freeing Scotland. It may be that God has willed it that this cruel blow, which has been struck at me, shall be the means of bringing this about. Hitherto, although I have hated the English and have fought against them, it has been fitfully and without order and method, seeing that other things were in my heart. Henceforth I will live but for vengeance and Scotland. Hitherto the English have regarded me as an outlaw and brigand. Henceforth they shall view me as an enemy to be dreaded. Sound the signal of assembly at once.

Signify that as many as are within reach shall gather below in two hours. There will be but few, for, not dreaming of this, the bands two days since dispersed. But even were there none but ourselves it would suffice. Tonight we will take Lanark."

Chapter 4

The Capture of Lanark

A low shout of enthusiasm rose from Wallace's followers, and they repeated his words as though it had been a vow: "Tonight we will take Lanark." The notes of bugle rang through the air, and Archie could hear them repeated as by an echo by others far away in the woods.

The next two hours were spent in cooking and eating a meal; then the party on the ledge descended the narrow path, several of their number bearing torches were soon met by fifteen men who were found gathered together.

In a few words the sad news of what had taken place at Lanark was related to them and the determination which had been arrived at, and then the whole party marched away to the west. Archie's heart beat with excitement as he felt himself engaged in one of the adventures which had so filled his thoughts and excited his admiration. An adventure, too, far surpassing in magnitude and importance any in which Wallace had hitherto been engaged.

It seemed almost like an act of madness for twenty-five men to attack a city garrisoned by over five hundred English troops, defended by strong walls; but Archie never doubted for a moment that success would attend the enterprise, so implicit was his confidence in his leader. When at some little distance from the town they halted, and Wallace ordered a tree to be felled and cleared of its branches. It was some eight inches in diameter at the butt and thirty feet long. A rope had been brought, and this was cut into lengths of some four feet. Wallace placed ten of his men on each side of the tree, and the cords being placed under it, it was lifted and carried along with them.

Before they started, Wallace briefly gave them his orders, so that no word need be spoken when near the town. The band were, when they entered, to divide in three. Sir John Grahame, with a party, was to make for the dwelling of Sir Robert Thorne. Auchinleck, who had arrived with a party summoned by the bugle, was to arouse the town and attack any parties of soldiers in the street, while Wallace himself was to assault the house of Hazelrig. He requested that Archie accompany him.

Knowing the town well, Wallace led the party to the moat at a spot facing a sally-port. They moved without a word being spoken. The men bearing the tree laid it noiselessly to the ground. Wallace himself sprang into the moat and swam across. The splash in the water attracted the attention of a sentry over the gate, who at once challenged. There was no answer, and the man again shouted, peering over the wall to endeavor to discover what had caused the splash. In a few vigorous strokes, Wallace was across, hauled himself up to the door, and with his heavy battle-ax beat on the chains which held up the drawbridge. Two mighty blows and the chains yielded, and the drawbridge fell with a crash across the moat.

Instantly, the men lifted the tree, and dashing across swung it like a battering-ram against the door—half a dozen blows, and the oak and iron yielded before it. The door was burst in and the party entered Lanark. The sentry on the wall had fled at once to arouse the garrison. Instantly the three leaders started to perform the tasks assigned to them. As yet the town lay in profound sleep, although near the gate, windows were opening and heads were being put out to ascertain the cause of the din. As the Scots ran forward they shouted "Death to the English, death to the bloody Hazelrig!" The governor had long been odious for his cruelty and tyranny, and the murder of Marion Bradfute had that day roused the indignation of the people to the utmost. Not knowing how small was the force that had entered the town, but hoping only that deliverers had arrived, numbers of the townspeople rose and armed themselves, and ran into the streets to aid their countrymen. Wallace soon arrived at the governor's house, and with a few blows with his ax broke in the door; then he and his followers rushed into the house, cutting down the frightened men as they started up with sudden alarm, until he met Sir John Hazelrig, who had snatched up his arms and hurried from his chamber.

"Villain!" Wallace exclaimed, seizing him by his throat; "your time has come to make atonement for the murder of my wife."

Then dragging him into the street he called upon the towns-people, who were running up, to witness the execution of their tyrant, and stepping back a pace smote off his head with his sword. Young Hazelrig was also killed, as were all soldiers found in the house. The alarm-bells were ringing, now, and in a few minutes the armed citizens swarmed in the street. As the English soldiers, as yet but scarce awake, and bewildered by this sudden attack, hurried from their houses, they were fallen upon and slain by Wallace and the townspeople. Some of those in the larger houses issuing forth together were able to cut their way through and to make their escape by the gates; many made for the walls, and dropping in the moat swam across and escaped; but two hundred and fifty of their number were left dead in the streets. The town, once cleared of the English, gave itself up to wild rejoicing; bonfires were lit in the streets, the bells were rung, and the wives and daughters of the citizens issued out to join in their rejoicing and applaud their liberators.

Wallace held council at once with the chief citizens of Lanark. Their talk was a grave one, for though rejoicing in the liberation of the city, they could not but perceive that the situation was a serious one. By the defeat and destruction of the garrison, and the slaying of the governor, the town would bring upon itself the terrible wrath of King Edward, and of what he was capable the murdered thousands at Berwick sufficiently attested. However, the die was cast and there was no drawing back, and the town leaders undertook to put their town in a state of full defense. They determined to furnish a contingent of fighting men to Wallace, and to raise a considerable sum of money to aid him in the carrying on of the war; while he on his part undertook to endeavor, as fast as possible, to prevent the English from concentrating their forces for a siege of the town, by so harassing their garrisons elsewhere that none would be able to spare troops for any general purposes.

Proclamations were immediately made out in the name of Wallace, and were sent off by mounted messengers throughout the country. In these he announced to the people of Scotland that he had raised the national banner and had commenced a war for the freeing of the country from the English, and that as a first step he had captured Lanark. He called upon all true Scots to rally round him.

While the council was being held, the wives of the town leaders had taken the body of Marion from the place where it had been cast, and where hitherto none had dared to touch it, and had prepared it for burial, placing it in a stone coffin, such as were in use in those days, upon a cart which was covered with trappings of white and green boughs. Soon after daybreak a great procession was formed, and accompanied by all the matrons and maids of Lanark the body was conveyed to the church. This sad duty ended, Wallace mounted his horse and rode for Cart Lane Craigs, which he had named as the rendezvous where all who loved Scotland and would follow him, were to assemble. Archie rode first to Sir Robert Gordon's. His uncle received him kindly.

"Ah! my boy," he said, "I feared that your willful disposition would have its way. You have embarked young on a stormy course, and none can say where it will end. I myself have no hope that it can be successful. Did the English rule depend solely on the troops which garrison our towns and fortresses; I should believe that Wallace might possibly expel them; but this is as nothing. Edward can march a hundred and fifty thousand trained soldiers hither, and how will it be possible for any gathering of Scotsmen to resist these? However, you have chosen your course, and as it is too late to draw back now, I would not dispirit you. Take the best of my horses from the stable, and such arms and armor as you may choose from the walls. Here is a purse for your own private needs, which I pray you would share with Sir William Wallace. Fighting never was in my way, and I am too old to begin now. Tell him, however, that my best wishes are with him. I have already sent word to all my tenants that they are free, if they choose, to follow his banner."

"You have plenty of pikes and swords in the armory, uncle; weapons will be very useful; can I take some of them?"

"Certainly, Archie, as many as you like. But your aunt wants you to ride at once to Glen Cairn, to ask your mother to come over here and take up her abode till the stormy times are over. The news of last night's doings in Lanark will travel fast, and she will be terribly anxious. Besides, as the Kerrs are heart and soul with the English faction, they will likely take the opportunity during these turbulent times, and of your being involved in the rising, to destroy your castle altogether, seeing that so long as it stands there it is a sort of symbol that their lordship over the lands is disputed."

"The very thing that I was going to ask you, uncle. My mother's position at Glen Cairn would always be on my mind. As to the Kerrs, let them burn the castle if they will. If the rising fail, and I am killed, the line will be extinct, and it matters little about our hold. If we succeed, then I shall reign on my own, and shall turn the tables on the Kerrs, and will rebuild Glen Cairn twice as strong as before. And now can I take a cart to convey the arms?"

"Certainly, Archie; and may they be of service in the cause. You will, I suppose, conduct your mother hither?"

Archie replied that he would do so, and then at once made his preparations for the start. His uncle's armory was well supplied, and Archie had no difficulty in suiting himself. For work like that which he would have to do he did not care to encumber himself with heavy armor, but chose a light but strong steel cap, with a curtain of mail falling so as to guard the neck and ears, leaving only the face exposed, and a shirt of the same material. It was of fine workmanship and of no great weight, and did not hamper his movements. He also chose some leg-pieces for wearing when on horseback. He had already his father's sword, and needed only a light battle-ax and a dagger to complete his offensive equipment. Then he took down from the racks twenty swords and as many short pikes, and bonnets strengthened with iron hoops, which, although light, were sufficient to give much protection to the head. These were all placed in a light cart, and with one of his uncle's followers to drive, he took his seat in the cart, and started for Cart Lane Craigs.

Here he concealed the arms in a thicket, and then went up to speak to his leader.

"May I take ten men with me to Glen Cairn, Sir William? I am going to fetch my mother to reside with my uncle until the storm is over. He has sent you a hundred pounds toward the expenses of the struggle. I want the guard because it is possible that the Kerrs may be down there. I hear Sir John was carried away three hours after the fight, in a litter; it was well for him that he was not in Lanark when we took it. But if he is well enough to give orders, he may decide to send troops down to Glen Cairn to see if I have returned, and may burn the hold over my mother's head."

"Certainly," Sir William replied. "Henceforth I will put twenty men under your special orders, but for today Sir John Grahame shall lend you some of his own party. Of course they will go well-armed."

Half riding in the cart and half walking by turns, the party reached Glen Cairn late in the afternoon. The news of the fall of Lanark had already penetrated even to that quiet village, and there was great excitement as Archie and his party came in. One of Wallace's messengers had passed through, and many of the men were preparing to join him. Dame Forbes was at once proud and grieved when Archie told her of the share which he had had in the street fray at Lanark, and in the capture of the town. She was proud that her son had distinguished himself, at so young an age, but was grieved to see that he had become committed to a movement of whose success she had but little hope. However, she could not blame him, as it seemed as if his course had been forced upon him. She agreed to leave her home early the next morning.

It was well for Archie that he had brought a guard with him, for before he had been an hour in the hold a boy ran in from the village saying that a party of the Kerrs was close at hand, and would be there in a few minutes. Archie set his men at once to pile up a barricade of stones breast-high at the outer gate, and took his position there with his men. He had barely completed his preparations when the trampling of horses was heard and a party of ten men, two of whom bore torches, headed by young Allan Kerr, rode up. They drew rein abruptly as they saw the barricade with the line of pikes behind it.

"What do you want here, Allan Kerr?" Archie said.

"I came in search of you, little traitor," young Kerr replied angrily.

"Here I am," Archie said; "why don't you come and take me?"

Allan saw that the number of the defenders of the gate exceeded that of his own party, and there might, for all he knew, be more within.

"I will take you tomorrow," he said.

"Tomorrow never comes," Archie replied with a laugh. "Your father thought to take me yesterday. How is the good knight? Not suffering, I trust, greatly, either in body or temper?"

"You shall repent this, Archibald Forbes," Allan Kerr exclaimed furiously. "It will be my turn next time."

And turning his horse he rode off at full speed, attended by his followers.

"We had best start at once, Master Archie," Sandy Grahame said, "it is eight miles to the Kerr's hold, and when Allan Kerr returns there you may be sure they will call out their vassals and will be here early in the morning. Best get another cart from the village, for your men are weary and footsore, seeing that since last night they have been marching without ceasing. Elspie will by this time have gotten supper ready. There was a row of ducks and chickens on the spit when I came away."

"That is a good plan, Sandy. Please begin to assemble the men and help my mother pack up those things she most values, and I will go down to the village for the cart, for I wish to speak with someone there."

Archie had no difficulty in locating two carts, as he thought that one would be needed for his mother and what possessions she might take. Then he went from house to house and saw his old companions, and told them of his plans, which filled them with delight. Having done this he returned to the hold, hastily ate the supper which had been put aside for him, and then saw that his mother's chests, which contained all her possessions save a few articles of heavy furniture, were placed in one of the carts. A bed was then laid on its floor upon which she could sit comfortably. Elspie mounted with her. Archie, Sandy, and the men took their places in the other carts, and the party drove off. They had no fear of interruption, for the Kerrs, ignorant of the number who had arrived with Archie at Glen Cairn, would not venture to attack until they had gathered a considerable force, and would not be likely to set out till morning, and long before that time Dame Forbes would have arrived at her sister's.

The journey was indeed performed without incident, the escort leaving them when they came within two or three miles of Lanark. The moment Archie had seen his mother safely to Sir Robert Gordon's, he began to return to Glen Cairn.

As soon as it was daylight he walked out a mile on the road toward Glen Cairn. He soon saw a party approaching in military order. They halted when they reached him. They were twenty in number, and were the lads of his band at Glen Cairn, ranging between the ages of sixteen and eighteen. They had originally been stronger, but some of the elders had already joined Wallace's followers.

"Now," Archie said, "I can explain matters further than I did last night. I have procured arms for you all, and I hope that you will have opportunities of using them. But though some of you are old enough to join Wallace's band, there are others whom he might not deem fit to take part in such desperate enterprises. Therefore at first make but little show of your arms. I shall present you to Sir William, telling him that I have brought you hither to serve as messengers, and to enter towns held by the English and gather news, seeing that lads would be less suspected than men. But I suppose further, what I shall not tell him, that you shall form a sort of bodyguard to him. He takes not sufficient care of himself, and is ever getting into perils. I propose that without his knowing, you shall be ever at hand when he goes into danger of any sort, and may thus prevent his falling into the hands of his enemies. Now mind, lads, this is a great and honorable mission. You must be discreet as well as brave and ready, all of you, to give your lives, if need be, for that of Scotland's champion. Your work as messengers and scouts will be arduous and wearisome. You must be quiet and well-behaved—remember that boys' tricks and play are out of place among men engaged in a desperate enterprise. Mingle not much with the others. Be active and prompt in obeying orders, and be assured that you will have opportunities of winning great honor and credit, and of having your full share of hard knocks. You will, as before, be divided into two companies, William Orr and Andrew Macpherson being your lieutenants in my absence. You will obey their orders as implicitly as mine. Cluny, you have, I suppose brought, as I bade you last night, some of your sister's garments?"

"Yes, Sir Archie," the boy who was fair and slight, said, with a smile on his face.

"That is right. I know you are as handsome and strong as the rest; but seeing that your face is the smoothest and softest of any, you will do best should we need one in disguise as a girl. And now come with me. I will show you where your arms are placed; but at present you must not take them. If I led you as an armed band to Wallace, he might deem you too young. I must present you merely as lads whom I know to be faithful and trustworthy, and who are willing to act as a messengers and scouts to his force."

So saying, Archie led the band to the thicket where he had placed their arms; and the lads were pleased when they saw the pikes, swords, and headpieces. Then he led them up the craig to Wallace.

"Why, whom have you here?" Sir William exclaimed in surprise. "This will not do, Sir Archie. All lads are not like yourself, and were I to take such boys into my ranks I should have all the mothers in Scotland calling out against me."

"I have not brought them to join your ranks, Sir William, although many of them are stout fellows who might do good service at a pinch. I have brought them to act as messengers and scouts. They can carry orders whithersoever you may have occasion to send. They can act as scouts to warn you of the approach of an enemy; or if you need news of the state of any of the enemy's garrisons, they can go thither and enter without being suspected, when a man might be questioned and stopped. They are all sons of my father's vassals at Glen Cairn, and I can answer for their fidelity. I will take them specially under my own charge, and you will ever have a fleet and active messenger at hand when you desire to send an order."

"The idea is not a bad one," Sir William replied; "and in such a way a lad may well do the work of a man. Very well, Sir Archie, since you seem to have set your mind upon it I will not say nay. At any rate, we can give the matter a trial, understanding that you take the charge of them and are responsible for them in all ways. Now lads," he said turning, "you have heard that your lord, for he is your rightful lord, and will, if Scotland gains the day, be your real lord again, has answered for you. It is no boys' play in which you have taken service, for the English, if they conquer us, will show no further mercy to you than to others of my band. I understand then that you are all prepared, if need be, to die for Scotland. Is this so?"

"We are, sir," the lads exclaimed together.

"Then so be it," Sir William said. "Now, Sir Archie, do begin to fix a place for their encampment, and make such other arrangements as you may think fit. You will, of course, draw rations and other necessaries for them as regular members of the band."

Archie descended with his troop from the craigs, and chose a spot where they would be apart from the others. It was a small piece of ground cut off by the stream which wound at the foot of the craigs, so that to reach it, it was necessary to wade knee-deep through the water. This was no inconvenience to the lads, all of whom, as was common with their class at the time, were accustomed to go barefoot, although they sometimes wore a sort of sandal. Bushes were cut down, and arbors made capable of containing them. The spot was but a little distance from the foot of the path up the craigs, and any one descending the path could be seen from it.

Archie gave orders that one was always to be above in readiness to start instantly with a message; that a sentry was to be placed at the camp, who was to keep his eyes upon the path, and the moment the one on duty above was seen to leave, the next upon the list was to go up and take his place. None were to wander about the wood, but all were to remain in readiness for any duty which might be required. The two lieutenants were charged to drill them constantly at their exercises so as to accustom them to the weight and handle of their arms. Two were to be sent off every morning to the depot where the provisions were issued, to draw food for the whole for the day, and four were to be posted five miles away on the roads leading toward the craigs to give warning of the approach of any enemies. These were to be relieved every six hours. They were to be entirely unarmed, and none were to issue from the camp with arms except when specially ordered.

Having made these arrangements, and taking with him one of the band as the first on duty above, he rejoined Wallace at his post on the craigs.

Wallace's numbers now increased fast. On hearing of the fall of Lanark, and on the receipt of the proclamation calling upon all true Scots to join him in his effort to deliver their country from its yoke, the people began to flock in great numbers. Richard Wallace of Riccarton and Robert Boyd came in with such force as they could collect from Kyle and Cunningham, among them were not less than one thousand horsemen. Sir John Grahame, Sir

John of Tinto and Auchinleck assembled about three thousand mounted troops and a large number of footmen, many of whom, however, were imperfectly armed. Sir Ronald Crawford, Wallace's uncle, being so close to Ayr, could not openly join him, but secretly sent reinforcements and money. Many other gentlemen joined with their followers.

The news of the fall of Lanark and of the numbers who were flocking to join Wallace paralyzed the commanders of the English garrisons, and for a time no steps were taken against him; but news of the rising was instantly sent to King Edward, who, furious at this fresh trouble in Scotland, which he had deemed finally conquered, instantly commenced preparations for another invasion. A body of troops was at once sent forward from England, and being strengthened by bodies drawn from all the garrisons, assembled at Biggar. The army was commanded by the Earl of Kent. Heralds were sent to Wallace offering him not only pardon but an honorable post if he would submit, but warning him that if he refused this offer he should, when taken, be treated as a rebel and hung.

Wallace briefly refused submission, and said that he should be ready to give battle on the following morning.

At daybreak the army set forth, divided into three parts. Wallace, with Boyd and Auchinleck, commanded one; Sir John Grahame, with Wallace of Riccarton, the second; Sir Walter of Newbigging, with his son David and Sir John Clinto, the third. The cavalry were placed in front. The footmen, being imperfectly armed and disciplined, and therefore unable to withstand the first charge of the English, followed the cavalry.

Before marching forward Wallace called the commanders round him and charged them earnestly to restrain their men from plunder until the contest was decided, pointing out that many a battle had been lost owing to the propensity of those who gained the first advantage to scatter for plunder. Just as the Scots were moving, a body of three hundred horsemen, well armed and equipped, from Annandale and Eskdale, led by Halliday, Kirkpatrick, and Jardine, joined them; and with this accession of strength they marched forward confidently against the enemy.

Chapter 5

A Treacherous Plot

So rapid was the advance of Wallace's army that the English had little time to form before the Scots were upon them. The bold Scots charged with extreme impetuosity among the English ranks, directing the onslaught principally against the center, commanded by the Earl of Kent.

The English resisted stoutly; but the Earl of Kent was struck down by Wallace himself, and was with difficulty borne off the field; and after severe fighting the whole English army was thrown into disorder and retreated. Some hundreds were killed in the action and many more in the pursuit which followed; this, however, Wallace would not allow to be pushed too far lest the fugitives should rally and turn. Then the victorious Scots returned to the English camp. In this was found a great abundance of provisions, arms, and other valuable booty. Many of the cattle were killed, and a sumptuous feast prepared. Then Wallace had the whole of the spoil carried off into a place of safety in the heart of a neighboring bog, and he himself fell back to that shelter.

In the morning the English, who had rallied when the pursuit had ceased, again advanced, hoping to find Wallace unprepared. They were now commanded by the Earl of Lancaster, and had received some reinforcements in the night. They passed over the scene of the previous day's battle, and at last came in sight of the Scottish army. Wallace at first advanced, and then, as if dismayed at their superior strength, retired to the point where, in order to reach them, the English would have to cross a portion of the bog. The surface was covered with moss and long grass, and the treacherous nature of the ground was unperceived by the English, who, filled with desire to wipe out their defeat of the preceding day, charged impetuously against the Scottish line. The movement was fatal, for as soon as they reached the treacherous ground their horses sunk to the saddle-girths. The Scots had dismounted on firmer ground behind, and now advanced to the attack, some working round the flanks of the morass, others crossing on tufts of grass, and so fell upon the struggling mass of English. The Earl of Westmoreland and many others of note were killed, and the Earl of Lancaster, with the remains of his force, at once retreated south and recrossed the border.

Archie had taken no part in the first battle. Wallace had asked him whether he would fight by his side or take the command of a body of infantry; and he chose the latter alternative. Almost all the knights and gentlemen were fighting on horse with their followers, and Archie thought if these were repulsed the main burden would fall upon the infantry. On this occasion, then, he gathered with his band of lads a hundred or so pikemen,[4] and formed them in order, exhorting them, whatever happened, to keep together and to stand stoutly even against a charge of horse. As the victory was won entirely by the cavalry he had no opportunity of distinguishing himself. Upon the second day, however, he did good service, as he and his lightly armed footmen were able to cross the bog with relative ease.

The victory at Biggar still further swelled Wallace's forces. Sir William Douglas joined him, and other gentlemen. A great meeting was held at Forest Kirk, when all the leaders of Wallace's force were present; and these agreed to acknowledge him as general of the Scottish forces against England, with the title of Guardian of Scotland.

King Edward was at this time busied with his wars in France, and was unable to dispatch an army capable of effecting the reconquest of that portion of Scotland now held by Wallace; and as the English forces in the various garrisons were insufficient for such a purpose, the Earl of Percy and the other leaders proposed a truce. This proposal was agreed to. Although Wallace was at the head of a considerable force, Sir William Douglas was the only one among the Scottish nobles of importance who had joined him; and although the successes which he had gained were considerable, but little had been really done toward freeing Scotland, all of whose strong places were still in the hands of the English, and King Edward had not as yet unleashed his full strength.

---

4. Soldiers armed with pikes—weapons formerly used by foot soldiers, consisting of metal spearheads on long wooden shafts.

The greater portion of the army of Wallace was not dispersed. Shortly afterward the governor of Ayr issued a notice that a great council would be held at that town, and all the Scottish gentlemen of importance in the district were desired to attend. Wallace was one of those invited; and deeming that the governor might have some proposition of Edward to lay before them, he agreed to do so. Although a truce had been arranged, he himself with a band of his most devoted followers still remained under arms in the forest, strictly keeping the truce, but holding communications with his friends throughout the country, urging them to make every preparation, by collecting arms and exercising their vassals, to take the field with a better appointed force at the conclusion of the truce. Provisions and money were in abundance, so large had been the captures effected; but Wallace was so accustomed to the free life of the woods that he preferred to remain there to taking up abode in a town. Moreover, here he was safe from treachery; for he felt sure that although the English nobles and leaders would be incapable of breaking a truce, yet that there were many of lower degree who would not hesitate at any deed of treachery by which they might gain reward and credit from their king. Archie's band provided the greatest service as messengers; and although he sometimes spent a few days at Sir Robert Gordon's with his mother, he generally remained by the side of Wallace. The spot where the Scottish leader was now staying lay about half way between Lanark and Ayr.

Archie heard with uneasiness the news of the approaching council, and Wallace's acceptance of the invitation. The fact that the Earl of Percy, a very noble knight and gentleman, had been but lately recalled by one of somewhat low degree, Arlouf of Southampton, still further increased his doubts. It seemed strange that the governorship of so important a town—a post deemed fitting for Earl Percy—should be bestowed on such a man, were it not that one was desired who would not hesitate to perform an action from which any honorable English gentleman would shrink.

Two days before the day fixed for the council Archie called Cluny Campbell and another lad named Jock Farrel to him.

"I have a most important mission for you," he said. "You have heard of the coming council at Ayr. I wish to find out if any evil is intended by the governor. For this purpose you two will proceed thither. You Cluny, will put on the garments which you brought with you; while you, Jock, had best go as his brother. Here is money. On your way procure baskets and buy chickens and eggs, and take them in with you to sell. Go hither and thither among the soldiers and hear what they say. Find out among the townspeople if there is any thought that foul play may be intended by the English. Two of the band will accompany you to within a mile of Ayr, and will remain there in order that you may from time to time send news by them of whatever that you have gathered. Remember that the safety of Wallace, and with it the future of Scotland, may depend upon your care and vigilance. I would myself have undertaken the task; but the Kerrs are now, I hear, in Ayr, and a chance meeting might ruin all; for whatever the truce between England and Scotland, they would assuredly keep no truce with me did they meet me. Mind, it is a great honor that I have done you in choosing you, and is a proof that I regard you as two of the shrewdest of my band, although the youngest among them."

Greatly impressed with the importance of their mission, the lads promised to use their utmost vigilance to discover the intentions of the governor. A few minutes later, Cluny was dressed in his sister's clothes, and looked, as Archie laughingly said, "a better looking girl than she was herself." This odd couple soon started for Ayr, accompanied by two of their companions. They were to remain there until the conclusion of the council, but their companions would be relieved every six hours. During the journey, Cluny and Jock procured two baskets, which they filled with eggs and chickens; and then, leaving their comrades a mile outside Ayr, fearlessly entered the town.

The council was to take place in a large wooden building some short distance outside the town, which was principally chosen because it was thought by the governor that the Scottish gentlemen would have less reluctance to meet him there than if they were asked to enter a city with a strong garrison of English.

The first day the lads succeeded in finding out nothing which could give any validity to the suspicion that treachery was intended. They had agreed to work separately, and each mingled among the groups of citizens and soldiers, where the council was the general topic of conversation. There was much wonder and speculation as to the object for which the governor had summoned it, and as to the terms which he might be expected to propound, but to none did the idea of treachery or foul play in any way occur; and when at night they left the town and sent off their message to Archie, the lads could only say that all seemed fair and honest, and that none either of the townspeople or soldiers appeared to have the least expectation of trouble arising at the council.

The following morning they agreed that Jock should hang around the building in which the council was to be held, and where preparations for the meeting and for a banquet which was afterward to take place were being made, while Cluny should continue his inquiries within the walls. Jock hid away his basket and joined those looking on at the preparations. Green boughs were being carried in for decorating the walls, tables, and benches for the banquet. These were brought from the town in country carts, and a party of soldiers under the command of an officer carried them in and arranged them. Several of the rustics looking on gave their aid in carrying in the tables, in order that they might take home to their wives an account of the appearance of the place where the grand council was to be held. Jock thrust himself forward, and seizing a bundle of green boughs, entered the barn. Certainly there was nothing here to justify any suspicions. The soldiers were laughing and joking as they made the arrangements; clean rushes lay piled against a wall in readiness to strew over the floor at the last moment; boughs had been nailed against the walls, and the tables and benches were sufficient to accommodate a considerable number. Several times Jock passed in and out, but still without gathering a word to excite his suspicions. Presently Arlouf himself, a powerful man with a forbidding countenance, rode up and entered the barn. He approached the officer in command of the preparations, while Jock tried to keep near so as to catch something of their conversation.

"Is everything prepared, Harris?"

"Yes, sir; another half-hour's work will complete everything."

"Do you think that is strong enough?" the governor asked.

"Ay, strong enough for half-a-dozen of these half-starved Scots."

"One at a time will do," the governor said; and then, after a few more words, left the barn and rode off to Ayr.

Jock puzzled his head in vain over the meaning of the words he had heard. The governor had while speaking been facing the door; but to what he alluded, or what it was that the officer had declared strong enough to hold half-a-dozen Scots, Jock could not in the slightest degree make out. Still the words were strange and might be important; and he resolved, therefore, to return himself to Archie instead of sending a message, as much might depend upon his repeating, word for word, what he had heard, as there was somehow, he felt, a significance in the manner in which the question had been asked and answered more than in the words themselves.

Cluny had all day endeavored in vain to gather any news. He had the day before sold some of his eggs and chickens at the governor's house, and toward the evening he determined again to go thither and to make an attempt to enter the house, where he had heard that the officers of the garrison were to be entertained that evening at a banquet. "If I could but overhear what is said there, my mind would be at rest. Certainly nothing is known to the soldiers; but it may well be that if treachery is intended tomorrow, the governor will this evening explain his plans to his officers."

He had, before entering the town, again filled up his basket with the unsold portion of Jock's stock, for which the latter had no further use. The cook at the governor's, when he had purchased the eggs on the previous day, told him to call again, as Cluny's prices were considerably below those in the market. It was late in the afternoon when he again approached the house. The sentry at the gate asked no questions, seeing a girl with a basket, and Cluny went round again to the door of the kitchen.

"How late you are, girl!" the cook said angrily. "You told me you would come again today, and I relied upon you, and when you did not come it was too late, for the market was closed."

"I was detained, sir," Cluny said, dropping a curtsey; "my mother is ill, and I had to look after the children and get the dinner before they went away."

"There, don't waste time talking," the cook said, snatching the basket from him. "I have no time to count the eggs now; let me know the tale of them and the chickens at the same price as you charged yesterday, and come for your money tomorrow; I have no time to pay now. Here," he called to one of the scullions, "take out these eggs and chickens quickly, but don't break any, and give the basket to the girl here."

So saying he hurried off to attend to his cooking.

Cluny looked round, and immediately noticed a half-open door leading into the interior of the house. His resolution was taken in a moment. Seeing that none were looking at him he stole through the door, his bare feet falling noiselessly on the stones. He was now in a spacious hall. On one side was an open door, and within was a large room with tables spread for a banquet. Cluny entered at once and looked round for a place of concealment; none was to be seen. Tablecloths in those days were almost unknown luxuries. The tables were supported by trestles, and were so narrow that there was no possibility of hiding beneath them; nor were there hangings or other furniture behind which he could be concealed. With a beating heart he turned the handle of a door leading into another apartment, and found himself in a long and narrow room, used apparently as the private office of the governor. There were many heavy chairs in the room, arranged along the wall, and Cluny crouched in a corner behind one of the chairs. The concealment was a poor one, and one searching would instantly detect him; but he had no fear of a search, for he doubted not that the cook, on missing him, would suppose that he had left at once, intending to call for his money and basket together the next morning. It was already growing dusk, and should no one enter the room for another half hour he would be hidden in the shadow in the corner of the room; but it was highly unlikely that anyone would enter.

The time passed slowly on, and the darkness rapidly increased. Through the door, which Cluny had drawn to but had not tightly closed on entering, he could hear the voices of the servants as they moved about and completed the preparations in the banquet hall. Presently all was quiet, but a faint light gleaming in through the crack of the door showed that the lights were lit and that all was in readiness for the banquet. Half an hour later, and there was a heavy trampling of feet and the sound of many voices. The door was suddenly closed, and Cluny had no doubt that the dinner was beginning. Rising to his feet he went to the door and listened attentively.

A confused din met his ears, but no distinct words were audible. He could occasionally faintly hear the clattering of plates and the clinking of glasses. All this continued for almost two hours, and then a sudden quiet seemed to fall upon the assembly. Cluny heard the door close, and guessed that the banquet was at an end and the servants dismissed. Now, if ever, would something of importance be said within, Cluny would have given his life to be able to hear it. Many times he thought of turning the handle and opening the door an inch or two. Locks in those days were but roughly made; the slightest sound might attract attention, and in that case not only would his own life be forfeited, but no news of the governor's intentions—no matter what they might be—could reach Wallace; so, almost holding his breath, he lay on the ground and listened with his ear at the sill of the door. The silence was succeeded by a steady, monotonous sound, as of one addressing the others. Cluny groaned in spirit, for no word could be heard. After some minutes the murmur ceased, and then many voices were raised together; then one rose above the rest, and then, distinct and clear, came a voice evidently raised in anger.

"As you please, Master Hawkins; but if you disobey my orders, as King Edward's governor here, you will suffer the consequences. I shall at once place you in prison, and shall send report to the king of your mutinous conduct."

"Be that as it may," another voice replied; "whatever befall me, I tell you, sir, that Thomas Hawkins will take no part in an act of such foul and dastardly treachery. I am a soldier of King Edward. I am paid to draw my sword against his enemies, and not to do the bloody work of a murderer."

"Seize him!" the governor shouted, "Give him in charge to the guard, to lay in the castle dungeon."

There was some movement of feet or noise in the banquet hall, but Cluny waited no longer. The angry utterances had reached his ear, and knowing that his mission was accomplished, he thought only now of escape before detection might take place. He had noticed when he entered the room that the windows were, as was usually the case with rooms on the lower floors, barred; but he saw also that the bars were wide enough apart for a lad of his slimness to crawl through. The banqueting-room was raised three steps above the hall, and the room that he was in was on the same level; the window was four feet from the floor, and would therefore be probably seven or eight above the ground without, which would account for its not being more closely barred. He speedily climbed up to it and thrust himself through the bars, but not without immense difficulty and great destruction to his feminine garments.

"Poor Janet!" Cluny laughed to himself as he dropped from the window to the ground. "Whatever would she say were she to see the state of her lace and petticoats!"

The moon was young, but the light was sufficient to enable Cluny to see where he was. The window opened into a lane which ran down by the side of the governor's house, and he was soon in the principal street. Already most of the citizens were within their houses. A few, provided with lanterns, were picking their way along the uneven pavement. Cluny knew that it was impossible for him to leave the town that night; he would have given anything for a rope by which he might lower himself from the walls, but there was no possibility of his obtaining one. The appearance of a young girl wandering in the streets alone at night would at once have attracted attention and remarks. So Cluny withdrew into a dark archway, and then sat down until the general silence told him that all had retired to rest. Then he made his way along the street until he neared the gateway, and there lying down by the wall he went to sleep.

When the gate was opened in the morning, Cluny waited until a few persons had passed in and out, and then he approached it.

"Halloo! lass," the sergeant of the guard, who was standing there, said. "You are a pretty figure with your torn clothes!" Why, what has happened to you?"

"If you please, sir," Cluny said timidly, "I was selling my eggs to the governor's cook, and he kept me waiting, and I did not know that it was so late, and when I got to the gates they were shut, and I had nowhere to go; and then, please sir, as I was wandering about a rough soldier seized me and wanted to kiss me, and of course I would not let him, and in the struggle he tore my clothes dreadfully; and some citizens, who heard me scream, came up and the man left me. I don't know what mother will say about my clothes," and Cluny lifted the hem of his petticoat to his eyes.

"It is a shame, lass," the sergeant said good-temperedly; "had I been there I would have broke the fellow's skull for him; but in the future, lass, you should not overstay the hour; it is not good for young girls to be roaming at night in a town full of soldiers. There, I hope your mother won't beat you, for, after all, it is the fault of the governor's cook rather than yours."

Cluny pursued his way with a quiet and depressed manner until he was almost out of sight of the gates. Then he lifted his petticoats to a height which would have shocked his sister Janet, to give free play to his limbs, and at the top of his speed dashed down the road toward Lanark. He found his two companions waiting at the appointed spot, but he did not pause a moment.

"Are you mad, Cluny?" they shouted.

And indeed the wild figure, with its tucked-up garments, tearing at full speed along the road, would have been deemed that of a mad girl by any who had met it.

"Come on!" he shouted. "Come on, it is for life or death!" and without further word he kept on at full speed. It was some time before his companions overtook him, for they were at first too convulsed by laughter at Cluny's extraordinary appearance to be able to run. But presently, sobered by the conviction that something of extreme importance must have happened, they too started at their best speed, and presently caught up with Cluny, upon whose pace the mile he had already run told heavily.

"For the sake of goodness, Cluny, go slower," one of them panted out as they came up to him. "We have nine miles yet to run, and if we go on like this we shall break down in another half mile, and have to walk the rest."

Cluny himself, with all his anxiety to get on, was beginning to feel the same, and he slackened his pace to a slinging trot, which in little over an hour brought them to the wood.

Chapter 6

The Barns of Ayr

Archie was anxiously awaiting the arrival of his messenger, for the three lads were met two miles out by another who had been placed on watch, and had come on ahead at full speed with the news of their approach. The report brought in by Jock Farrel of the words that he had overheard in the barn prepared for the meeting, had been reported by Archie to Wallace. Sir John Grahame and other gentlemen with him all agreed that they were strange, and his friends had strongly urged their leader not to proceed to the meeting. Wallace, however, persisted in his resolution to do so, unless he received stronger proofs than those afforded by the few words dropped by the governor and his officer, which might really have no evil meaning whatever. He could not throw doubt upon the fair intentions of King Edward's representative, for it might well be said that it was the grossest insult to the English to judge them as guilty of the intention of a foul act of treachery upon such slight a foundation as this. "It would be a shame indeed," he said, "were I, the Guardian of Scotland, to shrink from appearing at a council upon such excuse at this." The utmost that Archie could obtain from him was that he would delay his departure in the morning until the latest moment, in order to see if any further news came from Ayr.

The meeting was to be held at ten o'clock, and until a little before nine he would not set out. He was in the act of mounting his horse when Cluny Campbell arrived.

"What is your news, Cluny?" Archie exclaimed, as the lads, panting and exhausted, ran up.

"There is treachery intended. I overheard the governor say so."

"Come along with me," Archie exclaimed; "you are just in time, and shall yourself tell the news. Draw your bridle, Sir William," he exclaimed as he ran up to the spot where Sir William Wallace, Grahame, and several other gentlemen were in the act of mounting. "Treachery is intended; my messenger has over-heard it. I know not his tale, but question him yourself."

Important as was the occasion, the Scottish chiefs could not resist a smile at the wild appearance of Archie's messenger.

"Is it a boy or a girl?" Wallace asked Archie, "for it might be either."

"He is one of my band, sir. I sent him dressed in this disguise as it would be the least suspected. Now, Cluny, tell your own story."

Cluny told his story briefly, but giving word for word the sentences that he had heard spoken in anger by the governor and his officer.

"I fear there can be no doubt," Wallace said gravely when the lad had finished, "that foul play of some kind is intended, and that it would be madness to trust ourselves in the hands of this treacherous governor. Would that we had the news twenty-four hours earlier; but even now some may be saved. Sir John, you will gallop, with all your mounted men, at full speed toward Ayr. Send men on all the roads leading to the council, and warn any who may not yet have arrived against entering."

Sir John Grahame instantly gave orders to all those who had horses, to mount and follow him at the top of their speed; and he himself, with the other gentlemen whose horses were prepared, started at once at full gallop.

"Sir Archie, cause the 'assembly' to be sounded, and send off your runners in all directions to bid every man who can be collected to gather here this afternoon at three o'clock. If foul play has been done we can avenge, although we are too late to save, and, by heavens, a full and bloody revenge will I take."

It was not until two in the afternoon that Sir John Grahame returned.

"The worst has happened; I can read it in your face," Wallace exclaimed.

"It is but too true," Sir John replied. "For a time we could obtain no information. One of my men rode forward until close to the barns, and reported that all seemed quiet there. A guard of soldiers were standing round the gates, and he saw one of those invited, who had arrived a minute before him, dismount and enter quietly. Fortunately, I was in time to stop many gentlemen who were proceeding to the council, but more had entered before I reached there. From time to time, I sent forward men on foot who talked with those who were standing without to watch the arrivals. Presently, a terrible rumor began to spread among them whether the truth was known from some coarse jest by one of the soldiers, or how it came out, I know not. But as time went on, and the hour was long past when any fresh arrivals could be expected, there was no longer any motive for secrecy and the truth was openly told. Each man as he entered was stopped just inside the door. A noose was dropped over his neck, and he was hauled up to a hook over the door. All who entered are dead."

A cry of indignation and rage broke from Wallace and those standing round him, and the Scottish leader again repeated his oath to take a bloody vengeance for the deed.

"And who are among the murdered?" he asked, after a pause.

"Alas! Sir William," Grahame said, "your good uncle, Sir Ronald Crawford, the sheriff of Ayr, is one; and also Sir Richard Wallace of Riccarton; Sir Bryce Blair and Sir Neil Montgomery, Boyd, Barclay, Steuart, Kennedy, and many others."

Wallace was overwhelmed with grief at the news that both his uncles, to whom he was greatly attached, had perished. Most of those around had also lost relatives and friends, and none could contain their grief and indignation.

"Was my uncle, Sir Robert Gordon, among the victims?" Archie inquired.

"No," Sir John replied; "happily he was one of the last who came along the road."

"Thank God for that!" Archie said earnestly; "my uncle's slowness has saved his life. He was ever late for business or pleasure, and my aunt was always rebuking him for his lack of punctuality. She will not do so again, for assuredly it has saved his life."

The men came in but slowly, for the bands had all dispersed to their homes, and it was only those who lived within a few miles who could arrive in time. Little over fifty men had come in by the hour named. With these Wallace started at once toward Ayr. Archie's band fell in with their arms, for they too burned to revenge the massacre, and Wallace did not refuse Archie's request that they might join.

"Let them come," he said, "we shall need every sword and pike tonight."

This was the first time that Wallace had seen the band under arms, for at the battle of Biggar, Archie had kept them from his sight, fearing that he might order them from the field.

"They look well, Sir Archie, and in good military order. Hitherto I have regarded them but as messengers, and as such they have done good service indeed; but I see now that you have them in good order, and that they can do other service in a pinch."

One member of Wallace's band was left behind, with orders to wait until seven o'clock, and then to bring on as fast as they could march all who might arrive before that hour. The band marched to within a mile of the barns. They then halted at a stack of straw, and sat down while one of Archie's band went forward to see what was being done. He reported that a great feast, at which the governor and all the officers of the garrison, with other English dwelling in the town, were present, was just beginning in the great barn where the massacre had taken place.

Soon after nine o'clock the man who had been left behind, with ten others, who had come in after Wallace had marched, came up. Each man, by Wallace's directions, drew a great truss of straw from the stack, and then the party, now eighty in all, marched toward the barn. Wallace's instructions were that as soon as the work had fairly begun, Grahame, with Archie and half the band, was to hurry off to seize the gate of Ayr, pretending to be a portion of the guard at the barn.

When they approached the spot they saw that the wooden building was brightly lit up with lights within, and the English guard, some fifty in number, were standing carelessly outside, or, seated round fires, were carousing on wine which had been sent out by the revelers within.

The Scots crept up quietly. Wallace's party, composed of half the strength, handed their bundles of straw to the men of Grahame's company; then with a sudden shout they fell upon the English soldiers, while Grahame's men, running straight to the door of the barn threw down their trusses of straw against it, and Sir John, snatching down a torch which burned beside the entrance, applied fire to the mass, and then, without a moment's delay, started at a run toward the town. Taken wholly by surprise the English soldiers were slain by Wallace and his men almost before they had time to seize their arms. Then the Scots gathered round the barn. The flames were already leaping up high, and a terrible din of shouts and cries issued from within. The doors had been opened now, but those within were unable to force their way across the blazing mass of straw. Many appeared at the windows and screamed for mercy, and some leaped out preferring to fall by the Scottish swords rather than to await for death by fire within.

The flames rose higher and higher, and soon the whole building was enveloped, and in minutes all those who had carried out, if not planned, the massacre of Ayr had perished. In the meantime, Grahame and his party had reached the gate of Ayr. Bidding the others follow him at a distance of about a hundred yards, he himself, with Archie and ten of his followers, ran up at full speed.

"Quick!" he shouted to the sentry on the gate. "Lower the bridge and let us in. We have been attacked by Wallace and the Scots, and they will speedily be here."

The attention of the guard had already been attracted by the sudden burst of light by the barns. They had heard distant shouts, and deemed that a conflagration had broken out in the banqueting-hall. Not doubting for an instant the truth of Grahame's story, they lowered the drawbridge instantly, and Sir John and his companions rushed across.

The guards were only undeceived when Grahame and his followers fell upon them with their heavy broadswords. They had left their weapons behind when they had assembled on the walls to look at the distant flames, and were cut down to a man by the Scots. By this time the rest of Grahame's band had arrived.

So short and speedy had been the struggle that no alarm had been given in the town. The inmates of a few houses near opened their windows and looked out.

"Come down as quickly as you may," Sir John said to them; "we have taken Ayr."

Several of the townspeople were soon in the street. "Now," Sir John said, "two of you who know the town well, go with me and point out the houses in which the English troops are quartered; let the others go from house to house, and bid every man come quickly with his sword to strike a blow for freedom."

Sir John now went round the town with the guides and posted two or more men at the door of each house occupied by the English. Soon the armed citizens flocked into the streets, and obtained brief instructions. The blowing of a horn gave the signal. The doors of the houses were beaten in with axes, and pouring in, the Scots slew the soldiers before they had scarce awakened from sleep. Very few of the English in the town escaped to tell about the massacre of Ayr.

One of the few who were saved was Captain Thomas Hawkins. Archie, mindful of the part which he had taken, and to which indeed, the discovery of the governor's intention was due, had hurried direct to the prison, and when this was, with the rest of the town, taken, discovered the English officer in chains in a dungeon, and protected him from harm.

The next morning he was brought before Wallace, who expressed to him his admiration for the honorable course which he had adopted, gave him a rich present out of the booty which had been captured, and placed him on a ship bound for England.

A week after the capture of Ayr one of Archie's band came into his hut. Tears were running down his cheeks, and his face was swollen with weeping.

"What is it, Jock?" Archie asked kindly.

"Ah! Sir Archie! we had bad news from Glen Cairn. One has come hither who says that a few days since the Kerrs, with a following of their own retainers, came down to the village. Having heard that some of us had followed you to the wars, they took a list of all that were missing, and Sir John called our fathers up before him. They all swore, truly enough, that they knew nought of our intentions, and that we had left without saying a word to them. Sir John refused to believe them, and at first threatened to hang them all. Then after a time he said they might draw lots, and that two should die. My father and Allan Cunningham drew the evil numbers, and Kerr hung them up to the old tree on the green and put fire to the roof-trees of all the others. Ah! but there is weeping and wailing in Glen Cairn!"

Archie was for awhile speechless with indignation. He knew well that this wholesale vengeance had not been taken by the Kerrs because the sons of the cottagers of Glen Cairn had gone to join the army of Wallace, but because he deemed them to be still

attached to their old lord; and it was to their fidelity to the
Forbeses rather than to Scotland that they owed the ruin which
had befallen them.

"My poor Jock!" he said, "I am grieved, indeed, at this misfortune. I cannot restore your father's life, but I can from the spoils
of Ayr send a sufficient sum to Glen Cairn to rebuild the cottages
which the Kerrs have destroyed. But this will not be enough—we
will have vengeance for the foul deed. Order the band to assemble
at dusk this evening, and tell Orr and Macpherson to come here
to me at once."

Archie had a long consultation with this two young lieutenants, whose fathers' cottages had with the others been destroyed.

"What we have to do," Archie said, "we must do alone. Sir William has ample employment for his men, and I cannot ask him to
weaken his force to aid me in a private broil; nor, indeed, would
any aid short of his whole band be of use, seeing that the Kerrs
can put three hundred retainers in the field. It is not by open force
that we must fight them, but by fire and harassment. Fighting is
out of the question; but we can do him some damage without giving him a chance of striking a blow at us. As he has burned Glen
Cairn, so shall he see fires blazing round his own castle of Aberfilly. We will not retaliate by hanging his crofters[5] and vassals;
but if he or any of his men-at-arms falls into our hands, we will
have blood for blood."

In the course of the afternoon Archie saw his chief and begged
leave to take his troop away for some time, telling Sir William of
the cruel treatment which the Kerrs had dealt at Glen Cairn, and
his determination to retaliate for the deed.

"Aberfilly is a strong castle, Archie." Wallace said; "at least so
people say, for I have never seen it, so far does it lie removed from
the main roads. But unless by stratagem, I doubt if my force is
strong enough to capture it; nor would I attack were I sure of capturing it without the loss of a man. The nobles and land-owners
stand aloof from me; but it may be that after I have wrested some
more strong places from the English, they may join me. But I
would not on any account war against one of them now. Half the
great families are united by ties of blood or marriage. The Kerrs,

---

5. Those who worked small fields or farms owned by overlords.

we know, are related to the Comyns and other powerful families; and did I lift a hand against them, adieu to my chance of being joined by the great nobles. No; openly hostile as many of them are, I must let them go their way, and confine my efforts to attacking their friends, the English. Then they will have no excuse of personal feud for taking side against the cause of Scotland. But this does not apply to you. Every one knows that there has long been a blood feud between the Forbeses and the Kerrs, and any damage you may do them will be counted as a private feud. I think it is a rash adventure that you are undertaking with but a handful of boys, although it is true that a boy can fire a roof or drive off a bullock as well as a man. However, this I will promise you, that if you should get into any scrape I will come with what speed I can to your rescue, even if it embroil me with half the nobles of Scotland. You embroiled yourself with all the power of England in my behalf, and you will not find me slack in the hour of need. But if I join in the fray it is to rescue my friend Archie Forbes, and not to war against John Kerr, the ally of the English, and my own enemy."

Archie warmly thanked his leader, but assured him that he had no thought of placing himself in any great peril.

"I am not going to fight," he said, "for the Kerr and his retainers could eat us up; we shall trust to our legs and our knowledge of the mountains."

Archie and his band started after dark, and arrived within ten miles of Aberfilly on the following morning. They rested till noon, and then again set out. When they approached one of the outlying farms of the Kerrs, Archie halted his band, and accompanied by four of the strongest and tallest of their number, went to visit the farmer's home. The man came to the door.

"What would you, young sir?" he said to Archie.

"I would," Archie said, "that you bear a message from me to your lord."

"I know not what your message may be; but frankly, I would rather that you bore it yourself, especially if it be of a nature to anger Sir John."

"The message is this," Archie said quietly: "tell him that Archibald Forbes bids him defiance, and that he will retort upon him and his the cruelties which he had wrought in Glen Cairn, and that he will rest not night nor day until he has revenge for innocent blood shed and roof-trees ruthlessly burned."

"Then," the tenant farmer said bluntly, "if you be Archibald Forbes, you may even take your message yourself. Sir John cares not much upon whose head his wrath lights, and I care not to appear before him as a willing messenger on such an errand."

"You may tell him," Archie said quietly, "that you are no willing messenger; for that I told you that unless you did my errand your house should, before morning, be a heap of smoking ashes. I have a following hard by and will keep my word."

The crofter or tenant farmer hesitated.

"Do my bidding; and I promise you that whatever may befall the other vassals of the Kerrs, you shall go free and unharmed."

"Well, if needs must, it must," the crofter said; "and not to avoid seeing my house in ruins, but more because I have heard of you as a valiant youth who fought stoutly by the side of Wallace at Lanark and Ayr—though, seeing that you are but a lad, I marvel much that you should be able to hold your own in such wild company. Although as a vassal of the Kerrs I must needs follow their banner, I need not tell you since you have lived so long at Glen Cairn, that the Kerrs are feared rather than loved. There is many a man among us who would leave if our lord did not have the English by his side. However, we must needs dance as he plays; and now I will put on my bonnet and do your errand. Sir John can hardly blame me greatly for doing what I needs must."

Great was the wrath of Sir John Kerr when his vassal reported to him the message with which he had been charged, and in his savage fury he was with difficulty dissuaded from ordering him to be hung for bringing such a message. His principal retainers ventured, however, to point out that the man had acted upon compulsion, and that the present was not the time, when he might at any moment have to call upon them to take the field, to anger his vassals, who would assuredly resent the undeserved death of one of their number.

"It is past all bearing," the knight said furiously, "that an insolent boy like this should first wound me in the streets of Lanark, and should then cast his defiance in my teeth—a landless rascal, whose father I killed, and whose den of a castle I but a month ago gave to the flames. He must be mad to dare to set his power against mine. I was a fool that I did not stamp him out long ago; but woe betide him when we next meet! Had it not been that I was served by a fool"—and here the angry knight turned to his henchman, Red Boy—"this would not have happened. Who could have thought that a man of your years could have suffered himself to be fooled by a boy, and to bring me tales that this insolent upstart was a poor stupid lout! By heavens! to be thus badly served is enough to make one mad!"

"Well, Sir John," the man grumbled, "the best man will be sometimes in error. I have done good service for you and yours, and yet ever since we met this boy outside the gates of Lanark you have never ceased to vex me concerning him. Rest secure that no such error shall occur again, and that the next time I meet him I will pay him alike for the wound he gave you and for the anger he has brought upon my head. If you will give orders I will start at daybreak with twenty men. I will take up his trail at the cottage of John Frazer, and will not give up the search until I have overtaken and slain him."

"Do so," the knight replied, "and I will forgive your having been so easily fooled. But this fellow may have some of Wallace's followers with him, and contemptible as the rabble are, we had best be on our guard. Send round to all my vassals, and tell them to keep good watch and ward, and keep a party of retainers under arms all night in readiness to sally out in case of alarm."

The night, however, passed quietly. The next day the knight sallied out with a strong party of retainers and searched the woods and lower slopes of the hill, but could find no signs of Archie and his followers, and at nightfall returned to the castle in a rage, declaring that the defiance sent him was a mere piece of insolent bravado. Nevertheless, he kept the horses again saddled all night ready to issue out at the slightest alarm. Soon after midnight flames suddenly burst out at a dozen of the homesteads. At the vassal's shout of alarm Sir John Kerr and his men-at-arms instantly mounted. The gate was thrown open and the drawbridge lowered, and Sir John rode out at the head of his following. He was within a few feet of the outer end of the drawbridge when the chains which supported this suddenly snapped. The drawbridge fell into the moat, plunging all those upon it into the water.

Archie, with his band, after detaching some of their number to fire the homesteads, had crept up unperceived in the darkness to the end of the drawbridge, and had noiselessly cut the two projecting beams upon which its end rested when it was lowered. He had intended to carry out this plan on the previous night, but when darkness set in not a breath of wind was stirring, and the night was so still that he deemed that the operation of sawing through the beams could not be effected without attracting the attention of the warders on the wall, and had therefore retreated far up in the recesses of the hills. The next night, however, was windy, and well attracting the attention of the warders. When Kerr and his men-at-arms rode out, the whole weight of the drawbridge and of the horsemen crossing it was thrown entirely upon the chains, and these yielded to a strain far greater than they were calculated to support.

The instant the men-at-arms were precipitated into the moat, Archie and his companions, who had been lying down near its edge, leaped to their feet, and opened fire with their bows and arrows upon them. It was well for Sir John and his retainers that they had not stopped to buckle on their defensive armor. Had they done so every man would have been drowned in the deep waters. As it was, several were killed with the arrows, and two or three by the hoofs of the struggling horses. Sir John himself, with six of the eighteen men who had fallen into the moat, succeeded in climbing up the drawbridge and regaining the castle. A fire of arrows was at once opened from the walls, but Archie and his followers were already out of bowshot;[6] and knowing that the fires would call in a few minutes to the spot a number of the Kerr's vassals more than sufficient to crush them without the assistance of those in the castle, they again made for the hills, well satisfied with the first blow they had struck at their enemies.

The rage of Sir John Kerr was beyond all expression. He had himself been twice struck by arrows, and the smart of his wounds added to his fury. By the light of the burning barns the garrison were enabled to see how small was the party which had made this audacious attack upon them; and this increased their wrath. Men were instantly set at work to raise the drawbridge from the

---

6. The distance that an arrow can travel when shot from a bow.

A Successful Stratagem

moat, to repair the chains, and to replace the timbers upon which it rested; and a summons was despatched to the whole of the vassals to be at the castle in arms by daybreak.

Again the woods were searched without success, and the band then divided into five parties, each forty strong. They proceeded to explore the hills; but the Pentlands afforded numerous hiding places to those, like Archie and most of his band, well acquainted with the country; and after searching till nightfall the parties retired, worn out and disheartened, to the castle. That night three of the outlying farms were in flames, and the cattle were slaughtered in their stalls, but no attack was made upon the dwelling-houses. The following night Sir John distributed that whole of his vassals among the farms lying farthest from the castle, putting twenty men in each; but to his fury this time it was five homesteads nearer at hand which were burned. The instant the first outburst of flame was discovered the retainers hurried to the spot; but by the time they reached it no sign of the assailants was visible; the flames had however taken too good a hold of the various barns and outbuildings to be extinguished.

Chapter 7

The Cave in the Pentlands

Sir John Kerr was well-nigh beside himself with fury. If this was to go on, the whole of his estate would be harried, his vassals ruined, and his revenues stopped, and this by a mere handful of foes. Again he started with his vassals to explore the hills, this time in parties of ten only, so as to explore thoroughly a larger space of ground. When at evening the men returned, it was found that but two men of one of the parties, composed entirely of men-at-arms from the castle, came back. They reported that when in a narrow ravine showers of rocks were hurled down upon them from both sides. Four of their number were killed at once, and four others had fallen pierced by arrows from an unseen foe as they fled back down the ravine.

"Methinks, Sir John," Red Roy said, "that I know the place where the Forbeses may have taken up their abode. When I was a boy I was tending a herd of goats far up in the hills, and near the pass where this mischance has today befallen us I found a cave in the mountain's side. Its entrance was hidden by bushes, and I should not have found it had not one of the goats entered the bush and remained there so long that I went to see what it was doing. There I found a cave. The entrance was but three feet high, but inside it widened out into a great cavern, where fifty men could shelter. Perchance Archie Forbes or some of his band may also have discovered it; and if so, they might well think that no better place of concealment could be found."

"We will search it tomorrow," the knight said. "Tell the vassals to gather here three hours before daybreak. We will start so as to be there soon after sunrise. If they are on foot again tonight they will then be asleep. Did you follow the cave and discover whether it had any other entrances beyond that by which you entered?"

"I know not," the henchman replied; "it goes a long way into the hills, and there are several inner passages; but these I did not explore, for I was alone and feared being lost in them."

The next night some more homesteads were burnt, but this time the vassals did not turn out, as they had been told to rest until the appointed hour whatever might befall.

Three hours before daybreak a party of fifty picked men assembled at the castle, for this force was deemed to be ample. The two men who had escaped from the attack on the previous day led the way to the ravine, and there Red Roy became the guide and led the band far up the hillside. Had it been possible they would have surrounded the cave before daylight, but Roy said that it was so long since he had first found the cave that he could not lead them there in the dark, but would need daylight to enable him to recognize the surroundings. Even when daylight came he was for some time disoriented, but he at last pointed to a clump of bushes, growing on a broken and precipitous face of rock, as the place where the cave was situated.

Red Roy was right in his conjecture. Archie had once when wandering among the hills, shot at a wild cat and wounded it, and had followed it to the cave to which it had fled, and seeing it an advantageous place of concealment had, when he determined to harry the district of the Kerrs, fixed upon it as the hiding place for his band. Deeming it possible, however, that its existence might be known to others, he always placed a sentry on watch; and on the approach of the Kerrs, Cluny Campbell, who happened to be on guard, ran in and roused the band with the news that the Kerrs were below. Archie immediately crept out and reconnoitered them; from the bushes he could see that his foes were still disorganized. Sir John himself was standing apart from the rest, with Red Roy, who was narrowly scrutinizing the face of the cliff, and Archie guessed at once that they were aware of the existence of the cavern, though at present they could not determine the exact spot where it was situated. It was too late to retreat now, for the face of the hill was too steep to climb to this crest, and their retreat below was cut off by the Kerrs. He therefore returned to the cave, leaving Cluny on guard.

"They are not sure as to the situation of the cave yet," he said, "but they will find it. We can hold the mouth against them for some time, but they might smoke us out, that is our real danger; or if they fail in that, they may try starvation. Several of us must take brands at once from the embers and explore all the passages behind us; they are so narrow and low that hitherto we have not deemed it worth while to examine them, but now they are really our only hope; some of them may lead round to the face of the hill, and in that case we may find some way by which we may circumvent the Kerrs."

Six of the lads at once started with flaming pineknots,[7] while Archie returned to the entrance. Just as he took his place there he saw Red Roy pointing toward the bushes. A minute or two later Sir John and his followers began to advance. Archie now called out the rest of his band, who silently took their places in the bushes beside him. Led by Sir John and personal retainers, the assailants approached the foot of the rocks and began to make their way up, using the utmost precaution to avoid any noise. There was no longer any need for concealment, and as the foremost of the assailants began to climb the great boulders at the foot of the precipice, a dozen arrows from bush above alighted among them, killing three and wounding several others. Sir John Kerr shouted to his men to follow him, and began to clamber up the hill. Several arrows struck him, but he was sheathed in mail, as were his men-at-arms, and although several were wounded in the face and two slain they succeeded in reaching the bushes, but they could not penetrate further, for as they strove to tear the bushes aside and force an entry, those behind pierced them with their spears, and as but four or five assailants at a time could gain a footing and use their arms they were outnumbered and finally driven back by the defenders. When Sir John, furious at his discomfiture, rejoined his vassals below, he found that the assault had already cost him eight of his best men. He would, however, have again led them to the attack, but Red Roy said:

"It were best, my lord, to summon fifty of the vassals to come up hither at once, with bows and arrows. They can so riddle those bushes that the defenders will be unable to occupy them to resist our advance."

---

7. Pine branches with knots which are used for torches.

"That is a good step," Sir John said; "but even when we gain the ledge I know not how we shall force our way through the hole, which you say is but three feet high."

"There is no need to force our way in," Red Roy replied; "each man who climbs shall carry with him a bundle of wood, and we will smoke them in their holes like wolves."

"'Tis well thought of, Roy; that assuredly is the best plan. Send off at once one of the most fleet-footed of the party."

Archie, watching from above, saw the assailants draw back out of bowshot, and while one of their number started at full speed down the hillside, the others sat down, evidently prepared to pass some time before they renewed the attack. Leaving two of the party on guard, Archie, with the rest, re-entered the cavern. The searchers had just returned and reported that all the various passages came to nothing save one, which ascended rapidly and terminated in a hole which looked as if it had been made by rabbits, and through which the light of day could be seen.

"Then it is there we must work," Archie said. "I will myself go and examine it."

The passage, after ascending to a point which Archie judged to be almost a hundred feet above the floor of the cave, narrowed to a mere hole, but two feet high and as much wide. Up this he crawled for a distance of four or five yards, then it narrowed suddenly to a hole three or four inches in diameter, and through this, some three feet further, Archie could see the daylight through a clump of heather. He backed himself down the narrow passage again until he joined his comrades. "Now," he said, "do four of you stay here, and take it by turns one after the other, to enlarge the hole forward to the entrance. As you scrape the earth down you must pass it back handful by handful. Do not enlarge the outer entrance or disturb the roots of the heather growing there. Any movement might be noticed by those below. It is lucky, indeed, that the rock ends just when it gets to its narrowest, and that it is but sandy soil through which we have to scrape our way. It will be hard work, for you have scarce room to move your arms, but you have plenty of time since we cannot leave until nightfall."

The hours passed slowly, and about noon the lookout reported that a number of bowmen were approaching.

"They are going to attack this time under cover of their fire," Archie said, "and as I do not wish to risk the loss of any lives, we will keep within the cave and let them gain the ledge. They can never force their way through the narrow entrance. The only thing I fear is smoke. I purpose that if they light a fire at the mouth of the cave, we shall retire at once up the passage where we are working, and block it up the narrow place a short distance after it leaves this cavern, with our clothes. You had best take off some of your things, scrape up the earth from the floor of the cavern, and each make a stout bundle, so that we can fill up the hole solidly."

This was soon done, and the bundles of earth were laid in readiness at the point upon which their leader had fixed. In the meantime Archie had rejoined the lookout.

"They have been scattered for some time," the guard said, "and have been cutting down bushes and making them into bundles."

"Just what I expected," Archie exclaimed. "The bowmen are joining them now. We shall soon see them at work."

Sir John Kerr now marshaled his retainers. He and his men-at-arms drew their swords, and the rest, putting the bundles of wood on their shoulders, prepared to follow, while the bowmen fitted their arrows to the string.

"Fall back inside the cave," Archie said; "it is of no use risking our lives."

The band now gathered in a half circle, with level spears, round the entrance. Soon they heard a sharp tapping sound as the arrows struck upon the rock, then there was a crashing among the bushes.

"Come on!" Sir John Kerr shouted to the vassals. "The foxes have slunk into their hole." Then came low thuds as the bundles of wood were cast down. The light which had streamed in through the entrance gradually became obscure, and the voices of those without muffled. The darkness grew more intense as the bundles were piled thicker and thicker; then suddenly a slight odor of smoke was perceived.

"Come along now," Archie said; "they have fired the pile and there is no fear of their entrance."

Two of their number, with blazing pine-knots, led the way. When they reached the narrow spot all passed through, Archie and Andrew Macpherson last; these took the bundles of earth, as the others passed them along from behind, and built them up like a wall across the entrance, beating them down as they piled them, so as to make them set close and fill up every crevice. Several remained open after the wall was completed; these were closed as the earth was crammed into the crevices between the bags. The smell of the smoke had grown strong before the wall was completed, but it was not too oppressive to breathe. Holding the torch close to the wall, Archie and his comrade closed the few places through which they saw that the smoke was still making its way, and soon had the satisfaction of seeing that the barrier was completely smoke-tight.

There was plenty of air in the passage to support life for some time, but Archie called back to those who were laboring to enlarge the exit, in order to allow as much fresh air as possible to enter. A strong guard with spears was placed at the barrier, although Archie deemed that some hours at least would elapse before the Kerrs could attempt to penetrate the cave. The fire would doubtless be kept up for some time, and after it had expired it would be long before the smoke cleared out sufficiently from the cave to allow any one to enter it. After a time, finding that there was no difficulty in breathing, although the air was certainly close and heavy, Archie again set the lads at work widening the entrance, going up himself to superintend the operation. Each in turn crept forward, loosened a portion of the earth with his knife, and then filling his cap with it, crawled backward to the point where the passage widened.

It was not yet dark when the work was so far done that there now remained only a slight thickness of earth, through which the roots of the bush protruded, at the mouth of the passage, and a vigorous push would make an exit into the air. The guard at the barrier had heard no movement within. Archie withdrew one of the bags; but the smoke streamed through so densely that he hastily replaced it, satisfied that some hours must still elapse before the assailants would enter the cave. They watched impatiently the failing light through the hole, and at last, when night was completely fallen, Archie pushed aside the earth and heather, and looked around. They were, it seemed to him, on the side of the hill a few yards from the point where it fell steeply away. The ground was thickly covered with heather. He soon made his way out and ordered Andrew Macpherson, who followed him, to remain lying at the entrance, and to enjoin each, as he passed out, to crawl low among the heather, so that they might not show against the sky line, where dark as it was, they might attract the attention of those below. Archie himself led the way until so far back from the edge as to be well out of sight of those in the valley. Then he gained his feet, and was soon joined by the whole of his band.

"Now," he said, "we will make for Aberfilly; they think us all cooped up here and will be rejoicing in our supposed deaths. We will strike one more blow, and then driving before us a couple of score of oxen for the use of the army, rejoin Wallace. Methinks we shall have taken a fair vengeance for Kerr's doings at Glen Cairn."

The consternation of the few men left in the castle was great when, three hours after sunset, eight homesteads burst suddenly into flames. They dared not sally out, and remained under arms until morning, when Sir John and his band returned more furious than ever, as they had penetrated the cavern, discovered the barrier which had cut off the smoke, and the hole by which the foe had escaped; and their fury was brought to a climax when they found the damage which had been inflicted in their absence. Many a week passed before the garrison of Aberfilly and the vassals of the Kerrs were able to sleep in peace; so great was the scare which Archie's raid had inflicted upon them.

The truce was now at an end. The indignation excited by the treachery of the English spread widely through Scotland, and the people flocked to Wallace's standard in far greater numbers than before, and he was now able to undertake operations on a greater scale. Perth, Aberdeen, Brechin, and other towns fell into his hands, and the castle of Dundee was taken over. In the south Sir William Douglas captured the castles of Sanquhar, Desdeir, and others, and the rapid successes of the Scots induced a few of the greater nobles to take the field, such as the Steward of Scotland, Sir Andrew Moray of Bothwell, Sir Richard Lundin, and Wishart, Bishop of Glasgow.

Wallace was one day lamenting to Archie and his friend Grahame that the greater nobles still held aloof. "Above all," he said,

"I would gladly see on our side either Comyn or the young Bruce. Baliol is a captive in London, and it is to Comyn or Bruce that Scotland must look for her king. So long as only I, a poor knight, am at the head of this rising, it is but a rebellion against Edward, and its chances are still so weak that but few men who have much to lose, join us; but if Bruce or Comyn should raise his banner all would receive him as our future king. Both are lords of wide territories, and besides the forces they could bring into the field, they would be joined by many of the principal nobles, although it is true that the adherents of the other would probably arm for Edward. Still the thought of a king of their own would inflame the popular mind, and vast numbers who now hesitate to join a movement supported by so little authority, would then take up arms."

"Which of the two would you rather?" Archie asked.

"I would rather the Bruce," Wallace said. "His father is an inert man and a mere cipher, and the death of his grandfather, the competitor, has now brought him prominently forward. It is true that he is said to be a strong adherent of England and a personal favorite of Edward; that he spends much of his time in London; and is even at the present moment the king's lieutenant in Carrick and Annandale, and is waging war for him against Sir William Douglas. Still Comyn is equally devoted to England; he is older, and less can be hoped from him. Bruce is young; he is said to be of great strength and skill in arms, and to be one of the foremost knights in Edward's court. He is, I hear, of noble presence, and is much loved by those with whom he comes in contact. Did such a man determine to break with Edward, and to strive to win the crown of Scotland as a free gift of her people, instead of as a nominee of Edward, and to rule over an independent kingdom instead of an English province, he would attract all hearts to him, and may well succeed where I, as I foresee, must sooner or later fail."

"But why should you fail when you have succeeded so far?" Archie asked.

"Because I have with me but a small portion of the people of Scotland. The whole of the northern lords hold aloof, and in the south Carrick and Annandale and Galloway are hostile. Against me I have all the power of England, Wales, and Ireland; and although I may for a time win victories and capture towns, I am certain, Archie, in the end to be crushed."

"And will all our efforts have been in vain?" Archie said with tears in his eyes.

"By no means, my brave lad; we shall have lighted the fire of a national resistance, we shall have shown the people that if Scotland, divided against herself, and with all her great nobles and their vassals standing sullenly aloof, can yet for a long time make head against the English, assuredly when the time shall come, and she shall rise as one man from the Solway to Caithness, her freedom will be won. Our lives will not have been thrown away, Archie, if they have taught this lesson."

Wallace had by this time returned from his expedition further north, and his force was in camp near Lanark, which town, when not engaged in distant enterprises, was regarded as the center of the movement. That evening Archie said, that as his leader purposed to give his troops rest for a week or two, he should go to his uncle's for a short time.

"And if you can spare them, Sir William, I would gladly let my band go away for the same time. They have now been six months from home."

"Certainly," Wallace said, "they need a rest after their hard work. They are ever afoot, and have been of immense service."

Having obtained this permission, Archie went to the spot where his band were encamped. "I have another expedition for you," he said, "this time all together; when that is over you will be able to go home for a few days for a rest. They will all be glad to see you, and may well be proud of you, and I doubt not that the spoil which you gathered at Ayr and elsewhere will create quite a sensation at Glen Cairn. There are some of you who are, as I remember in the old days, good shots with the bow and arrow. Ten of you who were the best at home should get bows and arrows from the store. Here is an order for you to receive them, and be all in readiness to march at daylight."

The next morning the band set out in a southwesterly direction, and after a long day's march halted near Cumnock. In the morning they started at the same time observing more caution as they went, for by the afternoon they had crossed the stream and were within the boundaries of Carrick. They halted for the night near Crossraguel Abbey. Here for the first time Archie confided to his followers the object of their march.

"We are now," he said, "within a few miles of Turnberry Castle, the residence of Bruce. Sir William has a great desire to speak with him; but, seeing that Bruce is at present fighting for King Edward against Douglas there is little chance of such a meeting coming about with his good will. He has recently returned from Douglasdale. Here, in the heart of his own country, it is like enough that he may ride near his castle with but a few horsemen. In that case we will seize him, without, I trust, having to do him hurt, and will bear him with us to Lanark. We may have to wait some time before we find an opportunity; but even if the ten days for which I have asked lengthen to as many weeks, Sir William will not grudge the time we have spent if we succeed. Tomorrow morning let those who have bows go out in the forest, and see if they can shoot a deer; or failing that, bring in a sheep or two from some of the folds. As each of you has brought with you a meal for ten days, we shall be able to keep an eye on Turnberry for some time."

The next day Archie, with Andrew Macpherson and Cluny Campbell, made their way through the woods until within sight of the castle, which was but a mile distant. The strongholds of the lords of Carrick stood on a bold promontory washed by the sea.

"It would be a hard nut to crack, Sir Archie," his lieutenant said. "Unless by famine, the place could scarce be taken."

"No," Archie replied, "I am glad that our mission is rather to capture the earl than his castle. It is a grand fortalice. Would that its owner were but a true Scot! This is a good place on which we are standing, Andrew, to place a scout. Among the trees here he can watch the road all the way from the castle to the point where it enters the forest. It would be good, if you, Cluny take post here at once. Search well all that passes, and what is doing, and all bodies of men who enter or leave the castle. There is no occasion to bring news to me, for it would be unlikely that we should meet in the forest; you have therefore only to watch. Tomorrow I shall return with the band, and encamp in the woods further back. As soon as we arrive you will be relieved of your guard."

The following day the band moved up to a spot within half a mile of the seaward edge of the forest, and a few hundred yards from the road to Crossraguel Abbey. It was only on this road that Archie could hope to effect a capture; for the country near the coast was free of trees, and no ambush could be set. The lords of Carrick were, moreover, patrons of the abbey, and Bruce might ride over thither with but a small party, whereas, if journeying south, or southeast toward Douglasdale, he would probably be marching with a strong force. For several days they watched the castle; bodies of mounted men entered and departed. Twice parties, among whom ladies could be seen, came out with their hawks; but none came within reach of their lurking foes.

On the fifth morning, however, the lad on watch ran into the glade in which they were encamped and reported that a small body of seemingly two or three knights, with some ladies, followed by four mounted men, had left the castle and were approaching toward the abbey.

Not a moment was lost. Archie placed six of his company, with pike and sword, close to the road, to form across it when he gave the order, and to bar the retreat of any party who had passed. Another party of equal strength he placed one hundred yards further on, and followed with this group. Archie then placed four young men, armed with bows and arrows, on either side, near the party which he commanded. Scarcely had his preparations been made when a trampling of horses was heard, and the party were seen approaching. They consisted of Robert Bruce, his brother Nigel, and three of his sisters—Isabel, Mary and Christina. Behind them rode four men-at-arms. From the description which he had heard of him Archie had no doubt that the elder of the two knights was Robert Bruce himself, and when they approached within thirty yards he gave a shout, and, with his band, with leveled spears, drew up across the road. At the same moment the other party closed in behind the horsemen; and the eight archers, with bent bows and arrows drawn to the head, rose among the trees. The party reined in their horses suddenly.

"Hah! what have we here?" Bruce exclaimed. "An ambush— and on all sides, too!" he added as he looked round. "What means this?" are you robbers who thus dare attack the Bruce within a mile of Turnberry? Why, they are but lads," he added scornfully.

"Rein back, girls; we and the men-at-arms will soon clear a way for you through these varlets. Nay, I can do it single-handed myself."

"Halt! Sir Robert Bruce," Archie exclaimed in a loud clear voice. "If you move I must then give the word, and it may well be that some of the ladies with you may be struck with the arrows. Young though my followers may be, you would not find them so easy a conquest as you imagine. They have stood up before the English ere now; and you and your men-at-arms will find it hard work to get through their pikes; and we outnumber you three-fold. We are not robbers. I myself am Sir Archibald Forbes."

"You!" exclaimed Robert Bruce, lowering his sword, which he had drawn at the first alarm and held uplifted in readiness for a charge; "you Sir Archibald Forbes! I have heard the name often as that of one of Wallace's companions, who, with Sir John Gra-hame, fought with him bravely at the captures of Lanark, Ayr, and other places, but surely you cannot be he!"

"I am Sir Archibald Forbes, I pledge you my word," Archie said quietly; "and Sir Robert Bruce, methinks that if I, who am, as you see, but yet a lad—not yet having reached my seventeenth year—can have done good service for Scotland, how great the shame that you, a valiant knight and a great noble, should be in the ranks of her oppressors, and not of her champions! My name will tell you that I have come hither for no purpose of robbery. I have come on a mission from Wallace—not sent thereon by him, but acting of myself in consequences of words which dropped from him. He said how sad it was that you, who might be king of a Scotland free and independent, by the choice of her people, should prefer the chance of reigning, a mere puppet of Edward, over an enslaved land. He spoke in the highest terms of your per-son, and held that, did you place yourself at its head, the move-ment which he commands would be a successful one. Then I determined, unknown to him, to set out and bring you to him face to face—honorably and with courtesy if you would, by force if you would not. I would hope it shall be the former; but believe me, you would not find it easy to break away through the hedge of pikes now around you."

By this time the whole party had gathered round the horsemen. Bruce hesitated; his mind was not yet made up as to his future course. Hitherto he had been with England, since upon Edward only his chances seemed to depend; but recently he had begun to doubt whether even Edward could place him on the throne in opposition to the wishes of his countrymen. His sisters, who, taking after their mother, were all true Scottish patriots, now urged upon him to comply with Wallace's request and accompany him to Lanark. Their hearts and wishes were entirely with the champion of their country.

"Go with him, Robert," Isabel, the eldest, exclaimed. "Neither I nor my sisters fear being struck with the arrows, although such might well be the case should a conflict begin; but, for your own sake, and Scotland's, go and see Wallace. No harm can arise from such a journey, and much good may come of it. Even should the news of your having had an interview with him come to the ears of Edward, you can truly say that you were taken thither a captive and that we being with you, you were unable to make an effort to free yourself. This young knight, of whose deeds of gallantry we have heard"—and she smiled approvingly at Archie— "will doubtless give you a safeguard, on his honor, to return hither free and unpledged when you have seen Wallace."

"Willingly, lady," Archie replied. "One hour's interview with my honored chief is all I ask for. That over, I pledge myself that the Earl of Carrick shall be free at once to return hither, and that an escort shall be provided for him to protect him from all dangers on the way."

Chapter 8

The Council at Stirling

A rchie had not been mounted during his confrontation with Bruce, so one of his followers brought his horse forward. He soon started with Robert Bruce, young Nigel and the ladies saluting him cordially.

"I trust," said Nigel, "that Wallace will succeed in converting my brother. I am envious of you, Sir Archie. Here are you, many years younger than I am, and yet you have won a name throughout Scotland as one of her champions; while I am eating my heart out, with my brother, at the court of Edward."

"I trust it may be so, Sir Nigel," Archie answered. "If Sir Robert will but join our cause, heart and soul, the battle is as good as won."

The journey passed without adventure until they arrived within two miles of Lanark, where Archie found Wallace was now staying. On the road Bruce had much conversation with Archie, and learned the details of many adventures of which before he had only heard vaguely by report. He was impressed by the lad's modesty and loyal patriotism.

"If ever I come to my kingdom, Sir Archie," he said, "you shall be one of my most trusted knights and counselors; and I am well assured that any advice you may give will be ever what you think to be right and for the good of the country. That is more than I could look for in most counselors. And now methinks as we are drawing near to Lanark, it will be well that I waited here in this wood, under the guard of your followers, while you ride forward and inform Wallace that I am here. I care not to show myself in Lanark, for busy tongues would soon take the news to Edward; and as I know not what may come of our interview, it were well that it should not be known to all men."

Archie agreed, and rode into the town.

"Why, where have you been, truant?" Sir William exclaimed as Archie entered the room in the governor's house which had been set apart for the use of Wallace since the expulsion of the English. "Sir Robert Gordon has been here several times, and tells me that they have seen naught of you; and although I have made many inquiries I have been able to obtain no news, save that you and your band have disappeared. I even sent to Glen Cairn, thinking that you might have been repairing the damages which the fire, lighted by the Kerrs, did to your home. I found, however, not only that you were not there yourself, but that none of your band had returned thither. This made it more mysterious; for had you alone disappeared I should have supposed that you had been following up some love adventure, though, indeed, you have never told me that your heart was in any way touched."

Archie laughed. "There will be time enough for that, Sir William, ten years hence; but in truth I have been on an adventure on my own account."

"So, in sober earnest, I expected, Archie, and feared that your enterprise might lead you into some serious scrape, since I deemed that it must have been well-nigh a desperate one or you would not have hidden it from my knowledge."

"It might have led to some blows, Sir William, but happily it did not turn out so. Knowing the importance you attached to the adhesion to the cause of Scotland of Robert the Bruce, I determined to fetch him hither to see you; and he is now waiting with my band for your coming, in a wood some two miles from the town."

"Are you jesting with me?" Wallace exclaimed. "Is the Bruce really waiting to see me? Why, this would be well-nigh a miracle."

"It is a fact, Sir William; if you will cause your horse to be brought to the door I will tell you on the road how it has come about."

In another five minutes Sir William and his young followers were on their way, and the former heard how Archie had entrapped Robert Bruce while riding to Crossraguel Abbey.

"It was well done, indeed," the Scottish leader exclaimed; "and it may well prove, Archie, that you have done more toward freeing Scotland by this adventure of yours than we have by all our months of marching and fighting."

"Ah! Sir William, but had it not been for our marching and fighting Bruce would never have waved in his allegiance to Edward. It was only because he begins to think that our cause may be a winning one that he decides to join it."

The meeting between Wallace and Bruce was a cordial one. Each admired the splendid proportions and great strength of the other, for it is probable that in all Europe there were no two more doughty champions; although, indeed, Wallace was far the superior in personal strength, while Bruce was famous throughout Europe for his skill in knightly exercise.

Archie withdrew to a distance while the leaders conversed. He could see that their talk was animated as they strode together up and down among the trees, Wallace being the principal speaker. At the end of half an hour they stopped, and Wallace ordered the horses to be brought, and then called Archie to them.

"Sir Robert has decided to throw in his lot with us," he said, "and will at once call out his father's vassals of Carrick and Annandale. Seeing that his father is at Edward's court, it may be that many will not obey the summons. Still we must hope that, for the love of Scotland and their young lord, many will quickly follow him. And, indeed, there is need for haste, seeing that Percy and Clifford have already crossed the border with an English army, and are marching north through Annandale toward Ayr."

"Good-bye, my captor," Bruce said to Archie as he mounted his horse; "whatever may come of this strife, remember that you will always find a faithful friend in Robert Bruce."

Wallace had, at Archie's request, brought six mounted men-at-arms with him from Lanark, and these now rode behind Bruce as his escort back to his castle of Turnberry. There was no time now for Archie and his band to take the rest they had looked for, for messengers were sent out to gather the bands together again, and as soon as a certain portion had arrived Wallace marched for the south. The English army was now in Annandale, near Lochmaben. They were far too strong to be openly attacked, but on the night following his arrival in their neighborhood Wallace broke in upon them in the night. Surprised by this sudden and unexpected attack, the English fell into great confusion. Percy at once ordered the camp to be set on fire. By its light the English were able to see how small was the force of their assailants, and gathering together soon showed so formidable a front that Wallace called off his men, but not before a large number of the English had been killed. Many of their stores, as well as the tents, were destroyed by the conflagration. The English army now proceeded with slow marches toward Ayr.

At Irvine the Scottish leaders had assembled their army—Douglas, Bruce, The Steward, Sir Richard Loudon, Wishart, Bishop of Glasgow, and others. Their forces were about equal to those of the English marching against them. Wallace was collecting troops further north, and Archie was of course with him.

"I fear," the lad said one day, "that we shall not be able to reach Irvine before the armies join the battle."

"Sir William Douglas and Bruce are there, and as it lies in their country it were better to let them win the day without my meddling. But, Archie, I fear there will be no battle. News has reached me that messengers are riding to and fro between Percy's army and the Scots, and I fear me that these half-hearted barons will make peace."

"Surely that cannot be! It were shame indeed to have taken up the sword, and to lay it down after scarce striking a blow."

"Methinks, Archie, that the word shame is not to be found in the vocabulary of the nobles of this unhappy land. But let us hope for the best; a few days will bring us the news."

The news when it came was of the worst. All the nobles, headed by Wishart, Douglas, and Bruce, with the exception only of Sir Andrew Moray of Bothwell, had made their submission, acknowledging their guilt of rebellion, and promising to make every reparation required by their sovereign lord. Percy, on his part, guaranteed their lives, lands, goods, and chattels, and that they should not be imprisoned or punished for what had taken place.

Sir William Douglas and Bruce were ordered to find guarantees for their good conduct; but Sir William Douglas, finding himself unable to fulfill his engagements, surrendered, and was thrown into prison in Berwick Castle, and there kept in irons until he died, his death being attributed, by contemporary historians, to poison.

The surrender of the leaders had little result upon the situation. The people had won their successes without their aid, and beyond the indignation excited by their conduct, the treaty of Irvine did nothing toward ensuring peace, and indeed heightened the confidence of the people in Wallace. The movement spread over the whole of Scotland. Skirmishes and unimportant actions took place in all quarters. The English were powerless outside the walls of their fortresses, and in Berwick and Roxburgh alone was the English power paramount. Most of the great nobles, including Comyn of Buchan, Comyn of Badenoch, and twenty-six other powerful Scottish lords, were at Edward's court, but many of their vassals and dependents were in the field with Wallace.

About this time it came to the ears of the Scottish leader that Sir Robert Cunninghame, a Scottish knight of good family, who had hitherto held aloof from any part in the war, had invited some twelve other residents in the counties round Stirling, to meet at his house in that city that they might talk over the circumstances of the times. All these had, like himself, been neutral, and as the object of the gathering was principally to discover whether some means could not be hit upon for calming down the disorders which prevailed, the English governor had willingly granted safe conducts to all.

"Archie," Sir William said, "I mean to be present at the interview. They are all Scottish gentlemen, and though but lukewarm in the cause of their country, there is not fear that any will be base enough to betray me; and surely if I can get speech with them I may rouse them to cast in their lot with us."

"It were a dangerous undertaking, Sir William, to trust yourself within the walls of Stirling," Archie said gravely. "Remember how many are the desperate passes into which your adventurous spirit has brought you, and your life is of too great a consequence to Scotland to be rashly endangered."

"I would not do it for a lesser cause," Sir William said; "but the gain may be greater than the risk. So I shall go, Archie, your wise counsel notwithstanding; and you shall journey with me to see that I get not into scrapes, and to help me out of them should I, in spite of your care, fall into them."

"When is the day for the meeting?" Archie asked.

"In three days' time. The day after tomorrow we will move in that direction, and enter the town early the next day."

No sooner had he left Wallace than Archie called his band together. They still numbered twenty, for although three or four had fallen, Archie had always filled up their places with fresh recruits, as there were numbers of boys who deemed it the highest honor to be enrolled in their ranks. Archie drew aside his two lieutenants, Andrew Macpherson and William Orr.

"I have an enterprise on hand," he said, "which will need all your care, and may call for your bravery. Sir William Wallace purposes to enter Stirling in disguise, to attend a meeting of notables to be held at the residence of Sir Robert Cunninghame. I am to accompany him thither. I intend that the band shall watch over his safety, and this without his having knowledge of it, so that if naught comes of it he may not chide me for being over careful of his person. You will both, with sixteen of the band, accompany me. You will choose two of your most trusty men to carry out the important matter of securing our retreat. They will procure a boat capable of carrying us all, and will take their place in the bend of the river nearest to the castle, and will hoist, when the time comes, a garment on an oar, so that we may make straight for the boat. The ground is low and swampy, and if we get a fair start even mounted men would scarce overtake us across it. I think, William, that the last recruit who joined was from Stirling?"

"He was, Sir Archie. His parents reside there. They are vendors of wood, as I have heard him say."

"It could not be better," Archie replied; "and seeing that they have allowed their son to join us, they must surely be patriots. My purpose is, that on the morning of the interview you shall appear before the gates with a cart laden with firewood, and this you will take to Campbell's father. There you will unload the firewood, and store the arms hidden beneath it, placing them so that they may be readily caught up in case of necessity. In twos and threes, carrying eggs, fowls, firewood, and other articles, as for sale, the rest of the band will come into the town, joining themselves with parties of country people, so that the arrival of so many lads unaccompanied will not attract notice. James Campbell will go with you, and will show you the way to his father's house. He will remain near the gate, and as the others enter he will guide them there, so that they will know where to run for their arms should there be need. You must start tomorrow, so as to enter Stirling on the next day and arrange with his father for the keeping of the arms. His mother had best leave the town that evening. Should nothing occur she can return unsuspected; but should a tumult arise, and the arms have to be used, his father must leave the town with us. He shall be handsomely rewarded, and provision made for him in the future.

"When you see me enter with Sir William, bid Jock Farrel follow me at a little distance; he will keep me always in sight, and if he see me lift my hand above my head he will run with all speed to give you the news. On his arrival, you, Andrew, with the half you command, will hurry up to my assistance; while you, William, with the others, will fall suddenly upon the guard at the gate, and will at all hazards prevent them from closing it, and so cutting off our retreat. Seize, if you can, the moment when a cart is passing in or out and slay the horse in the shafts, so that as he falls the cart will prevent the gate from being closed, and so keep the way open, even should you not be able to resist the English until we come up. Have all the band outside Stirling on the night before, so that you will be able to make every arrangement and obtain a cart in readiness for taking in the wood and arms in the morning. Let all bring their bows and arrows, in addition to pike and sword, for the missiles may aid us to keep the soldiers at bay. Now, Andrew, repeat all my instructions, so that I may be sure that you thoroughly understand my wishes, for any small error in the plan might ruin the whole adventure."

On the morning of the day fixed for the meeting, Sir William Wallace, accompanied by Archie, entered the gates of Stirling. Both were attired as young farmers, and they attracted no special attention from the guards. For a time they strolled about the streets. They saw the gentlemen who had been invited by Sir Robert Cunninghame arrive one by one. Others, too, known as being specially attached to the English party, rode in, for the governor had invited those who assembled at Cunninghame's to meet him afterward in the castle in order that he might hear the result of their deliberations; and he had asked several others attached to the English party to be present.

When most of the gentlemen invited had entered Sir Robert Cunninghame's, Wallace boldly followed them; and Archie sat down on a doorstep nearly opposite. Presently he saw two figures which he recognized riding up the street, followed, as the others had been, by four armed retainers. They were Sir John Kerr and his son. Archie rose at once, and turned down at a side street before they came up, as a recognition of him would be fatal to all their plans. When they had passed up the street to the castle he returned and resumed his seat, feeling more uneasy than before, for the Kerrs had seen Wallace in the affray at Lanark, and a chance meeting now would betray him. An hour and a half passed, and then Archie saw the Kerrs riding down the street from the castle. Again he withdrew from sight, this time down an archway, where he could still see the door on the opposite side. A short time before, he had been wishing to see it open and for Wallace to appear; and now he dreaded this above all things. His worst fears, however, were realized, for just as the horsemen reached the spot the door opened and Wallace stepped out. His figure was too remarkable to avoid notice; and no sooner did Sir John Kerr's eye fall upon him than he exclaimed, "The traitor Wallace! seize him, men; there is a high reward offered for him; and King Edward will give honor and wealth to all who capture him."

As Sir John spoke Archie darted across the street and placed himself by Wallace's side, holding his hand high above his head as he did so. At this same moment he saw Jock Farrel, who had been lounging at a corner a few yards away, dart off down the street at top speed.

Sir John and his retainers drew their swords and spurred forward; but the horses recoiled from the flashing swords of Wallace and his companion.

"Dismount," Sir John shouted, setting the example; "cut them both down; one is as bad as the other. Ten pounds to the man who slays the young Forbes."

Wallace cut down two of the retainers as they advanced against them, and Archie badly wounded a third. Then they began to retreat down the street; but by this time the sound of the fray had called together many English soldiers who were informed by Sir John's shouts of "Down with Wallace! slay! slay!" As they came running up from both sides Wallace and Archie could retreat no further, but with their backs against the wall they kept their foes at bay in a semicircle by the sweep of their swords.

The fight continued but two or three minutes, when a sudden shout was heard, and William Orr, with eight young fellows, fell upon the English soldiers with their pikes. The latter, astonished at this sudden onslaught, and several of their number being killed before they had time to turn and defend themselves, fell back for a moment. Wallace and Archie joined their allies, and began to retreat, forming a line of pikes across the narrow street. Wallace, Archie, William Orr, and three of the most stout of the band were sufficient for the line, and the other five shot between them. So hard and fast flew their arrows that several of the English soldiers were slain, and the others drew back from the assault.

Andrew Macpherson's sudden attack at the gate overpowered the guard, and for awhile he held possession of it, and following Archie's instructions, slew a horse drawing a cart laden with flour in the act of entering. Then the guard rallied, and, joined by other soldiers who had run up, made a fierce attack upon him; but his line of pikes drawn up across the gate defied their efforts to break through. Wallace and his party were within fifty yards of the gate when reinforcements from the castle arrived. Sir John Kerr, furious at the prospect of his enemies again escaping him, headed them in their furious rush. Wallace stepped forward beyond the line and met him. With a great sweep of his mighty sword he beat down Sir John's guard, and the blade descending clove helmet and skull, and the knight fell dead in his tracks.

"That is one for you, Archie," Wallace said, as he cut down a man-at-arms.

In vain did the English try to break through the line of pikes. When they arrived within twenty yards of the gate, Wallace gave the order, and the party burst through the English who were attacking its defenders. Once again, Wallace was united with his entire troop.

"Fall back!" Wallace shouted, "and form without the gates. Your leader and I will cover the retreat." Passing between the cart and the posts of the gates, the whole party fell back. Once through, Wallace and Archie made a stand, and even the bravest of the English did not venture to pass the narrow portals, where but one could pass at a time.

The band formed in good order and retreated at rapid step. When they reached a distance of about three hundred yards, Wallace and Archie, deeming that sufficient start had been gained, sprang away, and running at top speed soon rejoined them.

"Now, Archie, what next?" Sir William asked; "since it is you who have formed this army, doubtless your plans are complete as to what shall next be done. They will have horsemen in pursuit as soon as they remove the cart."

"I have a boat in readiness on the river bank, Sir William. Once across and we shall be safe. They will hardly overtake us when we get there, seeing how swampy is the ground below."

At a slinging trot the party ran forward, and soon gained the lower ground. They were halfway across when they saw a large body of horsemen following in pursuit.

"A little to the right, Sir William," Archie said; "you see that coat flying from an oar; there is the boat."

As Archie had expected, the swampy ground impeded the speed of the horsemen. In vain the riders spurred and shouted, the horses, fetlock deep, could make but slow advance, and before they reached the bank the fugitives had reached the boat and were already halfway across the stream. Then the English had the mortification of seeing them land and march away quietly on the other side.

**As Archie expected, the swampy ground
impeded the English horsemen**

Chapter 9

The Battle of Stirling Bridge

Upon rejoining his force Sir William Wallace called together the few knights and gentlemen who were with him and said to them:

"Methinks, gentlemen, that the woes of this contest should not fall upon one side only. Every one of you here is outlawed, and if you are taken by the English will be executed or thrown in prison for life, and your lands and all belonging to you forfeited. It is time that those who fight upon the other side should learn that they too run some risk. Besides leading his vassals in the field against us, Sir John Kerr twice in arms has attacked me, and done his best to slay me or deliver me over to the English. He fell yesterday by my hand at Stirling, and I hereby declare forfeit the land which he held in the county of Lanark, part of which he wrongfully took from Sir William Forbes, and his own fief adjoining. Other broad lands he owns in Ayrshire, but these I will not now touch; but the lands in Lanark, both his own fief and that of the Forbeses, I, as Guardian of Scotland, hereby declare forfeit and confiscated, and bestow them upon my good friend, Sir Archie Forbes. Sir John Grahame, I hereby direct you to proceed tomorrow with five hundred men and take possession of the property of the Kerrs. Sir Allan Kerr is still at Stirling, and will not be there to defend it. In all likelihood, the vassals will make no resistance, but will gladly accept the change of masters. The Kerrs have the reputation of being hard lords, and their vassals cannot like being forced to fight against the cause of their country. The hired men-at-arms may resist, but you will know how to make short work of these. I ask you to go rather than Sir Archibald Forbes, because I would not that it were said that he took the Kerr's hold on his private quarrel.

"Your new possessions, Archie, will, as you know, be held on doubtful tenure. If we conquer and Scotland is freed, I doubt in no way that the king, whoever he may be, will confirm my grant. If the English win, your land is lost, be it an acre or a county. And now let me be the first to congratulate you on having won by your sword and your patriotism the lands of your father, and on having repaid upon your family's enemies the measure which they meted to you. But you will still have to beware of the Kerrs. They are a powerful family, being connected by marriage with the Comyns of Badenoch, and other noble houses. Their lands in Ayr are as extensive as those in Lanark, even with your father's lands added to their own. However, if Scotland win the day the good work that you have done should well outweigh all the influence which they might bring to bear against you.

"And now, Archie, I can, for a time, release you. Ere long Edward's army will be pouring across the border, and then I shall need every good Scotsman's sword. Till then you had best retire to your new estates and spend the time in preparing your vassals to follow you in the field, and in putting one or other of your castles in the best state of defense you may. Methinks that the Kerr's hold may more easily be made to withstand a lengthened siege than Glen Cairn, seeing that the latter is commanded by the hill beside it. Kerr's castle, too, is much larger and more strongly fortified."

"I need no thanks," he continued, as Archie was about to express his warm gratitude; "it is the Guardian of Scotland who rewards your services to the country; but Sir William Wallace will not forget how you have twice stood beside him against overwhelming odds, and how yesterday, in Stirling, it was your watchful care and thoughtful precaution which alone saved his life."

Archie's friends all congratulated him warmly, and the next morning, with his own band, he started for Glen Cairn. Here the news that he was once more their lawful chief caused the greatest delight. It was evening when he reached the village, and soon great bonfires blazed in the street, and as the news spread new fires began at many an outlying farm. Before night all the vassals of the estate came in, and Glen Cairn and the village was a scene of great enthusiasm.

Much as Archie regretted that he could not establish himself in the home of his father, he felt that Wallace's suggestion was the right one. Glen Cairn was a mere shell, and could in no case be made capable of a prolonged resistance by a powerful force. Whereas, the castle of the Kerrs was very strong. It was a disappointment to his retainers when they heard that he could not at once return among them; but they saw the force of his reasons, and he promised that if Scotland was freed and peace restored, he would again make Glen Cairn habitable, and pass some of his time there.

"In the meantime," he said, "I shall be but eight miles from you, and the estate will be all one. But now I hope that for the next three months every man among you will aid me—some by personal labor, some by sending horses and carts—in the work of strengthening to the utmost my new castle of Aberfilly, which I wish to make so strong that it will long resist an attack. Should Scotland be permanently conquered, which may God forbid, it could not, of course, be held; but should we have temporary reverses we might well hold out until our cause again prospers."

Every man on the estate promised his aid to an extent far beyond that which Archie, as their feudal superior, had a right to demand from them. They had had a hard time under the Kerrs, who had raised all taxes, and greatly increased their feudal services. They were sure of good treatment should the Forbeses make good their position as their lords, and were ready to make any sacrifices to aid them to do so.

The next morning a messenger arrived from Sir John Grahame, saying that he had, during the night, stormed Aberfilly, and that with scarce an exception all the vassals of the Kerrs—when upon his arrival on the previous day they had learned of his purpose in coming, and of the disposition which Wallace had made of the estate—had accepted the change with delight, and had joined him in the assault upon the castle, which was defended by only thirty men-at-arms. These had all been killed, and Sir John invited Archie to ride over at once and take possession. This he did, and found that the vassals of the estate were all gathered at the castle to welcome him. He was introduced to them by Sir John Grahame, and they received Archie with shouts of enthusiasm, and all swore obedience to him as their feudal lord. Archie promised them to be a kind and lenient chief, to abate any unfair burdens which had been laid upon them, and to respect all their rights. "But," he said "just at first I must ask for sacrifices from you. This castle is strong, but it must be made much stronger, and must be capable of standing a continued siege in case temporary reverses should enable the English to endeavor to retake it for their friend, Sir Allan Kerr. My vassals at Glen Cairn have promised an aid far beyond that which I can command, and I trust that you also will extend your time of feudal service, and promise you a relaxation in future years equivalent to the time you may now give me."

The demand was readily assented to, for the tenants of Aberfilly were no less delighted than those of Glen Cairn to escape from the rule of the Kerrs. Archie, accompanied by Sir John Grahame, now made an inspection of the walls of his new hold. It stood just where the counties of Linlithgow and Edinburgh join that of Lanark. The castle was built on an island on a tributary of the Clyde. The stream was but a small one, and the island had been artificially made, so that the stream formed a moat on either side of it, the castle occupying a knoll of ground which rose somewhat abruptly from the surrounding country. The moat was but twelve feet wide, and Archie and Sir John decided that this should be widened to fifty feet and deepened to ten, and that a dam should be built just below the castle to keep back the stream and fill the moat. The walls should everywhere be raised ten feet, several strong additional flanking towers added, and a work built beyond the moat to guard the head of the drawbridge. With such additions Aberfilly would be able to stand a long siege by any force which might assail it.

Timber, stones, and rough labor there were in abundance, and Wallace had insisted upon Archie's taking from the treasures which had been captured from the enemy, a sum of money which would be ample to hire skilled masons from Lanark, and to pay for the cement, iron and other necessaries which would be beyond the resources of the estate. These matters in train, Archie rode to Lanark and fetched his proud and rejoicing mother from Sir Robert Gordon's to Aberfilly. She was accompanied by Sandy Grahame and Elspie; the former Archie appointed major-domo,[8] and to be in command of the garrison whenever he should be absent.

The vassals were as good as their word. For three months the work of digging, quarrying, cutting and squaring timber and building went on without intermission. There were upon the estates fully three hundred able-bodied men, and the work progressed rapidly. When, therefore, Archie received a message from Wallace to join him near Stirling, he felt that he could leave Aberfilly without any fear of a successful attack being made upon it in his absence.

There was need, indeed, for every Scot, capable of bearing arms, to gather round Wallace. Under the Earl of Surrey, the high treasurer Cressingham, and other leaders, an army of fifty thousand footmen and one thousand horse were advancing from Berwick, while eight thousand footmen and three hundred horse under Earl Percy advanced from Carlisle. Wallace was besieging the castle of Dundee when he heard of their approach, and leaving the people of Dundee to carry on the siege under the command of Sir Alexander Scrymgeour, he himself marched to defend the only bridge by which Edward could cross the Forth, near Stirling.

Thus far Surrey had experienced no resistance, and at the head of so large and well appointed a force he might well feel sure of success. A large proportion of his army consisted of veterans exposed to service in wars at home, in Wales, and with the French. These veterans, along with the mail-clad knights and men-at-arms looked with absolute contempt upon the rabble which was opposed to them. The Scottish army consisted solely of popular levies of men who had left their homes and taken up arms for the freedom of their country. They were rudely armed and hastily trained. Of all the feudal nobles of Scotland who should have led them but one, Sir Andrew Moray, was present. Their commander was still little more than a youth, who, great as was his individual valor and prowess, had had no experience in the art of war on a large scale; while the English were led by a general whose fame was known throughout Europe.

The Scots took up their station upon the high ground north of the Forth, protected from observation by the precipitous hill

---

8.   A man in charge of a great, royal, or noble household; a chief steward.

immediately behind Cambuskenneth Abbey and known as the Abbey Craig. In a bend of the river opposite the Abbey Craig stood the bridge by which the English army were preparing to cross. Archie stood beside Wallace on the top of the craig looking at the English array.

"It is a fair sight," he said; "the great camp, with its pavilions, its banners and pennons, lying there in the valley, with the old castle rising on the lofty rock behind them. It is a pity that such a sight should bode evil to Scotland."

"Yes," Wallace said; "I would that the camp lay where it is, but that the pennons and banners were those of Scotland's nobles, and that the royal lions floated over Surrey's tent. Truly that were a sight which would glad a Scot's heart. When shall we see aught like it? However, Archie," he went on in a lighter tone, "methinks that that will be a rare camp to plunder."

Archie laughed. "One must kill the lion before one talks of dividing his skin," he said; "and truly it seems well-nigh impossible that such a following as yours, true Scots and brave men though they be, yet altogether undisciplined and new to war, should be able to bear the brunt of such a battle."

"You are thinking of Dunbar," Wallace said; "and did we fight in such a field our chances would be poor; but with that broad river in front and but a narrow bridge for access, methinks that we can render an account of them."

"God grant it be so!" Archie replied; "but I shall be right glad when the day is over."

Three days before the battle the Steward of Scotland, and Earl of Lennox, and others of the Scottish contingent entered Surrey's camp and begged that he would not attack until they tried to induce the people to lay down their arms. They returned, however, on the third day saying that they would not listen to them, but that the next day they would themselves join his army with their men-at-arms. On leaving the camp that evening the Scottish nobles, riding homeward, were forced to fight with some English soldiers, of whom one was wounded by the Earl of Lennox. News being brought to Surrey, he resolved to wait no longer, but gave orders that the assault should take place on the following morning. At daybreak on the eleventh of September, 1297, one of the outposts woke Wallace with the news that the English

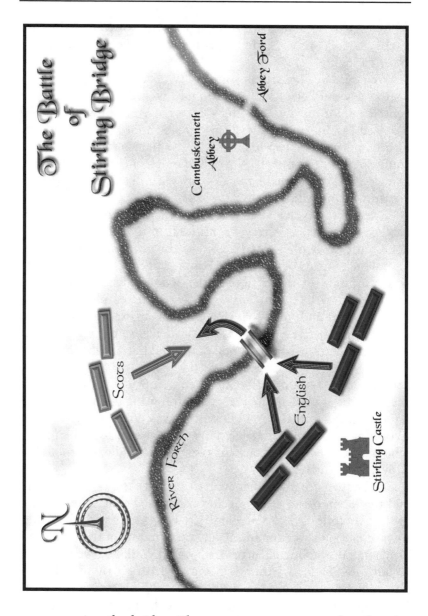

were crossing the bridge. The troops were at once placed under arms, and were eager to rush down to commence the battle, but Wallace restrained them. Five thousand Welsh foot-soldiers crossed the bridge, then there was a pause, and none were seen following them. "Were we to charge down now, Sir William?" Archie said, "surely we might destroy that body before aid could come to them."

"We could do, Archie, as you say," Wallace replied, "but such a success would be of little worth, nay, would harm rather than benefit us, for Surrey, learning that we are not altogether to be despised, as he now believes, would be more prudent in the future and would keep his army in the flat country, where we could do naught against it. No, to win much one must risk much, and we must wait until half of Surrey's army is across before we venture down against them."

Presently the Welsh were seen to retire again. Their movement had been premature. Surrey was still asleep, and nothing could be done until he awoke; when he did so the army armed leisurely, after which Surrey bestowed the honor of knighthood upon many young aspirants. The number of the Scots under Wallace is not certainly known; the majority of the estimates place it below twenty thousand, and as the English historian, who best describes the battle, speaks of it as the defeat of the many by the few; it can certainly be assumed that it did not exceed this number.

Only on the ground of his utter contempt for the enemy can the conduct of the Earl of Surrey, in attempting to engage in such a position, be understood. The bridge was wide enough for but two, or at most three, horsemen to cross abreast; and when those who had crossed were attacked, assistance could reach them but slowly from the rear.

The English knights and men-at-arms, with the Royal Standard and the banner of the Earl of Surrey, crossed first. The men-at-arms were followed by the infantry, who, as they passed, formed up on the tongue of land formed by the winding of the river.

When half the English army had passed Wallace gave the order to advance. First Sir Andrew Moray, with two thousand men, descended the hills further to the right, and on seeing these the English cavalry charged at once against them. The instant they did so Wallace, with his main army, poured down from the craig impetuously and swept away the English near the head of the bridge, taking possession of the end, and by showers of arrows and darts preventing any more from crossing. By this maneuver the whole of the English infantry who had crossed were cut off from their friends and enclosed in the narrow promontory.

The English men-at-arms had succeeded in overthrowing the Scots, against whom they had charged, and had pursued them some distance; but upon drawing rein and turning to rejoin the army, they found the aspect of affairs changed indeed. The troops left at the head of the bridge were overthrown and destroyed. The royal banner and that of Surrey were down, and the bridge was now in the possession of the enemy. The men-at-arms charged back and strove in vain to recover the head of the bridge. The greater proportion of the men-at-arms were killed. One valiant knight alone, Sir Marmaduke de Twenge, with his nephew and a squire, cut their way through the Scots, and crossed the bridge. Many were drowned in attempting to swim the river, only one succeeding in so gaining the opposite side.

The men-at-arms defeated, Wallace and the chosen band under him, who had been engaged with them, joined those who were attacking the English and Welsh, now cooped up in the promontory. Flushed with the success already gained the Scots were irresistible, and almost every man who had crossed was either killed or drowned in attempting to swim the river. No sooner had he seen that success in this quarter was secure than Wallace led a large number of his followers across the bridge. Here the English, who still outnumbered his army, and who had now all the advantage of position which had previously been on the side of the Scots, might have defended the bridge, or in good order have given him battle on the other side. The sight, however, of the terrible disaster which had befallen nearly half their number before their eyes, without their being able to render them the slightest assistance, had completely demoralized them, and as soon as the Scots were seen to be crossing the bridge they fled in terror. A hot pursuit was kept up by the fleet-footed and lightly-armed Scots, and great numbers of fugitives were slain.

More than twenty thousand English perished in the battle or flight, and the remainder crossed the border a mere herd of broken fugitives.

The Earl of Surrey, before riding off the field, committed the charge of the castle of Stirling to Sir Marmaduke de Twenge, promising him that he would return to his relief within ten weeks at the utmost. All the tents, wagons, horses, provisions, and stores of the English fell into the hands of their enemies, and every Scottish soldier obtained rich booty.

Cressingham was among the number killed. It was said by one English historian, and his account has been copied by many others, that Cressingham's body was flayed and his skin divided among the Scots; but there appears no good foundation for the story, although Cressingham, who had rendered himself peculiarly obnoxious and hateful to the Scots, was probably hewn in pieces. But even were it proved that the story is a true one, it need excite no surprise, seeing the wholesale slaying, plundering, and burning which had been carried on by the English, and that the Scottish prisoners falling into their hands were often mutilated and tortured before being executed and quartered. The English historians were fond of crying out that the Scots were cruel and barbarous people whenever they retaliated for the treatment which they suffered; but so far from this being the case, it is probable that the Scots before the first invasion of Edward, were a more enlightened and, for their numbers, a more well-to-do people than the English. They had for many years enjoyed peace and tranquillity, and under the long and prosperous reign of Alexander had made great advances, while England had been harassed by continuous wars and troubles at home and abroad. Its warlike barons, when not engaged under its monarchs in wars in Wales, Ireland, and France, occupied themselves in quarrels with each other, or in struggles against the royal supremacy; and although the higher nobles, with their mail-clad followers, could show an amount of chivalrous pomp unknown in Scotland, yet the condition of the middle classes and of the agricultural population was higher in Scotland than in England.

Archie, as one of the principal leaders of the victorious army, received a share of the treasure captured in the camp sufficient to repay the money which he had had for the strengthening of the castle of Aberfilly, and on the day following the battle he received permission from Sir William to return at once, with the two hundred and fifty retainers which he had brought into the field, to complete the rebuilding of the castle. In another three months this was completed, and stores of arms and munition of all kinds were collected.

Immediately after the defeat at Stirling Bridge, King Edward summoned the Scottish nobles to join Brian Fitzallan, whom he appointed governor of Scotland, with their whole forces, for the purpose of putting down the rebellion. Among those addressed as his allies were the Earls Comyn of Badenoch, Comyn of Buchan, Patrick of Dunbar, Umfraville of Angus, Alexander of Menteith, Malise of Strathearn, Malcolm of Lennox, and William of Sutherland, together with James the Steward, Nicholas de la Haye, Ingelram de Umfraville, Richard Fraser, and Alexander de Lindsay of Crawford. From this enumeration it is clear that Wallace had still many enemies to contend with at home as well as the force of England. Patrick of Dunbar, assisted by Robert Bruce and Bishop Anthony Beck, took the field, but was defeated. Wallace captured all the castles of the earl save Dunbar itself, and forced him to fly to England; then the Scottish army poured across the border and retaliated upon the northern counties for the deeds which the English had been performing in Scotland for the last eight years. The country was ravaged to the very walls of Durham and Carlisle, and only those districts which bought off the invaders were spared. The title which had been bestowed upon Wallace by a comparatively small number was now ratified by the commonalty of the whole of Scotland; and associated with him was the young Sir Andrew Moray of Bothwell, whose father had been the only Scottish noble who had fought at Stirling, and it is notable that in some of the documents of the time Wallace gives precedence to Andrew Moray.

They proceeded to effect a military organization for the country of Scotland, dividing it up into districts, each with commanders and lieutenants. Order was established and negotiations entered into for the mutual safeguard of traders with the Hanse towns. The nobles who ventured to oppose the authority of Wallace and his colleague were punished in some cases by the confiscation of lands, which were bestowed upon Sir Alexander Scrymgeour and other loyal gentlemen, and these grants were recognized by Bruce when he became king. In these deeds of grant Wallace and Moray, although acting as governors of Scotland, state that they did so in the name of Baliol as king, although a helpless captive in England. For a short time Scotland enjoyed peace, save that Earl Percy responded to the raids made by the

Scots across the border, by carrying fire and sword through Annandale. The English writers and historians who complain of the conduct of the Scots have no word of rebuke for the proclamation issued to the soldiers on crossing the border, that they were free to plunder where they chose, nor as to the men and women slain, nor the villages and churches committed to the flames.

Chapter 10

The Battle of Falkirk

While Wallace was endeavoring to restore order in Scotland, Edward was straining every nerve to renew his invasion. He himself was upon the Continent, but he made various concessions to his barons and great towns to induce them to aid him heartily, and issued writs calling upon the whole nobility remaining at home, as they valued his honor and that of England, to meet at York on January twentieth, "and proceed under the Earl of Surrey to repress and chastise the audacity of the Scots." At the same time he despatched special letters to those of the Scottish nobles who were not already in England, commanding them to appear at the rendezvous.

The call upon the Scottish nobles was not generally responded to. They had lost much of their power over their vassals, many of whom had fought under Wallace in spite of the abstention of their lords. It was clear, too, that if they joined the English, and another defeat of the latter took place, their countrymen might no longer condone their treachery, but their titles and estates might be confiscated. Consequently but few of them presented themselves at York. There, however, the English nobles gathered in force. The Earls of Surrey, Gloucester and Arundel; the Earl Mareschal and the great Constable were there; Guido, son of the Earl of Warwick, represented his father. Percy was there, John de Wathe, John de Seagrave, and very many other barons, the great array consisting of two thousand horsemen heavily armed, twelve hundred light horsemen, and one hundred thousand foot-soldiers.

Sir Aymer de Vallance, the Earl of Pembroke, and John Sieward, son of the Earl of March, landed with an army in Fife, and proceeded to burn and siege towns. They were met by a patriot force under Wallace in the forest of Black Ironside, and were totally defeated.

Surrey's army crossed the border, raised the siege of Roxburgh, and advanced as far as Kelso. Wallace did not venture to oppose so enormous a force, but wasted the country on every side so that they could draw no provisions from it, and Surrey was forced to fall back to Berwick; this town was being besieged by a Scottish force, which retired at his approach. Here the English army halted upon receipt of orders from Edward to wait his coming. He hastily patched up a peace with France, and, having landed at Sandwich, summoned the parliament, and on the twenty-seventh of May issued writs to as many as one hundred and fifty-four of his great barons to meet him at Roxburgh on the twenty-fourth of June. Here three thousand cavalry, men and horses clothed in complete armor, met with four thousand lighter cavalry, the riders being armed in steel but the horses being uncovered. They were joined by five hundred splendidly mounted knights and men-of-arms from Gascony; and at least eighty thousand infantry assembled together. This huge army marched from Roxburgh, keeping near the coast, receiving provisions from a fleet which sailed along beside them. But in spite of this precaution it was delayed for a month near Edinburgh, as Wallace so wasted the country that the army was almost famished. In spite of numerous attempts, the English were unable to bring on a battle with the Scots, whose rapid marches and intimate acquaintance with the country baffled all the efforts of the English leaders to force on an action.

Edward was about to retreat, being unable any longer to subsist his army, when the two Scottish Earls of Dunbar and Angus sent news to the king that Wallace was with his army in Falkirk forest, about six miles away, and had arranged to attack the camp on the following morning. The English at once advanced and that evening encamped at Linlithgow, and the next morning moved on against the Scots.

Late in the evening Archie's scouts brought in the news to Wallace that the English army was within three miles, and a consultation was at once held between the leaders. Most of them were in favor of a retreat; but Comyn of Badenoch, who had recently joined Wallace, and had been from his rank appointed to the command of the cavalry, with some of his associates, urged strongly the necessity for fighting, saying that the men would be utterly

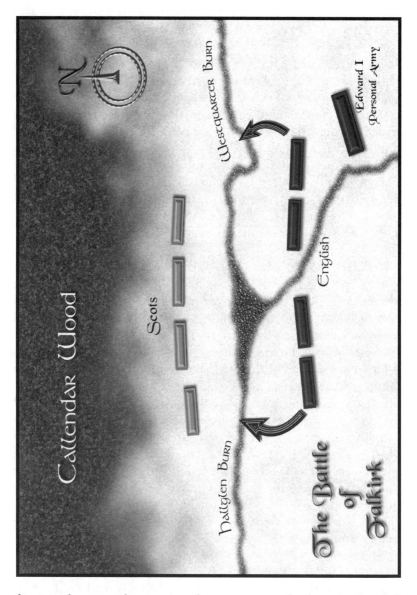

dispirited at such continual retreats, and that with such immensely superior cavalry the English would follow them up and destroy them. To these arguments Wallace, Sir John Grahame, and Sir John Stewart, yielded their own opinions, and prepared to fight. They took up their position so that their front was protected by a morass, and a fence of stakes and ropes was also fixed across so as to impede the advance or retreat of the English cavalry. The Scottish army consisted almost entirely of infantry. These were about a third the number of those of the English, while Comyn's cavalry were a thousand strong.

The infantry was formed in three great squares or circles, the front rank kneeling and the spears all pointing outward. In the space between these squares were placed the archers, under Sir John Stewart.

The English army was drawn up in three divisions. The first was commanded by the Earl Mareschal, the Earl of Lincoln and Hereford; the second by Beck, the warlike Bishop of Durham, and Sir Ralph Basset; the third by the king himself. The first two divisions consisted almost entirely of knights and men-at-arms; the third, of archers and slingers.

Wallace's plan of battle was that the Scottish squares should first receive the brunt of the onslaught of the enemy, and that while the English were endeavoring to break these, the Scottish cavalry, which were drawn up some distance in the rear, should fall upon them when in a confused mass and drive them against the fence or into the morass.

The first division of the English on arriving at the bog made a circuit to the west. The second division, seeing the obstacle which the first had encountered, moved round to the east, and both fell upon the Scottish squares. The instant they were seen rounding the ends of the morass, the traitor Comyn, with the whole of the cavalry, turned rein and fled from the field, leaving the infantry alone to support the whole brunt of the attack on the English. So impetuous was the charge of the latter that Sir John Stewart and his archers were unable to gain the shelter of the squares, and he was, with almost all his men, slain by the English men-at-arms. Thus the spearmen were left entirely to their own resources.

Encouraged by Wallace, Grahame, Archie Forbes, and their other leaders, the Scottish squares stood firmly, and the English cavalry in vain strove to break the hedge of spears. Again and again the bravest of the chivalry of England tried to hew a way through. The Scots stood firm and undismayed, and had the battle lain between them and the English cavalry, the day would have been theirs. But presently the king, with his enormous body of infantry, arrived on the ground, and the English archers and slingers poured clouds of missiles into the ranks of the Scots; while the English spearmen, picking up the great stones with which the ground was strewn, hurled them at the front ranks of their foes. Against this storm of missiles the Scottish squares could do nothing. Such armor as they had was useless against the English cloth-yard arrows and thousands fell as they stood.

Again and again they closed up the gaps in their ranks, but at last they could no longer withstand the hail of arrows and stones, to which they could offer no return. Some of them wavered. The gaps in the squares were no longer filled up, and the English cavalry, who had been waiting their opportunity, charged into the midst of them. No longer was there any thought of resistance. The Scots fled in all directions. Numbers were drowned in trying to swim the river Carron, which ran close by. Multitudes were cut down by the host of English cavalry.

Sir Archie Forbes was in the same square with Wallace with a few other mounted men. They dashed forward against the English as they broke through the ranks of the spearmen, but the force which opposed them was overwhelming.

"It is of no use, Archie; we must retire. Better that than throw away our lives uselessly. All is lost now."

Wallace shouted to the spearmen, who gallantly rallied round him, and, keeping together in spite of the efforts of the English cavalry, succeeded in withdrawing from the field. The other squares were entirely broken and dispersed, and scarce a man of them escaped.

Accounts vary as to the amount of the slaughter, some English writers placing it as double that of the army which Wallace could possibly have brought into the field, seeing that the whole of the great nobles stood aloof, and that Grahame, Stewart, and Macduff of Fife were the only three men of noble family with him. All these were slain, together with some twenty-five thousand infantry.

Wallace with about five thousand men succeeded in crossing a ford of the Carron, and the English spread themselves over the country. The districts of Fife, Clackmannan, Lanark, Ayr, and all the surrounding country were wasted and burned, and every man found put to the sword.

The Scots themselves in retreating destroyed Stirling and Perth, and the English found the town of St. Andre's deserted and burned it to the ground.

No sooner had Wallace retreated than he divided his force into small bands, which proceeded in separate directions, driving off the cattle and destroying all stores of grain, so that in a fortnight after the battle of Falkirk the English army were again brought to a stand by shortness of provisions, and were compelled to fall back again with all speed to the mouth of the Forth, there to obtain provisions from their ships. As they did so Wallace reunited his bands, and pressed hard upon them. At Linlithgow he fell upon their rear and inflicted heavy loss, and so hotly did he press them that the great army was obliged to retreat rapidly across the border, and made no halt until it reached the fortress of Carlisle.

That it was compulsion alone which forced Edward to make this speedy retreat we may be sure from the fact that after the victory of Dunbar, he was contented with nothing less than a clean sweep of Scotland to its northern coast, and that he repeated the same process when, in the year following the battle of Falkirk, he again returned with a mighty army. Thus decisive as was the battle of Falkirk, it ultimately had little impact on the towns of Scotland.

When the English had crossed the border, Wallace assembled the few gentlemen who were still with him, and announced his intention of resigning the guardianship of Scotland, and of leaving the country. The announcement was received with exclamations of surprise and regret.

"Surely, Sir William," Archie exclaimed, "you cannot mean it. You are our only leader; in you we have unbounded confidence, and in none else. Had it not been for the treachery of Comyn, the field of Falkirk would have been ours, for had the horse charged when the English were in confusion round our squares they would have assuredly been defeated. Moreover, your efforts have retrieved that disastrous field, and have driven the English across the border."

"My dear Archie," Wallace said, "it is because I am the only leader in whom you have confidence that I must needs go. I had vainly hoped that when the Scottish nobles saw what great things the commonalty were able to do, and how far, alone and unaided, they had cleared Scotland of her tyrants, they would have joined us with their vassals; but you see it is not so. The successes that I have gained have but excited their envy against me. Of them all only Grahame, Stewart, and Macduff stood by my side, while all the great earls and barons either stayed aloof or were like Bruce, in the ranks of Edward's army, or like Comyn and his friends who joined me solely to betray me. I am convinced now that it is only a united Scotland that can resist the power of England, and it is certain that so long as I remain here Scotland never can be united. Of Bruce, I have no longer any hope; but if I retire, Comyn may take the lead, and many at least of the Scottish nobles will follow him. Had we but horsemen and archers to support our spearmen, I would not fear the issue; but it is the nobles alone who can place mounted men-at-arms in the field. Of bowmen we must always be deficient, seeing that our people take not naturally to this arm as do the English; but with spearmen to break the first shock of English chivalry, and with horsemen to charge them when in confusion, we may yet succeed, but horsemen we shall never get so long as the nobles hold aloof. It is useless to try and change my decision, my friends. Some grief though it will be to me to sheath my sword and to stand aloof when Scotland struggles for freedom, I am convinced that only by my doing so has Scotland a chance of ultimate success in the struggle. Do not make it harder for me by your pleadings. I have thought long over this, and my mind is made up. My heart is well-nigh broken by the death of my dear friend and brother-in-arms, Sir John Grahame and I feel able to struggle no longer against the jealousy and hostility of the Scottish nobles."

Wallace's hearers were all in tears at his decision, but they felt that there was truth in his words that the Scottish nobles were far more influenced by feelings of personal jealousy than by patriotism, and that so long as Wallace remained the guardian of Scotland they would, to a man, side with the English. The next day Wallace assembled all his followers, and in a few words announced his determination, and the reasons which had driven him to take it. He urged them to let no feelings of resentment at the treatment he had experienced, or any wrath at the lukewarmness and treachery which had hitherto marked the Scottish nobles, overcome their feeling of patriotism, but to follow these leaders should they raise the banner of Scotland, as bravely and devotedly as they had followed him.

Then he bade them farewell, and mounting his horse rode to the seacoast and passed over to France.

Although he had retired from Scotland, Wallace did not cease from war against the English; but being warmly received by the French king fought against them both by sea and land, and won much renown among the French.

After returning to England, Edward, finding that the Scottish leaders still professed to recognize Baliol as king, sent him to the pope at Rome, having first confiscated all his great possessions in England, and bestowed them upon his own nephew, John of Brittany; and during the rest of his life Baliol lived in obscurity in Rome. A portion of the Scottish nobles assembled and chose John Comyn of Badenoch and John de Soulis as guardians of the kingdom. In the autumn of the following year Edward again assembled a great army and moved north, but it was late; and in the face of the approaching winter, and the difficulty of forage, many of the barons refused to advance. Edward himself marched across the border; but seeing that the Scots had assembled in force, and that at such a season of the year he could not hope to carry his designs fully into execution, he retired without striking a blow. Thereupon the castle of Stirling, which was invested by the Scots, seeing no hope of relief, surrendered, and Sir William Oliphant was appointed governor.

The next spring, Edward again advanced with an army even greater than that with which he had before he entered Scotland. With him were Alexander of Baliol, son of the late king, who was devoted to the English; Dunbar, Fraser, Ross, and other Scottish nobles. The vast army first laid siege to the little castle of Carlaverock, which, although defended by but sixty men, resisted for some time the assaults of the whole army, but was at last captured. The Scots fell back as Edward advanced, renewing Wallace's tactics of wasting the country, and Edward could get no further than Dumfries. Here, finding the enormous difficulties which beset him, he made a pretense of yielding with a good grace to the entreaties of the pope and the King of France that he would spare Scotland; he retired to England and disbanded his army, having accomplished nothing in the campaign save the capture of Carlaverock.

The following summer he again advanced with the army, this time supported by a fleet of seventy ships. The Scots resorted to their usual strategy, and, when winter came, the invaders had penetrated no further than the Forth. Edward remained at Linlithgow for a time, and then returned to England. Sir Simon Fraser, who had been one of the leaders of the English army at Carlaverock, now imitated Comyn's example, and deserting the English cause, joined his countrymen.

The greater part of the English army recrossed the border, and the Scots captured many of the garrisons left in the towns. Sir John Seagrave next invaded Scotland with from twenty thousand to thirty thousand men, mostly cavalry. They reached the neighborhood of Edinburgh when Comyn and Fraser advanced against them with eight thousand men, chiefly infantry. The English army was advancing in three divisions, in order better to obtain provisions and forage. After a rapid night march, the Scots came upon one of them, commanded by Seagrave in person; and conceiving himself sufficiently strong to defeat the Scots unaided by any of the other divisions, Sir John Seagrave immediately gave battle.

As at Falkirk, the English cavalry were unable to break through the Scottish pikes. Great numbers were killed or taken prisoners, Seagrave himself being severely wounded and captured, with twenty distinguished knights, thirty esquires, and many soldiers. Scarcely was the battle over when the second English division, even stronger than the first, arrived on the field. Encumbered by their prisoners, the Scots were at a disadvantage; and fearing to be attacked by these in the rear while engaged in front, they slaughtered the greater portion of the prisoners, and arming the camp-followers, prepared to resist the English onslaught. This failed as the first had done; the English cavalry were defeated with great loss by the spearmen, and many prisoners again taken—among them Sir Ralph Manton.

The third English division now appeared; and the Scots, worn out by their long march and the two severe conflicts they had endured, were about to fly from the field when their leaders exhorted them to one more effort. The second batch of prisoners were slaughtered, and the pikemen again formed line to resist the English charge. Again were the cavalry defeated, Sir Robert Neville, their leader, slain, with many others, and the whole dispersed and scattered. Sir Robert Manton, who was the king's treasurer, had had a quarrel with Fraser, when the latter was in Edward's service, regarding his pay; and Fraser is said by some historians to have now revenged himself by slaying his prisoner. Other accounts, however, represent Manton as having escaped.

The slaughter of the prisoners appears, although cruel, to have been unavoidable; as the Scots, having before them a well-appointed force fully equal to their own in number, could not have risked engaging, with so large a body of prisoners in their rear. None of the knights or other leaders were slain, these being subsequently exchanged or ransomed, as we afterward find them fighting in the English ranks.

Seeing by this defeat that a vast effort was necessary to conquer Scotland, King Edward advanced in the spring of 1303 with an army of such numbers that the historians of the time content themselves with saying that "it was great beyond measure." It consisted of English, Welsh, Irish, Gascons, and Savoyards. One division, under the Prince of Wales, advanced by the west coasts; that of the king, by the east; and the two united at the Forth. Without meeting with any serious resistance the great host marched north through Perth and Dundee to Brechin, where the castle, under the charge of Sir Thomas Maille, surrendered after twenty days.

The English then marched north through Aberdeen, Banff and Moray into Caithness, carrying utter destruction everywhere; towns and hamlets, villages and farmhouses were alike destroyed; crops were burned, forests and orchards cut down. Thus was the whole of Scotland wasted; and even the rich abbeys of Abberbredok and Dunfermline, the richest and most famous in Scotland, were destroyed, and the whole leveled to the ground. It was the intention of Edward to blot out the Scottish people, and to reduce the land to a condition of irrecoverable devastation, and thus to stamp out forever any further resistance in Scotland.

During the three years which had elapsed since the departure of Wallace, Archie had for the most part remained quietly in his castle, occupying himself with the comfort and well-being of his vassals. He had, each time the English entered Scotland, taken the field with a portion of his retainers, in obedience to the summons of Comyn. The latter was little disposed to hold valid the grants made by Wallace, especially in the case of Archie Forbes, the Kerrs being connections to his house; but the feeling of the people in general was too strongly in favor of the companion of Wallace for him to venture to set it aside, especially as the castle could not be captured without a long-continued siege. Archie and many of the nobles hostile to the claims of Comyn obeyed his orders, he being the sole possible leader, at present, of Scotland. Edward, however, had left them no alternative, since he had, in order to induce the English nobles to follow him, formally divided among them the lands of the whole of the Scottish nobles, save those actually fighting in his ranks.

Archie was now nearly twenty-three, and his frame had fully borne out the promise of his youth. He was over the average height, but appeared shorter from the extreme breadth of his shoulders; his arms were long and sinewy, and his personal strength immense.

From the time of his first taking possession of Aberfilly he had kept a party of men steadily engaged in excavating a passage from the castle toward a wood a mile distant. The ground was soft and offered but few obstacles, but the tunnel throughout its whole length had to be supported by massive timbers. Wood, however, was abundant, and the passage had by this time been completed. Whenever, from the length of the tunnel, the workmen began to suffer from lack of air, ventilation was obtained by way of a small shaft that ran up to the surface; in this was placed a square wooden tube about six inches in diameter, round which the earth was again filled in. A few rapidly-growing plants and bushes were planted round the orifice to prevent its being noticed by any passer-by.

Chapter 11

Robert the Bruce

During the last great invasion of Scotland by King Edward, Archie did not take the field, seeing that Comyn, in despair of opposing so vast a host, did not call out the levies. Upon the approach of the English army under the Prince of Wales, Archie called the whole of his tenants into the castle. Great stores of provisions had already been collected. The women and children were sent away up into the hills, where provisions had also been garnered, and the old men and boys accompanied them. As the Prince of Wales passed north, bands from his army spreading over the country destroyed every house in the district. Archie was summoned to surrender, but refused to do so; and the prince, being on his way to join his father on the Forth, after himself surveying the hold, and judging it far too strong to be carried without a prolonged siege, marched forward, promising on his return to destroy it.

Soon afterward Archie received a message that Wallace had returned. He at once took with him fifty men, and leaving the castle in charge of Sandy Grahame, with the rest of his vassals, two hundred and fifty in number, he rejoined his former leader. Many others gathered round Wallace's standard; and throughout Edward's march to the north and his return to the Forth Wallace hung upon his flanks, cutting off and slaying great numbers of the marauders, and striking blows at detached bands wherever these were in numbers not too formidable to be coped with.

Stirling was now the only great castle which remained in the hands of the Scots, and King Edward prepared to lay siege to this. Save for the band of Wallace there was no longer any open resistance in the field. A few holds like those of Archie Forbes still remained in the hands of their owners, their insignificance, or the time which would be wasted in subduing them, having protected them from siege. None of the nobles now remained in arms.

Bruce had for a short time taken the field; but had, as usual hastened to make his peace with Edward. Comyn and all his adherents surrendered upon promise of their lives and freedom, and that they should retain their lands, subject to a pecuniary fine. All the nobles of Scotland were included in this capitulation, save a few who were condemned to suffer temporary banishment. Sir William Wallace alone was by name specially exempted from the surrender.

Stirling Castle was besieged on the twentieth of April, 1304, and for seventy days held out against all the efforts of Edward's army. Warlike engines of all kinds had been brought from England for the siege. The religious houses of St. Andrews, Brechin, and other churches were stripped of lead for the catapults. The sheriffs of London, Lincoln, York, and the governor of the Tower were ordered to collect and forward all the mangonels,[9] quarrels, and bows and arrows they could gather; and for seventy days missiles of all kinds, immense stones, leaden balls, and javelins were rained upon the castles; and Greek fire—a new and terrible mode of destruction—was also used in the siege. But it was only when their provisions and other resources were exhausted that the garrison capitulated; and it was found that the survivors of the garrison which had defended Stirling Castle for upward of three months against the whole force of England numbered, including its governor, Sir William Oliphant, and twenty-four knights and gentlemen, but a hundred and twenty soldiers, two monks, and thirteen females.

During the siege Wallace had kept the field, but Archie had, at his request, returned to his castle, which being but a day's march from Stirling, might at any moment be besieged. Several times, indeed, parties appeared before it, but Edward's hands were too full, and he could spare none of the catapults needed to undertake such a siege. After Stirling finally fell, Edward and his army were in too great haste to return to England to undertake another prolonged siege, especially as Aberfilly, standing in a retired position, and commanding none of the principal roads, was a hold of no political importance.

---

9. Ancient military apparatuses for hurling heavy stones and other missiles.

A short time afterward to Archie's immense grief, Sir William Wallace was betrayed into the hands of the English. Several Scottish nobles took part in this base act, the principal being Sir John Menteith. Late historians, in their ardor to whitewash those who have for ages been held up to infamy, have endeavored to show that Sir John Menteith was not concerned in the matter; but the evidence is overwhelming the other way. Scottish historians at the time, and for generations afterward, universally imputed the crime to him. Fordun, who wrote in the reign of Robert Bruce, Bowyer, and Langtoft, all Scottish historians, say that it was he who betrayed Wallace, and their account is confirmed by contemporary English writings. Sir Francis Palgrave had discovered in the memoranda of the business of the privy-council that forty marks were bestowed upon the young man who spied out Wallace, sixty marks were divided among some others who assisted in his capture, and that to Sir John Menteith was given land of the annual value of one hundred pounds—a very large amount in those days.

The manner in which Wallace was seized is uncertain; but he was at once handed by Sir John Menteith to Sir John Seagrave, and carried by him to London. He was taken on horseback to Westminster, the mayor, sheriffs, and aldermen, with a great number of horse and footmen, accompanying him. There the mockery of a trial was held, and he was in one day tried, condemned, and executed. He defended himself nobly, urging truly that, as a native-born Scotsman, he had never sworn allegiance to England, and that he was perfectly justified in fighting for the freedom of his country.

Every cruelty attended his execution. He was drawn through the streets at the tails of horses; he was hung for some time by a halter, but was taken down while yet alive; he was mutilated and disemboweled. The head of Wallace was then cut off, his body divided in four, his head impaled over London Bridge, and his quarters distributed to four principal towns in Scotland. Such barbarities were common at executions in the days of the Norman kings, who have been described by modern writers as chivalrous monarchs.

A nobler character than Wallace is not to be found in history. Alone, a poor and landless knight, by his personal valor and energy he aroused the spirit of his countrymen, and in spite of the opposition of the whole of the nobles of his country banded the people in resistance against England, and for a time wrested all Scotland from the hands of Edward. His bitter enemies the English were unable to adduce any proofs that the epithets of ferocious and bloodthirsty, with which they were so fond of endowing him, had even a shadow of foundation. We have more reason to believe the Scottish accounts that his gentleness and nobility of soul were equal to his valor. Of his moderation and wisdom while acting as governor of Scotland there can be no doubt, while the brilliant strategy which first won the battle of Stirling, and would have gained that of Falkirk had not the treachery and cowardice of the cavalry ruined his plans, show that under other circumstances he would have taken rank as one of the greatest commanders of his own or any age.

He first taught his countrymen, and indeed Europe in general, that steady infantry can repel the assaults even of mail-clad cavalry. The lesson was followed at Bannockburn by Bruce, who won under precisely the same circumstances as those under which Wallace had been defeated, simply because at the critical moment he had five hundred horse at hand to charge the disordered mass of the English archers, while at Falkirk, Wallace's cavalry, who should have struck the blow, was galloping far away from the battlefield. Nor upon his English conquerors was the lesson lost, for at Cressy, when attacked by vastly superior numbers, Edward III, dismounted his army, and ordered them to fight on foot, and the result gave a death-blow to that mailed chivalry which had come to be regarded as the only force worth reckoning in a battle. The conduct of Edward to Wallace, and later to many other distinguished Scotsmen who fell into his hands, is a foul blot upon the memory of one of the greatest of the kings of England.

Edward might now well have believed that Scotland was crushed forever. In ten years, no less than twelve great armies had marched across the border; and twice the whole country had been ravaged from sea to sea, the last time so effectually, that Edward had good ground for his belief that the land would never again raise its head from beneath his foot.

He now proceeded, as William of Normandy after Hastings had done, to settle his conquest, and appointed thirty-one commissioners, of whom twenty-one were English and ten so-called Scots, among them Sir John Menteith, to carry out his ordinances. All the places of strength were occupied by English garrisons. The high officers and a large proportion of the justiciaries and sheriffs were English, and Edward ruled Scotland from Westminster as he did England.

Among the commissioners was Robert Bruce, now, through the death of his father, Lord of Annandale and Carrick; and Edward addressed a proclamation to him, headed: "To our faithful and loyal Robert de Bruce, Earl of Carrick, and all others who are in his company greeting;" and went on to say that he possessed the king's fullest confidence. But though Scotland lay prostrate, the spirit of resistance yet lingered in the hearts of the commonalty. Although conquered, now the memory of their past successes still inspired them, but until some leader presented himself none could stir. It was in August that Wallace had been executed. Archie had received several summonses from the English governors of Stirling and Lanark to come in and do homage to Edward, but he had resolutely declined, and the task of capturing his castle was too heavy a one to be undertaken by any single garrison; still he saw that the time must come, sooner or later, when he would have to choose between surrender and death. When matters settled down it was certain that a great effort would be made to root out the one recalcitrant south of the Forth. For some time he remained gloomy and thoughtful, a mood most unusual to him, and his mother, who was watching him anxiously, was scarcely surprised when one day he said to her:

"Mother, I must leave you for a time. Matters can no longer continue as they are. Surrender to the English I will not, and there remains for me but to defend this castle to the last, and then to escape to France; or to cross thither at once, and enter the service of the French king, as did Wallace. Of these courses I would gladly take the latter, seeing that the former would bring ruin and death upon our vassals, who have ever done faithful service when called upon, and whom I would not see suffer for my sake. In that case I should propose that you should return and live quietly with Sir Robert Gordon until times change."

Dame Forbes agreed with her son, for she had long felt that further resistance would only bring ruin upon him.

"There is yet one other course, mother, and that I am about to take; it is well nigh a desperate one, and my hopes of success are small, yet would I attempt it before I leave Scotland and give Aberfilly back again to the Kerrs. Ask me not what it is, for it were best that if it fail you should not know of it. There is no danger in the enterprise, but for a month I shall be absent. On my return you shall hear my final resolve."

Having attired himself as a lowland farmer, Archie proceeded to Edinburgh, and there took ship for London; here he took lodgings at an inn, which he had been told in Edinburgh was frequented by Scots who had to go to London on business. His first care was to purchase the garments of an English gentlemen of moderate means, so that he could pass through the streets without attracting attention.

He was greatly impressed with the bustle and wealth of London.

"It is wonderful," he said to himself, "that we Scots, who were after all but an army of peasants, could for nigh ten years have supported a war against such a country as England. Still, it seems like madness to think that we can yet win our struggle. If my present errand fails I will assuredly hold firm to my resolve and seek a refuge in France."

Archie ascertained that Robert the Bruce lodged at Westminster, and that great celebrations were taking place at the court on account of the final termination of hostilities with Scotland, now secured by the execution of Wallace. He despatched a letter to the earl by a messenger from the inn, saying that one who had formerly known him in Scotland desired earnestly to speak to him on matters of great import, and begging him to grant a private interview with him at his lodging at as early an hour as might be convenient to him. The man returned with a verbal reply, that the earl would see the writer at his lodging at nine o'clock on the following morning.

At the appointed time, Archie presented himself at the house inhabited by Bruce. To the request of the earl's retainer for his name and business he replied that his name mattered not, but that he had received a message from the earl appointing him a meeting at that hour.

Two minutes later, he was ushered into the private cabinet of Robert Bruce. The latter was seated writing, and looked up at his unknown visitor.

"Do you remember me, Sir Robert Bruce?" Archie asked.

"Methinks I know your face, sir," the earl replied, "but I cannot recall where I have seen it."

"It is five years since," Archie said, "and as that time has changed me from a youth into a man I wonder not that my face has escaped you,"

"I know you now!" the earl exclaimed, rising suddenly from his seat. "You are Sir Archibald Forbes?"

"I am," Archie replied, "and I have come now on the same errand I came then—the cause of our country. The English think she is dead, but though faint and bleeding, Scotland yet lives; but there is one man only who can revive her, and that man is yourself."

"Your mission is a vain one," Bruce replied. "Though I honor you, Sir Archibald, for your faith and constancy; though I would give much, ay, all that I have, were my record one of as true patriotism and sacrifice as yours, yet it were madness to listen to you. Have I not," he asked bitterly, "earned the hatred of my countrymen? Have I not three times raised my standard only to lower it again without striking a blow? Ah!" he said in a changed tone, "Never shall I forget the horror which I felt as I passed over that field strewn with Scottish corpses. Truly my name must be loathed in Scotland; and yet, Sir Archibald, irresolute and false as I have hitherto proved myself, believe me, I love Scotland, the land of my mother."

"I believe you, sir," Archie said, "and it is therefore that I implore you to listen to me. You are now our only possible leader, our only possible king. Baliol is a captive at Rome, his son a courtier of Edward. Wallace is dead. Comyn proved weak and incapable, and was unable to rally the people to offer any opposition to Edward's last march. Scotland needs a leader strong and valiant as Wallace, capable of uniting around him a large body, at least, of the Scottish nobles, and having some claim to her crown. You know not, sir, how deep is the hatred of the English. The last terrible incursion of Edward has spread that feeling far and wide, and while before it was but in a few counties of the lowlands that

Archie's Interview with Sir Robert Bruce

the flame of resistance really burnt, this time, believe me, that all
Scotland, save perhaps the Comyns and their adherents, would
rise at the call. I say not that success would at once attend you,
for, forgive me for saying so, the commonalty would not at first
trust you; but when they became convinced that you were fighting for Scotland as well as for your own crown, that you had, by
your action, definitely and forever broken with the English, I am
sure they would not hold back. Your own vassals of Carrick and
Annandale are a goodly array in themselves, and the young Douglas might be counted on to bring his dalesmen[10] to your banner.
There are all the lords who have favored your cause, and so stood
aloof from Comyn. You will have a good array to commence
with; but above all, even if unsuccessful at first, all Scotland
would come in time to regard you as her king and champion.
Resistance will never cease, for even as Wallace was ever able to
assemble bands and make head against the English, so will it be
with you, until at last freedom is achieved, and you will reign a
free king over a free Scotland, and your name will be honored to
all time as the champion and deliverer of our country. "Think
not, sir," he went on earnestly as Bruce paced up and down the

---

10. Men who live in dales or valleys, especially in northern England.

little room, "that it is too late. Other Scotsmen, Fraser and many others, who have warred in the English ranks, have been joyfully received when at length they drew sword for Scotland. If you will but stand forth as our champion, believe me, the memory of your former weakness will be forgotten in the admiration of present patriotism."

For two or three minutes Bruce strode up and down the room, then he paused before Archie.

"By heavens," he said, "I will do it! I am not so sanguine as you, I do not believe that success can ever finally attend the enterprise, but, be that as it may, I will attempt it, win or die. The memory of Robert Bruce shall go down in the hearts of Scottish patriots as one who whatever his early errors, atoned for them at last by living and dying in her cause. My sisters and brothers have long urged me to take such a step, but I could never bring myself to face the power of England. Your words have decided me. The die is cast. Henceforward, Robert Bruce is a true Scot. And now, Sir Archibald, what do you think my first step should be?"

"The English in Scotland are lulled in security, and a sudden blow upon them will assuredly at first be wholly successful. You must withdraw suddenly and quietly from here."

"It is not easy to do so," Bruce replied. "Although high in favor with Edward, he has yet some suspicions of me—not," he said bitterly, "without just cause—and would assuredly arrest me did he know that I were going north. My only plan will be to appear at court as usual, while I send down relays of horses along the northern road. You will ride with me, Sir Archie, will you not? But I must tell you that I have already, in some degree, prepared for a movement in Scotland. Comyn and I have met and have talked over the matter. Our mutual claims to the crown stood in the way, but we have agreed that one shall yield to the other, and that whoso takes the crown shall give all his lands to be the property of the other, in consideration of his waiving his claim and giving his support. This we have agreed to, and have signed a mutual bond to that effect, and though it is not formally written we have further agreed that I shall have the crown and that Comyn shall take Carrick and Annandale; but this was for the future, and we thought not of any movement for the present."

"It were a bad bargain, sir," Archie said gravely; "and one that I trust will never be carried out. The Comyns are even now the most powerful nobles in Scotland, and with Carrick and Annandale in addition to their own broad lands, would be masters of Scotland, no matter who would be called her king. If you were king, they could with their vassals and connections, place a stronger army in the field than that which you could raise; and could at any moment, did you anger them, call in the English to his aid, and so again lay Scotland under the English yoke."

"I will think of it, Sir Archie. There is much in what you say, and I will rethink my views regarding the Comyns. Henceforth do not fear to give me your advice freely. You possessed the confidence of Wallace, and have shown yourself worthy of it. Should I ever free Scotland and win me a kingdom, believe me you will not find Robert Bruce ungrateful. I will give orders tomorrow for the horses to be privately sent forward, so that at any hour we can ride if the moment seem propitious; meanwhile I pray you to move from the hostelry in the city, where your messenger told me you were staying, to one close at hand, in order that I may instantly communicate with you in case of need. I cannot ask you to take up your abode here, for there are many Scots among my companions who might know your face."

That afternoon Archie took up his abode at Westminster. A week later one of Bruce's retainers came in just as Archie was about to retire to bed, and said that the Earl of Carrick wished immediately to see Master Forbes. Sir Archie had retained his own name while dropping the title. He at once crossed to Bruce's lodging.

"We must mount at once!" the earl exclaimed as he entered. "What think you? I have but now received word from a friend, who is a member of the council, to say that this afternoon a messenger arrived from the false Comyn with a letter to the king, containing a copy of the bond between us. Whether the coward feared the consequences, or whether he has all along acted in treachery with the view of bringing me into disgrace, and so ridding himself of a rival, I know not; but the result is the same, he has disclosed our plans to Edward. A council was hastily called, and it has but just separated. It is to meet again in the morning, and the king himself will be present. I am to be summoned before it, being as it is supposed, in ignorance of the betrayal of my plans. It was well for me that Edward himself had pressing engagements and was unable to be present at the council. Had he been, prompt steps would have been taken, and I should by this time be lying a prisoner in the Tower. Even now I may be arrested at any moment. Have you aught for which you wish to return to your inn?"

"No," Archie replied. "I have but a change of clothing there, which is of no importance, and we had best lose not a moment's time. But there is the reckoning to discharge."

"I will give orders," the earl said, "that it shall be discharged in the morning. Now let us without a moment's delay make to the stables and mount there. Here is a cloak and valise."

The earl struck a bell, and a retainer appeared.

"Allan, I am going out to pay a visit. Take these two valises to the stable at once and order Roderick to saddle the two bay horses in the stalls at the end of the stables. Tell him to be speedy, for I shall be with him anon. He is not to bring them round here. I will mount in the court."

Five minutes later Bruce and Archie, enveloped in thick cloaks with hoods drawn over their faces, rode north from Westminster. At first they went slowly, but as soon as they were out in the field they set spur to their horses and galloped on in the darkness.

The snow lay thick upon the ground, and the roads were entirely deserted.

"Farewell to London!" Bruce exclaimed. "Except as a prisoner I shall never see it again. The die is cast this time, Sir Archie, and for good; even if I would I can never draw back again. Comyn's treachery has made my action irrecoverable—it is now indeed death or victory!"

All night they rode without drawing rein, save that they once changed horses where a relay had been provided. They had little fear of pursuit, for even when Bruce's absence was discovered none of his household would be able to say where he had gone, and some time must elapse before the conviction that he had ridden for Scotland, in such weather, would occur to the king. Nevertheless they traveled fast, and on the tenth of February entered Dumfries.

Chapter 12

The Battle of Methven

Bruce had, during the previous week, sent messages to several of his friends in Annandale and Carrick saying that he might at any time be among them, and at Dumfries he found many of them prepared to see him. The English justiciaries for the southern district of the conquered kingdom were holding a judicial assembly, and at this most of the nobles and principal men of that part were present. Among these were, of course, many of Bruce's vassals; among them also was John Comyn of Badenoch who held large estates in Galloway, in virtue of which he was now present.

As soon as the news that Bruce had arrived in town spread, his adherents and vassals there speedily gathered round him, and as, accompanied by several of them, he went through the town he met Comyn in the precincts of the Grey Friars. Concerning this memorable meeting there has been great dispute among historians. Some have charged Bruce with inviting Comyn to meet him, with the deliberate intention of slaying him; others have represented the meeting as accidental, and the slaying of Comyn as the result of an outburst of passion on the part of Bruce; but no one who weighs the factors, and considers the circumstances in which Comyn was placed, can feel the least question that the latter is the true hypothesis.

Bruce, whose whole course shows him to have been a man who acted with prudence and foresight, would have been nothing short of mad had he, just at the time when it was necessary to secure the goodwill of the whole of the Scottish nobles, chosen that moment to slay Comyn, with whom were connected, by blood or friendship, the larger half of the Scottish nobles. Still less, had he decided upon so suicidal a course, would he have selected a sanctuary as the scene of the deed. To slay his rival in such a place would be to excite against himself the horror and aversion of the whole people, and to enlist against him the immense authority and influence of the church. Therefore, unless we should conclude that Bruce—whose early career showed him to be a cool and calculating man, and whose future course was marked throughout with wisdom of the highest character—was suffering from an absolute aberration of intellect, we must accept the account by those who represent the meeting as accidental, and the slaying as the result of an outburst of passion provoked by Comyn's treachery.

When Bruce saw Comyn approaching, he ordered his followers to stop where they were. Then he advanced toward Comyn, who was astonished at his presence.

"I would speak with you aside, John Comyn," Bruce said; and the two withdrew into the church apart from the observation of the others.

Then Bruce broke into a torrent of accusations against Comyn for his gross act of treachery in betraying him by sending to Edward a copy of their agreement.

"You sought," he said "to send me to the scaffold, and so clear the way for yourself to the throne of Scotland."

Comyn, finding that dissimulation was useless, replied as hotly. Those without could hear the voices of the angry men rise higher and higher; then there was silence, and Bruce hurried out alone.

"What has happened?" Archie Forbes exclaimed.

"I fear that I have slain Comyn," Bruce replied in an agitated voice.

"Then I will make sure," Kirkpatrick, one of his retainers, said; and accompanied by Lindsay and another of his companions he ran in and completed the deed.

Scarcely was this done than Sir Robert Comyn, uncle of the earl, ran up, and seeing what had taken place, furiously attacked Bruce and his party. A fierce fray took place, and Robert Comyn and several of his friends were slain.

"The die is cast now," Bruce said when the fight was over; "but I would give my right hand had I not slain Comyn in my passion; however, it is too late to hesitate now. Gather together, my friends, all your retainers, and let us hurry at once to attack the justiciaries."

In a few minutes Kirkpatrick brought together those who had accompanied him and his companions to the town, and they at once moved against the courthouse. The news of Bruce's arrival and of the fray with the Comyns had already reached the justiciaries, and with their retainers and friends they had made hasty preparations for defense; but seeing that Bruce's followers outnumbered them, and that a defense might cost them their lives, they held parley and agreed to surrender upon Bruce promising to allow them to depart at once for England. Half an hour later the English had left Dumfries.

Bruce called a council of his companions.

"My friends," he said, "we have been hurried into a terrible strife, and deeply do I regret that by my own mad passion at the treachery of Comyn I have begun it by an evil deed; but when I tell you of the way in which that traitor sought to bring me to an English block, you will somewhat absolve me for the deed, and will grant that unhappy and unfortunate as it was, my passion was in some degree justified."

He then informed them of the bond into which he and Comyn had entered, and of its betrayal by Comyn to Edward.

"Thus it is," he said, "that the deed has taken place, and it is too late to mend it. We have before us a desperate enterprise, and yet I hope that we may succeed in it. At any rate, this time there can be no drawing back, and we must conquer or die. It was certain in any case that Comyn and his party would oppose me, but now their hostility will go to all lengths, while Edward will never forgive the attack upon his justiciaries. Still we shall have some breathing time. The king will not hear for ten days of events here, and it will take him two months at least before he can assemble an army on the border, and Comyn's friends will probably do naught till the English approach. However, let us hurry to Lochmaben Castle; there we shall be safe from any sudden attack by Comyn's friends in Galloway. First let us draw out papers setting forth the cause of my enmity to Comyn, and of the quarrel which led to his death, and telling all Scots that I have now cut myself loose forever from England, and that I have come to free Scotland and to win the crown which belongs to me by right, or to die in attempt."

Many of these documents being drawn out, messengers were despatched with them to Bruce's friends throughout the country, and he and his followers rode to Lochmaben.

Archie Forbes went north to his own estate, and at once gave notice to his retainers to prepare to take the field, and to march to Glasgow, which Bruce had named as the rendezvous for all well disposed toward him. From time to time messages came from Bruce, telling him that he was receiving many promises of support; the whole of the vassals of Annandale and Carrick had assembled at Lochmaben, where many small landowners with their retainers also joined him. As soon as his force had grown to a point when he need fear no interruption on his march toward Glasgow, Bruce left Lochmaben. On his way he was joined by the first influential nobleman who had espoused his cause; this was Sir James Douglas, whose father, Sir William, had died in an English prison. At the time of his capture his estates had been bestowed by Edward upon Lord Clifford, and the young Douglas, then but a lad, had sought refuge in France. After awhile he had returned, and was living with Lamberton, Bishop of St. Andrews, who had been one of Wallace's most active supporters.

The young Douglas on receiving the news that Bruce was marching north, at once mounted, rode off, and joined him. He was joyfully received by Bruce, as not only would his own influence be great among his father's vassals of Douglasdale, but his adhesion would induce many others to join. Receiving news of Bruce's march, Archie moved to Glasgow with his retainers. The English garrison and adherents in Glasgow fled at his approach. Upon arriving there Bruce solemnly proclaimed the independence of Scotland, and set out notices to all the nobles and gentry, calling upon them to join him.

Fortunately the Bishop of St. Andrews, and Wishart, Bishop of Glasgow, another of Wallace's friends, at once declared strongly for him, as did the Bishop of Moray and the Abbot of Scone. The adhesion of these prelates was of immense importance to Bruce, as to some extent the fact of their joining him showed that the church felt no overwhelming indignation at the act of sacrilege which he had committed, and enabled the minor clergy to advocate his cause with their flocks.

Many of the great nobles hostile to the Comyn faction also joined him; among these were the Earls of Athole, Lennox, Errol, and Menteith; Christopher Seaton, Sir Simon Fraser, Sir Thomas Randolph, and Sir Neil Campbell. Bruce's four brothers, Edward, Nigel, Thomas, and Alexander, were of course, with him. Bruce now moved from Glasgow to Scone, and was there crowned King of Scotland on the twenty-seventh of March, 1306, six weeks after his arrival at Dumfries.

Since the days of Malcolm Canmore the ceremony of placing the crown on the head of the monarch had been performed by the representative of the family of Macduff, the earls of Fife; the present earl was in the service of the English; but his sister Isobel, wife of Comyn, Earl of Buchan, rode into Scone with the train of followers upon the day after the coronation, and demanded to perform the office which was the privilege of the family. To this Bruce gladly assented, seeing that many Scots would hold the coronation to be irregular because it was not performed by the hereditary functionary, and that as Isobel was the wife of Comyn of Buchan, her open adhesion to him might influence some of that faction. Accordingly on the following day the ceremony was again performed, Isobel of Buchan placing the crown on Bruce's head, an act of patriotism for which the unfortunate lady was afterward to pay dearly. Thus, although the great majority of the Scottish nobles still held aloof, Bruce was now at the head of a considerable force, and he at once proceeded to overrun the country. The numerous English who had come across the border, under the belief that Scotland was finally conquered, or to take possession of lands granted them by Edward, were all compelled either to take refuge in the fortified towns and castles held by English garrisons, or to return hastily to England.

When the news of the proceedings at Dumfries and the general rising in the south of Scotland reached Edward he was at the city of Winchester. He had been lately making a sort of triumphant passage through the country, and the unexpected news that Scotland which he had believed crushed beyond all possibility of further resistance was again in arms, is said for a time to have driven him almost out of his mind with rage.

Not a moment was lost. Aylmer de Valence, Earl of Pembroke, was at once commissioned to proceed to Scotland, to "put down the rebellion and punish the rebels," the whole military array of the northern counties was placed under his orders, and Clifford and Percy were associated with him in the commission. Edward also applied to the pope to aid him in punishing the sacrilegious rebels who had violated the sanctuary of Dumfries.

As Clement V was a native of Guienne, and kept his court at Bordeaux within Edward's dominions, his request was, of course, promptly complied with, and a bull issued instructing the Archbishop of York and the Bishop of Carlisle to excommunicate Bruce and his friends, and to place them and their possessions under an interdict. It was now that the adhesion of the Scottish prelates was of such vital consequence to Bruce. Had the interdict been obeyed, the churches would have been closed, all religious ceremonies suspended, the rites of the church would have been refused even to dying men, and the dead would have been buried without service in unconsecrated ground. So terrible a weapon as this was almost always found irresistible, and its terrors had compelled even the most powerful monarchs to yield obedience to the pope's orders; but the Scottish prelates set the needs of their country above the commands of the pope and in spite of repeated bulls the native clergy continued to perform their functions throughout the whole struggle, and thus nullified the effect of the popish anathema.

King Edward was unable himself to lead his army against the Scots, for he was now sixty-seven years old and the vast fatigues and exertions which he had undergone in the course of a life spent almost continually in war had worn upon him. He had partially lost the use of his limbs, and was forced to travel in carriage or litter; but when he reached London from Winchester a grand ceremony was held, at which the order of knighthood was conferred by the king upon the Prince of Wales, and three hundred aspirants belonging to the principal families of the county. Orders were then given that the whole military array of the kingdom should, in the following spring gather at Carlisle, where Edward himself would meet them and accompany them to Scotland.

The Earl of Pembroke, with Clifford and Percy, lost no time in following the orders of Edward, and with the military power of the northern counties marched into Scotland. They advanced unopposed to the Forth, and crossing this river proceeded toward Perth, near which town the Scottish army were gathered.

Archie Forbes, who stood very high in favor with Bruce, had urged upon him the advantage of carrying out the tactics formerly adopted by Wallace, and of compelling the enemy to fall back by cutting off all food supplies, but Bruce would not, in this instance, be guided by his counsel.

"When the king advances next spring with his great army, Sir Archie, I will assuredly adopt the course which you point out, seeing that we could not hope to withstand so great an array in a pitched battle; but the case is different now. In the first place all the castles and towns are in the hands of the English, and from them Pembroke can draw such provision as he needs. In the second place his force is not so superior to our own but that we may fight him with a fair hope of victory; and whereas Wallace had never any cavalry with him, save at Falkirk when they deserted him at the beginning of the battle, we have a strong body of mounted men-at-arms. The retainers of the nobles are with me, therefore, I do not fear to give them battle in the open field."

In pursuance of this determination Bruce sent a challenge to Pembroke to meet him with his army in the open field the next day. Pembroke accepted the challenge, and promised to meet his opponent on the following morning, and the Scots retired for the night to the wood of Methven, near Perth. Here many of them set out on foraging excursions, the knights laid aside their armor, and the army prepared for sleep.

Archie Forbes was much dissatisfied at the manner in which Bruce had endangered all the fortunes of Scotland on a pitched battle, thereby throwing away the great advantage which their superior mobility and knowledge of the country gave to the Scots. He had disarmed like the rest, and was sitting by a fire chatting with William Orr and Andrew Macpherson, who, as they had been his lieutenants in the band of lads he had raised seven years before, now occupied the same position among his retainers, each having the command of a hundred men. Suddenly one who had been wandering outside the lines in search of food among the farmhouses ran hastily in, shouting that the whole English army was upon them.

A scene of the utmost confusion took place. Bruce and his knights hastily armed, and mounting their horses rode to meet the enemy. There was no time to form ranks or to make any order of battle. Archie sprang to his horse. He directed his lieutenants to form the men into a compact body and move forward, keeping the king's banner ever in sight, and to cut their way to it whenever they saw it was in danger. Then followed by his two mounted squires, he rode after the king. The contest of Methven can scarce be called a battle, for the Scots were defeated before it began. Many, as has been said, were away; great numbers of the footmen instantly took flight and dispersed in all directions. Here and there small bodies stood and fought desperately, but being unsupported were overcome and slain. The king with his knights fought with desperate bravery, spurring hither and thither and charging furiously among the English men-at-arms. Three times Bruce was unhorsed and as often remounted by Sir Simon Fraser. Once he was so entirely cut off from his companions by the desperation with which he had charged into the midst of the English, that he was surrounded, struck from his horse, and taken prisoner.

"The king is taken!" Archie Forbes shouted; "ride in, my lords, and rescue him."

Most of the Scottish knights were so hardly pressed that they could do nothing to aid the king; but Christopher Seaton joined Archie, and the two knights charged into the midst of the throng of English and cut their way to Bruce. Sir Philip Mowbray, who was beside the captured monarch, was overthrown, and several others cut down. Bruce leaped into his saddle again and the three for a time kept at bay the circle of foemen; but such a conflict could have but one end. Archie Forbes vied with the king in the strength and power of his blows, and many of his opponents went down before him. There was, however, no possibility of extricating themselves from the mass of their foes, and Bruce, finding the conflict hopeless, was again about to surrender when a great shout was heard, and a close body of Scottish spearmen threw themselves into the ranks of the English horse. Nothing could withstand the impetuosity of the assault. The horsemen recoiled before the leveled spears, and the pikemen, sweeping onward, surrounded the king and his companions.

"Well done, my brave fellows!" Archie cried; "now keep together in a close body and draw off the field."

The darkness which had at first proved so disastrous to the Scots was now favorable to them. The English infantry knew not what was going on. The cavalry tried in vain to break through the ranks of the spearmen, and these keeping closely together, regained the shelter of the wood, and drew off by way of Dunkeld and Killiecrankie to the mountains of Athole. On their way they were joined by Edward Bruce, the Earl of Athole, Sir Neil Campbell, Gilbert de la Haye, and Douglas, and by many scattered footmen.

To his grief Bruce learned that Randolph, Inchmartin, Somerville, Alexander Fraser, Hugh de la Haye, and others had been captured, but the number killed had been small. When once safe from pursuit a council was held. It was agreed at once that it was impossible that so large a body could find subsistence in the mountains of Athole, cooped up as they were by their foes. The lowlands swarmed with the English; to the north was Badenoch, the district of their bitter enemies the Comyns; while westward lay the territory of the MacDougalls of Lorne, whose chieftain, Alexander, was a nephew by marriage of the Comyn killed by Bruce, and an adherent of the English.

Beyond an occasional deer, and the fish in the lochs and streams, the country afforded no means of subsistence; it was therefore decided to disband the greater portion of the force, the knights and nobles, with a few of their immediate retainers, alone remaining with the king. Meanwhile the main body of Bruce's army dispersed to regain their homes. This was done; but a few days later a messenger came saying that the queen, with the wives of many of the gentlemen, had arrived at Aberdeen and sought to join the king. Although an accession of numbers was by no means desirable, and the hardships of such a life immense for ladies to support, there was no other resource but for them to join the party as they would otherwise have speedily fallen into the hands of the English. Therefore Bruce, accompanied by some of his followers, rode to Aberdeen and escorted the queen and ladies to his mountain retreat.

It was a strange life that Bruce, his queen, and his little court led. Sleeping in rough arbors formed of boughs, the party supported themselves by hunting and fishing.

Gins and traps were set in the streams, and Douglas and Archie were specially active in this pursuit; Archie's boyish experience at Glen Cairn serving him in good stead. Between him and Sir James Douglas a warm friendship had sprung up. Douglas was four years his junior. As a young boy he had heard much of Archie's feats with Wallace, and his father had often referred to him as one who was as conspicuous for his bravery as well as his youth. The young Douglas therefore entertained the highest admiration for him, and had from the time of his joining Bruce become his constant companion.

Bruce himself was the life and soul of the party. He was ever hopeful and in high spirits, cheering his followers by his humor, and whiling away the long evenings by tales of adventure and chivalry, told when they were gathered round the fire.

Gradually the party made their way westward along Loch Tay and Glen Dochart until they reached the head of Strathfillan; here as they were riding along a narrow pass, they were suddenly attacked by Alexander MacDougall with a large gathering of his clansmen. Several of the royal party were cut down at once, but Bruce with his knights fought desperately. Archie Forbes with a few of the others rallied round the queen and her ladies, and repelled every effort of the wild clansmen to break through and continued to draw off gradually down the glen. Bruce, with Douglas, De la Haye, and some others, formed the rear guard and kept back the mass of their opponents. De la Haye and Douglas were both wounded, but the little party continued to show a face to their foes until they reached a spot where the path lay between a steep hill on one side and the lake on the other. Then Bruce sent his followers ahead, and himself covered the rear.

Suddenly three of the MacDougalls, who had climbed the hillside, made a spring upon him from above. One leaped on to the horse behind the king, and attempted to hold his arms, another seized his bridle rein, while the third thrust his hand between Bruce's leg and the saddle to hurl him from his horse. The path was too narrow for Bruce to turn his horse, and spurring forward he pressed his leg so close to the saddle that he imprisoned the arm of the assailant beneath it and dragged him along with him, while with a blow of his sword he smote off the arm of him who grasped the rein. Then, turning in his saddle, he seized his assailant who was behind him and by sheer strength wrenched him round to the pommel of the saddle and there slew him. Then he turned and having cut down the man whose arm he held beneath his leg, he rode on and joined his friends.

In the course of the struggle the brooch which fastened his cloak was lost. This was found by the MacDougalls and carried home as a trophy. It has been preserved by the family ever since, with apparently as much pride as if it had been a proof of the fidelity and patriotism of their ancestors, instead of being a memento of the time when, as false and disloyal Scotsmen, they fought with England against Scotland's king and deliverer.

Bruce Struggles with the MacDougalls

Chapter 13

The Castle of Dunstaffnage

Bruce's party were now more hungry than ever, since they had to depend almost entirely upon such fish as they might catch, as it was dangerous to stray far away in pursuit of deer. Archie, however, with his bow and arrows ventured several times to go hunting in order to relieve the sad condition of the ladies, and succeeded two or three times in bringing a deer home with him.

He had one day ventured much further away than usual. He had not succeeded in finding a stag, and the ladies had for more than a week subsisted entirely on fish. He therefore determined to continue the search, however long, until he found one. He had crossed several wooded hills, and was, he knew, leagues away from the point where he had left his party, when, suddenly emerging from a wood, he came upon a road just at the moment when a party some twenty strong of wild clansmen were traversing it. On a palfrey in their center was a young lady whom they were apparently escorting. They were but twenty yards away when he emerged from the wood, and on seeing him they drew their claymores and rushed upon him. Perceiving that flight from these swift-footed mountaineers would be impossible, Archie threw down his bow and arrows, and, drawing his sword, placed his back against a tree, and prepared to defend himself until the last.

Parrying the blows of the first two who arrived he stretched them dead upon the ground, and was then at once attacked by the whole of the party together. Two more of his assailants fell by his sword; but he would have been soon overpowered and slain, when the young lady, whose cries to her followers to cease had been unheeded in the din of the conflict, spurred her palfrey forward and broke into the ring gathered round Archie.

The clansmen drew back a pace, and Archie lowered his sword.

"Desist," she cried to the former in a tone of command, "or my uncle Alexander will make you rue the day when you disobeyed my orders. I will answer for this young knight. And now, sir," she said, turning to Archie, "do you surrender your sword to me, and yield yourself up a prisoner. Further resistance would be madness; you have done too much harm already. I promise you your life if you will make no further resistance."

"Then, lady," Archie replied, handing his sword to her, "I willingly yield myself your prisoner, and thank you for saving my life from the hands of your savage followers."

The young lady touched the hilt of his sword, and motioned him to replace it in its scabbard.

"You must accompany me," she said, "to the abode of my uncle Alexander MacDougall. I wish I could set you at liberty, but my authority over my uncle's clansmen does not extend so far; and did I bid them let you go free they would assuredly disobey me. You are, as I can see by your attire, one of the Bruce's followers, for no other knight could be found wandering alone through these woods."

"Yes, lady," Archie said, "I am Sir Archibald Forbes, one of the few followers of the King of Scotland."

The lady gave a sudden start when Archie mentioned his name, and for a time did not speak again.

"I would," she said at last in a low voice, "that you had been any other, seeing that Alexander MacDougall has a double cause of enmity against you—firstly, as being a follower of Bruce, who slew his kinsman Comyn, and who has done but lately great harm to himself and his clansmen; secondly, as having dispossessed Allan Kerr, who is also his relative, of his lands and castle. My uncle is a man of violent passions, and"—she hesitated.

"And he may not, you think," Archie went on, "respect your promise for my life. If that be so, lady—and from what I have heard of Alexander MacDougall it is like enough—I beg you to give me back my surrender, for I would rather die here, sword in hand, than be put to death in cold blood in the castle of Dunstaffnage."

"No," the lady said, "that cannot be. Think you I could see you butchered before mine eyes after having once surrendered yourself to me. No, sir. I beseech you act not so rashly—that were certain death; and I trust that my uncle, hostile as he may be against you, will not inflict such dishonor upon me as to break the pledge I have given for your safety."

Archie thought from what he had heard of the MacDougall that his chance was a very slight one. Still, as the young ever cling to hope, and as he would assuredly be slain by the clansmen, he thought it better to take the chance, small as it was, and so continued his march by the side of his captor's escorts.

After two hours' journey they neared the castle of Alexander of Lorne. Archie could not repress a thrill of apprehension as he looked at the grim fortress and thought of the character of its lord; but his bearing showed no fear, as, conversing with the young lady, he approached the entrance. The gate was thrown open, and Alexander of Lorne himself issued out with a number of retainers.

"Ah, Marjory!" he said, "I am glad to see your bonny face at Dunstaffnage. It is three months since you left us, and the time has gone slowly; the very dogs have been pining for your voice. But who have we here?" he exclaimed, as his eye fell upon Archie.

"It is a wandering knight, uncle," Marjory said lightly, "whom I captured in the forest on my way hither. He fought valiantly against Murdoch and your followers, but at last he surrendered to me on my giving him my pledge that his life should be safe, and that he should be treated honorably. Such a pledge I am sure, uncle," she spoke earnestly now, "you will respect."

Alexander MacDougall's brow was as black as night, and he spoke in Gaelic with his followers.

"What!" he said angrily to the girl; "he has killed four of my men, and is doubtless one of Bruce's party who slipped through my fingers the other day and killed so many of my kinsmen and vassals. You have taken too much upon yourself, Marjory. It is not by you that he has been made captive, but by my men, and you had no power to give such promise as you have made. Who is this young upstart?"

"I am Sir Archibald Forbes," Archie said proudly—"a name which may have reached you even here."

"Archibald Forbes!" exclaimed MacDougall furiously. "What! the enemy and despoiler of the Kerrs! Had you a hundred lives you should die. Didst know this, Marjory?" he said furiously to the girl. "Didst know who this young adventurer was when you asked his life of me?"

"I did, uncle," the girl said fearlessly. "I did not know his name when he surrendered to me, and afterwards, when he told me, what could I do? I had given my promise, and I renewed it; and I trust, dear uncle, that you will respect and not bring dishonor upon it."

"Dishonor!" MacDougall said savagely; "the girl has lost her senses. I tell you he should die if every woman in Scotland had given her promise for his life. Away with him!" he said to his retainers; "take him to the chamber at the top of the tower; I will give him till tomorrow to prepare for death, for by all the saints I swear he shall hang at daybreak. As to you, girl, go to your chamber, and let me not see your face again till this matter is concluded. Methinks a madness must have fallen upon you that you should thus venture to lift your voice for a Forbes."

The girl burst into tears as Archie was led away. His guards took him to the upper chamber in a turret, a little room of some seven feet in diameter, and there, having deprived him of his arms, they left him, barring and bolting the massive oaken door behind them.

Archie had no hope whatever that Alexander MacDougall would change his mind, and felt certain that the following dawn would be his last. Of escape there was no possibility; the door was solid and massive, the window a mere narrow loophole for archers, two or three inches wide; and even had he time to enlarge the opening he would be no nearer freedom, for the moat lay a full eighty feet below.

"I would I had died sword in hand!" he said bitterly; "then it would have been over in a moment."

Then he thought of the girl to whom he had surrendered his sword.

"It was a sweet face and a bright one," he said; "a fairer and brighter I never saw. It is strange that I should meet her now only when I am about to die." Then he thought of the agony which his mother would feel at the news of his death and at the extinction of their race. Sadly he paced up and down his narrow cell till night fell. None took the trouble to bring him food—considering, doubtless, that he might well fast till morning. When it became dark he lay down on the hard stone, and, with his arm under his head was soon asleep —his last determination being that if possible he would snatch a sword or dagger from the hand of those who came to take him to execution, and so die fighting; or if that were impossible, he would try to burst from them and to end his life by a leap from the turret.

He was awakened by a slight noise at the door, and sprang to his feet instantly, believing that day was at hand and his hour had come. To his surprise a voice, speaking scarcely above a whisper, said:

"Hush! my son, make no noise; I am here as a friend." Then the door closed, and Archie's visitor produced a lighted lantern from the folds of his garments, and Archie saw that a priest stood before him.

"I thank you, father," he said gratefully; "you have doubtless come to pray with me, and I would gladly listen to your ministrations. I would gladly intrust you, too, with a message to my mother if you will take it for me; and I would ask also that you tell the Lady Marjory that she must not grieve for my death, or feel that she is in any way dishonored by it, seeing that she strove to her utmost to keep her promise."

"You can even give her your message yourself, sir knight," the priest said, "seeing that the willful girl has herself accompanied me hither."

Thus saying, he stepped aside, and Archie perceived, standing behind the priest, a figure who, being in deep shadow, he had not hitherto seen. She came timidly forward, and Archie, bending on one knee, took the hand she held out and kissed it.

"Lady," he said, "you have heard my message; blame not yourself, I beseech you, for my death. Remember that after all you have lengthened my life and not shortened it, seeing that but for your interference I must have been slain as I stood, by your followers. It was kind and good of you thus to come to bid me farewell."

"But I have not come to bid you farewell. Tell him, good Father Anselm, our purpose here."

"'Tis a dangerous business," the priest said, shrugging his shoulders; "and, priest though I am, I shall not care to meet Mac-Dougall in the morning. However, since this willful girl wills it, what can I do? I have been her instructor since she was a child; and instead of being a docile and obedient pupil, she has been a tyrannical master to me; and I have been so accustomed to do her will in all things that I cannot say her nay now. I held out as long as I could; but what can a poor priest do against sobs and tears? So at last I have given in and consented to risk the MacDougall's anger, to bring smiles into her face again. I have tried in vain to persuade her that since it is the chief's doing, your death will bring no dishonor upon her. I have offered to absolve her from the promise, but I might as well have spoken to the wind. When a young lady makes up her mind, stone walls are less difficult to move; so you see here we are. Wound round my waist are a hundred feet of stout rope, with knots tied three feet apart. We have only now to ascend the stairs to the platform above and fix the rope, and in an hour you will be far away among the woods."

Archie's heart bounded with joy with the hope of life and freedom; but he said quietly, "I thank you, dear lady, with all my heart for your goodness; but I could not accept life at the cost of bringing your uncle's anger upon you."

"You need not fear for that," the girl replied. "My uncle is passionate and headstrong—unforgiving to his foes or those he deems so, but affectionate to those he loves. I have always been his pet; and though, doubtless, his anger will be hot just at first, it will pass away after a time. Let no scruple trouble you on that score; and I would rather put up with a hundred beatings than live with the knowledge that one of Scotland's bravest knights came to his end by a breach of my promise. Though my uncle and all my people side with the English, yet do not I; and I think the good father here, though from prudence he says but little, is a true Scotsman also. I have heard of your name from childhood as the companion and friend of Wallace, and as one of the champions of our country; and though by blood I ought to hate you, my feelings have been very different. But now stand talking no longer; the castle is sound asleep, but I tremble lest some trouble should mar our plans."

"That is good sense," Father Anselm said; "and remember, not a word must be spoken when we have once left this chamber. There is a sentry at the gate; and although the night is dark, and I deem not that he can see us, yet must we observe every precaution."

"Dear lady," Archie said, "henceforth Archie Forbes is your knight and servant. You have given me my life, and henceforth I regard it as yours. Will you take this ring as my token? Should you ever send it to me, in whatever peril or difficulty you may be, I will come to your aid instantly, even should it reach me in a desperate battle. Think not that I speak the language of idle gallantry. Hitherto my thoughts have been only on Scotland, and no maiden has ever for an instant drawn them from her. Henceforth, though I fight for Scotland, yet will my country have a rival in my heart; and even while I charge into the ranks of the English, the fair image of Marjory MacDougall will be in my thoughts."

Father Anselm gave a slight start of surprise as Archie concluded, and would have spoken had not the girl touched him lightly. She took the pledge from Archie and said, "I will keep your ring, Sir Archibald Forbes; and should I ever have occasion for help I will not forget your promise. As to your other words, I doubt not that you mean them now; but it is unlikely, though I may dwell in your thoughts, that you will ever in the flesh see Marjory MacDougall, between whose house and yours there is, as you know, bitter enmity."

"There! there!" Father Anselm said impatiently; "enough, and more than enough talk. Go to the door, Sir Archibald, and prepare to open it as soon as I have blown out the light. The way up the stairs lies on your right hand as you go out."

Not another word was spoken. Noiselessly the little party made their way to the roof; there one end of the rope was quickly knotted round the battlement. Archie grasped the priest's hand, and kissed that of the girl; and then, swinging himself off the battlement, disappeared at once in the darkness. Not a sound was heard for some time, then the listening pair above heard a faint splash in the water. The priest laid his hands on the rope and found that it swung slack in the air; he hauled it up and twisted it again round his waist. As he passed the door of the cell he replaced the bars and bolts, and then with his charge regained the portion of the castle inhabited by the family.

A few vigorous strokes took Archie across the moat, and an hour later he was deep in the heart of the forest. Before morning broke he was far beyond the risk of pursuit; and, taking the bearings of the surrounding hills, he found himself, after some walking, at the spot where he had left the royal party. As he had expected, it was deserted; he, however, set out on the traces of the party, and that night overtook them at their next encampment.

With the reticence natural to young lovers, Archie felt a disinclination to speak of what had happened, or of the services which Marjory MacDougall had rendered him. As it was naturally supposed that he had lost his way in the woods on the previous day, and had not reached the encampment in the morning, until after they had started, few questions were asked; and indeed the thoughts of the whole party were occupied with the approaching separation which the night before they had agreed was absolutely necessary. The ladies were worn out with their fatigues and hardships, and the Earl of Athole, and some of the other elder men, were also unable any longer to support it. Winter was close at hand, and the hardships would increase ten-fold in severity. Therefore it was concluded that the time had come when they must separate, and that the queen and her companions, accompanied by those who could still be mounted, should seek shelter in Bruce's strong castle of Kildrummy. The Earl of Athole and the king's brother Nigel were in charge of the party.

Bruce with his remaining companions determined to proceed into Kintyre, the country of Sir Neil Campbell, and thence to cross for a time to the north of Ireland. Sir Neil accordingly started to obtain the necessary vessels, and the king and his company followed slowly. To reach the Frith of Clyde it was necessary to cross Loch Lomond. This was a difficult undertaking; but after great search Sir James Douglas discovered a small boat sunk beneath the surface of the lake. On being pulled out it was found to be old and leaky, and would hold at best but three. With strips torn from their garments they stopped the leaks as best they could, and then started across the lake. There were two hundred to cross, and the passage occupied a night and a day; those who could not swim being taken over in the boat, while the swimmers kept alongside and when fatigued rested their hands on her gunwales. They were now in the Lennox country, and while Bruce and his friends were hunting, they were delighted to come across the Earl of Lennox and some of his companions, who had found refuge there after the battle of Methven. Although himself an exile and a fugitive the earl was in his own country, and was therefore able to entertain the king and his companions hospitably; and the rest and feeling of security were welcome indeed after the past labours and dangers.

After a time Sir Neil Campbell arrived with the vessels, and, accompanied by the Earl of Lennox, Bruce and his companions embarked at a point near Cardross. They sailed down the Clyde and round the south end of Arran, until, after many adventures and dangers, they reached the Castle of Dunaverty, on the south point of the Mull of Kintyre, belonging to Angus, chief of Isla. Here they waited for some time, but not feeling secure even in this secluded spot from the vengeance of their English and Scottish foes, they again set sail and landed at the Isle of Rathlin, almost midway between Ireland and Scotland.

Hitherto Robert Bruce had received but little of that support which was so freely given to Wallace by the Scottish people at large; nor is this a matter for surprise. Baliol and Comyn had in turn betrayed the country to the English, and Bruce had hitherto been regarded as even more strongly devoted to the English cause than they had been. Thus the people viewed his attempt rather as an effort to win a throne for himself than as one to free Scotland from English domination. They had naturally no confidence in the nobles who had so often betrayed them, and Bruce especially had, three or four times already, after taking up arms, made his peace with England and fought against the Scots. Therefore, at first the people looked on at the conflict with comparative indifference. They were ready enough to strike for freedom, as they had proved when they had rallied round Wallace, but it was necessary before they did so that they should possess confidence in their leaders. Such confidence they had certainly no cause whatever to feel in Bruce. The time was yet to come when they should recognize in him a leader as bold, as persevering, and as determined as Wallace himself.

The people of Rathlin were crude and ignorant, but simple and hospitable. The island contained nothing to attract either adventurers or traders, and it was seldom, therefore, that ships touched there. Consequently there was little fear that the news of the sojourn of the Scottish king and his companions would reach the mainland, and indeed the English remained in profound ignorance as to what had become of the fugitives, and deemed them to be still in hiding somewhere among the western hills.

Edward had in council issued a proclamation commanding "all the people of the country to pursue and search for all who had been in arms and had not surrendered and all who had been guilty of other crimes. They were to deliver them up dead or alive, and that whosoever were negligent in the discharge of their duty should forfeit their castles and be imprisoned."

Pembroke, the guardian, was to punish at his discretion all who harbored offenders. Those who abetted the slayers of Comyn, or who knowingly harboured them or their accomplices, were to be "drawn and hanged," while all who surrendered were to be imprisoned during the king's pleasure. The edict was carried out to the letter, and the English soldiery, with the aid of the Scottish of their party, scoured the whole country, putting to the sword all who were found in arms or under circumstances of suspicion.

Chapter 14

Colonsay

A rchie, having little else to do, spent much of his time fishing. As a boy he had learned to be fond of the sport in the stream of Glen Cairn; but the sea was new to him, and whenever the weather permitted he used to go out with the natives in their boats. The Irish coast was but a few miles away, but there was little traffic between Rathlin and the mainland. The coast there is wild and extremely dangerous in cases when a northerly gale blows up suddenly. The natives were a wild and savage race, and many of those who had fought to the last against the English refused to submit even when their chiefs laid down their arms. They took refuge in the many caves and hiding places afforded in the wild and broken country on the north coast.

Thus no profitable trade was to be carried on with the Irish mainland. The people of Rathlin were themselves primitive in their ways. Their wants were few and easily satisfied. The wool of their flocks furnished them with clothing, and they raised sufficient grain in sheltered spots to supply them with meal, while an abundance of food could always be obtained from the sea. In fine weather they took more than sufficient for their needs, and dried the surplus to serve them when the winter winds kept their boats from putting out. Once or twice in the year their largest craft, laden with dried fish, would make it across to Ayr, and there disposing of its cargo would bring back such articles as were needed, and more precious still, the news of what was going on in the world of which the simple islanders knew so little.

Even more than fishing, Archie loved, when the wind blew wildly, to go down to the shore and watch the great waves rolling in and dashing themselves into foam on the rocky coast. This to him was an entirely new pleasure, and he enjoyed it intensely. Perched on some projecting rock out of reach of the waves, he would sit for hours watching the grand scene, sometimes alone, sometimes with one or two of his comrades. The influx of a hundred visitors had somewhat burdened the islanders, and the fishermen were forced to put to sea in weather when they would not ordinarily have launched their boats, for in the winter they seldom ventured out unless the previous season had been unusually bad, and the stores of food laid by insufficient for winter consumption. Archie generally went out with an old man, who with two grown-up sons owned a boat. They were bold and skillful fishermen, and often put to sea when no other boat cared to go out.

One evening the old man, as usual before going to sea, came into the hut which Archie and Sir James Douglas inhabited, and told him that he was going out early the next morning. "Fish are scarce," he said, "and it would be a disgrace on us islanders if our guests were to run short of food."

"I shall be ready, Donald," Archie replied, "and I hope we shall have good sport."

"I can't see what pleasure you take, Sir Archie," the young Douglas said, when the fisherman had left, "in being tossed up and down on the sea in a dirty boat, especially when the wind is high and the sea rough."

"I like it best then," Archie replied; "when the men are rowing against the wind, and the waves dash against the boat and the spray comes over in blinding showers, I feel very much the same sort of excitement as I do in a battle. It is a strife with the elements instead of with men, but the feeling in both cases is akin, and I feel the blood dancing fast through my veins and my lips set tightly together, just as when I stand shoulder to shoulder with my retainers, and withstand a wave of English horsemen."

"Well, each to his taste, I suppose," Douglas said, laughing; "I have not seen much of war yet, and I envy you with all my heart the fights which you have gone through; but I can see no amusement in getting drenched to the skin by the sea. I think I can understand your feeling, though, for it is near akin to my own when I sit on the back of a fiery young horse, who has not yet been broken, and feel him battle with his will against mine, and bound, and rear, in his efforts to throw me, until at last he is conquered and obeys the slightest touch of the rein."

Archie at the Isle of Rathlin

"No doubt it is the same feeling," Archie replied; "it is the joy of strife in another form. For myself, I own I would rather fight on foot than on horseback; I can trust myself better than I can trust my steed, can wheel thrice while he is turning once, can defend both sides equally well; whereas on horseback, not only have I to defend myself but my horse, which is far more difficult, and if he is wounded and falls I may be entangled under him and be help-less at the mercy of an opponent."

"But none acquitted them better on horseback at Methven than you did, Sir Archie," the young fellow said, admiringly. "Did you not save the king, and keep at bay his foes till your retainers came up with their pikes and carried him off from the center of the English cavalry?"

"I did my best," Archie said, "as one should always do; but I felt even then that I would rather have been fighting on foot."

"That is because you have so much skill with your weapon, Sir Archie," Douglas said. "On horseback with mace or battle-axe it is mainly a question of sheer strength, and though you are very strong there are others who are as strong as you. Now, it is allowed that none of the king's knights and followers are as skill-ful as you with the sword, and even the king himself, who is regarded as the second best knight in Europe, owns that on foot and with a sword he has no chance against you. That we all saw when you practiced for the amusement of the queen and her ladies in the mountains of Lennox. None other could even touch you, while you dented all our helmets and armor finely with that sword of yours. Had we continued the sport there would not have been a whole piece of armor among us save your own harness."

Archie laughed. "I suppose, Douglas, we all like best that in which we most excel. There are many knights in the English army who would assuredly overthrow me either in the tilting ring or in the field, for I had not the training on horseback when quite young which is needed to make a perfect knight, while I had every advantage in the learning of sword-playing, and I stick to my own trade. The world is beginning to learn that a man on foot is a match for a horseman—Wallace taught Europe that lesson. They are slow to believe it, for hitherto armed knights have deemed themselves invincible, and have held in contempt all foot-soldiers. Stirling, and Falkirk, and Loudon Hill have taught

them the difference, but it will be a long time before they fairly
own a fact so mortifying to chivalry; but the time will come, be
well assured, when battles will be fought almost with infantry
alone. Upon them the brunt of the day will fall, and by them will
victory be decided, while horsemen will be used principally for
pursuing the foe when he is broken, for covering the retreat of
infantry by desperate charges, or by charging into the midst of a
fray when the infantry are broken."

"All the better for Scotland," James Douglas said, cheerfully.
"We are not a nation of horsemen, and our mountains and hills,
our forests and morasses, are better adapted for infantry than cavalry; so if ever the change you predict comes to pass we shall be
gainers by it."

The following morning Archie went down to the cove where
his friend the fisherman kept his boat. The old man and his two
sons were already there, but had not launched their craft.

"I like not the look of the weather," the fisherman said when
Archie joined him. "The sky is dull and heavy, the sea is black
and sullen, but there is a sound in the waves as they break against
the rocks which seems to tell of a coming storm. I think, however, it will be some hours before it breaks; and if we have luck
we may get a haul or two before it comes on."

"I am ready to go or stay," Archie said; "I have no experience
in your weather here, and would not urge you against your own
judgment, whatever it be; but if you put out I am ready to go with
you."

"We will try it," the fisherman said, "for food is running short;
but we will not go far from the shore, so that we can pull back if
the weather gets worse."

The boat was soon launched, the nets and oars were already on
board, and they quickly put out from the shore. The boat carried
a small square sail, which was used when running before the
wind. In those days the art of navigation was in its infancy, and
the art of tacking against the wind had scarcely begun to be
understood; indeed, so high were the ships out of water, with
their lofty poops and forecastles, that it was scarcely possible to
sail them on a wind, so great was the leeway they made. Thus
when contrary winds came, mariners anchored and waited as
patiently as they might for a change, and voyage to a port but two

days' sail with a favouring wind, was a matter of weeks when it was foul.

After rowing a mile from land the nets were put out, and for some time they drifted near these. From time to time the old fisherman cast an anxious eye at the sky.

"We must get in our nets," he said at last decidedly; "the wind is rising fast, and is backing from the west round to the south. Be quick, lads, for ere long the gale will be on us in its strength, and if 'tis from the south we may well be blown out to sea."

Without a moment's delay the fishermen set to work to get in the nets, Archie lending a hand to assist them. The younger men thoroughly agreed in their father's opinion of the weather, but they knew too well the respect due to age to venture upon expressing an opinion until he had first spoken. The haul was a better one than they had expected, considering that the net had been down but two hours.

"'Tis not so bad," the fisherman said, "and the catch will be right welcome—that is," he added, as he looked toward the land, "if we get it safely on shore."

The wind was now blowing strongly; but if it did not rise, the boat would assuredly make the land. Archie took the helm, having learned somewhat how to steer on previous excursions, while the three fishermen tugged at the oars. It was a cross sea, for although the wind now blew nearly in their teeth, it had until the last half hour been from the west, and the waves were rolling in from the Atlantic. The boat, however, made fair progress; and Archie began to think that the doubts of the fishermen as to their making it to shore were in no wise justified, when suddenly a gust, far stronger than those they had hitherto met, struck the boat. "Keep her head straight!" the fisherman shouted. "Don't let the wind take it one side or the other. Stick to it, boys; row your hardest; it is on us now and in earnest, I fear."

The three men bent to their oars, but Archie felt that they were no longer making headway. The boat was wide and high out of the water; a good sea boat, but very hard to row against the wind. Although the men strained at the oars, till Archie expected to see the tough staves crack under their efforts, the boat did not seem to move. Indeed it appeared to Archie that in the brief space when the oars were out of the water, the wind drove her further back than the distance she had gained in the last stroke. He hoped, however, that the squall was merely temporary, and that when it subsided there would still be no difficulty in gaining the land. His hope was not realized. Instead of abating, the wind appeared each moment to increase in force. Clouds of spray were blown on the top of the waves, so that at times Archie could not see the shore before him. For nearly half an hour the fishermen struggled on, but Archie saw with dismay that the boat was receding from the shore, and that they had already lost the distance they had gained before the squall struck them. The old fisherman looked several times over his shoulder.

"It is of no use," he said at last; "we shall never make Rathlin, and must even run before the gale. Put up the helm, young sir, and take her round. Wait a moment till the next wave has passed under us—now!" In another minute the boat's head was turned from land, and she was speeding before the gale.

"In with your oars, lads, and rig the mast, reef down the sail to the last point; we must show a little to keep her dead before the wind; we shall have a tremendous sea when we are once fairly away from the shelter of the island. This gale will soon knock up the sea, and with the cross swell from the Atlantic it will be as much as we can do to carry through it."

The mast was stepped and a mere rag of sail hoisted, but this was sufficient to drive the boat through the water at a great speed. The old fisherman was steering now, and when the sail was hoisted the four men all gathered in the stern of the boat.

"You will go between Islay and Jura, I suppose," one of the younger men said.

"Ay," his father said briefly; "the sea will be too high to windward of Islay."

"Could we not keep inside Jura?" Archie suggested; "and shelter in some of the harbors on the coast of Argyle."

"Ay," the old man said; "could we be sure of doing that it would be right enough, but, strong as the wind is blowing her, it will be stronger still when we get in the narrow waters between the islands and the mainland, and it would be impossible to keep her even a point off the wind; then if we missed making a harbor we should be driven up through the Strait of Corrievrekan, and the biggest ship which sails from a Scottish port would not live in the sea which will be running there. No, it will be bad enough passing between Islay and Jura; if we get safely through that I shall try to run into the narrow strait between Colonsay and Oronsay; there we should have good and safe shelter. If we miss that, we must run inside Mull—for there will be no getting without it —and either shelter behind Lismore island far up the strait, or behind Kerara, or into the passage to Loch Etive."

"It will not be the last, I hope," Archie said, "for there stands Dunstaffnage Castle, and the lands all belong to the MacDougalls. It is but two months back I was a prisoner there, and though I then escaped, assuredly if I again get within its walls I shall never go out again. As well be drowned here."

"Then we will hope," the fisherman said, "that 'tis into some other harbor that this evil wind may blow us; but as you see, young sir, the gale is the master and not we, and we must needs go where it chooses to take us."

Fiercer and fiercer blew the gale; a tremendous cross sea was now running, and the boat, stout and buoyant as she was, seemed every moment as if she would be engulfed in the chaos of water. Small as the sail had been it had been taken down and lashed with ropes to the yard, so that now only about three square feet of canvas was set.

"We can show a little more," the fisherman shouted in Archie's ear, "when we get abreast of Islay, for we shall then be sheltered from the sea from the west, and can run more boldly with only a following sea; but till we get out of this cross tumble we must not carry on, we only want steerageway to keep her head straight."

Never before had Archie Forbes seen a great gale in all its strength at sea, for those which had occurred while at Rathlin were as nothing to the present; and although on the hillside round Glen Cairn the wind sometimes blew with a force which there was no withstanding, there was nothing to impress the senses as did this wild confusion and turmoil of water. Buoyant as was the boat, heavy seas often broke on board her, and two hands were constantly employed in baling; still Archie judged from the countenance of the men that they did not deem the position desperate, and that they believed the craft would weather the gale. Toward mid day, although the wind blew as strongly as ever, there was a sensible change in the motion of the boat. She no longer was tossed up and down with jerky and sudden motion, as the waves seemed to rise directly under her, but rose and fell on the following waves with a steady and regular motion.

"We are well abreast of Islay," the old fisherman said when Archie remarked on the change to him. "There! do you not see that dark bank through the mist; that is Islay. We have no longer a cross sea, and can show a little more sail to keep her from being pooped. We will bear a little off toward the land—we must keep it in sight, and not too far on our left, otherwise we may miss the straits and run on to Jura."

A little more sail was accordingly shown to the gale, and the boat scudded along at increased speed.

"How far is it to Colonsay?" Archie asked.

"Between fifty and sixty miles from Rathlin," the fisherman said. "It was eight o'clock when we started, ten when the squall struck us; it will be dark by four, and fast as we are running we shall scarcely be in time to catch the last gleam of day. Come, boys," he said to his sons, "give her a little more canvas still, for it is life and death to reach Colonsay before nightfall, for if we miss it we shall be dashed on to the Mull long before morning."

A little more sail was soon shown, and the boat tore through the water at what seemed to Archie to be tremendous speed; but she was shipping but little water now, for though the great waves as they neared her stern seemed over and over again to Archie as if they would break upon her and send her instantly to the bottom, the stout boat always lifted lightly upon them until he at length felt free from apprehension on that score. Presently the fisherman pointed out a dark mass over their other bow.

"That is Jura," he said; "we are fair for the channel, lads, but you must take in the sail again to the smallest rag, for the wind will blow through the gap between the islands with a force fit to tear the mast out of her."

Through the rest of his life Archie Forbes regarded that passage between Islay and Jura as the most tremendous peril he had ever encountered. Strong as the wind had been before, it was as nothing to the force with which it swept down the strait—the height of the waves was prodigious, and the boat, as it passed over the crest of a wave, seemed to plunge down a very abyss. The old fisherman crouched low in the boat, holding the helm, while the other three lay on the planks in the bottom. Speech was impossible, for the loudest shouts would have been drowned in the fury of the storm. In half an hour the worst was over. They were through the straits and out in the open sea again, but Islay now made a lee for them, and the sea, high as it was, was yet calm in comparison to the tremendous waves in the Strait of Jura. More sail was hoisted again, and in an hour the fisherman said, "Thank God, there are the islands." The day was already fading, and Archie could with difficulty make out the slightly dark mass to which the helm pointed.

"Is that Colonsay?" he asked.

"It is Oronsay," the fisherman said. "The islands are close together and seem as if they had once been one, but have been cleft asunder by the arm of a giant. The strait between them is very narrow, and once within it we shall be perfectly sheltered. We must make as close to the point of the island as we can well go, so as not to touch the rocks, and then turn and enter the strait. If we keep out any distance we shall be blown past the entrance, and then our only remaining chance is to try and run her on to Colonsay, and take the risk of being drowned as she is dashed upon the rocks."

The light had almost faded when they ran along at the end of Oronsay. Archie shuddered as he saw the waves break upon the rocks and fly high up into the air, and felt how small was the chance of their escape should they be driven on a coast like that. They were but fifty yards from the point when they came abreast of its extremity; then the fisherman put down the helm and turned her head towards the strait, which opened on their left.

"Down with the sail and mast, lads, and out with your oars; we must row her in."

Not a moment was lost, the sail was lowered, the mast removed from its socket, and the oars got out, with a speed which showed how urgent was the occasion. Archie, who did not feel confidence in his power to manager her now in such a sea, took his seat by the other men, and double-banked his oar. Five minutes of desperate rowing and they were under shelter of Oronsay, and were rowing more quickly up the narrow strait and towards the shore of Colonsay, where they intended to land. A quarter of an hour more and they stepped ashore.

The old fisherman raised his hat reverently. "Let us thank God for His mercy," he said, "for He preserved us through such great danger. I have been nigh fifty years at sea, and never was out in so wild a gale."

For a few minutes all stood silent and bare-headed, returning fervent thanks for their escape.

"It is well," the old man said, as they moved inland, "that I have been so far north before; there are but few in Rathlin who have even been north of Islay, but sometimes when fish have been very plentiful in the island, and the boat for Ayr had already gone, I have taken up a boatload of fish to the good monks of Colonsay, who, although fairly supplied by their own fishermen, were yet always ready to pay a good price for them. Had you been in a boat with one who knew not the waters, assuredly we would have perished, for neither skill nor courage could have availed us. There! do you see that light ahead? That is the monastery, and you may be sure of a welcome there."

The monastery door was opened at their ring, and the monk who appeared was, greatly surprised at receiving visitors on such a night. He at once invited them to enter when he heard that they were fishermen whom the storm had driven to shelter on the island. The fishermen had to lend their aid to the monk to close the door again, so great was the power of the wind. The monk shut the bolts, saying, "We need expect no further visitors tonight;" and led them into the kitchen, where a huge fire was blazing.

"Quick, brother Austin," he said to the monk, who acted as cook, "warm up a hot drink for these poor souls, for they must assuredly be well-nigh perished with cold, seeing that they have been wet for many hours and exposed to all the violence of this wintry gale."

Archie and his companions were, indeed, stiff with cold and exposure, and could scarcely answer the questions which the monks asked them.

"Have patience, brother! have patience!" brother Austin said. "When their tongues are unfrozen doubtless they will tell you all that you want to know. Only wait, I pray you, till they have drunk this potion which I am preparing."

The monk's curiosity was not, however, destined to be so speedily satisfied, for just as the voyagers were finishing their hot drinks a monk entered with a message that the prior, having heard that some strangers had arrived, wished to welcome and speak with them in his apartment. They rose at once.

"When the prior has done questioning you," brother Austin said, "return hither at once. I will set about preparing supper for you, for I am certain that you must need food as well as drink. Fear not but, however great your appetite may be, I will have enough to satisfy it by the time you return."

"Welcome to Colonsay!" the prior said, as the four men entered his apartment; "but stay—I see you are drenched to the skin; and it were poor hospitality, indeed, to keep you standing thus even to assure you of your welcome. Take them," he said to the monk, "to the guest chamber at once, and furnish them with changes of attire. When they are warm and comfortable return with them hither."

In ten minutes Archie and his companions re-entered the prior's room. The prior looked with some astonishment at Archie; for in the previous short interview he had not noticed the difference in their attire, and had supposed them to be four fishermen. The monk, however, had marked the difference; and on inquiry, finding that Archie was a knight, had furnished him with appropriate attire. The good monks kept a wardrobe to suit guests of all ranks, seeing that many visitors came to the holy priory, and that sometimes the wind and waves brought them to shore in such sorry plight that a change of garments was necessary.

"Ah!" the prior said, in surprise; "I crave your pardon sir knight, that I noticed not your rank when you first entered. The light is somewhat dim, and as you stood there together at the door way I noticed not that you were of superior condition to the others."

"That might well be, holy prior," Archie said, "seeing that we were more like drowned beasts than Christian men. We have had a marvelous escape from the tempest—thanks be to God!—seeing that we were blown off Rathlin, and have run before the gale down past Islay and through the Straits of Jura. Next to the protection of God, our escape is due to the skill and courage of my brave companions here, who were as cool and calm in the tempest as if they had been sitting by the fires at home."

"From Rathlin!" the prior said in surprise, "and through the strait 'twixt Islay and Jura! Truly that was a marvelous voyage in such a gale—and as I suppose, in an open boat. But how comes it, sir knight—if I may ask the question without prying into your private affairs—that you, a knight, were at Rathlin? In so wild and lonely an island men of your rank are seldom to be found."

"There are many there now, holy prior, far higher in rank than myself," Archie replied, "seeing that Robert the Bruce, crowned King of Scotland, James Douglas, and others of his nobles and knights, are sheltering there with him from the English bloodhounds."

"The Bruce at Rathlin!" the prior exclaimed, in surprise. "The last ship which came hither from the mainland told us that he was a hunted fugitive in Lennox; and we deemed that seeing the MacDougalls of Lorne and all the surrounding chiefs were hostile to him, and the English scattered thickly over all the low country, he must long ere this have fallen into the hands of his enemies."

"Thanks to Heaven's protection," Archie said devoutly, "the king with a few followers escaped and safely reached Rathlin!"

"Thou shouldst not speak of Heaven's protection," the prior said, sternly, "seeing that Bruce has violated the sanctuary of the church, has slain his enemy within her walls, has drawn down upon himself the anathema of the pope, and has been declared excommunicated and accursed."

"The pope," Archie replied, "although supreme in the church at Rome, is but little qualified to judge of the matter, seeing that he draws his information from King Edward, who seldom gives honest reports. The good Bishops of St. Andrews and Glasgow, with the Abbot of Scone, and many other dignitaries of the Scottish church, have pardoned his offense, seeing that it was committed in hot blood and without prior intent. The king himself bitterly regrets the deed, which preys sorely upon his mind; but I can answer for it that Bruce had no thought of meeting Comyn at Dumfries." "You speak boldly, young sir," the prior said, sternly, "for one over whose head scarce two-and-twenty years can have rolled; but enough now. You are storm-staid and wearied; you are the guests of the monastery. I will not keep you further now, for you have need of food and sleep. Tomorrow I will speak with you again."

So saying, the prior sharply touched a bell which stood on a table near him. The monk re-entered. The prior waved his hand: "Take these guests to the kitchen and see that they have all they stand in need of, and that the bed-chambers are prepared. In the morning I would speak to them again."

Chapter 15

A Mission to Ireland

Father Austin was as good as his word, and it was long indeed, since Archie had sat down to such a meal as that which was spread for him. Hungry as he was, however, he could scarcely keep his eyes open to its conclusion, so great was the fatigue of mind and body; and on retiring to the chamber which the monks had prepared for him, he threw himself on a couch and instantly fell asleep. In the morning the gale still blew violently, but with somewhat less fury than on the preceding evening. He joined the monks at their morning meal in the refectory, and afterwards they gathered round him to listen to his news of what was going on in Scotland; for although at ordinary times pilgrims came not infrequently to visit the isle of Colonsay, in the present stormy times men stirred but little from home, and it was seldom that the monks obtained news of what was passing on the mainland. Presently a servitor brought word that the prior would see Archie.

"It was ill talking last night," the prior said, "with a man hungry and worn-out; but I gathered from what you said that you are not only a follower of Bruce, but that you were with him at that fatal day at Dumfries when he drew his dagger upon Comyn in the sanctuary."

"I was there, sir," Archie replied, "and can testify that the occurrence was wholly unpremeditated; but Bruce had received sufficient provocation from the Comyn to afford him fair reason for slaying him wheresoever they might meet. But none can regret more than he does that that place of meeting was in a sanctuary. The Comyn and Bruce had made an agreement together whereby the former relinquished his own claims to the throne of Scotland on condition that Bruce, on attaining the throne, would hand over to him all his lordships in Carrick and Annandale."

"It were a bad bargain," the prior said, "seeing that Comyn would then be more powerful than his king."

"So I ventured to tell the Bruce," Archie replied.

"Thou?" the prior said; "you are young, sir, to be in a position to offer counsel to Robert Bruce."

"I am young," Archie said modestly; "but the king is good enough to overlook my youth in consideration of my fidelity to the cause of Scotland. My name is Archibald Forbes."

"Sir Archibald Forbes!" the prior repeated, rising; "and are you really that loyal and faithful Scottish knight who fought ever by the side of Wallace, and have almost alone refused ever to bow the knee to the English? Even to this lonely isle tales have come of your valor, how you fought side by side with Wallace, and were, with Sir John Grahame, his most trusty friend and confidant. Many of the highest and noblest of Scotland have for centuries made their way to the shrine of Colonsay, but none more worthy to be our guest. Often have I longed to see so brave a champion of our country, little thinking that you would one day come a storm-driven guest. Truly am I glad to see you, and I say it even though you may have shared in the deed at Dumfries, for which I would gladly hope from your words there is fairer excuse to be made than I had hitherto deemed. I have thought that the Bishops of St. Andrews and Glasgow were wrong in giving their approval to a man whom the pope had condemned —a man whose prior history gives no ground for faith in his patriotism, who has taken up arms, now for, now against, the English, but has ever been ready to make terms with the oppressor, and to parade as his courtier at Westminster. In such a man I can have no faith, and deem that, while he pretends to fight for Scotland, he is in truth but warring for his own aggrandizement. But since you, the follower and friend of the disinterested and intrepid champion of Scotland, speak for the Bruce, it may be that my judgment has been too severe upon him."

Archie now related the incident of his journey to London to urge Bruce to break with Edward and to head the national movement. He told how, even before the discovery of his agreement with Comyn, brought about by the treachery of the latter, Bruce had determined definitely to throw in his cause with that of Scotland; how upon that discovery he had fled north, and, happening to meet Comyn at Dumfries, within the limits of the sanctuary, had, in his indignation at his treachery, drawn and slain him.

Then he told the tale of what had taken place after the rout of Methven, how bravely Bruce had borne himself, and had ever striven to keep up the hearts of his companions; how cheerfully he had supported the hardships, and how valiantly he had borne himself both at Methven and when attacked by the MacDougalls of Lorne.

"Whatever his past may have been," Archie concluded, "I hold that now the Bruce is as earnest in the cause of Scotland as was even my dear leader Wallace. In strength and in courage he rivals that valiant knight, for though I hold that Wallace was far more than a match for any man of his time, yet Bruce is a worthy second to him, for assuredly no one in Scotland could cross swords with him on equal chances. That he will succeed in his enterprise would be rash to say, for mighty indeed are the odds against him; but if courage, perseverance, and endurance can wrest Scotland from the hands of the English, Robert Bruce will, if he lives, accomplish the task."

"Right glad am I," the prior replied, "to hear what you have told me. Hitherto, owing to my memory of his past and my horror at his crime—for though from what you tell me there was much to excuse it, still it was a grievous crime—I have had but little interest in the struggle, but henceforth this will be changed. You may tell the king that from this day, until death or victory crown his efforts, prayers will be said to heaven night and day at Colonsay for his success."

It was four days before the storm was over and the sea sufficiently calmed to permit Archie's departure. During that time he remained as the honored guest of the priory, and the good monks vied with the prior in their attentions to the young knight, the tales of whose doings, as one of Scotland's foremost champions, had so often reached their lonely island. At the end of that time, the sea being now calm and smooth, with a light wind from the north, Archie bade adieu to his hosts and sailed from Colonsay.

Light as the wind was, it sufficed to fill the sail; and as the boat glided over the scarce rippled water Archie could not but contrast the quiet sleepy motion with the wild speed at which the boat had torn through the water on her northern way. It was not until the following morning that Rathlin again came in sight.

As the boat was seen approaching, and was declared by the islanders to be that which they had regarded as lost in the storm a week previously, the king, Douglas, and the rest of his followers made their way down to the shore; and loud was the shout of welcome which arose when Archie stood up and waved his hand.

"Verily, Archie Forbes," the king said as he warmly embraced the young knight, "I now think that the angels presided at your birth and gave you some charm to preserve your life alike against the wrath of men and of the elements. Never assuredly did anyone pass through so many dangers unscathed as you have done."

"I hope to pass through as many more, sire, in your service," Archie said smiling.

"I hope so, indeed," Bruce replied; "for it were an evil day for me and for Scotland that saw you fall; but henceforth I will fret no more concerning you. You alone of Wallace's early companions have survived. You got free from Dunstaffnage by some miracle which you have never fully explained to me, and now it would seem that even the sea refuses to swallow you."

"I trust," Archie said more gravely, "that the old saying is not true in my case, and that hanging is not to be my fate."

"Assuredly it will be if I ever fall into the hands of Edward, and I shall think it a hard end indeed if the mercy of Heaven, which has spared me so often in battle, leads me to that fate."

"I trust not indeed, Sir Archie," the king said, "though hanging now has ceased to be a dishonorable death when so many of Scotland's best and bravest have suffered it at the English hands. However, I cannot but think that God must have reserved for you the fate of the heroes of most of the stories of my old nurse, which always wound up with 'and so he married, and lived happily ever after.' And now, Archie, tell me all that has befallen you, where you have been, and how you fared, and by what miraculous gift you escaped the tempest. All our eyes were fixed on the boat when you laboured to reach the shore, and had you heard the groans we uttered when we saw you give up the effort as hopeless and fly away to sea before the wind you would have known how truly all your comrades love you. We gave you up as assuredly lost, for the islanders here agreed that you had no chance of weathering the gale, and that the boat would, ere many hours, be dashed to pieces either on Islay or Jura, should it even reach so far;

but the most thought that you would founder long before you came in sight of the land."

Accompanying the king with his principal companions to the hut which he occupied, Archie related the incidents of the voyage and of their final refuge at Colonsay.

Some days later the king said to Archie, "I have a mission for you; 'tis one of danger, but I know that that is no drawback in your eyes."

"I am ready," Archie said modestly, "to carry out to the best of my power any errand with which your majesty may intrust me."

"I have been thinking, Sir Archie, that I might well make some sort of alliance with the Irish chieftains. Many of these are, like most of our Scottish nobles, on terms of friendship with England; still there are others who hold aloof from the conquerors. It would be well to open negotiations with these, so that they by rising might distract Edward's attention from Scotland, while we, by our efforts, would hinder the English from sending all their force thither, and we might thus mutually be of aid to each other. At present I am, certainly, in no position to promise aid in men or money; but I will bind myself by an oath that if my affairs in Scotland prosper I will from my treasury furnish money to aid them in carrying on the struggle, and that if I clear Scotland of her oppressors I will either go myself or send one of my brothers with a strong force to aid the Irish to follow our example. The mission is, as you will see, Sir Archie, a dangerous one; for should any of the English, or their Irish allies, lay hands on you, your doom would be sealed. Still you may do me and Scotland great service should you succeed in your mission. Even minor risings would be of much utility, seeing that they would at any rate prevent Edward from bringing over troops from Ireland to assist in our conquest. I have thought the matter over deeply, and conclude that, young as you are, I can intrust it to you with confidence, and that you are indeed the best fitted among those with me to undertake it. Douglas is but a boy; my brother Edward is too hot and rash; Boyd is impatient and headstrong, trusty and devoted to me though he is; but I am sure that in you there is no lack either of prudence or courage. Hence, Sir Archie, if you will undertake it I will intrust it to you."

"I will willingly undertake it, sire, since you think me fitting for it, and deem it a high honor indeed that you have chosen me. When will you that I start?"

"It were best to lose no time," the king replied, "and if you have no reason for delay I would that you should embark tonight, so that before daybreak you may have gained the Irish shore. They tell me that there are many desperate men in refuge among the caves on the coast, and among these you might choose a few who might be useful to you in your project; but it is not in this part that a rising can be effected, for the country inland is comparatively flat and wholly in the hands of the English. It was on the west coast that the resistance to the English was continued to the last, and here from time to time it blazes out again. In those parts, as they tell me, not only are there wild mountains such as we have in Scotland, but there are great morasses and swamps, extending over wide tracts, where heavy-armed soldiers cannot penetrate, and where many people still maintain a sort of wild independence, defying all the efforts of the English to subdue them. The people are wild and savage, and ever ready to rise against the English. Here, then, is the country where you are most likely to find chiefs who may enter into our plans, and agree to second our efforts for independence. Here are some rings and gold chains, which are all that remain to me of my possessions. Money I have none; but with these you may succeed in winning the hearts of some of these savage chieftains. Take, too, my royal signet, which will be a guarantee that you have power to treat in my name. I need not tell you to be brave, Sir Archie; but be prudent—remember that your life is of the utmost value to me. I want you not to fight, but simply to act as my envoy. If you succeed in raising a great fire in the west of Ireland, remain there and act as counselor to the chiefs, remembering that you are just as much fighting for Scotland there as if you were drawing sword against her foes at home. If you find that the English arm is too strong, and the people too cowed and disheartened to rise against it, then make your way back here by the end of three months, by which time I hope to sail hence and to raise my standard in Scotland again."

On leaving the king, Archie at once conferred with Duncan the fisherman, who willingly agreed that night to set him ashore in Ireland.

"I will land you," he said, "at a place where you need not fear that any English will meet you. It is true that they have a castle but three miles away perched on a rock on the coast. It is called Dunluce, and commands a wide seaward view, and for this reason it would be well that our boat were far out at sea again before morning dawned, so that if they mark us they will not suppose that we have touched on the coast; else they might send a party to search if any have landed—not even then that you need fear discovery, for the coast abounds in caves and hiding places. My sons have often landed there, for we do a certain trade in the summer from the island in fish and other matters with the natives there. If it pleases you, my son Ronald, who is hardy and intelligent, shall land with you and accompany you as your retainer while you remain in Ireland. The people there speak a language quite different to that which you use in the lowlands of Scotland and in England, but the language we speak among ourselves closely resembles it; and we can be easily understood by the people of the mainland. You would be lost if you were to go among the native Irish without an interpreter."

Archie thankfully accepted the offer, and that night, after bidding adieu to his comrades, started in Duncan's boat.

"'Tis a strange place where I am going to land you," the fisherman said; "such a place as nowhere else have my eyes beheld, though they say that at the Isle of Staffa, far north of Colonsay, a similar sight is to be seen. The rocks, instead of being rugged or square, rise in close columns like the trunks of trees, or like the columns in the church of the priory of Colonsay. Truly they seem as if wrought by the hands of men, or rather of giants, seeing that no men could carry out so vast a work. The natives have legends that they are the work of giants of old times. Some of them are down by the level of the sea. Here their heads seem to be cut off so as to form a landing-place, to which the natives give the name of the Giant's Causeway. Others in low rows stand on the face of the cliff itself, though how any could have stood there to work them, seeing that no human foot can reach the base, is more than I can say. 'Tis a strange and wonderful sight, as you will say when the morning light permits you to see it."

It was fortunate that Duncan knew the coast so well, and was able by the light of the stars to find a landing-place, for quiet as the sea appeared a swell rose as they neared the shore, and the waves beat heavily on the wild and rocky coast. Duncan, however, steered his boat to the very foot of the Causeway, and then, watching his opportunity, Archie sprang ashore followed by Ronald. A few words of adieu were spoken, and then the boat rowed out to sea again, while Archie and Ronald turned away from the landing-place.

"It were best," the young fisherman said, "to find a seat among the rocks, and there to await the dawn, when I can guide you to some caves close by; but in the darkness we might well fall and break a limb should we try and make our way across the coast."

A niche was soon found, and Archie and his companion sat down for a while. Archie, however, soon discovered that the sides and back of his seat were formed of the strange columns of which Duncan had spoken, and that he was sitting upon the tops of others which had broken off. Eagerly he passed his hands over the surface of these strange pillars, and questioned his companion as to what he knew about them; but Ronald could tell him no more than his father had done, and Archie was forced to await the dawn to examine more closely the strange columns. Daylight only added to his wonder. On all sides of him stretched the columns, packed in a dense mass together, while range above range they stood on the face of the great cliffs above him. The more he examined them the more his wonder grew.

Ronald now urged that they had better be moving, as it was possible, although unlikely enough, that one passing along the top of the cliffs might get sight of them. They accordingly moved along the shore, and in a quarter of a mile reached the mouth of a great cave. The bottom was covered with rocks, which had fallen from the roof, thickly clustered over with wet sea-weed, which, indeed, hung from the sides far up, showing that at high tide the sea penetrated far into the cave.

"The ground rises beyond," Ronald said, "and you will find recesses there which the tide never reaches." They moved slowly at first until their eyes became accustomed to the darkness; then they kept on, the ground getting more even as they ascended, until they stood on a dry and level floor.

"Now I will strike a light," Ronald said, "and light the torch which I brought with me. We are sure to find plenty of drift-wood cast up at the highest point the tide reaches. Then we can make a fire, and while you remain here I will go out and find some of the natives, and engage a guide to take us forward tonight."

Taking out his flint and steel, Ronald proceeded to strike a light; and after several efforts he succeeded in doing so, igniting some dried moss which he had brought with him. The young fisherman had carefully shielded the moss from dampness in the folds of his garment. As a light flame rose he applied his torch to it; but as he did so, came an exclamation of astonishment, for gathered in a circle round them were a dozen wild figures. All were armed and stood in readiness to strike down the intruders into their hiding-place. They were barefooted, and had doubtless been asleep in the cave until, when awakened by the approaching footsteps and voices, they had silently arisen and prepared to fall upon the intruders.

"We are friends," Ronald said in the native language when he recovered from his start of surprise. "I am Ronald, a fisherman from Rathlin, and was over here in the summer exchanging fish for sheep."

"I recollect you," one of the men said; "but why are you here so strangely and secretly? Are the English hunting you too from your island as they have done us?"

"They have not come to Rathlin yet," Ronald said.

"Doubtless they would do so, but 'tis too poor to offer any temptation for their greed. But they are our enemies as they are yours. I am here to guide this Scottish knight, who is staying at Rathlin, a fugitive from their vengeance like yourself, and who is charged with a mission from the King of Scotland to your chiefs, whom he would gladly induce to join in a rising against the power of the English."

"He is welcome," the man who appeared to be the leader of the party replied, "and may he succeed in his object; but," he continued bitterly, "I fear that the chance is a small one. The Norman foot is on our necks, and most of those who should be our leaders have basely accepted the position of vassals to the English king. Still there are brave hearts yet in Ireland who would gladly rise did they see even a faint chance of success. Hundreds are there who, like us, prefer to live the lives of hunted dogs in caves, or in the bogs, rather than yield to the English yoke. Tell me your plans and whither you would go; and I will give you guides who know every foot of the country, and who can lead you to the western hills, where, though no open resistance is made, the English have scarce set foot. There we generally find refuge; and 'tis only at times, when the longing to see the homes of our childhood becomes too strong for us, that I and those you see—all of whom were born and reared between this and Coleraine—come hither for a time, when at night we can issue out and prowl round the ruins of the homes of our fathers."

While this conversation had been going on, the others, seeing that the visit was a friendly one, had set to work, and bringing up driftwood from below, piled it round the little blaze which Ronald had commenced, and soon had a great fire lighted. They then produced the carcass of a sheep which they had the evening before carried off. Ronald had brought with him a large pile of oaten-cakes, and a meal was speedily prepared.

Archie could not but look with surprise at the wild figures around him, lit up by the dancing glare of the fire. Their hair lay in tangled masses on their necks; their attire was of the most primitive description, consisting but of one garment secured round the waist by a strap of untanned leather; their feet and legs were bare. Their hair was almost black; their eyes small and glittering, with heavy overhanging brows; and they differed altogether in appearance even from the wildest and poorest of the Scottish peasantry. In their belts all bore long knives of rough manufacture, and most of them carried slings hanging from the belt, in readiness for instant use. In spite of the wildness of their demeanor they seemed kindly and hospitable; and many were the questions which they asked Ronald concerning the King of Scotland and his knights who were in refuge at Rathlin.

When the meal was over all stretched themselves on the sand like so many animals, and without further preparation went off to sleep. Archie, knowing that nothing could be done until nightfall, followed their example. The fire had by this time burned low, and soon perfect stillness reigned in the great cavern, save that far away at its mouth the low thunder of the waves upon the rocks came up in a confused roar.

Chapter 16

An Irish Rising

When night came on Archie started for the west, accompanied by Ronald and two of the Irish as guides. They crossed the country without question or interference, and reached the wild mountains of Donegal in safety. Archie had asked that his conductors should lead him to the abode of the principal chieftain of the district. The miserable appearance of the sparsely scattered villages through which they had passed had prepared him to find that the superiors of such a people would be in a very different position from the feudal lords of the Highlands of Scotland. He was not surprised, therefore, when his attendants pointed out a small hold, such as would appertain to a small landowner on the Scottish border, as the residence of the chief. Around it were scattered a number of low huts composed of turf, roofed with reeds. From these, when the approach of strangers was reported, a number of wild-looking figures poured out, armed with weapons of the most primitive description. A shout from Archie's guides assured these people that the newcomer was not, as his appearance labeled him, a Norman knight, but a visitor from Scotland who sought a friendly interview with the chief.

Insignificant as was the hold, it was evident that something like feudal discipline was kept up. Two men, armed with pikes, were stationed on the wall, while two others leant in careless fashion against the posts of the open gate. On the approach of Archie an elderly man, with a long white beard, came out to meet them. Ronald explained to him that Archie was a knight who had come as an emissary from the King of Scotland to the Irish chieftains, and desired to speak with the great Fergus of Killeen. The old man bowed deeply to Archie, and then escorted him into the house.

The room which they entered occupied the whole of the ground floor of the hold, and was some thirty feet wide by forty long. As apparently trees of sufficient length to form the beams of so wide an apartment could not be obtained, the floor above was supported by two rows of roughly squared posts extending down from end to end. The walls were perfectly bare. The beams and planks of the ceiling were stained black by the smoke of a fire which burned in one corner; the floor was of clay beaten hard. A strip some ten feet wide, at the further end, was raised eighteen inches above the general level, forming a sort of platform. Here, in a seat carved out of black wood, sat the chief. Some females, evidently the ladies of his family, were seated on piles of sheepskins, and were plying their distaffs; while an aged man was seated on the end of the platform with a harp of quaint form on his knee; his fingers touched a last chord as Archie entered. He had evidently been playing while the ladies worked.

The chief was a fine-looking man about fifty years old. He was clad in a loose-fitting tunic of soft dark-green cloth, confined at the waist by a broad leathern band with silver clasp and ornaments, and reaching to his knees. His arms were bare; on his feet he wore sandals, and a heavy sword rested against the wall near his hand. The ladies wore dresses of similar material and of somewhat similar fashion, but reaching to the feet. They wore gold armlets; and the chief's wife had a light band of gold round her head. The chief rose when Archie entered; and upon the sentry informing him of the rank and mission of his visitor he stepped from the platform, and greeted him warmly. Then he led him back to the platform, where he presented to him the ladies of his family, ordering the retainers, of whom about a score were gathered in the hall, to place two piles of sheepskins near the fire. On one of these he sat down, and motioned to Archie to take his place on the other—his own chair being removed to a corner. Then, through the interpreter named Ronald, the conversation began.

Archie related to the chief the efforts which the Scots were making to win their freedom from England, and urged in the king's name that a similar effort should be made by the Irish; as the forces of the English, being thereby divided and distracted, there might be better hope of success. The chief heard the communication in grave silence. The ladies of the family stood behind the chief with deeply-interested faces; and as the narrative of the long-continued struggle which the Scots were making for freedom continued it was clear, by their glowing cheeks and their animated faces, how deeply they sympathized in the struggle.

The wife of the chief, a tall and stately lady, stood immediately behind him with her two daughters, girls of some seventeen or eighteen years of age, beside her. As Ronald was translating his words Archie glanced frequently at the group, and thought he had never seen one fairer or more picturesque. There was a striking likeness between mother and daughters; but the expression of staid dignity in the one was in the other's replaced by a bright expression of youth and happiness. Their beauty was of a kind new to Archie. Their dark glossy hair was kept smoothly in place by the fillet of gold in the mother's case, and by purple ribbons in that of the daughters. Their eyebrows and long eyelashes were black, but their eyes were gray, and as light as those to which Archie was accustomed under the fair tresses of his countrywomen. The thing that struck him most in the faces of the girls was their variety, the expression changing as it seemed in an instant from serious to happy—flushing at one moment with interest at the tale of deeds of valor, paling at the next at the recital of cruel oppression and wrong. When Archie had finished his narrative he presented to the chief a beautifully wrought chain of gold as a token from the King of Scotland.

The chief was silent for some time after the interpreter concluded Archie's narrative; then he said:

"Sir knight, it almost seems to me as if I had been listening to the tale of the wrongs of Ireland, save that it appears that the mastery of the English here has been more firmly established than with you. This may be from the nature of the country; our hills are, for the most part, bare, while yours, you say, are covered with forest. Thus the Normans could more easily, when they had once gained the upper hand, crush out the last vestiges of opposition than they could with you. As I judge from what you say, the English in Scotland hold all the fortresses, and when the people rise they remain sheltered in them until assistance comes from England. With us it is different. First they conquer all the country; then from a wide tract, a third perhaps of the island, they drive out the whole of the people, and establish themselves firmly there, portioning the land among the soldiery while repopulating the country with an English race. Outside this district the Irish chieftains, like myself, retain something of independence; we pay a tribute, and are in the position of feudatories,[11] being bound to furnish so many men for the King of England's wars if called upon to do so. The English seldom come beyond their pale so long as the tribute is paid, and the yoke, therefore, weighs not so heavy upon us; but were we to rise, the English army would pour out from its pale and carry fire and sword throughout the country.

"We, like you, have been without one who would unite us against the common enemy. Our great chiefs have, for the most part, accepted English titles, and since their power over the minor chiefs is extended, rather than decreased by the changed circumstances, they are well content; for they rule now over their districts, not only as Irish chieftains, but as English lieutenants. You have seen, as you journeyed here, how sparse is the population of our hills, and how slight would be the opposition which we could offer, did the Earl of Ulster sweep down upon us with trained English soldiers.

"Were there a chance of success, Fergus of Killeen would gladly draw the sword again; but I will not bring ruin upon my family and people by engaging in a hopeless enterprise. Did I raise my standard, all Donegal would take up arms; but Donegal alone is powerless against England. I know my people—they are ready for the fray, they would rush to battle and perish in thousands to win victory, but one great defeat would crush them. The story of the long fight which your Wallace, with a small following, made against the power of England, will never be told of an Irish leader. We have bravery and reckless courage, but we have none of the stubborn obstinacy of your Scottish folk. Were the flag raised the people would flock to it, and would fight desperately; but if they lost, there would be utter and complete collapse. The fortitude to support repeated defeats, to struggle on when the prospect seems darkest, does not belong to my people.

"It is for this reason that I have no hope that Ireland will ever regain its independence. She may struggle against the yoke, she may blaze out again and again in bloody risings, our sons may die

---

11. People who held land by feudal tenure.

in tens of thousands for her; but never, I believe, as long as the men of the two countries remain what they are, will Ireland recover her independence, for, in the long run, English perseverance and determination will overcome the fitful courage of the Irish. I grieve that I should say it. I mourn that I feel it my duty to repress rather than to encourage the eager desire of my people to draw the sword and strike for freedom; but such is my conviction.

"But understand, sir knight, that whatever I may think, I shall not be backward in doing my part. If Ireland again rises, should the other native chieftains determine to make one more effort to drive the English across the channel, be sure that Fergus of Killeen and the men of Donegal will be in the front of the battle. No heart beats more warmly for freedom than mine; and did I stand alone I would take to the bogs and join those who shelter there, defying the might of England. But I have my people to think of. I have seen how the English turn a land to desolation as they sweep across it, and I will not bring fire and sword into these mountain valleys unless all Ireland is banded in a common effort. You have seen Scotland wasted from sea to sea, her cities burned, her people slain by thousands, her dales and valleys wasted; and can you tell me that after these years of struggle you have gained any such advantage as would warrant your advising me to rise against England?"

Archie was silent. He began to think over the struggle in which he had taken part for so many years, and remembered the woes that it had brought on Scotland. This young knight also thought about the fact that Bruce and the handful of fugitives at Rathlin were the sole survivors of the patriotic party. Archie could not but acknowledge at heart the justice of the chief's words. His sole hope for Scotland now rested in the perseverance and personal valor of the king, and the stubborn character of the people, which he felt assured would lead them to rise again and again, in spite of disaster and defeat, until freedom was won. The Irish possessed no Bruce; their country was less defendable than Scotland; and if, as Fergus said, they had none of that indomitable perseverance which enabled the Scottish people again and again to rise against the yoke, what hope could there be of final success; how could he be justified in urging upon the chieftain a step which would bring fire and sword into those quiet valleys! For some time, therefore, after Ronald had translated the chief's speech he remained silent.

"I will not urge you further, sir," he said, "for you are surely the best judge of what is good for your people, and I have seen such ruin and desolation in Scotland, so many scores of ruined towns and villages, so many thousands of leveled homesteads, that I will not say a single word to urge you to alter your resolution. It is enough for me that you have said that if Ireland rises you will also draw the sword. I must carry out my instructions, and hence shall travel south and visit other chiefs; they may view matters differently, and may see that what Ireland cannot do alone she may do in conjunction with Scotland."

"So be it!" Fergus said. "Believe me, if you raise a flame through the west the north will not hang back. And now I trust that you will remain here for a few days as my guest. All that I have is yours, and my wife and daughters will do their best to make the time pass pleasantly for you."

Archie remained three days at the chief's hold, where the primitive life interested him greatly. A lavish hospitality was exercised. Several sheep were killed and roasted each day, and all comers were free to join the feast. The chief's more immediate retainers, some twenty in number, ate, lived, and slept in the great hall; while tables were spread outside, at which all who came sat down without question. The upper rooms of the hold were occupied by the chief, the ladies of his family, and the female domestics. Here they retired when they felt disposed, but their meals were served with special care. In the evening the harper played and sang legends of deeds of bravery in the day of Ireland's independence; and as Ronald translated the songs to him Archie could not but conclude privately that civil war, strife, and massacre must have characterized the country in those days.

At the conclusion of his stay Fergus appointed two of the retainers to accompany Archie south, and to give assurance to the various wild people through whom he might pass, that Archie's mission was a friendly one to Ireland, and that he was an honored friend and guest of the chief of Killeen.

On his arrival in Mayo, Archie found matters more favorable to his mission. An insurrection had already broken out, headed by some of the local chieftains, originating in a broil between the

English soldiers of a garrison and the natives. The garrison had been surprised and massacred, and the wild Irish were flocking to arms. By the chieftains here Archie, on explaining his mission, was warmly welcomed. As they were already in arms no urging on his part was needed, and they despatched messengers throughout the country, saying that an emissary from Scotland had arrived, and calling upon all to rise and to join with the Scots in shaking off the yoke of England.

Archie had therefore to travel no farther, and decided that he could best carry out his mission by assisting to organize and lead the Irish forces. These he speedily discovered were beyond all comparison inferior, both in arms, in discipline, and in methods of fighting, to the Scots. For a dashing foray they would be excellent. Hardy, agile, and full of impetuosity, they would bear down all resistance instantly, were that resistance not too strong; but against stubborn and well-armed troops they would break like a wave against a rock. Archie saw that with such troops anything like regular war would be impossible, and that the struggle must be one of constant surprises, attacks, and forays, and that they could succeed only by wearing out and not by defeating the enemy. With such tactics as these they might by long perseverance succeed; but this was just what Fergus had warned him they would not practice, and that their courage was rather of a kind which would lead them to dash desperately against the line of leveled spears, rather than continue a long and weary struggle under apparently hopeless circumstances.

The chiefs, hearing from Archie that he had acted as one of Wallace's lieutenants in battles where the English had been heavily defeated, willingly consented that he should endeavour to instill the tactics by which those battles had been won into their own followers; but when they found that he proposed that the men should remain stationary to withstand the English charges, they shook their heads.

"That will never do for our people," they said. "They must attack sword in hand. They will rush fearlessly down against any odds, but you will never get them steadily to withstand a charge of men-at-arms."

Archie, however, persuaded them to allow him to organize a band of two hundred men under his immediate orders. These were armed with long pikes, and were to form a sort of reserve, in order that if the wild charge of the main body failed in its object these could cover a retreat, or serve as a nucleus around which they could rally. The army swelled rapidly; every day fresh chiefs arrived with scores of wild tribesmen. Presently the news came that an English force was advancing from the Pale against them.

A council was held at which Archie was present. He strongly urged his views upon the chieftains, and recommended that they should avoid a pitched battle. The young Scottish knight advised that they should divide into numerous parties, and move against the Pale, destroying weak garrisons and ravaging the country, in an effort to wear out the English by constant skirmishes and night attacks, but refusing always to allow themselves to be tempted into an engagement.

"The English cannot be everywhere at once," he urged. "Let them hold only the ground on which their feet stand. As they advance or retire, close ever in on their rear, drive off their cattle and destroy their crops and granaries in the Pale; force them to live wholly in their walled towns, and as you gain in strength capture these one by one, as did we in Scotland. So, and so only, can you hope for ultimate success."

His advice was received with a silence which he at once recognized as disapproval. One after another of the Irish chieftains rose and declared that such a war could not be sustained.

"Our retainers," they said, "are ready to fight, but after fighting they will want to return to their homes; besides, we are fifteen thousand strong, and the English men-at-arms marching against us are but eight hundred; it would be shameful and cowardly to avoid a battle, and were we willing to do so our followers would not obey us. Let us first destroy this body of English, then we shall be joined by others, and can soon march straight upon Dublin."

Archie saw that it was hopeless to persevere, and set out the following day with the wild rabble, for they could not be termed an army, to meet the English. The leaders yielded so far to his advice as to take up a position where they would fight with the best chance of success. The spot lay between a swamp extending a vast distance, and a river, and they were thus open only to an attack in front, and could, if defeated, take refuge in the bog, where horsemen could not follow them.

On the following morning the English were seen approaching. In addition to the eight hundred men-at-arms were one thousand lightly-equipped footmen; for experience had taught the English commanders that in such a country, lightly-armed men were necessary to operate where the wide extending morasses prevented the employment of cavalry. The English advanced in solid array: three hundred archers led the way; these were followed by seven hundred spearmen, and the men-at-arms brought up the rear. The Irish were formed in disordered masses, each under its own chieftain. The English archers commenced the fight with a shower of arrows. Scarcely had these began to fall when the Irish with a tremendous yell rushed forward to the assault. The English archers were swept like chaff before them. With reckless bravery they threw themselves next upon the spearmen. The solid array was soon broken by the onslaught, and in a moment both parties were mixed up in wild confusion.

The sight was too much for Archie's band to view unmoved, and these, in spite of his shouts, left their ground and rushed at full speed after their companions and threw themselves into the fight.

Archie was mounted, having been presented with a horse by one of the chiefs, and he now, although hopeless of the final result, rode forward. Just as he joined the confused and struggling mass the English men-at-arms burst down upon them. As a torrent would cleave its way through a mass of loose sand, so the English men-at-arms burst through the mass of Irish, trampling and cutting down all in their path. Not unharmed, however, for the Irish fought desperately with ax and knife, hewing at the men-at-arms, stabbing at the horses, and even trying by sheer strength to throw the riders to the ground. After passing through the mass the men-at-arms turned and again burst down upon them. It was a repetition of the first charge. The Irish fought desperately, but it was each for himself; there was neither order nor cohesion, and each man strove only to kill a foe before being himself slain. Archie and the chiefs, with the few mounted men among the retainers, strove in vain to stem the torrent. Under the orders of their leaders the English kept in a compact mass, and the weight of the horses and armor bore down all opposition. Four times did the men-at-arms burst through the struggling mass of Irish. As they formed to charge the fifth time the latter lost heart, and as if acting under a simultaneous influence they turned and fled.

The English horsemen burst down on the rear of the mass of fugitives, hewing them down in hundreds. Those nearest to the river dashed in, and numbers were drowned in striving to cross it. The main body, however, made for the swamp, and though in the crush many sank in and perished miserably here, the great majority, leaping lightly from tuft to tuft, gained the heart of the morass, the pursuing horsemen reining up on its edge.

Ronald had kept near Archie in the fight, and when all was lost ran along by the side of his horse, holding fast to the stirrup leather. The horsemen still pressed along between the river and the morass, and Archie, following the example of several of the chiefs, alighted from his saddle, and with his companion entered the swamp. It was with the greatest difficulty that he made his way across it, and his lightly-armed companion did him good service in assisting several times to drag him from the treacherous mire when he began to sink in it. At last they reached firmer ground in the heart of the swamp, and here some five thousand or six thousand fugitives were gathered. At least four thousand had fallen on the field. Many had escaped across the river, although numbers had lost their lives in the attempt. Others scattered and fled in various directions. A few of the chiefs were gathered in council when Archie arrived. They agreed that all was lost and there was nothing to do but scatter to their homes. Archie took no part in the discussion. That day's experience had convinced him that nothing like a permanent and determined insurrection was possible; and only by such a movement could the Scottish cause be aided, by forcing the English to send reinforcements across St. George's Channel. After seeing the slaughter which had taken place, he was rejoiced at heart that the rising had commenced before he joined it. It was in no way the result of his mission, but was one of the sporadic insurrections which frequently broke out in Ireland, only to be instantly and sternly repressed.

"We have failed, Sir Knight," one of the chiefs said to him, "but it was not for want of courage on the part of our men."

"No, indeed," Archie replied through his interpreter; "never did I see men fight more fiercely, but without discipline and organization victory is well-nigh impossible for lightly-armed footmen against heavy mail-clad cavalry."

"The tactics you advised were doubtless good," the chief said; "I see their wisdom, but they are well-nigh impossible to carry out with troops like ours. They are ever impatient for the fray, but quickly wearied by effort; ready to die, but not to wait; to them prudence means cowardice, and their only idea of fighting is to rush full at a foe. See how they broke the English spearmen!"

"It was right well done," Archie replied, "and someday, when well trained and disciplined, Irish soldiers will be second to none in the world; but unless they will submit to training and discipline they can never hope to conquer the English."

"And now, Sir Knight, what do you propose doing?" the chief said.

"I shall make my way north," Archie replied, "and shall rejoin my king at Rathlin."

"I will send two of my men with you. They know every foot of the morasses of this neighborhood, and when they get beyond the point familiar to them they will procure you two others to take their places. It will take all your prudence and courage to get through, for the English men-at-arms will be scouring the country in groups of four, hunting all those they come across like wolves. See, already!" and he pointed to the horizon; "they are scattering round the edge of the morass to inclose us here; but it is many miles round, and before tomorrow is gone not a man will be left here."

When darkness fell, Archie, accompanied by Ronald and his guides, set out on his journey. Alone he could never have found his way through the swamps, but even in the darkness his guides moved along quickly, following tracks known to them with the instinct of hounds; Archie kept close on their heels, as a step only a few inches from the track might plunge him in a deep morass, in which in a few seconds he would sink out of sight. On nearing the edge of the bog the guides slackened their pace. Motioning to Archie to remain where he was, they crept forward noiselessly into the darkness. Not far off he could hear the calls of the English horsemen. The sounds were repeated again and again until they died away in the distance, showing that an encirclement had been drawn round the morass so as to inclose the fugitives from the battle of the previous day.

In a quarter of an hour the guides resumed marching as noiselessly as before, and Archie continued the march at their heels. Even greater caution than before was now necessary in walking, for the English, before darkness had set in, had narrowly examined the edge of the morass, and had placed three or four men wherever they could discover the slightest signs of a track. Thus Archie's guides were obliged to leave the path by which they had previously traveled. Their progress was slow now, the party only moving for a few yards at a time, and then halting while the guides searched for ground solid enough to carry their weight. At last Archie felt the ground grow firmer under his foot, and a reconnaissance by the guides having shown them that none of the English were stationed opposite to them, they left the morass, and noiselessly made their way across the country until far beyond the English line.

All night they walked, and at daybreak entered another swamp, and lay down for the day in the long coarse grass growing on a piece of firm ground deep in its recesses. In the evening one of the guides stole out and returned with a native of the neighborhood, who undertook to show Archie the way on his further journey.

Ten days, or rather nights, of steady journeying brought Archie again to the rocky shore where he had landed. Throughout he had found faithful guides, whom he had rewarded by giving, as was often the custom of the time, in lieu of money, a link or two of one of his gold chains. He and Ronald again took refuge in the cave where they had passed the first night of their landing. It was empty now.

Here they abode for a fortnight, Ronald going up every two or three days to purchase provisions at the scattered cottages. On Saturday night they lit a great fire just inside the mouth of the cave, so that while the flames could be seen far out at sea the light would be unobserved by the garrison of Dunluce or any straggler on the cliff above. It had been arranged with Duncan that every

Saturday night, weather permitting, he should sail across and look for a signal fire. The first Saturday night was wild and stormy, and although they lit the fire they had but slight idea that Duncan would sail out. The following week, however, the night was calm and bright, and after piling up the fire high they proceeded to the causeway, and two hours later saw to their joy a boat approaching. In a few minutes they were on board, and by the following morning reached Rathlin.

The king and his companions welcomed Archie's return warmly, although the report which he made showed that there was no hope of obtaining any serious diversion of the English attack by a permanent rising in Ireland; and the king, on hearing Archie's account of all that had passed, assured him that he felt that, although he had failed, no one, under the circumstances, could have done otherwise.

Chapter 17

The King's Blood-Hound

The only other event which occurred throughout the winter was the arrival of a fishing boat with a messenger from one of the king's adherents, and the news which he brought filled them with sorrow and dismay. Kildrummy had been threatened with a siege, and the queen, Bruce's sisters Christine and Mary, his daughter Marjory, and the other ladies accompanying them, deemed it prudent to leave the castle and take refuge in the sanctuary of St. Duthoc, in Ross-shire.

The sanctuary was violated by the Earl of Ross and his followers, and the ladies and their escort delivered up to Edward's lieutenants and sent to England. The knights and squires who formed the escort were all executed, and the ladies committed to various places of confinement, where most of them remained in captivity of the strictest and most rigorous kind until after the battle of Bannockburn, eight years later. The Countess of Buchan, who had crowned Bruce at Scone, and who was one of the party captured at St. Duthoc, received even fouler treatment, by Edward's especial orders being placed in a cage on one of the turrets of Berwick Castle so constructed that she could be seen by all who passed; and in this cruel imprisonment she was kept like a wild beast for seven long years by a Christian king whom his admirers love to hold up as a model of chivalry.

Kildrummy had been besieged and taken by treachery. The king's brother, Nigel Bruce, was carried to Berwick, and was there hanged and beheaded. Christopher Seaton and his brother Alexander, the Earl of Atholle, Sir Simon Fraser, Sir Herbert de Moreham, Sir David Inchmartin, Sir John Somerville, Sir Walter Logan, and many other Scotsmen of noble degree, had also been captured and executed, their only offense being that they had fought for their country.

In all the annals of England there is no more disgraceful page than that which chronicles the savage ferocity with which King Edward behaved to the Scottish nobles and ladies who fell into his hands. The news of these murders excited the utmost fury as well as grief among the party at Rathlin, and only increased their determination to fight till the death against the power of England.

The spring was now at hand, and Douglas, with Archie Forbes and a few followers, left in a boat, and landed on the Isle of Arran. In the bay of Brodick was a castle occupied by Sir John Hastings and an English garrison. The Scots concealed themselves near the castle, awaiting an opportunity for an attack. A day or two after their arrival several vessels arrived with provisions and arms for the garrison. As these were being landed Douglas and his followers sallied out and captured the vessels and stores. The garrison of the castle made a sortie to assist their friends, but were driven in with slaughter, and the whole of the supplies remained in the hands of the Scots, causing great rejoicing to the king and the rest of the party when a few days later they arrived from Rathlin.

Bruce now proposed an immediate descent upon Carrick, there, in the midst of his family possessions, to set up his banner in Scotland. The lands had been forfeited by Edward and bestowed upon some of his own nobles. Annandale had been given to the Earl of Hereford, Carrick to Earl Percy, Selkirk to Aymer de Valence. The castle of Turnberry was occupied by Percy with three hundred men. Bruce sent on his cousin Cuthbert to reconnoitre and see whether the people would be ready to rise, but Cuthbert found the Scots sunk in despair. All who had taken up arms had perished in the field or on the scaffold. The country swarmed with the English, and further resistance seemed hopeless. Cuthbert had arranged to light a beacon on a point at Turnberry visible at Lamlash Bay in Arran, where the king with his two hundred men and eighty-three boats, awaited the sight of the smoke which should tell them that circumstances were favorable for their landing.

Cuthbert, finding that there was no chance of a rising, did not light the bonfire; but as if fortune was determined that Bruce should continue a struggle which was to end finally in the freedom of Scotland, some other person lit a fire on the very spot where Cuthbert had arranged to show the signal. On seeing the smoke the king and his party at once got into their boats and rowed across to the mainland, a distance of seventeen miles. On reaching land they were met by Cuthbert, who reported that the fire was not of his kindling, and that the circumstances were altogether unfavorable. Bruce consulted with his brother Edward, Douglas, Archie, and his principal friends as to what course had better be pursued. Edward declared at once that he for one would not take to sea again; and this decision settled the matter.

The king without delay led his followers against the village outside the castle, where a considerable portion of the garrison were housed. These were assailed so suddenly that all save one were slain. Those in the castle heard the sounds of the conflict, but being unaware of the smallness of the assailant's force, did not venture to sally out to their assistance.

Percy, with his followers, remained shut up in the castle, while Bruce overran the neighboring country; but an English force under Sir Roger St. John, far too powerful to be resisted, advanced to Turnberry, and Bruce and his followers were obliged to seek refuge in the hills. Thomas and Alexander, the king's brothers, with Sir Reginald Crawford, had gone to the islands to beat up recruits, and returning in a vessel with a party who had joined them, landed at Loch Ryan. They were attacked at once by Macdowall, a chieftain of Galloway, and routed. The king's brothers, with Sir Reginald Crawford, were carried to Carlisle severely wounded, and delivered over to King Edward, who at once sent them to the scaffold.

These wholesale and barbarous executions saddened the Scots, and, as might be expected, soon roused them to severe reprisals. Bruce himself, however, although deeply stirred by the murder of his three brothers and many dear friends, and by the captivity and harsh treatment of his wife and female relatives, never attempted to take vengeance for them upon those who fell into his hands, and during the whole of the war in no single instance did he put a prisoner to death. He carried magnanimity, indeed, almost to the extent of impolicy; for had the nobles of England found that those of their number who fell into Bruce's hands suffered the penalty of death, which Edward inflicted upon the Scottish prisoners, they would probably have remonstrated with the king and

insisted upon his conducting the war in a less barbarous and ferocious fashion.

Sir James Douglas was so stirred by the murder of the three
Bruces and so many of his friends and companions, that he
resolved henceforth to wage an exterminating war against the
English, and by the recapture of his own stronghold, known as
Castle Douglas, began the series of desperate deeds which won
for him the name of the Black Douglas, and rendered his name for
generations a terror among the English on the border. The castle
had been conferred by Edward on Sir Robert de Clifford, and was
occupied by an English garrison. Douglas revealed his intention
only to Archie Forbes, who at once agreed to accompany him. He
asked leave from the king to quit their hiding-place for a time,
accompanied by Archie, in order to revisit Douglas Hall, and see
how it fared with his tenants and friends. The king acquiesced
with difficulty, as he thought the expedition a dangerous one, and
feared that the youth and impetuosity of Douglas might lead him
into danger; before consenting he strongly urged on Archie to
keep a strict watch over the doings of the young noble.

Accompanied by but one retainer, the friends set out for Douglasdale. When they arrived there Douglas went to the cottage of
an old and faithful servant named Thomas Dickson, by whom he
was joyfully received. Dickson went out among the retainers and
revealed to such as could be most surely depended upon the
secret of their lord's presence, and one by one took them in to see
him. The friends had already determined upon their course, and
the retainers all promised to take part in the scheme. They were
not numerous enough to assault the castle openly, but they chose
the following Sunday for the assault. This was Palm Sunday and
a festival, and most of the garrison would come to the Church of
St. Bride, in the village of the same name, a short distance from
the castle.

Dickson with some of his friends went at the appointed time,
with arms concealed under their clothes, to the church; and after
the service had commenced Douglas and some of his followers
gathered outside. Unfortunately for the plan, some of those outside set up the shout, "A Douglas!" prematurely before the whole
party had arrived and were ready to rush into the church. Dickson with his friends at once drew out their arms and attacked the

The Black Douglas' Revenge

English; but being greatly outnumbered and for a time unsupported, most of them, including their leader, were slain. Sir James and his followers then fought their way in, and after a desperate fight all the garrison save ten were killed.

The party then proceeded to the castle, which they captured without resistance. Douglas and his companions partook of the dinner which had been prepared for the garrison; then as much money, weapons, armor, and clothing as they could carry away was taken from the castle. The whole of the vast stores of provisions were carried into the cellar and the heads struck out of the ale and wine casks, the prisoners were also slain and their bodies thrown down into the cellar, and the castle was then set on fire. Archie Forbes in vain begged Douglas to spare the lives of the prisoners, but the latter would not listen to him. "No, Sir Archie," he exclaimed; "the King of England held my good father a prisoner in chains until he died; he has struck off the heads of every one of our friends who have fallen into his hands; he has wasted Scotland from end to end with fire and sword, and has slain our people in tens of thousands. So long as this war continues, so long will I slay every prisoner who falls into my hands, as King Edward would slay me should I fall into his; and I will not desist unless this cruel king agrees to show quarter to such of us as he may capture. I see not why all the massacring and bloodshed should be upon one side."

Archie did not urge him further, for he too was half beside himself with indignation and grief at the murder of the king's brothers and friends, and at the cruel captivity which, by a violation of the laws of sanctuary, had fallen upon the ladies with whom he had spent so many happy hours in the mountains and forests of Athole.

Douglas and Archie now rejoined the king. For months Bruce led the life of a hunted fugitive. His little following dwindled away until but sixty men remained in arms. Of these a portion were with the king's brother in Galloway, and with but a handful of men Bruce was lying among the fastnesses of Carrick when Sir Ingram de Umfraville, with a large number of troops sent by the Earl of Pembroke from Edinburgh, approached. Wholly unable to resist so large a force, Bruce's little party scattered, and the king himself, attended only by a page, lay hidden in the cottage of a peasant. The English in vain searched for him, until a traitorous Scot went to Umfraville and offered, for a reward of a grant of land to the value of £40 annually, to slay Bruce.

The offer was accepted, and the traitor and his two sons made their way to Bruce's place of concealment. As they approached, Bruce snatched his bow from his page and shot the traitor through the eye. One son attacked him with an ax, but was slain with a blow from the king's sword. The remaining assailant rushed at him with a spear; but the king with one blow cut off the spearhead, and before the assailant had time to draw his sword, stretched him dead at his feet.

After this the king with his adherents eluded the search of the English and made their way into Galloway. The people here who were devoted to the English cause determined to hunt him down, and two hundred men, accompanied by some bloodhounds, set off toward the king's retreat; but Bruce's scouts were on the watch and brought him news of their coming. The king with his party retired until they reached the morass, through which flowed a running stream, while beyond a narrow passage led through a deep quagmire.

Beyond this point the hunted party lay down to rest, while the king with two followers returned to the river to keep watch. After listening for some time they heard the baying of the hounds coming nearer and nearer, and then, by the light of a bright moon, saw their enemies approaching.

The king sent his two followers to rouse the band. The enemy, seeing Bruce alone, pressed forward with all haste; and the king, knowing that if he retired his followers would be attacked unprepared, determined alone to defend the narrow path. He retired from the river-bank to the spot where the path was narrowest and the morass most impassable, and then drew his sword. His pursuers, crossing the river, rode forward against him; Bruce charged the first, and with his lance slew him; then with a blow with his mace he stretched his horse beside him, blocking the narrow passage. One by one his foes advanced, and five fell beneath his blows, before his companions ran up from behind. The Galloway men then took to flight, but nine more were slain before they could cross the ford.

The admiration and confidence of Bruce's followers were greatly aroused by this new proof of his courage and prowess. Sir James Douglas, his brother Edward, and others soon afterwards returned from the expeditions on which they had been sent, and the king had now four hundred men assembled. This force, however, was powerless to resist an army of English and Lowland Scots who marched against him, led by Pembroke in person. This force was accompanied by John, son of Alexander MacDougall of Lorne, with eight hundred of his mountaineers. While the heavily armed troops occupied all the Lowlands, Lorne and his followers made a circuit in the mountains so as to inclose the royal fugitive between them.

Bruce, seeing that resistance was impossible, caused his party to separate into three divisions, and Douglas, Edward Bruce, and Sir Archibald Forbes were charged to lead their bands, if possible, through the enemy without fighting. The king tried to escape by a different route with a handful of men. John of Lorne had obtained from Turnberry a favorite blood-hound belonging to Bruce, and the hound being put upon the trace persistently followed the king's party. Seeing this, Bruce ordered them all to disperse, and, accompanied only by his foster brother, attempted to escape by speed.

As they sped along the mountain side they were seen by Lorne, who directed his henchman, with four of his bravest and swiftest men, to follow him. After a long chase the MacDougalls came up with Bruce and his foster brother, who drew their swords and stood on the defense. The henchman, with two of his followers, attacked Bruce, while the other two fell on his foster brother. The combat was a desperate one, but one by one the king cut down his three assailants, and then turned to the assistance of his foster brother, who was hardly pressed. The king's sword soon rid him of one of his assailants, and he slew the other. Having thus disembarrassed themselves of the whole of their immediate assailants, Bruce and his companion continued their flight. The main body of their hunters, with the hound, were but a short distance away, but in a wood the fugitives came upon a stream, and, marching for some distance down this, again landed, and continued their flight.

The hound lost their scent at the spot where they had entered the water, and being unable to recover it, Lorne and his followers abandoned the chase. Among the king's pursuers on this occasion was his nephew Randolph, who had been captured at the battle of Methven, and having again taken the oath of allegiance to Edward had been restored to that monarch's favor, and was now fighting among the English ranks.

The search was actively kept up after Bruce, and a party of three men-at-arms came upon him and his foster brother. Being afraid to attack the king, whom they recognized, openly, they pretended they had come to join him.

The king suspected treachery; and when the five lay down for the night in a cottage which they came upon, he and his companion agreed to watch alternately. Overcome by fatigue, however, both fell asleep, and when they were suddenly attacked by the three strangers, the foster brother was killed before he could offer any resistance. The king himself, although wounded, managed to struggle to his feet, and then proved more than a match for his three treacherous assailants, all of whom, after a desperate struggle, he slew.

The next morning he continued his way, and by nightfall succeeded in joining the three bands, who had safely reached the rendezvous he had appointed.

A few hours after this exploit of Bruce, Archie with two or three of his followers joined him.

"This is indeed a serious matter of the hound," Archie said when Bruce told him how nearly he had fallen a victim to the affection of his favorite. "Methinks, sire, so long as he remains in the English hands your life will never be safe, for the dog will always lead the searchers to your hiding-places; if one could get near enough to shoot him, the danger would be at an end."

"I would not have him shot, Archie, for a large sum. I have had him since he was a little pup; he has for years slept across my door, and would give his life for mine. 'Tis but his affection now that brings danger upon me."

"I should be sorry to see the dog killed myself," Archie said, "for he is a fine fellow, and he quite admitted me to his friendship during the time we were together. Still, sire, if it were a question between their lives and yours, I would not hesitate to kill any number of dogs. The whole future of Scotland is wrapped up in you; and as there is not one of your followers but would gladly give his life for yours, it were no great thing that a hound should do the same."

"I cannot withstand you in argument, Archie," the king said smiling; "yet I would gladly that my favorite should, if possible, be spared. But I grant you, should there be no other way, and the hound should continue to follow me, he must be put to death. But it would grieve me sorely. I have lost so many and so dear friends in the last year, that I can ill spare one of the few that are left me."

Archie was himself fond of dogs, and knowing how attached Bruce was to his faithful hound he could quite understand how reluctant he was that harm should come to him. Still, he felt it was necessary that the dog should, at all hazards, be either killed or taken from the English, for if he remained in their hands he was almost certain sooner or later to lead to Bruce's capture. He determined then to endeavour to avert the danger by abstracting the dog from the hands of the English, or, failing that, by killing him. To do this it would be absolutely necessary to enter the

English camp. There was no possibility of carrying out his purpose without running this risk, for when in pursuit of the king the hound would be held by a leash, and there would be many men-at-arms close by, so that the difficulty of shooting him would be extremely great, and Archie could see no plan save that of boldly entering the camp.

He said nothing of his project to Bruce, who would probably have refused to allow him to undertake it; but the next morning when he parted from him—for it was considered advisable that the fugitives should be divided into the smallest groups, and that only one or two of his retainers should remain with Bruce—he started with his own followers in the direction of Pembroke's camp. He presently changed clothes with one of these, and they then collected a quantity of firewood and made it into a great bundle. Archie gave them orders where they should await him, and lifting the bundle on his shoulders boldly entered the camp. He passed with it near the pavilion of Pembroke. The earl was standing with some knights at the entrance.

"Come hither, Scot," he said as Archie passed.

Archie laid his bundle on the ground, and doffing his bonnet strode with an awkward and abashed air toward the earl.

"I suppose you are one of Bruce's men?" the earl said.

"My father," Archie replied, "as well as all who dwell in these dales, were his vassals; but seeing that, as they say, his lands have been forfeit and given to others, I know not whose man I am at present."

"Dost know Bruce by figure?"

"Surely," Archie said simply, "seeing that I was employed in the stables at Turnberry, and used to wash that big hound of his, who was treated as a Christian rather than a dog."

"Oh, you used to tend the hound!" Pembroke said. "Then perhaps you could manage him now. He is here in camp, and the brute is so savage and fierce he has already well-nigh killed two or three men; and I would have had him shot but that he may be useful to us. If he knows you he may be quieter with you than others."

"Doubtless he would know me," Archie said; "but seeing that I have the croft to look after, as my father is old and infirm, I trust that you will excuse me the service of looking after the hound."

"Answer me not," Pembroke said angrily. "You may think yourself lucky, seeing that you are one of Bruce's retainers, that I do not have you hung from a tree. "Take the fellow to the hound," he said to one of his retainers, "and see if the brute recognizes him; if so, put him in charge of him for the future. And see you Scot, that you attempt no tricks, for if you try to escape I will quickly hang you."

Archie followed the earl's retainer to where, behind his pavilion, the great dog was chained up. He leapt to his feet with a savage growl on hearing footsteps approaching. His hair bristled and he tugged at his chain.

"What a savage beast it is!" the man said; "I would sooner face a whole company of you Scots than get within reach of his jaws. Dickon," he went on as another soldier, on hearing the growl, issued from one of the smaller tents which stood in the rear of the pavilion, "the earl has sent this Scot to relieve you of your charge of the dog; he is to have the care of him from now on."

"That is the best turn the earl has done me for a long time," the man replied. "Never did I have a job I fancied less than the tending of that evil-tempered brute."

"He did not use to be evil-tempered," Archie said; "but was a quiet beast when I had to do with him before. I suppose the strangeness of the place and so many strange faces have driven him half wild. Besides, he is not used to being chained up. Hector, old fellow," he said approaching the dog quietly, "don't you know me?"

The great hound recognized the voice and his aspect changed at once. The bristling hair lay flat on his back; the threatening jaws closed. He gave a short deep bark of pleasure, and then began leaping and tugging at his chain to reach his acquaintance. Archie came close to him now. Hector reared on his hind legs, and placed his great paws on his shoulders, and licked his face with whines of joy.

"He knows you, sure enough," the man said; "and maybe we shall get on better now. At any rate there may be some chance of sleep, for the brute's howls every night since he has been brought here have kept the whole camp awake."

"No wonder!" Archie said, "when he has been accustomed to be petted and cared for; he resents being chained up."

"Would you unchain him?" the man asked.

"That would I," Archie replied; "and I doubt not that he will stay with me."

"It may be so," the man replied; "but you had best not unchain him without leave from the earl, for were he to take it into his head to run away, I would not give a groat for your life. But I will go and inform the earl that the dog knows you, and ask his orders as to his being unchained."

In two or three minutes he returned.

"The earl says that on no account is he to be let free. He has told me to have a small tent pitched here for you. The hound is to be chained to the post, and to share the tent with you. You may, if you will, walk about the camp with him, but always keeping him in a chain; but if you do so it will be at your peril, for if he gets away your life will answer for it."

In a short time two or three soldiers brought a small tent and erected it close by where the dog was chained up. Archie unloosed the chain from the post round which it was fastened, and led Hector to the tent, the dog keeping close by his side and wagging his tail gravely, as if to show his appreciation for the change, to the satisfaction of the men to whom hitherto he had been a terror. Some heather was brought for a bed, and a supply of food, both for the dog and his keeper. The men then left the two friends alone. Hector sat up on his haunches and gazed affectionately at Archie, his tail beating the ground with slow and regular strokes.

"I know what you want to ask, old fellow," Archie said to him; "why I don't lead you at once to your master? Don't you be impatient, old fellow, and you shall see him ere long;" and he patted the hound's head.

Hector, with a great sigh expressive of content and satisfaction, lay down on the ground by the side of the couch of heather on which Archie threw himself—his nose between his forepaws, clearly expressing that he considered his troubles were over, and could now afford to wait until in due time he should be taken to his master. That night the camp slept quietly, for Hector was silent. For the next two days Archie did not go more than a few yards from his tent, for he feared that he might meet someone who would recognize him.

Chapter 18

The Hound Restored

On the third day after his arrival at the camp Archie received orders to prepare to start with the hound, with the earl and a large party of men-at-arms, in search of Bruce. A traitor had just come in and told them where Bruce had slept the night before. Reluctantly Archie unfastened the chain from the pole, and holding the end in his hand went round with Hector to the front of the pavilion. He was resolved that if under the dog's guidance the party came close up with Bruce, he would kill the dog and then try to escape by fleetness of foot, though of this, as there were so many mounted men in the party, he had but slight hope. Led by the peasant they proceeded to the hut, which was five miles away in the hills. On reaching it Hector at once became greatly excited. He sniffed here and there, eagerly hunted up and down the cottage, then made a circuit round it, and at last, with a loud deep bay he started off with his nose to the ground, pulling so hard at the chain that Archie had difficulty in keeping up with him. Pembroke and his knights rode a little behind, followed by their men-at-arms.

"I pray you, Sir Earl," Archie said, "keep not too close to my traces, for the sound of the horse's hoofs and the jingling of the equipments make him all the more impatient to get forward, and even now it taxes all my strength to hold him in."

The earl reined back his horse and followed at a distance of some fifty yards. He had no suspicion whatever of any hidden design on Archie's part. The fact that the hound had recognized him had appeared to him a sure proof of the truth of his tale, and Archie had put on an air of such stupid simplicity that the earl deemed him to have but imperfect possession of his wits. Moreover, in any case he could overtake him in case he attempted flight.

Archie proceeded at a trot behind the hound, who was with difficulty restrained at that pace, straining eagerly on the chain and occasionally sending out his deep bay. Archie anxiously regarded the country through which he was passing. He was waiting for an opportunity, and was determined, whenever they passed near a steep hillside unscalable by horsemen, he would stab Hector to the heart and take to flight. Presently he saw a man, whose attire showed him to be a Highlander, approaching at a run; he passed close by Archie, and as he did so stopped suddenly, exclaiming, "Archibald Forbes!" and drawing his broadsword sprang at him. Archie, who was unarmed save by a long knife, leapt back. In the man he recognized the leader of the MacDougall's party, who had captured him near Dunstaffnage. The conflict would have terminated in an instant had not Hector intervened. Turning round with a deep growl the great hound sprang full at the throat of the Highlander as with uplifted sword he rushed at Archie. The impetus of the spring threw the MacDougall on his back, with the fangs of the hound fixed in his throat. Archie's first impulse was to pull the dog off, the second thought showed him that, were the man to survive he would at once denounce him. Accordingly, though he appeared to tug hard at Hector's chain, he in reality allowed him to have his way. Pembroke and his knights instantly galloped up. As they arrived Hector loosed his hold, and with his hair bristly with rage prepared to attack those whom he regarded as fresh enemies.

"Hold in that hound," Pembroke shouted, "or he will do more damage. What means all this?" For a minute Archie did not answer, being engaged in pacifying Hector who, on seeing that no harm was intended, strove to return to his first foe.

"It means," Archie said, when Hector was at last pacified, "that that Highlander came the other day to our cottage and wanted to carry off a cow without making payment for it. I withstood him, he drew his sword, but as I had a stout cudgel in my hand I hit him on the wrist ere he could use it, and well nigh broke his arm. So he made off, cursing and swearing, and vowing that the next time he met me he would have my life."

"And that he would have done," Pembroke said, "had it not been for Bruce's dog, who has turned matters the other way. He is dead assuredly. It is John of Lorne's henchman, who was doubtless on his way with a message from his lord to me. Could not the fool have postponed his grudge till he had delivered it? I tell you, Scot, you had best keep out of the MacDougalls' way, for assuredly they will revenge the death of their clansman upon you if they have the chance, though I can testify that the affair was none of your seeking. Now let us continue our way."

"I doubt me, Sir Earl, whether our journey ends not here," Archie said, "seeing that these hounds, when they taste blood, seem for a time to lose their fineness of scent; but we shall see."

Archie's opinion turned out correct. Do what they would they could not induce Hector again to take up his master's trail, the hound again and again returning to the spot where the dead Highlander still lay. Pembroke had the body carried off; but the hound tugged at his chain in the direction in which it had gone, and seemed to have lost all remembrance of the track upon which he was going. At last Pembroke was obliged to acknowledge that it was useless to pursue longer, and, full of disappointment at their failure, the party returned to camp, Pembroke saying: "Our chase is but postponed. We are sure to get tidings of Bruce's hiding-place in a day or two, and next time we will have the hound muzzled, lest any hot-headed Highlander should again interfere to mar the sport."

It was some days before further tidings were obtained of Bruce. Archie did not leave his tent during this time, giving as a reason that he was afraid if he went out he should meet some of Lorne's men, who might take up the quarrel of the man who had been killed. At length, however, another traitor came in, and Pembroke and his party set out as before, Hector being this time muzzled by a strap round his jaw, which would not interfere with his scent, but would prevent him from widely opening his jaws.

The scent of Bruce was again taken up at a lonely hut in the hills. The country was far more broken and rough than that through which they had followed Bruce's trail on the preceding occasion. Again Archie determined, but most reluctantly, that he would slay the noble dog; but he determined to postpone the deed to the latest moment. Several places were passed where he might have succeeded in effecting his escape after stabbing the hound, but each time his determination failed him. It would have been of no use to release the dog and make himself up the hillside, for a bloodhound's pace when on the track is not rapid, and the horsemen could have kept up with Hector, who would of course have continued his way upon the trail of the king. Presently two men were seen in the distance; they had evidently been alarmed by the bay of the hound, and were going at full speed. A shout of triumph broke from the pursuers, and some of the more eager would have set spurs to their horses and passed the hound.

"Rein back, rein back," Pembroke said, "the country is wild and hilly here, and Bruce may hide himself long before you can overtake him. Keep steadily in his track till he gains flatter country, where we can keep him in sight, then we shall have no more occasion for the hound and can gallop on at full speed."

Archie observed, with satisfaction, that Bruce was making up an extremely steep hillside, deeming probably that horsemen would be unable to follow him here, and that he would be able to distance pursuers on foot. Ten minutes later his pursuers had reached the foot of the hill. Pembroke at once ordered four knights and ten men-at-arms to dismount.

"You must," he said, "with the dog, follow hard upon the traces of Bruce. When you reach the top signal to us the direction in which he has gone. Follow ever on his track without stopping; he must ultimately take to the low country again. Some of my men shall remain here, others a mile further on, and so on round the whole foot of the hills. When you see that he has distanced you, which he may well do being more lightly armed and flying for his life, send men in different directions to give me warning. The baying of the dog will act as a signal to us."

While the men had been dismounting and Pembroke was giving his orders Archie had proceeded up the hill with the hound. The path was exceedingly steep and difficult.

"Do not hurry, sirrah," Pembroke called; "hold in your hound till the others join you." But Archie paid no attention to the shout, but kept up the steep path at the top of his speed. Shouts and threats followed him, but he paused not till he reached the top of the ascent; then he unfastened Hector's collar, and the dog, relieved from the chain which had so long restrained him, bounded away with a deep bay in pursuit of his master, whose scent was now strong before him. As Archie looked back, the four knights and their followers, in single file, were, as yet, scarce halfway up the ascent. Lying round were numbers of loose boulders, and Archie at once began to roll these down the hillside. They went but slowly at first, but as they reached the steeper portion they gathered speed, and taking great bounds crashed down the hillside. As these formidable missiles burst down from above, the knights paused.

"On!" Pembroke shouted from below; "the Scot is a traitor, and he and the hound will escape if you seize him not." Again the party hurried up the hill. Three of them were struck down by the rocks, and the speed of all was impeded by the pauses made to avoid the great boulders which bounded down toward them. When they were within a few yards of the top Archie turned and bounded off at full speed. He had no fear of being himself overtaken. Lightly clad and unarmed, the knights and men-at-arms, who were all in full armor, and who were already breathless with the exertions they had made, would have no chance of overtaking him; indeed he could safely have fled at once when he loosed Hector, but he had stopped to delay the ascent of his pursuers solely to give the hound as long a start as possible. He himself could have kept up with the hound; the men-at-arms could assuredly not do so, but they might for a long time keep him in sight, and his baying would afterwards indicate the line the king was taking, and Bruce might yet be cut off by the mounted men. The delay which his bombardment had caused had given a long start to the hound, for it was more than five minutes from the time when it had been loosed before the pursuers gained the crest of the hill. Archie, in his flight, took a different line to that which the dog had followed. Hector was already out of sight, and although his deep baying might for a time afford an index to his direction this would soon cease to act as a guide, as the animal would rapidly increase his distance from his pursuers, and would, when he had overtaken the king, cease to emit his warning note. The pursuers, after a moment's pause for consultation on the crest of the hill, followed the line taken by the hound.

The men-at-arms paused to throw aside their defensive armor, breast, back, and leg pieces, and the knights relieved themselves of some of their iron gear; but the delay, short as it was, caused by the unbuckling of straps and unlacing of helms, increased the distance which already existed between them and the hound, whose

Archie Baffles His Pursuers

deep notes, occasionally raised, grew fainter and fainter. In a few minutes it ceased altogether, and Archie judged that the hound had overtaken his master, who, on seeing the animal approaching alone, would naturally have checked his flight. Archie himself was now far away from the men-at-arms, and after proceeding until beyond all reach of pursuit, slackened his pace, and breaking into a walk continued his course some miles across the hills until he reached a lonely cottage where he was kindly received, and remained until the next day.

The following morning he set out and journeyed to the spot, where, on leaving his retainers more than a week before, he had ordered them to await his coming. It was another week before he obtained such news as enabled him again to join the king, who was staying at a woodcutter's hut in Selkirk Forest. Hector came out with a deep bark of welcome.

"Well, Sir Archie," the king said, following his dog to the door, "and how has it fared with you since we last parted a fortnight ago? I have been hotly chased, and thought I should have been taken; but, thanks to the carelessness of the fellow who led my hound, Hector somehow slipped his collar and joined me, and I was able to shake off my pursuers, so that danger is over, and without sacrificing the life of my good dog."

Archie smiled. "Perchance, sir, it was not from any clumsiness that the hound got free, but that he was loosed by some friendly hand."

"It may be so," the king replied; "but they would scarcely have intrusted him to a hand friendly to me. Nor would his leader, even if so disposed, have ventured to slip the hound, seeing that the horsemen must have been close by at the time, and that such a deed would cost him his life. It was only because Hector got away, when the horsemen were unable to follow him, that he escaped, seeing that, good dog as he is, speed is not his strong point, and that horsemen could easily gallop alongside of him even were he free. What are you smiling at, Sir Archie? The hound and you seem on wondrous friendly terms;" for Hector was now standing up with his great paws on Archie's shoulder.

"So we should be, sire, seeing that for eight days we have shared bed and board."

"Ah! is it so?" Bruce exclaimed. "Was it you, then, that loosed the hound?"

"It was, sir," Archie replied; "and this is the history of it; and you will see that if I have done you and Hector a service in bringing you together again the hound has repaid it by saving my life."

Entering the hut, Archie sat down and related all that had happened, to the king.

"You have done me great service, Sir Archie," Bruce said when he concluded his tale, "for assuredly the hound would have wrought my ruin had he remained in the hands of the English. This is another of the long list of services you have rendered me. Some day, when I come to my own, you will find that I am not ungrateful."

The feats which have been related of Bruce, and other personal adventures in which he distinguished himself, won the hearts of great numbers of the Scottish people. They recognized now that they had in him a champion as valiant as Wallace himself. The exploits of the king filled their imaginations, and the way in which he continued the struggle after the capture of the ladies of his family and the cruel execution of his brothers and so many of his adherents, convinced them that he would never desist until he was dead or a conqueror. Once persuaded of this, larger numbers gathered round his banner, and his fortunes henceforth began steadily to rise.

Lord Clifford had rebuilt Douglas Castle, making it larger and much stronger than before, and had committed it to the charge of Captain Thirlwall, with a strong garrison. Douglas took a number of his retainers, who had now joined him in the field, and some of these, dressing themselves as drovers and concealing their arms, drove a herd of cattle within sight of the castle toward an ambuscade in which Douglas and the others were laying in ambush. The garrison, seeing what they believed a valuable prize within their grasp, sallied out to seize the cattle. When they reached the ambuscade the Scots sprang out upon them, and Thirlwall and the greater portion of his men were slain. Douglas then took and destroyed the castle and marched away. Clifford again rebuilt it more strongly than before, and placed it in charge of Sir John Walton. It might have been thought that after the disasters which had befallen the garrison they would not have suffered themselves to be again entrapped. Douglas, however, ordered a number of his men to ride past within sight of the castle with sacks upon their horses, apparently filled with grain, but in reality with grass, as if they were countrymen on their way to the neighboring market town, while once more he and his followers placed themselves in ambush. Headed by their captain, the garrison poured out from the castle, and followed the apparent countrymen until they had passed the ambush where Douglas was lying. Then the drovers threw off their disguises and attacked them, while Douglas fell upon their rear, and Walton and his companions were all slain. The castle was then attacked, and the remainder of the garrison being cowed by the fate which had befallen their leader and comrades, made but a poor defense. The castle was taken, and was again destroyed by its lord, the walls being, as far as possible, overthrown.

Shortly after the daring adventures of Bruce had begun to rouse the spirit of the country Archie Forbes found himself at the head of a larger following than before. Foreseeing that the war must be a long one he had called upon his tenants and retainers to furnish him only with a force one-third of that of their total strength. Thus he was able to maintain sixty men always in the field—all the older men on the estate being exempted from service unless summoned to defend the castle.

One day when he was in the forest of Selkirk with the king a body of fifty men were seen approaching. Their leader inquired for Sir Archibald Forbes, and presently approached him as he was talking to the king.

"Sir Archibald Forbes," he said, "I am bidden by my mistress, the lady Mary Kerr, to bring these, a portion of the retainers of her estates in Ayrshire, and to place them in your hands to lead and govern."

"In my hands!" Archie exclaimed in astonishment. "The Kerrs are all on the English side, and I am their greatest enemy. It were strange, indeed, were one of them to choose me to lead their retainers in the cause of Scotland."

"Our young lord Sir Allan was slain at Methven," the man said, "and the lady Mary is now our lady and mistress. She sent to us months ago to say that she willed not that any of her retainers should any longer take part in the struggle, and all who were in the field were summoned home. Then we heard that no hindrance would be offered by her should any wish to join the Bruce; and now she has sent by a messenger a letter under her hand ordering that a troop of fifty men shall be raised to join the king, and that it shall fight under the leading and order of Sir Archibald Forbes."

"I had not heard that Sir Allan had fallen," Archie said to the king as they walked apart from the place where the man was standing; "and in truth I had forgotten that he even had a sister. She must have been a child when I was a boy at Glen Cairn, and could have been but seldom at the castle— which, indeed, was no fit abode for so young a girl, seeing that Sir John's wife had died some years before I left Glen Cairn. Perhaps she was with her mother's relations. I have heard that Sir John Kerr married a relation of the Comyns of Badenoch. 'Tis strange if, being of such bad blood on both sides, she should have grown up a true Scottish patriot—still more strange she should send her vassals to fight under the banner of one whom she must regard as the unlawful holder of her father's lands of Aberfilly."

"Think you, Sir Archie," the king said, "that this is a stratagem, and that these men have really come with a design to seize upon you and slay you, or to turn traitors in the first battle?"

Archie was silent. "Treachery has been so much at work," he said after a pause, "that it were rash to say that this may not be a traitorous device; but it were hard to think that a girl —even a Kerr—would lend herself to it."

"There are bad women as well as bad men," the king said: "and if a woman thinks she has grievances she will often stop at nothing to obtain revenge."

"It is a well-appointed troop," Archie said looking at the men, who were drawn up in order, "and not to be despised. Their leader looks an honest fellow; and if the lady means honestly it were churlish indeed, to refuse her aid when she ventures to break with her family and to declare for Scotland. No; methinks that, with your permission, I will run the risk, such as it may be, and will join this band with my own. I will keep a sharp watch over them at the first fight, and will see that they are so placed that, should they mean treachery, they shall have but small opportunity of doing harm."

Chapter 19

The Convent of St. Kenneth

Bruce, as the result of his successes, was now able to stop wandering and establish himself in the districts of Carrick, Kyle, and Cunningham. Pembroke had established himself at Bothwell Castle, and sent a challenge to Bruce to meet him with his force at Loudon Hill. Although his previous experience with such challenges was unfortunate, Bruce accepted the offer. He had learned much since the battle of Methven, and was not likely again to be caught asleep; on the ninth of May he assembled his forces at Loudon Hill.

It was but a small following. Douglas had brought one hundred men from Douglasdale, and Archie Forbes had as many under his banner. Bruce's own vassals had gathered two hundred strong, and as many more of the country people had joined; but in all, the Scottish force did not exceed six hundred men, almost entirely on foot and armed with spears. Bruce at once reconnoitred the ground to discover a spot where his little force might best withstand the shock of Pembroke's cavalry. He found that at one place near the hill the road crossed a level meadow with deep morasses on either side. He strengthened the position with trenches, and calmly awaited the approach of his enemy.

Upon the following day Pembroke's army was seen approaching, numbering three thousand knights and mounted men-at-arms, all in complete armor. They were formed in two divisions. The battle was almost a repetition of that which had been fought by Wallace near the same spot. The English cavalry leveled their spears and charged with proud confidence in their ability to sweep away the rabble of spearmen in front of them. Their front ranks became entangled in the morasses; their center tried in vain to break through the hedge of Scottish spears, and when they were in confusion, the king, his brother Edward, Douglas, Archie

Forbes, and some twenty other mounted men dashed through a gap in the spearmen and fell upon them. The second division, seeing the first broken and in confusion, turned and took to flight at once. A short time later Pembroke and his attendants rode, without drawing rein, to Bothwell Castle.

A few days later Bruce encountered and defeated Ralph de Monthermer, Earl of Gloucester, and compelled him to seek refuge in the Castle of Ayr.

Archie Forbes was not present at the second battle, for upon the morning after the fight at Loudon Hill he was aroused by his servant entering his tent.

"A messenger has just brought this," he said, handing him a small packet. "He bids me tell you that the sender is a prisoner in the convent of St. Kenneth, on Loch Leven, and prays your aid."

Archie opened the packet and found within it the ring he had given to Marjory at Dunstaffnage. Without a moment's delay he hurried to the king and begged permission to leave him for a short time on urgent business, taking with him twenty of his retainers.

"What is your urgent business, Sir Archie?" the king asked. "A lady is, in the case, I warrant me. Whenever a young knight has urgent business, be sure that a lady is in question. Now mind, Sir Archie, I have, as I have told you, set my heart upon marrying you to Mistress Mary Kerr, and so at once putting an end to a long feud and doubling your possessions. Her retainers fought well yesterday, and the least I can do to reward so splendid a damsel is to bestow upon her the hand of my bravest knight."

"I fear, sire," Archie said laughing, "that she must be content with another. There are plenty who will deem themselves well paid for their services in your cause by the gift of the hand of so rich an heiress. But I must gladly be excused; for as I told you, sire, when we were together in Rathlin Island, my heart was otherwise bestowed."

"What! to the niece of that malignant enemy of mine, Alexander of Lorne?" the king said laughing. "Her friends would rather see you on the gibbet than at the altar."

"I care naught for her friends," Archie said, "if I can get herself. My own lands are wide enough, and I need no dowry with my wife."

"I see you are hopeless," the king replied. "Well, go, Archie; but whatever be your errand, beware of the Lornes. Remember I have scarce begun to win Scotland yet, and cannot spare you."

"A quarter of an hour later Archie, with twenty picked men, took his way northward. Avoiding all towns and frequented roads, Archie marched rapidly north to the point of Renfrew and crossed the Firth of Clyde by boat; then he kept north round the head of Loch Fyne, and avoiding Dalmally skirted the head of Loch Etive and the slopes of Ben Nevis, and so came down on Loch Leven.

The convent stood at the extremity of a promontory jutting into the lake. The neck was very narrow, and across it were strong walls, with a gate and flanking towers. Between this wall and the convent was a garden where the inmates walked and enjoyed the air free from the sight of men, with the exception of fishermen who might be passing in their boats.

Outside the wall, on the shore of the lake, stood a large village; and here a strong body of the retainers of the convent were always on guard, for at St. Kenneth were many of the daughters of Scottish nobles, sent there either to be out of the way during the troubles or to be educated by the nuns. Although the terrors of the religious leaders at Rome might well deter any from laying hands upon the convent, yet even in those days of superstition some were found so fierce and irreverent as to dare even the anger of religious leaders to carry out their wishes; and the possession of some of these heiresses might well enable them to make good terms for themselves both with the church and the relations of their captives. Therefore a number of the retainers were always under arms, a guard was placed on the gate, and lookouts on the flanking towers—their duty being not only to watch the land side, but to shout orders to keep at a distance to any fisherman who might approach too closely to the promontory.

Archie left his party in the forest under the command of William Orr. He dressed himself as a mountaineer, and, accompanied by Cluny Campbell, and carrying a buck which they had shot in the forest, went boldly down into the village. He soon got into conversation with an old fisherman, and offered to exchange the deer for dried fish. The bargain was quickly struck, and then Archie said, "I have never been out on the lake, and would gladly have a view of the convent from the water. Will you take me and my brother out for a row?"

The fisherman, who had made a good bargain, at once assented, and rowed Archie and Cluny far out into the lake.

As they passed along at some distance, Archie saw that the shore was in several places smooth and shelving, and that there would be no difficulty in effecting a landing. He saw also that there were many clumps of trees and shrubs in the garden.

"And do the nuns and the ladies at the convent often walk there?" he asked the fisherman.

"Oh yes," he answered; "most evenings as I come back from fishing I can see numbers of them walking there. When the vesper-bell rings they all go in. That is the chapel adjoining the convent on this side."

"It is a strong building," Archie said as when past the end of the promontory they obtained a full view of it. "It is more like a castle than a convent."

"It had need be strong," the old man said; "for some of the richest heiresses in Scotland are shut up there. On the land side I believe there are no windows on the lower story, and the door is said to be of solid iron. The windows on that side are all strongly barred; and he would have hard work, indeed, who wanted by force or stratagem to steal one of the pretty birds out of that cage."

Archie had no idea of using force; and although he had been to some extent concerned in the breach of sanctuary at Dumfries, he would have shrunk from the idea of violating the sanctuary of St. Kenneth. But to his mind there was no breach whatever of that sanctuary in aiding one kept there against her will to make her escape. Having ascertained all that he wished to know, he bade the boatman return to shore.

"Keep a lookout for me," he said, "for I may return in a few days with another buck, and may bring a comrade or two with me who would like an afternoon's fishing on the lake. I suppose you could lend me your boat and nets?"

"Assuredly," the fisherman replied. "You will not mind taking into consideration the hire of the boat in agreeing for the weight of fish to be given for the stag?"

Archie nodded, secretly amused at the old man's covetousness, for he knew that the weight of fish he had given him for the stag which he had brought down was not one-fourth the value of the meat.

He then returned with Cluny to the band. Some time before daybreak he came down to the place again, and, entering the water quietly, at a distance from the promontory, swam noiselessly out, and landed at the garden, and there concealed himself in a clump of bushes.

Daylight came. An hour later some of the nuns of the second order, who belonged to poor families and acted as servants in the convent, came out into the garden, and busied themselves with the cultivation of the flowers, vegetables, and herbs. Not till the afternoon did any of the other inmates appear; but at about four o'clock the great door of the convent opened, and a number of women and girls streamed out. The former were all in nuns' attire, as were a few of the latter, but their garb was somewhat different from that of the elder sisters; these were the novices. The greater number, however, of the girls were dressed in ordinary attire, and were the pupils of the convent. While the nuns walked quietly up and down or sat on benches and read, the pupils scattered in groups laughing and talking merrily together. Among these Archie looked eagerly for Marjory. He felt sure that her imprisonment could be detention only, and not rigorous seclusion. Suddenly he saw her. She was walking with two of the nuns and three or four of the elder residents at the convent, for many of these were past the age of pupildom; and were there simply as a safe place of refuge during troublesome times. The conversation appeared to be an animated one. It was not for some time that the group passed within hearing of Archie's place of concealment. Then Archie heard the voice of one of the nuns raised in anger.

"It is monstrous what you say, and it is presumptuous and wicked for a young girl of eighteen to form opinions for herself. What should we come to if every young woman were to venture to think and judge for herself? Discord and disorder would be wrought in every family. All your relations and friends are opposed to this sacrilegious murderer, Robert Bruce. The church has solemnly banned him, and yet you venture to uphold his cause."

"But the Bishop of Glasgow," Marjory said, "and many other good prelates of our church side with him, and surely they must be good judges whether his sins are unpardonable."

"Do not argue with me," the sister said angrily. "I tell you this obstinacy will be permitted no longer. Had it not been that Alexander of Lorne begged that we would not be harsh with you, steps would long since have been taken to bring you to reason; but we can no longer permit this advocacy of rebellion, and the last unmaidenly step which you took of setting at defiance your friends and relatives, and even of sending messages hence, must be punished. The abbess bade me reason with you and try and turn your obstinate will. Your cousins of Badenoch here have appealed to you in vain. This can no longer be tolerated. The lady abbess bids me tell you that she gives you three days to renounce the rebel opinions you have so forwardly held, and to accept the husband whom your uncle and guardian has chosen for you, your cousin John of Lorne, his son. During that time none will speak to you. If at the end of three days you are still siding with rebels you will be confined to your cell on bread and water until better thoughts come to you."

While the conversation had been going on, the little group had halted near the bushes, and they now turned away, leaving Marjory standing by herself. The girl sat down on a bench close to where she had been standing, exclaiming to herself as she did so, "They may shut me up as a prisoner for life, but I will never consent to take sides against the cause of Scotland or to marry John of Lorne. Oh! who is there?" she exclaimed, starting suddenly to her feet as a man's voice behind her said:

"Quite right, Mistress Marjory, well and bravely resolved; but pray sit down again, and assume an attitude of indifference."

"Who is it that speaks?" the girl asked with a trembling voice, resuming her seat.

"It is your true knight, lady, Archibald Forbes, who has come to rescue you from this captivity."

"But how can you rescue me?" the girl asked after a long pause. "Do you know the consequences if you are found here within the bounds of the convent?"

"I care nothing for the consequences," Archie said. "I have in the woods twenty stout followers. I propose tomorrow to be with three of them on the lake fishing. If you, when the bell rings for your return in the evening, will enter that little path by the side of the lake, and will show yourself at the water's edge, we will row straight in and take you off long ere the guards can come hither to hinder us. The lake is narrow, and we can reach the other side before any boat can overtake us. There my followers will be awaiting us, and we can escort you to a place of safety. It is fortunate that you are ordered to be apart from the rest; none therefore will mark you as you linger behind when the bell rings for vespers."

Marjory was silent for some time.

"But, Sir Knight," she said, "whither am I to go? for of all my friends not one, save the good priest, but is leagued against me."

"I can take you either to the Bishop of Glasgow, who is a friend of the Bruce and whom I know well—he will, I am sure, take charge of you—or, if you will, lady, I can place you with my mother, who will receive you as a daughter."

"But what," the girl said hesitatingly, "will people say at my running away from a convent with a young knight?"

"Let them say what they will," Archie said. "All good Scots, when they know that you have been in prison here solely from the love of your country, will applaud the deed; and should you prefer it, the king will, I know, place you in charge of the wife of one of the nobles who adheres to him, and will give you his protection and countenance. Think, lady, if you do not take this opportunity of gaining your freedom, it may never occur again, for if you are once shut up in your cell, as I heard threatened, nothing save an attack by force of arms, which would be sheer sacrilege, can rescue you from it. Surely," he urged, as the girl still remained silent, "you can trust yourself with me. Do I not owe my life to you? and I swear that so long as you remain in my charge I will treat you as my sister in all honor and respect."

For some minutes the girl made no answer. At length she said, standing up, and half turning toward the bushes:

"I will trust you, Sir Archie. I know you to be a brave and honorable knight, and I will trust you. I know 'tis a strange step to take, and the world will blame me; but what can I do? If I refuse

your offer I shall be kept a prisoner here until I consent to marry
John of Lorne, whom I hate, for he is as rough and cruel as his
father, without the kindness of heart, which, save in his angry
moments, the latter has ever had toward me. All my relations are
against me, and struggle against my fate as I may, I must in the
end bend to their will if I remain here. 'Tis a hard choice to make;
but what can I do? Yes, I will trust to your honor; and may God
punish you if you are false to the trust! Tomorrow evening, as the
vespers are chiming, I will be at the water's edge, behind yonder
clump of bushes."

Then, with head bent down and slow steps, Marjory returned
to the convent, none addressing her as she passed through the
groups of her companions, the order that she was to be shut out
from the rest having been already issued. Archie remained in his
place of concealment until the gardens were deserted and night
had fallen. Then he left his hiding-place, and, entering the lake,
swam quietly away, and landed far beyond the village. An hour's
walk brought him to the encampment of his comrades.

At daybreak the next morning, the band, under the command
of William Orr, started for their long march round the head of the
lake to the position which they were to take up on the opposite
side facing the convent, Archie choosing three of the number
most accustomed to the handling of oars to remain with him.
With these he set out on a hunt as soon as the main body had left,
and by mid-day had succeeded in killing a stag. With this animal
dangling on a pole carried by his followers, Archie proceeded to
the village. He speedily found the fisherman with whom he had
before bargained.

"I did not expect you back again so soon," the old man said.

"We killed a buck this morning," Archie said carelessly, "and
my friends thought that the afternoon would be fine for fishing."

"You can try if you like," the fisherman said, "but I fear that
you will have but little sport. The day is too bright and clear, and
the fish will be sulking at the bottom of the lake."

"We will try," Archie said, "nevertheless. Even if the sport is
bad it will be pleasant out on the lake, and if we catch nothing we
will get you to give us some fresh fish instead of dry. The folks in
the hills will be no wiser, and it will not do for us to return
empty-handed."

The fisherman assented, and placed the oars and nets in the boat, and Archie and his companions entering rowed out into the middle of the lake, and then throwing over the nets busied themselves with fishing.

As the old man had predicted, their sport was but small, but this concerned them little. Thinking that they might be watched, they continued steadily all the afternoon casting and drawing in the nets, until the sun neared the horizon. Then they gathered the nets into the boat and rowed quietly towards the shore. Just as they were abreast the end of the promontory the bell of the chapel began to ring the vespers. A few more strokes and Archie could see the clump of bushes.

"Row quietly now," he said, still steering toward the village.

He was about a hundred yards distant from the shore of the convent garden. Just as he came abreast of the bushes the foliage was parted and Marjory appeared at the edge of the water. In an instant the boat's head was turned toward shore, and the three rowers bent to the oars.

A shout from the watchman on the turret showed that he had been watching the boat and that this sudden change of its course had excited his alarm. The shout was repeated again and again as the boat neared the shore, and just as the keel grated on the sand the outer gate was opened and some armed men were seen running into the garden, but they were still two hundred yards away. Marjory leapt lightly into the boat; the men pushed off, and before the retainers of the convent reached the spot the boat was speeding away over the lake. Archie gave up to Marjory his seat in the stern, and himself took an oar.

Loch Leven, though of considerable length, is narrow, and the boat was nearly a third of the way across it before two or three craft were seen putting out from the village in pursuit, and although these gained somewhat, the fugitives reached the other shore a long distance in advance. William Orr and his men were at the landing place, and soon the whole party were hurrying through the woods. They had no fear of instant pursuit, for even in the fast-gathering gloom those in the boats would have perceived the accession of force which they had received on landing, and would not venture to follow. But before morning the news of

the evasion would spread far and wide, and there would be a hot
pursuit among the mountains.

Scarcely a word had been spoken in the boat. Marjory was pale
and agitated, and Archie thought it best to leave her to herself.
On the way through the woods he kept beside her, assisting her
over rough places, and occasionally saying a few encouraging
words. When darkness had completely set in three or four torches
were lit, and they continued their way until midnight. Several
times Archie had proposed a halt, but Marjory insisted that she
was perfectly able to continue her way for some time longer.

At midnight, however, he halted.

"We will stop here," he said. "My men have been marching
ever since daybreak, and tomorrow we must journey fast and far.
I propose that we keep due east for some time and then along by
Loch Rannoch, then across the Grampians by the pass of
Killiecrankie, when we can make down to Perth, and so to
Stirling. The news of your escape will fly fast to the south, and
the tracks to Tarbert and the Clyde will all be watched; but if we
start at daybreak we shall be far on our way east before they begin
to search the hills here; and even if they think of our making in
this direction, we shall be at Killiecrankie before they can cut us
off."

Chapter 20

The Heiress of the Kerrs

While Archie was speaking Marjory had sat down on a fallen tree. She had not slept the night before, and had been anxious and agitated the whole day. The excitement had kept her up; but she now felt completely worn out, and accepted without protest Archie's decision that a halt must be made.

The men were already gathering sticks, and a bright fire soon blazed near the spot where she had seated herself. A short time later some venison steaks were broiled in the flames. At Archie's earnest request Marjory tried to eat, but could with difficulty swallow only a few morsels. A bed of green boughs was quickly made for her, and the ground thickly piled with fresh ferns. Marjory was soon sound asleep as a result of the fatigue and excitement of the day.

With the first dawn of morning the men were on their feet. Fresh sticks were thrown on the fire and breakfast prepared, for the march would be a long and wearisome one.

"Breakfast is ready, Mistress Marjory," Archie said, approaching the bower.

"And I am ready too," the girl said blithely as she appeared at the entrance. "The sleep has done wonders for me, and I feel brave and fresh again. I fear you must have thought me a terrible coward yesterday; but it all seemed so dreadful, such a wild and wicked thing to do, that I felt quite overwhelmed. Today you will find me ready for anything."

"I could never think you a coward," Archie said, "after you faced the anger of that terrible uncle of yours for my sake; or rather," he added, "for the sake of your word. And now I hope you will eat something, for we have a long march through the forest and hills before us."

"Don't fear that I shall tire," she said. "I am half a mountaineer myself, and, methinks, can keep on my feet as long as any man."

The meal was hastily eaten, and then the party started on their way.

"I have been wondering," the girl said, as with light steps she kept pace with Archie's longer strides, "how you came to know that I was in the convent."

Archie looked surprised.

"How should I know, Mistress Marjory, but through your own messenger?"

"My own messenger!" Marjory exclaimed. "You are jesting, Sir Archie."

"I am not so, fair lady," he said. "Surely you must remember that you sent a messenger to me, with word that you were captive at St. Kenneth and needed my aid?"

The girl stopped for a moment in her walk and gazed at her companion as if to assure herself that he was in earnest. "You must be surely dreaming, Sir Archie," she said, as she continued the walk, "for assuredly I sent you no such message."

"But, lady," Archie said, holding out his hand, "the messenger brought me as token that he had come from you this ring which I had given you, vowing that should you call me to your aid I would come immediately, even from a battlefield."

The blood had rushed into the girl's face as she saw the ring. Then she turned very pale. "Sir Archibald Forbes," she said in a low tone, after walking for a minute or two in silence, "I feel disgraced in your eyes. How forward and unmaidenly must you have thought me thus to take advantage of a vow made from the impulse of sudden gratitude."

"No, indeed, lady," Archie said hotly. "No such thought ever entered my mind. I should as soon doubt my own mother as to deem you capable of aught but what was sweet and womanly. The matter seemed to me simple enough. You had saved my life at great peril to yourself, and it seemed but natural to me that in your trouble, having none others to befriend you, your thoughts should turn to one who had sworn to be to the end of his life your faithful knight and servant. But," he went on more lightly, "since you yourself did not send me the ring and message, what good soul could have brought them to me?"

"The good soul was a very bad one," the girl said shortly, "and I will rate him soundly when I see him for thus adventuring without my consent. It is none other than Father Anselm; and yet," she added, "he has suffered so much on my behalf that I shall have to forgive him. After your escape my uncle in his passion was close to hanging the good priest in spite of his holy office, and drove him from the castle. He kept me shut up in my room for many weeks, and then urged upon me the marriage with his son. When he found that I would not listen to it he sent me to St. Kenneth, and there I have remained ever since. Three weeks ago Father Anselm came to see me. He had been sent for by Alexander of Lorne, who, knowing the influence he had with me, begged him to undertake the mission of inducing me to bend to his will. As he knew how much I hated John of Lorne, the good priest wasted not much time in entreaties; but he warned me that it had been resolved that unless I gave way my captivity, which had hitherto been easy and pleasant, would be made hard and rigorous, and that I would be forced into accepting John of Lorne as a husband. When he saw that I was determined not to give in, the good priest certainly hinted" (and here she again became agitated) "that you would, if sent for, do your best to carry me off. Of course I refused to listen to the idea, and chided him for suggesting so unmaidenly a course. He urged it no further, and I thought no more of the matter. The next day I missed my ring, which, to avoid notice, I had worn on a little ribbon round my neck. I thought at the time the ribbon must have broken and the ring been lost, and for a time I made diligent search in the garden for it; but I doubt not now that the traitor priest, as I knelt before him to receive his blessing on parting, must have severed the ribbon and stolen it."

"God bless him!" Archie said fervently. "Should he ever come to Aberfilly the warmest corner by the fire, the fattest capon, and the best bottle of wine from the cellar shall be his so long as he lives. Why, but for him, Lady Marjory, you might have worn out months of your life in prison, and have been compelled at last to wed your cousin. I should have been a miserable man for life."

The girl laughed.

"I would have given you a week, Sir Archie, and no more; that is the extreme time which a knight in our days can be expected to mourn for the fairest lady; and now," she went on, changing the subject, "think you we shall reach the pass across the Grampians before night?"

"If all goes well, lady, and your feet will carry you so far, we shall be there by eventide. Unless by some chance encounter, we need have no fear whatever of pursuit. It will have been daylight before the news of your flight fairly spread through the country, though, doubtless, messengers were sent off at once in all directions; but it would take an army to scour these woods, and as they know not whether we have gone east, west, north, or south, the chance is faint indeed of any party meeting us, especially as we have taken so straight a line that they must march without a pause in exactly the right direction to come up with us."

At nightfall the party camped again on the slope of the Grampians, and the following morning crossed by the pass of Killiecrankie and made toward Perth.

The next night Marjory slept in a peasant's cottage, Archie and his companions lying down without. Wishing to avoid attention, Archie purchased from the peasant the Sunday clothes of his daughter, who was about the same age and size as Marjory.

When they reached Perth he bought a strong horse, with saddle and pillion; and with Marjory behind him, and his band accompanying him on foot, he rode for Stirling. When he neared the town he heard that the king was in the forest of Falkirk, and having consulted Marjory as to her wishes rode directly thither.

Bruce, with his followers, had arrived but the day before, and had taken up his abode at the principal house of a village in the forest. He came to the door when he heard the trampling of a horse.

"Ah! Sir Archie, is it you safely returned, and, as I half expected, a lady?"

"This, sire," Archie said, dismounting, "is Mistress Marjory MacDougall, of whom, as you have heard me say, I am the devoted knight and servant. She has been put in duress by Alexander of Lorne because in the first place she was a true Scots woman and favored your cause, and because in the second place she refused to espouse his son John. I have borne her away from the convent of St. Kenneth, and as I used no force in doing so no sacrilege has been committed. I have brought her to you in all honor and courtesy, as I might a dear sister, and I now pray you to place her under the protection of the wife of one of your knights, seeing that she has no friends and natural protectors here. Then, when she has time to think, she must herself decide upon her future."

The king assisted Marjory to dismount.

"Fair mistress," he said, "Sir Archibald Forbes is one of the bravest and truest of my knights, and in the hands of none might you more confidently place your honor. Assuredly I will do as he asks me, and will place you under the protection of Dame Elizabeth Graham, who is now within, having ridden hither to see her husband but this morning. But I trust," he added, with a meaning smile, "that you will not long require her protection."

The king entered the house with Marjory, while Archie, with his band, rejoined the rest of his party, who were still with the king. After having seen that the wants of those who had accompanied him had been supplied he returned to the royal quarters. The king met him at the door, and said, with a merry smile on his face:

"I fear me, Sir Archie, that all my good advice with regard to Mistress Mary Kerr has been wasted, and that you are resolved to make this Highland damsel, the niece of my arch enemy Alexander of Lorne, your wife."

"If she will have me," Archie said stoutly, "such assuredly, is my intent; but of that I know nothing, seeing that, while she was under my protection, it would have been dishonorable to have spoken of love; and I know naught of her sentiments toward me, especially seeing that she herself did not, as I had hoped, send for me to come to her aid, and was indeed mightily indignant that another should have done so in her name."

"Poor Sir Archie!" the king laughed. "Though a man, and a valorous one in stature and in years, you are truly but a boy yet in these matters. It needed but half an eye to see by the way she turned pale and red when you spoke to her that she loves you. Now look you, Sir Archie," he went on more seriously; "these are troubled days, and one knows not what a day may bring forth. Graham's tower is neither strong nor safe, and the sooner this Mistress Marjory of yours is safely in your stronghold of Aberfilly the better for both of you, and for me also, for I know that you

will be of no more good to me so long as your brain is running on
her. Look you now, she is no longer under your protection, and
your scruples on that head are therefore removed; best go in at
once and ask her if she will have you. If she says, yes, we will ride
to Glasgow tomorrow or the next day. The bishop shall marry
you, and I myself will give you your bonny bride. This is no time
for wasting weeks with courtship and match-makers. What say
you?"

"Nothing would more surely suit my wishes, sire," Archie
said; "but I fear she will think me presumptuous."

"Not a bit of it," the king laughed. "Highland lassies are accustomed to sudden wooing, and I doubt not that when she freed you
last autumn from Dunstaffnage her mind was just as much made
up as yours is as to the state of her heart. Come along, sir."

So saying, the king passed his arm through that of Archie, and
drew him into the house. In the room which they entered Marjory was sitting with Lady Graham. Both rose as the king entered.

"My Lady Graham," the king said, "this my good and faithful
knight Sir Archie Forbes, whose person as well as repute is favor-
ably known to you, desires to speak alone with the young lady
under your protection. I may say he does so at my special begging,
seeing that at times like these the sooner matters are put in a
straight course the better. Will you let me lead you to the next
room while we leave the young people together?"

"Marjory," Archie said, when he and the girl were alone, "I fear
that you will think my wooing rude and hasty, but the times
must excuse it. I would gladly have waited that you might have
seen more of me before I tried my fate; but in these troubled days
who can say where I may be a week hence, or when I can see you
again were I once separated from you! Therefore, dear, I speak at
once. I love you, Marjory, and since the day when you came like
an angel into my cell at Dunstaffnage I have known that I loved
you, and should I never see you again could love none other. Will
you wed me, love?"

"But the king tells me, Sir Archie," the girl said, looking up
with a half smile, "that he wishes you to wed the Lady Mary
Kerr."

"It is a dream of the good king," Archie said, laughing, "and he
is not in earnest about it. He knows that I have never set eyes on

the lady or she on me, and he was but jesting when he said so to you, having known from me long ago that my heart was wholly yours."

"Besides," the girl said hesitating, "you might have objected to wed Mistress Kerr because her father was an enemy of yours."

"Why dwell upon it?" Archie said a little impatiently. "Mistress Kerr is nothing in the world to me, and I had clean forgotten her very existence, when by some freak or other she sent her retainers to fight under my command. She may be a sweet and good lady for what I know; she may be the reverse. To me she is absolutely nothing; and now, Marjory, give me your answer. I love you, dear, deeply and truly; and should you say, yes, will strive all my life to make you happy."

"One more question, Archie, and then I will answer yours. Tell me frankly, had I been Mary Kerr instead of Marjory MacDougall, could you so far forget the ancient feud between the families as to say to me, I love you."

Archie laughed.

"The question is easily answered. Were you your own dear self it would matter naught to me were your name Kerr, or MacDougall, or Comyn, or aught else. It is you I love, and your ancestors or your relations matter to me not one single jot."

"Then I will answer you," the girl said, putting her hand in his. "Archie Forbes, I love you with my whole heart, and have done so since I first met you; but," she said, drawing back, as Archie would have clasped her in his arms, "I must tell you that you have been mistaken, and that it is not Marjory MacDougall whom you would wed, but Mary, whom her uncle Alexander always called Marjory, Kerr."

"Marjory Kerr!" Archie repeated, in astonishment.

"Yes, Archie, Marjory or Mary Kerr. The mistake was none of my making; it was you who called me MacDougall; and knowing that you had reason to hate my race I did not undeceive you, thinking you might even refuse the boon of life at the hands of a Kerr. But I believed that when you thought it over afterwards you would suspect the truth, seeing that it must assuredly come to your ears if you spoke of your adventure, even if you did not already know it, that Sir John Kerr and Alexander of Lorne married twin sisters of the house of Comyn. You are not angry, I hope, Archie?"

"Angry!" Archie said, taking the girl, who now yielded unresistingly, in his arms. "It matters nothing to me who you were; and truly I am glad that the long feud between our houses will come to an end. My conscience, too, pricked me somewhat when I heard that by the death of your brother you had succeeded to the estates, and that it was in despite of a woman, and she a loyal and true-hearted Scotswoman, that I was holding Aberfilly. So it was you who sent the retainers from Ayr to me?"

"Yes," Marjory replied. "Father Anselm carried my orders to them. I longed to know that they were fighting for Scotland, and was sure that under none could they be better led."

"And you have told the king who you are?" Archie asked.

"Yes," the girl said, "shortly after we entered."

"And you agree that we shall be married at once at Glasgow, as the king has suggested to me?"

"The king said as much to me," Marjory said, blushing; "but oh! Archie, it seems dreadful, such an unseemly bustle and haste, to be betrothed one day and married the next! Whoever heard of such a thing?"

"But the circumstances, Marjory, are exceptional. We all carry our lives in our hands, and things must be done which at another time would seem strange. Besides, what advantage would there be in waiting? I should be away fighting the English, and you would see no more of me. You would not get to know me better than you do now."

"Oh! it is not that, Archie."

"Nor is it anything else," Archie said smiling, "but just surprise. With the King of Scotland to give you away and the Bishop of Glasgow to marry you, none can venture to hint that there is anything that is not in the highest degree orthodox in your marriage. Of course I shall have to be a great deal away until the war is over and Scotland freed of her tyrants. But I shall know that you are safe at Aberfilly, which is quite secure from any sudden attack. You will have my mother there to pet you and look after you in my absence, and I hope that good Father Anselm will soon find his way there and take up his abode. It is the least he can do, seeing that, after all, he is responsible for our marriage, and having, as it were, delivered you into my hands, ought to do his best to make you happy in your captivity."

Marjory raised no further objection. She saw, in truth, that, having once accepted Archie Forbes as her husband, it was in every way the best plan for her to marry him without delay, since she had no natural protectors to go to, and her powerful relations might stir up the church to view her evasion from the convent as a defiance of its authority.

Upon the following day the king moved with his force to Glasgow, which had already been evacuated by the English garrison, and the next morning Marjory—for Archie through life insisted upon calling her by the pet name under which he had first known her—was married to Sir Archibald Forbes. The Bruce gave her away, and presented her with a splendid necklace of pearls. His brother Edward, Sir James Douglas, and other companions of Archie in the field also made the bride handsome presents. Archie's followers from Aberfilly and the contingent from Marjory's estates in Ayr were also present, together with a crowd of the townspeople, for Archie Forbes, the companion of Wallace, was one of the most popular characters in Scotland, and the good city of Glasgow celebrated his marriage.

Suddenly as it was arranged, a number of the daughters of the wealthiest citizens attired in white attended the bride in procession to the altar. Flowers were strewn and the bride and bridegroom were heartily cheered by a concourse of people as they left the cathedral.

The party then mounted, and the king, his brother, Sir James Douglas, and some other knights, together with a strong escort, rode with them to Aberfilly. Archie had despatched a messenger to his mother with the news as soon as the arrangements had been made; and all was prepared for their coming. The tenants had assembled to give a hearty welcome to their lord and new mistress. Dame Forbes received her as she dismounted from the pillion on which she had ridden behind Archie, and embraced her tenderly.

It was the dearest wish of her life that Archie should marry; and although, when she first heard the news, she regretted in her heart that he should have chosen a Kerr, still she saw that the union would put an end to the long feud, and might even, in the event of the final defeat of Bruce, be the means of safety for Archie himself and security for his possessions.

She soon, however, learned to love Marjory for herself, and to be contented in every way with her son's choice. There was high feasting and revelry at Aberfilly that evening. Bonfires were burned in the castle yard, and the tenants feasted there, while the king and his knights were entertained in the hall of the castle.

The next morning the king and his companions again mounted and rode off. Sir James Douglas was going south to harry Galloway and to revenge the assaults which the people had made upon the king. There was a strong English force there under Sir Ingram Umfraville and Sir John de St. John.

"I will give you a week, Sir Archie, to take holiday, but can spare you no longer. We have as yet scarce begun our work, for well-nigh every fortress in Scotland is in English hands, and we must take as many of them as we can before Edward moves across the border again."

"I will not outstay the time," Sir Archie said. "As we arranged last night, I will march next week with my retainers to join Sir James Douglas in Galloway."

Chapter 21

The Siege of Aberfilly

Punctual to his agreement, Archie Forbes marched south with his retainers. He was sad, indeed, to leave Marjory, but he knew well that many days must elapse before he could hope to settle down quietly at home, and that it was important to renew the work at once before the English made another great effort to stamp out the movement. Marjory did not attempt to induce him to overstay his time. She was too proud of his position as one of the foremost knights of Scotland to say a word to detain him from the field. So she bade him adieu with a brave face, reserving her tears until after he had ridden away.

It had been arranged that Archie should operate independently of Douglas, the two joining their forces only when threatened by overwhelming numbers or when any great enterprise was to be undertaken. Archie took with him a hundred and fifty men from his estates in Lanark and Ayr. He marched first to Loudon Hill, then down through Cumnock and the border of Carrick into Galloway. Contrary to the usual custom, he enjoined his retainers on no account to burn or harass the villages and granges.

"The people," he said, "are not responsible for the conduct of their lords, and as I would not see the English harrying the country round Aberfilly, so I am loathed to carry fire and sword among these poor people. We have come hither to punish their lords and to capture their castles. If the country people oppose us we must needs fight them; but beyond what is necessary for our provisions let us take nothing from them, and show them, by our conduct, that we hold them to be Scotsmen like ourselves, and that we pity rather than blame them, inasmuch as by the orders of their lords they are forced to fight against us."

Archie had not advanced more than a day's march into Galloway when he heard that Sir John de St. John was marching with four hundred men-at-arms to meet him.

There were no better soldiers in the following of Bruce than the retainers of Aberfilly and Glen Cairn. They had now for many years been frequently under arms, and were thoroughly trained to fight together. They had the greatest confidence in themselves and their leader, and having often with their spears withstood the shock of the English chivalry, Archie knew that he could rely upon them to the fullest. He therefore took up a position on the banks of a river where a ford would enable the enemy to cross. Had he been less confident as to the result he would have defended the ford, which could be only crossed by two horsemen abreast. He determined, however, to repeat the maneuver which had proved so successful at Stirling Bridge, and to let half of the enemy cross before he fell upon them.

The ground near the river was stony and rough. Great boulders, which had rolled from the hillside, were thickly scattered about it, and it would be difficult for cavalry to charge up the somewhat steeply sloping ground in anything like unbroken order.

With eighty of his men Archie took up a position one hundred yards back from the stream. With great exertions some of the smaller boulders were removed, and rocks and stones were piled to make a wall on either flank of the ground, which, standing two deep, he occupied. The remaining seventy men he divided equally, placing one company under the command of each of his two faithful lieutenants, Andrew Macpherson and William Orr. These took post near the river, one on each side of the ford, and at a distance of about one hundred yards therefrom. Orr's company were hidden among some bushes growing by the river. Macpherson's lay down among the stones and boulders, and were scarce likely to attract the attention of the English, which would naturally be fixed upon the little body drawn up to oppose them in front. The preparations were scarcely completed when the English were seen approaching. They made no halt at the river, but at once commenced crossing at the ford, confident in their power to overwhelm the little body of Scots, whose number had, it seemed to them, been exaggerated by the fears of the country people. As soon as a hundred of the men-at-arms had passed, their leader marshalled them in line, and with level spears charged up the slopes against Archie's force. The large stone wall hindered the English ranks, and it was but in straggling order that they reached the narrow line of Scottish spears.

These they in vain endeavored to break through. Their numbers were of no avail to them, as, being on horseback, but twenty men at a time could attack the double row of spearmen. While the conflict was at its height Archie's trumpet was sounded, for he saw that another hundred men had now crossed the ford.

At the signal the two hidden parties leapt to their feet, and with leveled pikes rushed towards the ford. The English had no force there to resist the attack, for as the men-at-arms had passed, each had ridden on to join the fray in front. The head of the ford was therefore seized with but little difficulty. Orr, with twenty men, remained at the bridge to hold it and prevent others from crossing, while Macpherson, with fifty, ran up the hill and fell upon the rear of the confused masses of cavalry, who were striving in vain to break the lines of Archie's spears.

The attack was decisive; the English, surprised and confused by the sudden attack, were unable to offer any effectual resistance to Macpherson's pikemen, and at the same moment that these fell upon the rear, Archie gave the word and his men rushed forward upon the struggling mass of cavalry. The shock was irresistible; men and horses fell in numbers under the Scottish spears, and in a few minutes those who could manage to extricate themselves from the struggling mass rode off in various directions. These, however, were few in number, for ninety were killed and seventy taken prisoners. St. John himself succeeded in cutting his way through the spearmen, and, swimming the river below the ford, rejoined his followers, who had in vain endeavoured to force the passage of the ford. With these he rapidly retired.

A detachment of fifty men were sent off with the prisoners to Bruce. In the meantime, Archie with the main body of his followers, joined the force under Sir James Douglas two days later.

Upon the following morning a messenger from Aberfilly reached Archie.

"My lord," he said, "I bring you a message from the Lady Marjory. I have spent five days in searching for you, and have never but once laid down during that time, therefore do not blame me if my message is long in coming."

"What is it, Evan? naught is wrong there, I trust?"

"The Lady Marjory bade me tell you that news has reached her, that from each of the garrisons of Ayr, Lanark, Stirling and Bothwell, a force is marching toward your hold, which the governor of Bothwell has sworn to destroy. When I left they were expected hourly in sight, and this is full a week since."

"Aberfilly can hold out for longer than that," Archie said, "against aught but surprise, and the vassals would have had time to gather."

"Yes," the man replied, "they were flocking in when I came away; the men of Glen Cairn had already arrived; all the women and children were taking to the hills, according to the orders which you gave."

"And now, good Evan, please eat some supper, and then rest. No wonder you have been so long in finding me, for I have been wandering without ceasing. I will start at once with my followers here for Aberfilly; by tomorrow evening we will be there."

Archie hurried to the hut occupied by Douglas, told him the news, and said he must hurry away to the defense of his castle.

"Go, by all means, Archie," Douglas replied. "If I can gather a force sufficient to relieve you I will myself march thither; but at present I fear that the chances of my doing so are small, for the four garrisons you have named would be able to spare a force vastly larger than any with which I could meet them in the field, and the king is no better able to help you."

"I will do my best," Archie said. "The castle can stand a stout siege; and fortunately I have a secret passage by which we can escape."

"Never mind the castle," Douglas replied. "When better days come we will rebuild it again for you."

A few notes on a horn brought Archie's little band of followers together. Telling them the danger which threatened Glen Cairn, Archie placed himself at their head, and at a rapid step they marched away. It was forty-five miles across the hills, but before morning they approached it, and made their way to the woods in which was the entrance to the subterranean passage leading to the castle. Archie had feared that they might find the massive doors which closed it, a short distance from the entrance, securely fastened as usual. They were shut, indeed, but as they approached them they heard a challenge from within.

"It is I, Sir Archie Forbes."

The door was opened at once. "Welcome, Sir Archie!" the guard said. "The Lady Marjory has been expecting you for the last five days, and a watch has been kept here constantly, to open the doors should you come."

"The messenger could not find me," Archie said. "Is all well at the castle?"

"All is well," the man replied. "The English have made two attacks, but have been beaten back with loss. This morning some great machines have arrived from Stirling and have begun battering the walls. Is it your will that I remain here on guard, now that you have come?"

"Yes," Archie answered. "It were best that one should be always stationed here, seeing that the entrance might perchance be discovered by one wandering in the woods, or they might obtain the secret of its existence from a prisoner. If footsteps are heard approaching retire at once with the news. There is no danger if we are warned in time, for we can turn the water from the moat into it."

Archie and his followers now made their way along the passage until they entered the castle. As they issued out from the entrance a shout of joy rose from those near, and the news rapidly flew through the castle that Archie had arrived. In a moment Marjory ran down and threw herself into his arms.

"Welcome back, Archie, a thousand times! I have been grievously anxious as the days went on and you did not return, and had feared that some evil must have befallen you. It has been a greater anxiety to me than the defense of the castle; but I have done my best to be hopeful and bright, to keep up the spirits of our followers."

"It was no easy task for your messenger to find me, Marjory, for we are ever on the move. Is my mother here?"

"No, Archie, she went a fortnight since on a visit to Lady Gordon."

"It is well," Archie said, "for if in the end we have to leave the castle, you, who have proved yourself so strong and brave, can, if needs be, take to the hills with me; but she could not support the fatigues of such a life. And now, dear, we have marched all night and shall be glad of food; while it is preparing I will go to the walls and see what is going on."

As Archie reached the battlement a loud cheer broke from the defenders gathered there, and Sandy Grahame hurried up to him.

"Welcome back, Sir Archie; glad am I to give up the responsibility of this post, although, indeed, it is not I who have been in command, but Lady Marjory. She has been always on the walls, cheering the men with her words and urging them to deeds of bravery; and, indeed, she has frightened me sorely by the way in which she exposed herself where the arrows were flying most thickly, for as I told her over and over again, if the castle were taken I knew that you would be sure that I had done my best, but what excuse should I be able to make to you if I had to bear you the news that she had been killed?"

"And what did she say to that, Sandy?"

"Truth, Sir Archie, she's a woman and willful, and she just laughed and said that you would know you could not keep her in order yourself, and could not therefore expect me to rule her."

"That is so, Sandy," Archie laughed; "but now that I am back I will for once exert my authority, and will see that she runs into no further danger. And now, how goes the siege?"

"So far they have done but little damage, Sir Archie; but the machines which they brought up yesterday will, I fear, play havock with our walls. They have not yet begun their work, for when they brought them up yesterday afternoon our men shot so fiercely that they had to fall back again; but in the night they have thrown up high banks of earth, and have planted the engines under their shelter, and will, ere long, begin to send their messengers against our walls. Thrice they assaulted the works beyond the drawbridge and twice we beat them back; but last night they came on with all their force. I was myself there, and after fighting for a while and seeing they were too strong for us, I thought it best to withdraw before they gained footing in the work, and so had time to draw off the men and raise the drawbridge."

"Quite right, Sandy! The defenders of the post would only have been slaughtered, and the assailants might have rushed across the drawbridge before it could have been raised. The post is of little importance save to defend the castle against a sudden surprise, and would only have been a source of constant anxiety and loss. How many do you reckon them? Judging by their tents there must be three or four thousand."

"About three thousand, Sir Archie, I make it; and as we had no time to get the tenants in from my lady's Ayrshire estate, we have but two hundred men in the castle, and many of these are scarce more than boys."

"I have brought a hundred and fifty with me, Sandy, so we have as many as we can use on the walls, though I could wish I had another hundred or two for sorties."

Half an hour later the great machines began to work, hurling vast stones with tremendous force against the castle wall. Strongly as this was built, Archie saw that it would not take many days for his castle to crumble before the blows.

"I did not reckon on such machines as these," he said to Sandy. "Doubtless they are some of the huge machines which King Edward had constructed for the siege of Stirling, and which have remained there since the castle was taken. Fortunately we have still the moat when a breach is made, and it will be hard work to cross that."

All day the great stones thundered against the wall. The defenders were not idle, but kept up a shower of arrows at the edge of the mound behind which the machines were hidden; but although many of those working there were killed, fresh relays came constantly up, and the machines never ceased their work. By nightfall the face of the wall was bruised and battered. Many of the stones in front had fallen from their places.

"Another twenty-four hours," Archie said to Marjory, as he joined her in the great hall, "and the breach will be begun, forty-eight and it will be completed. They will go on all night, and we may expect no rest until the work is done. In an hour's time I shall sally out from the passage into the wood and beat up their camp. Expecting no attack from the rear, we shall do them great damage before they can gather to oppose us. As soon as they do so we shall be off again, and, scattering in various directions, gather again in the woods and return here."

An hour later Archie, with two hundred men, started. No sooner had he left than Marjory called Sandy Grahame and

Andrew Macpherson, whom he had left in joint command during his absence.

"Now," she said, "I am not going to remain quiet here while Sir Archie does all the fighting, therefore you will gather all the garrison together, leaving only twenty to hold the gate. See that the wheels of the drawbridge are well oiled, and the hinges of the gate. Directly, when we see that the attack has begun upon the camp we will lower the drawbridge quietly, open the gates, and sally out. There is no great force in the outer work. When we have cleared that—which, if we are quick, we can do without alarming the camp, seeing what a confusion and uproar will be going on there—we will make straight along to the point where the machines are placed. Let some of the men take axes and cut the ropes, and let others carry bundles of wood well steeped in oil; we will pile them round the machines and light them, and thus having ensured their destruction, we will fall back again."

"But, Lady Marjory—" Sandy began.

"I will have no buts, Sandy; you must just do as I order you, and I will answer to Sir Archie. I shall myself go forth with you and see that the work is properly done."

The two men looked doubtfully at each other.

"Now, Andrew," Marjory said briskly, "let us have no hesitation or talk, the plan is a good one."

"I do not say that it is not a good one," Sandy replied cautiously, "or that it is not one that Sir Archie might have carried out if he had been here."

"Very well, Andrew, then that is quite enough. I give you the orders and I am responsible, and if you and Sandy do not choose to obey me, I shall call the men together myself and lead them without you."

As Sandy and Andrew were quite conscious that their lady would be as good as her word, they at once proceeded to carry her orders into effect. The wheels of the portcullis and drawbridge were oiled, as were the bolts and hinges of the gate. The men were formed up in the courtyard, where presently they were rejoined by Marjory who had put on a light steel cap and a shirt of mail, and who had armed herself with a light sword. The men gathered round her enthusiastically, and would have burst into cheers had she not held up her hand to command silence.

"I will to the wall now," she said, "to watch for the signal. The instant the attack begins and the attention of those in the outwork is called that way, draw up the portcullis noiselessly and open the gate, oil the hinges of the drawbridge and have everything in readiness; then I will join you. Let the drawbridge be lowered swiftly, and as it falls we will rush across. You have, I suppose, briefed the men who are to remain behind. Tell them that when the last of us have crossed they are to raise the drawbridge a few feet, so that none can cross it until we return."

Then, accompanied by Macpherson, she ascended the walls. All was quiet in the hostile camp, which was about a quarter of a mile distant, and only the creaking of the wheels of the machines, the orders of those directing them, and the dull crash as the great stones struck the wall, broke the stillness of the night. For half an hour they watched, and then a sudden uproar was heard in the camp. The Scottish war cry pealed out, followed by shouts and yells, and almost instantly flames were seen to mount up.

"My lord is at work," Marjory said, "it is time for us to be doing also." So saying she ran down to the courtyard. Sandy Grahame, Macpherson, and a few picked men took their place around her, then the drawbridge was suddenly run down, and the Scots dashed across it. As Marjory had anticipated, the English in the outwork had gathered on the farther side and were watching the sudden outbreak in the camp. Alarmed at the prospect of an attack, perhaps by the Bruce, in that quarter, they were suddenly startled by the rush of feet across the drawbridge, and before they had time to recover from their surprise the Scots were upon them. The latter were superior in numbers, and the English, already alarmed by the attack upon their camp, offered but a feeble resistance. Many were cut down, but the greater part leapt from the wall and fled towards the camp. The moment resistance ceased the outer gate was thrown open, and at full speed the Scots moved toward the machines. The party here had suspended their work and were gazing toward the camp, where the uproar was now great. The wind was blowing briskly and the fire had spread with immense rapidity, and already half the camp was in flames. Suddenly from the bank above, the Scots poured down upon them like a torrent. There was scarcely a thought of resistance.

The Defence of Aberfilly Castle

Stricken with dismay and astonishment at this unexpected attack, the soldiers working the machines fled hastily, only a few falling beneath the swords of the Scots. The men with axes at once fell upon the machines, cutting the ropes and smashing the wheels and levers which worked them, while those with the bundles of wood piled them round. In less than two minutes the work was done, lighted torches were applied to the bundles, and the flames soon shot up hotly.

The Scots waited but a minute or two to see that the work was thoroughly done and that the flames had gained fair hold, and then, keeping in a close body, they retired to the castle. Not a soul was met with by the way, and leaving Andrew Macpherson with fifty men to hold the outwork until Archie should return and decide whether it should be occupied, Marjory, with the rest, re-entered the castle.

She at once ascended to the walls again, where Sandy also posted the men to be in readiness to open fire with their arrows should the English return and endeavour to extinguish the flames round the machines. The sound of fighting had ceased at the camp. By the light of the flames numbers of the English could be seen pulling down the tents which the fire had not yet reached and endeavoring to check the conflagration, while a large body of horsemen and footmen were rapidly advancing toward the castle.

As soon as they came within bow-shot range the archers opened fire, and the English leaders, seeing that it was already too late to save the machines, which were by this time completely enveloped in flames, and that men would only be sacrificed to no good purpose, halted the troops. They then moved towards the outwork, but finding this in possession of the Scots, they fell back again to the camp to take council as to the next steps to be adopted.

Archie's attack had been crowned with complete success. Apprehending no danger from behind, the English had neglected to place sentries there, and the Scots were already among the tents before their presence was discovered. Numbers of the English were cut down and the tents fired, and as soon as the English recovered from their first surprise and began to form, Archie gave the word for a retreat. This was effected without molestation, for the first thought of the English was to save the camp from total destruction. The reports of the men who escaped from the castle outwork and the outburst of flames around the machines added to the confusion which reigned; and the leaders, who had by the light of the flames ascertained that the assault upon the camp had been made by a small body of the enemy, deemed it of the first importance to move at once to save the machines if it were still possible.

The Scots regained the entrance to the passage without the loss of a single man, and passing through, soon re-entered the castle. Marjory had laid aside her warlike trappings and awaited her husband's return at the inner entrance of the passage.

"We have had good success, Marjory," Archie said as he greeted her, "as you will have seen from the walls. The greater part of the English camp is destroyed; we have killed great numbers, and have not lost a man."

"That is good news indeed, Archie. We, too, have not been quite idle while you have been away."

"Why, what have you been doing, Marjory?" Archie asked in surprise.

"Come up to the walls and I will show you."

Archie mounted with her, and gave a start of surprise as he looked towards the machines. The great body of fire had died down now, but the beams of the machines stood up red and glowing, while a light flickering flame played round them.

"You see we have not been idle, Archie. We have destroyed the machines, and retaken the outwork, which is now held by Andrew Macpherson with fifty men."

"Why, what magic is this, wife?"

"No magic at all, Sir Knight. We have been carrying out the work which you, as a wise and skillful commander, should have ordered before you left. We have taken advantage of the confusion of the enemy by the fire in their camp, and have made a sortie, and a successful one, as you see."

"I am delighted, indeed," Archie said; "and the destruction of those machines is indeed a great work. Still Sandy and Macpherson should not have undertaken it without orders from me; they might have been cut off and the castle stormed before I came back."

"They had orders from me, sir, and that was quite sufficient. To do them justice, they hesitated about obeying me, and I was well-nigh ordering them to the dungeon for disobedience; and they only gave way at last when I said they could stop at home if they liked, but that I should lead out the retainers. Of course I went in your place with armor and sword; but perhaps it was as well that I had no fighting to do."

"Do you mean, Marjory, that you really led the sortie?"

"I don't think I led it, Archie; but I certainly went out with it, and very exciting it was. There, dear, don't look troubled. Of course, as chatelaine of the castle, I was bound to animate my men."

"You have done bravely and well, indeed, Marjory, and I am proud of my wife. Still, dear, I tremble at the thought of the risk you ran."

"No more risk than you are constantly running, Archie; and I am rather glad you tremble, because in future you will understand my feelings better, left here all alone while you are risking your life perpetually with the king."

The success of the sally and the courage and energy shown by Marjory raised the spirits of the garrison to the highest pitch; and had Archie given the word they would have sallied out and fallen upon the besiegers. Two days later fresh machines arrived from Stirling, and the attack again commenced, the besiegers keeping a large body of men near the gate to prevent a repetition of the last sally. Archie now despatched two or three fleet-footed runners through the passage to find the king, and tell him that the besiegers were making progress, and to pray him to come to his assistance. Two days passed, and the breach was now fairly practicable, but the moat, fifty feet wide, still barred the way to the besiegers. Archie had noticed that for two or three days no water had come down from above, and had no doubt that they had diverted the course of the river. Upon the day after the breach was completed the besiegers advanced in great force up the stream from below.

"They are going to try to cut the dam," Archie said to Sandy; "place every man who can draw a bow on that side of the castle."

As the English approached, a rain of arrows was poured into them; but covering themselves with their shields and with large mantlets[12] formed of hurdles covered with hides, they pressed forward to the dam. Here those who had brought with them picks and mattocks set to work upon the dam, the men with mantlets shielding them from the storm of arrows, while numbers of archers opened fire upon the defenders. Very many were killed by the Scottish arrows, but the work went on. A gap was made through the dam. The water, as it rushed through, aided the efforts of those at work; and after three hours' labor and fighting the gap was so far deepened that the water in the moat had fallen eight feet. Then, finding that this could now be waded, the assailants desisted, and drew off to their camp.

A council was held that evening in the castle as to whether the hold should be abandoned at once or whether one attack on the breach should be withstood. It was finally determined that the breach should be held. The steep sides of the moat, exposed by the subsidence of the water, were slippery and difficult. The force in the castle was amply sufficient at once to man the breach and to furnish archers for the walls on either side, while in the event of the worst, were the breach carried by the English, the defenders might fall back to the central keep, and thence make their way through the passage. Had it not been for the possibility of an early arrival of the king to their relief all agreed that it would be as well to evacuate the castle at once, as this in the end must fall, and every life spent in its defense would thus be a useless sacrifice. As, however, troops might at any moment appear, it was determined to hold the castle until the last.

The next morning a party of knights in full defensive armor came down to the edge of the moat to see whether passage could be effected. They were not molested while making their examination, as the Scottish arrows would only have dropped harmlessly off their steel harness. Archie was on the walls.

"How like you the prospect, Sir Knights?" he called out merrily. "I fear that the sludge and slime will sully your bright armor and smirch your plumes, for it will be difficult to hold a footing on those muddy banks."

"It were best for you to yield, Sir Archibald Forbes, without giving us the trouble of making our way across your moat. You

---

12. A moveable roof or screen used to protect besiegers from the enemy.

have made a stout resistance, and have done enough for honor, and you must see that sooner or later we must win our way in."

"Then I would rather it should be later," Archie replied. "I may have done enough for honor, but it is not for honor that I am fighting, but for Scotland. Your work is but begun yet, I can assure you. We are far from being at the end of our resources yet. It will be time enough to talk about surrendering when you have won the breach and the outer walls."

The knights retired; and as some hours passed without the besiegers seeing any preparation for an assault they judged that the report carried back to camp was not an encouraging one. Large numbers of men were, however, seen leaving the camp, and these toward sunset came back staggering under immense loads of brushwood which they had cut in the forest.

"They intend to fill up the moat," Archie said; "it is their wisest course."

He at once directed his men to make up large trusses of straw, over which he poured considerable quantities of oil. Early the next morning the English drew out of their camp, and advanced in martial array. Each man carried a great bundle of wood, and, covering themselves with these as they came within bowshot, they marched down to the moat. Each in turn threw in his bundle, and when he had done so returned to the camp and brought back another. Rapidly the process of filling up the moat opposite to the breach continued. The besieged kept up a rain of arrows and darts, and many of the English were killed; but the work was continued without intermission until well-nigh across the moat a broad crossway was formed level with the outer bank. A narrow gap remained to be filled, however, and the English leaders advanced to the front to prevent the Scots on the breach from rushing down to assault those placing the bundles of wood.

Somewhat to the surprise of the English the defenders remained stationary, contenting themselves with hurling great stones at their busy enemy. Suddenly there was a movement. Archie and a party of his best men dashed down the breach, and, climbing on the causeway, for a moment drove the workers and their guards back. They were followed by twenty men carrying great trusses of straw. These were piled against the bundles of wood forming the end of the causeway. Archie and his band leapt back as a torch was applied to the straw. In a moment the hot flames leapt up, causing the knights who had pressed after the retreating Scots to fall back hastily. A shout of triumph rose from the garrison and one of dismay from the besiegers. Saturated with oil, the trusses burnt with fury, and the bundles were soon alight. A fresh wind was blowing, and the flames crept rapidly along the causeway. In a few minutes this was in a blaze from end to end, and in half an hour nothing remained of the great pile save charred ashes and the saturated bundles which had been below the water in the moat, and which now floated upon it.

The besiegers had drawn off when they saw that the flames had gained a fair hold of the causeway. The smoke had scarcely ceased to rise when a great outcry arose from the English camp, and the lookout from the top of the keep perceived a strong force marching toward it. By the bustle and confusion which reigned in the camp Archie doubted not that the new-comers were Scots. The garrison were instantly called to arms. The gates were thrown open, and leaving a small body only to hold the gates, he sallied out at the head of his men and marched toward the English camp.

At the approach of the Scottish force the English leaders had marched out with their men to oppose them. Bruce had been able to collect but three hundred and fifty men, and the English, seeing how small was the number advancing against them, prepared to receive them boldly. Scarcely had the combat begun when Archie with his band entered the English camp, which was almost deserted. They at once fired the tents, and then advanced in a solid mass with level spears against the rear of the English. These, dismayed at the destruction of their camp, and at finding themselves attacked both front and rear, lost heart and fell into confusion. Their leaders strove to rally them, and dashed with their men-at-arms against the spearmen, but their efforts to break through were in vain, and their defeat increased the panic of the footmen. Archie's party broke away through their disordered line and joined the body commanded by the king, and the whole rushed so fiercely upon the English that these broke and fled in all directions, pursued by the triumphant Scots.

"I am but just in time I see, Sir Archie," Bruce said, pointing to the breach in the wall; "a few hours more and methinks that I should have been too late."

"We could have held out longer than that, sire," Archie replied. "We have repulsed an attack this morning and burnt a causeway of wood bundles upon which they attempted to cross the moat; still, I am truly glad that you have arrived, and thank you with all my heart for coming so speedily to my rescue, for sooner or later the hold must have fallen; the great machines which they brought with them from Stirling proved too strong for the wall."

"And how has the Lady Marjory borne up during the siege?" the king inquired.

"Right nobly," Archie replied; "ever in good spirits and showing a brave face to the men; and one night when I made a sortie through my secret passage, and fell upon the English camp from the other side, having left the castle in her charge, she headed the garrison and issuing out, recaptured the outworks, and destroyed the machines by fire."

"Bravely done," the king said, "and just what I should expect from your wife. You did well to take my advice in that matter."

"We shall never agree there, sire, for as you know I followed my own will and wed the bride I had fixed upon for myself."

"Well, well, Sir Archie, as we are both satisfied we will then let it be; and now, I trust that you still have some supplies left, for to tell you the truth I am hungry as well as weary, as my men have marched fast and far."

"There is an abundance," Archie replied; "to last them all for a month, and right willingly is it at their service."

The king remained a week at Aberfilly, his men aiding Archie's retainers in repairing the gap in the dam and in rebuilding the wall; and as five hundred men working willingly and well can effect wonders, by the time Bruce rode away the castle was restored to its former appearance. Archie marched on the following day, and rejoined Douglas in Galloway.

Chapter 22

A Prisoner

After some consultation between the leaders, it was agreed to make an attempt to capture the castle of Knockbawn. It was known to possess a garrison of some sixty men only, and although strong, Archie and Sir James believed that it could be captured by assault. It was arranged that Archie should ride to reconnoitre it, and taking two mounted retainers he started, the force remaining in the forest some eight miles distant. The castle of Knockbawn stood on a rocky promontory, jutting a hundred and fifty yards into the sea. When he neared the neck of the point, which was but some twenty yards wide, Archie bade his followers fall back a short distance.

"I will ride," he said, "close up to the castle walls. My armor is good, and I care not for arrow or crossbow bolt. It were best you fell back a little, for they may have horses and may sally out in pursuit. I am well mounted and fear not being overtaken, but it were best that you should have a good start."

Archie then rode forward toward the castle. Seeing a knight approaching alone, the garrison judged that he was friendly; and it was not until it was seen that instead of approaching the drawbridge he turned aside and rode to the edge of the fosse,[13] that they suspected that he was a foe. Running to the walls they opened fire with arrows upon him, but by this time Archie had seen all that he required. Across the promontory ran a sort of fissure, some ten yards wide and as many deep. From the opposite edge of this the wall rose abruptly. Here assault would be difficult, and it was upon the gateway that an attack must be made. Several arrows had struck his armor and glanced off; and Archie now turned and quietly rode away, his horse being protected by mail like himself. Scarce had he turned when he saw a sight which caused him for a moment to draw rein. Coming at full gal-

---

13.A ditch used in fortifications.

lop toward the promontory was a strong body of English horsemen, flying the banner of Sir Ingram de Umfraville. They were already nearer to the end of the neck than he was. There was no mode of escape, and drawing his sword he galloped at full speed to meet them. As he neared them Sir Ingram himself, one of the doughtiest of Edward's knights, rode out with leveled lance to meet him. At full gallop the knights charged each other. Sir Ingram's spear was pointed at the bars of Archie's helmet, but as the horses met each other Archie, with a blow of his sword, cut off the head of the lance and dealt a tremendous back-handed blow upon Sir Ingram's helmet as the latter passed him, striking the knight forward on to his horse's neck; then without pausing a moment he dashed into the midst of the English ranks.

The horsemen closed around him, and although he cut down several with his sweeping blows he was unable to break his way through them. Such a conflict could not last long. Archie received a blow from behind which struck him from his horse. Regaining his feet he continued the fight, but the blows rained thick upon him, and he was soon struck senseless to the ground.

When he recovered he was in a room in the keep of the castle. Two knights were sitting at a table near the couch on which he was lying. "Ah!" exclaimed one, on seeing Archie open his eyes and move, "I am glad to see your senses coming back to you, sir prisoner. Truly, sir, I regret that so brave a knight should have fallen into my hands, seeing that in this war we must needs send our prisoners to King Edward, whose treatment of them is not gentle; for indeed you fought like any champion. I deemed not that there was a knight in Scotland, save the Bruce himself, who could have so borne himself; and never did I, Ingram de Umfraville, come nearer to losing my seat than I did from that backhanded blow you dealt me. My head rings with it still. My helmet will never be fit to wear again, and as the leech said when plastering my head, 'had not my skull been of the thickest, you had assuredly cut through it.' May I crave the name of so brave an antagonist?"

"I am Sir Archibald Forbes," Archie replied.

"By St. Jago!" the knight said, "but I am sorry for it, seeing that, save Bruce himself, there is none in the Scottish ranks against whom King Edward is so bitter. In the days of Wallace there was no one whose name was more often on our lips than that of Sir Archibald Forbes, and now, under Bruce, it is ever coming to the front. I had thought to have asked Edward as a boon that I should have kept you as my prisoner until exchanged for one on our side, but being Sir Archibald Forbes I know that it were useless indeed; nevertheless, sir knight, I will send to King Edward, begging him to look mercifully upon your case, seeing how bravely and honorably you have fought."

"Thanks for your good offices, Sir Ingram," Archie replied, "but I shall ask for no mercy for myself. I have never owed or paid him allegiance, but, as a true Scot, have fought for my country against a foreign enemy."

"But King Edward does not hold himself to be a foreign enemy," the knight said, "seeing that Baliol, your king, with Comyn and all your great nobles, did homage to him as Lord Paramount of Scotland."

"It were an easy way," Archie rejoined, "to gain a possession to nominate a puppet from among the nobles already your vassals, and then to get him to do homage. No, sir knight, neither Comyn nor Baliol, nor any other of the Anglo Norman nobles who hold estate in Scotland, have a right to speak for her, or to barter away her freedom. That is what Wallace and thousands of Scots have fought and died to protest against, and what Scottish patriots will do until their country is free."

"It is not a question for me to argue upon," Sir Ingram said arrogantly. "King Edward bids me fight in Scotland, and as his knight and vassal I put on my harness without question. But I own to you that seeing I have fought beside him in Gascony, when he, as a feudal vassal of the King of France, made war upon his lord, I cannot see that the offense is an unpardonable one when you Scots do the same here. Concerning the lawfulness of his claim to be your lord paramount, I own that I neither know nor care one jot. However, sir, I regret much that you have fallen into my hands, for to Carlisle, where the king has long been lying, as you have doubtless heard, grievously ill, I must forthwith send you. I must leave you here with the governor, for in half an hour I mount and ride away with my troop. He will do his best to make your sojourn here easy until such time as I may have an opportunity of sending you by ship to Carlisle; and now farewell, sir," he said, giving Archie his hand. "I regret that an unkind chance has thrown so gallant a knight into my hands, and that my duty to the king forbids me from letting you go free."

"Thanks, Sir Ingram," Archie replied. "I have ever heard of you as a brave knight, and if this misfortune must fall upon me, would sooner that I should have been captured by you than by one of less fame and honor."

The governor then had a meal with some wine set before Archie, and soon left him alone.

"I am not at Carlisle yet," Archie said to himself. "Unless I am mistaken, we shall have Sir James thundering at the gate before morning. Cluny will assuredly have ridden off at full speed to carry the news when he saw that I was cut off, and even now he will be marching towards the castle."

As he expected, Archie was roused before morning by a tremendous outburst of noise. Heavy blows were given, followed by a crash, which Archie judged to be the fall of the drawbridge across the moat. He guessed that some of Douglas's men had crept forward noiselessly, and managed to climb up to the gate, and had then suddenly attacked with their axes the chains of the drawbridge.

A prodigious uproar raged in the castle. Orders were shouted, and the garrison, aroused from their sleep, snatched up their arms and hastened to the walls. Outside rose the war cry, "A Douglas! A Douglas!" mingled with others of, "Glen Cairn to the rescue!" For a few minutes all was confusion, then a light suddenly burst up and grew every instant more and more bright.

"Douglas has piled bundles of wood against the gates," Archie said to himself. "Another quarter of an hour and the castle will be his."

Three or four minutes later the governor with six soldiers, two of whom bore torches, entered the room. "You must come along at once, Sir Knight," the governor said. "The attack is of the fiercest, and I know not whether we shall make head against it, but at any rate I must not risk your being recaptured, and must therefore place you in a boat and send you off without delay to the castle at Port Patrick."

It was in vain for Archie to think of resistance, he was unarmed and helpless. Two of the soldiers laid hands on him and hurried him along until they reached the lower chambers of the castle. The governor unlocked a door, and with one of the torchbearers led the way down some narrow steps. These were some fifty in number, and then a level passage ran along for some distance. Another door was opened, and a fresh breeze blew upon them as they issued forth. They stood on some rocks at the foot of the promontory on which the castle stood. A large boat lay close at hand, drawn to the shore. Archie and the six soldiers entered her; four of the latter took the oars, and the others seated themselves by their prisoner, and then the boat rowed away, while the governor returned to aid in the defence of the castle.

The boat was but a quarter of a mile away when on the night air came the sound of a wild outburst of triumphant shouts which told that the Scots had won their way into the castle. With muttered curses the men bent to their oars and every minute took them further away from Knockbawn.

Archie was bitterly disappointed. He had reckoned confidently on the efforts of Douglas to deliver him, and the possibility of his being sent off by sea had not entered his mind. It seemed to him now that his fate was sealed. He had noticed on embarking that there were no other boats lying at the foot of the promontory, and pursuit would therefore be impossible.

After rowing eight hours the party reached Port Patrick, where Archie was delivered by the soldiers to the governor with a message from their commander saying that the prisoner, Sir Archibald Forbes, was a captive of great importance, and was, by the orders of Sir Ingram de Umfraville who had captured him, to be sent on to Carlisle to the king when a ship should be going thither. A fortnight passed before a vessel sailed. Archie was placed in irons and so securely guarded in his dungeon that escape was altogether impossible. So harsh was his confinement that he longed for the time when a vessel would sail for Carlisle, even though he was sure that the same fate which had attended so many of Scotland's best and bravest knights awaited him there.

The winds were contrary, and the vessel was ten days upon the voyage. Upon reaching Carlisle, Archie was handed to the governor of the castle, and the next morning was conducted to the presence of the king himself. The aged monarch, in the last extremity of sickness, lay upon a couch. Several of his nobles stood around him.

"So," he said as the prisoner was brought before him, "this is Archibald Forbes, the one companion of the traitor Wallace who has hitherto escaped my vengeance. So, young sir, you have ventured to brave my anger and to think yourself capable of coping with the Lion of England."

"I have done my utmost, sir king," Archie said firmly, "such as it was, for the freedom of my country. No traitor am I, nor was my leader Wallace. Nor he, nor I, ever took vow of allegiance to you, maintaining ever that the kings of England had neither claim nor right over Scotland. He has been murdered, foully and dishonorably, as you will doubtless murder me, and as you have killed many nobler knights and gentlemen; but others will take our places, and so the fight will go on until Scotland is free."

"Scotland will never be free," the king said with angry vehemence. "Rather than that, she shall cease to exist, and I will slay till there is not one of Scottish blood, man, woman, or child, to bear the name. Let him be taken to Berwick," he said; "there let him be exposed for a week in a cage outside the castle, that the people may see what sort of a man this is who matches himself against the might of England. Then let him be hung, drawn, and quartered, his head sent to London, and his limbs distributed between four Scottish cities."

"I go, sir king," Archie said, as the attendants advanced to seize him, "and at the end of the week I will meet you before the throne of God, for you, methinks, will have gone thither before me, and there will I tax you with all your crimes, with the slaughter of tens of thousands of Scottish men, women, and children, with cities destroyed and countries wasted, and with the murder in cold blood of a score of noble knights whose sole offense was that they fought for their native country."

With these words Archie turned and walked proudly from the king's presence. An involuntary murmur of admiration at his fearless bearing escaped from the knights and nobles assembled round the couch of the dying monarch.

When, two days later, Archie entered the gates of Berwick Castle the bells of the city were tolling, for a horseman had just ridden in with the news that Edward had expired on the evening before, being the sixth day of July, 1307, just at the moment when he was on the point of starting with the great army he had assembled to stamp out the insurrection in Scotland.

So deep was his hatred for the people who had dared to oppose his will that when dying he called before him his eldest son, and in the presence of his barons caused him to swear upon the saints that as soon as he should be dead his body should be boiled in a cauldron until the flesh should be separated from the bones, after which the flesh should be committed to the earth, but the bones preserved, and that, as often as the people of Scotland rebelled, the military array of the kingdom should be summoned and the bones carried at the head of the army into Scotland. His heart he directed should be conveyed to and deposited in the Holy Land.

So died Edward I, a champion of the Holy Sepulchre, King of England, Lord of Ireland, Duke of Aquitaine, conqueror of Wales, and would-be conqueror of Scotland. In many respects his reign was a great and glorious one, for he was more than a fierce conqueror, he was, to England, a great king. In the sight of Almighty God, however, Edward was a wicked man and a vessel fit for destruction in the eternal fires of hell.

English historians have striven to excuse and ignore his conduct toward Scotland. They have glossed over his crimes and tried to explain away the records of his deeds of savage atrocity. Such lies were designed to show that Edward's claims to Scotland, which had not a shadow of foundation except from the traitorous submission of her Anglo-Norman nobles, almost all of whom were his own vassals and owned estates in England, were just and righteous. The justification of blind and sinful ambition is not the true function of history, for history must be rooted in the heavenly standards of truth and righteousness. Edward's sole claim to Scotland was that he was determined to unite under his rule England, Scotland, Wales, and Ireland, and he failed because the people of Scotland, deserted as they were by all their natural leaders, preferred death to such a slavery as that under which Ireland and Wales helplessly groaned. His dying wishes were not observed. Edward's body was laid in rest in Westminster Abbey, and on the tomb was inscribed, "Edward I the mallet of the Scots."

Chapter 23

The Escape from Berwick

Upon entering the castle Archie was at once escorted to a sort of cage which had been constructed for a previous prisoner. On the outside of a small cell a framework of stout beams had been erected. It was seven feet in height, six feet wide, and three feet deep. The bars were four inches round, and six inches apart. There was a door leading into the cell behind. This was closed in the daytime, so that the prisoner remained in the cage in sight of passers-by, but at night the governor, who was a humane man, allowed the door to remain unlocked, so that the prisoner could enter the inner cell and lie down there.

The position of the cage was about twenty-five feet above the moat. The moat itself was some forty feet wide, and a public path ran along the other side, and people passing here had a full view of the prisoner. There were still many of Scottish birth in the town in spite of the efforts which Edward had made to convert it into a complete English colony; and although the English were in the majority, Archie was subject to but little insult or annoyance. Although for the present in English possession, Berwick had always been a Scottish town, and might yet again from the fortune of war fall into Scottish hands. Therefore even those most hostile to them felt that it would be prudent to restrain from any demonstrations against the Scottish prisoners, since in the event of the city again changing hands a bloody retaliation might be dealt them. Occasionally a passing boy would shout out an epithet of contempt or hatred or throw a stone at the prisoner, but such trifles were unheeded by him. More often men or women passing would stop and gaze up at him with pitying looks, and would go away wiping their eyes.

Archie, after the first careful examination of his cell, at once abandoned any idea of escape from it. The massive bars would have defied the strength of twenty men, and he had no instrument of any sort with which he could cut them. There was, he felt, nothing before him but death; and although he feared this little for himself, he felt sad indeed as he thought of the grief of Marjory and his mother.

The days passed slowly. Five had gone without an incident, and but two remained, for he knew that there was no chance of any change in the sentence which Edward had passed, even were his son more disposed than he toward merciful measures to the Scots, which Archie had no warrant for supposing. The new king's time would be too closely engaged in the affairs entailed by his accession to rank, the arrangement of his father's funeral, and the details of the army advancing against Scotland, to give a thought to the prisoner whose fate had been determined by his father.

Absorbed in his own thoughts Archie seldom looked across the moat, and paid no heed to those who passed or who paused to look at him. On the afternoon of the fifth day, however, his eye was caught by two women who were gazing up at the cage. It was the immobility of their attitude and the length of time which they continued to gaze at him, which attracted his attention.

In a moment he recognized the women and almost gave a cry, for in one of them he saw his wife, Marjory. The instant that the women saw that he had observed them they turned away and walked carelessly and slowly along the road. Archie could hardly believe that his eyesight had not deceived him. It seemed impossible that Marjory, whom he deemed a hundred miles away, in his castle at Aberfilly, should be here in the town of Berwick, and yet when he thought it over he saw that it might well be so. There was indeed ample time for her to have made the journey two or three times while he had been lying in prison at Port Patrick awaiting a ship. She would be sure, when the news reached her of his capture, that he would be taken to Edward at Carlisle, and that he would be either executed there or at Berwick. It was then by no means impossible, strange and wondrous as it appeared to him, that Marjory should be in Berwick.

She was attired in the garment of a peasant woman of the better class, such as the wife of a small crofter or farmer, and remembering how she had saved his life before at Dunstaffnage, Archie felt that she had come hither to try to rescue him.

Archie's heart beat with delight and his eyes filled with tears at the devotion and courage of Marjory, and for the first time since he had been hurried into the boat on the night of his capture a feeling of hope entered his breast. Momentary as the glance had been which he had obtained of the face of Marjory's companion, Archie had perceived that it was in some way familiar to him. In vain he recalled the features of the various servants at Aberfilly, and those of the wives and daughters of the retainers of the estate; he could not recognize the face of the woman accompanying Marjory as belonging to any of them. His wife might, indeed, have brought with her some one from the estates at Ayr whom she had known from childhood, but in that case Archie could not account for his knowledge of her. This, however, did not occupy his mind many minutes; it was assuredly one whom Marjory trusted, and that was sufficient for him. Then his thoughts turned wholly to his wife.

Anyone who had noticed the prisoner's demeanor for the last few days would have been struck with the change which had come over it. Prior to the visit from Marjory he had stood often for hours leaning motionless, with his arms crossed, in the corner of his cage; now he paced restlessly up and down his narrow limits, two steps each way and then a turn, like a caged beast.

The sun sank. An hour later a jailer brought his jug of water and piece of bread, and then, without a word, retired, leaving, as usual, the door into the cell open, but carefully locking and barring the inner door. Archie had a longer walk now, from the front of the cage to the back of the cell, and for three hours he paced up and down. Sometimes he paused and listened attentively. The sounds in the town gradually died away and all became still, except that he could hear the calls of the warder on the battlement above him. The night was a very dark one and he could scarcely make out the gleam of water in the moat below.

Suddenly something struck him a sharp blow on the face and fell at his feet. He stooped and picked it up, it was an arrow with a wad of wool fastened round its point to prevent it from making a noise should it strike the wall or cage; to the other end was attached a piece of string. Archie drew it in until he felt that it

Archie a Prisoner in the Cage at Berwick

was held firmly, then after a moment the hold relaxed somewhat, and the string again yielded as he drew it. It was now, he felt, taut from the other side of the moat. Presently a stout rope, amply sufficient to bear his weight, came into his hands. At the point of junction was attached some object done up in flannel. This he opened, and found that it was a fine saw and a small bottle containing oil. He fastened the rope securely to one of the bars and at once commenced to saw asunder one of the others. In five minutes two cuts had been noiselessly made, and a portion of the bar five feet long came away. He now tried the rope and found that it was tightly stretched, and evidently fixed to some object on the other side of the moat. He grasped it firmly with his arms and legs and slid rapidly down it.

In another minute he was grasped by some strong arms which checked his rapid progress and enabled him to gain his feet without the slightest noise. As he did so a woman threw her arms round him, and he exchanged a passionate but silent embrace with Marjory. Then she took his hand and with noiseless steps they proceeded down the road. He had before starting removed his shoes and put them in his pockets. Marjory and her companion had also removed their shoes, and even the keenest ears upon the battlements would have heard no sound as they proceeded along the road. Fifty yards farther and they were among the houses. Here they stopped a minute and put on their shoes, and then continued their way. Not a word was spoken until they had traversed several streets and stopped at the door of a house in a quiet lane; it yielded to Marjory's touch, she and Archie entered, and their follower closed and fastened it after them.

The moment this was done Marjory threw her arms round Archie's neck with a burst of tears of joy and relief. While Archie was soothing her the third person stirred up the embers on the hearth and threw on a handful of dry wood.

"And who is your companion?" Archie asked, after the first transports of joy and thankfulness were past.

"What! don't you recognize Cluny?" Marjory asked, laughing through her tears.

"Cluny! of course," Archie exclaimed, grasping his follower's hand in his. "I only caught a glimpse of your face and knew that is was familiar to me, but in vain tried to recall its owner. Why,

Cluny, it is a long time since you went dressed as a girl into Ayr? And so it is my good friend who had shared my wife's dangers."

"He has done more than that, Archie," Marjory said, "for it was to him that I owe my first idea of coming here. The moment after the castle was taken and it was found that you had been carried off in a boat by the English, Cluny started to tell me the news. Your mother and I were beside ourselves with grief, and Cluny, to comfort us, said, 'Do not despair yet, my lady; my lord shall not be killed by the English if I can prevent it. The master and I have been in a good many dangers, and have always come out of them safely; it shall not be my fault if he does not slip through their hands yet.' 'Why, what can you do, Cluny?' I said. 'I don't know what I can do yet,' he replied; 'that must depend upon circumstances. My lord is sure to be taken to Carlisle, and I shall go south to see if I cannot get him out of prison. I have often gone among the English garrisons disguised as a woman, and no one in Carlisle is likely to ask me my business there.' It was plain to me at once that if Cluny could go to your aid, so could I, and I at once told him that I should accompany him. Cluny raised all sorts of objections, but to these I would not listen, but brought him to my will by saying, that if he thought my being with him would add to his difficulties I would go alone, but that go I certainly would. So without more ado we got these dresses and made south. We had a few narrow escapes of falling into the hands of parties of English, but at last we crossed the frontier and made to Carlisle. Three days later we heard of your arrival, and the next morning all men were talking about your defiance of the king, and that you had been sent to Berwick for execution at the end of the week. So we journeyed hither and got here the day after you arrived. The first step was to find a Scotswoman whom we might trust. This, by God's grace, we did, and Mary Martin, who lives in this house, is a true Scottish patriot, and will help us to the extent of her power; she is poor, for her husband, who is an Englishman, had for some time been ill, and died but yesterday. Mary will, if she can, return with her daughter to Roxburgh, where her relations live, and where she married her husband, who was a soldier in the English garrison there."

"But, Marjory," Archie said, "have you thought how we are to escape hence; though I am free from the castle I am still within the walls of Berwick, and when, tomorrow, they find that I have escaped, they will search every nook and corner of the town. I had best without delay try and make my way over the walls."

"That was the plan Cluny and I first thought of," Marjory replied; "but owing to the raids of the Douglas on the border, so strict a watch is kept on the walls that it would be difficult indeed to pass. Cluny has tried a dozen times each night, but the watch is so vigilant that he has each time failed to make his way past them, but has been challenged and has had several arrows discharged at him. The guard at the gates is extremely strict, and all carts that pass in and out are searched. Could you have tried to pass before your escape was known you might no doubt have done so in disguise, but the alarm will be given before the gates are open in the morning, and your chance of passing through undetected then would be small indeed. The death of the man Martin suggested a plan to me. I have proposed it to his wife, and she has fallen in with it. I have promised her a pension for her life should we succeed, but I believe she would have done it even without reward. When she heard who it was that I was trying to rescue, she said at once she would risk anything to save the life of one of Scotland's best and bravest champions."

"But what are your plans, Marjory?"

"All the neighbors know that Martin is dead; they believe that Cluny is Mary's sister and I her niece, and she has told them that she shall return with us to Roxburgh. Martin was a native of a village four miles hence, and she is going to bury him with his fathers there. Now I have proposed to her that Martin shall be buried beneath the wood store here, and that you shall take his place in the coffin."

"It is a capital idea, Marjory," Archie said, "and will assuredly succeed if any plan can do so. The only fear is that the search will be so hot in the morning that the soldiers may even insist upon looking into the coffin."

"We have thought of that," Marjory said, "and dare not risk it. We must expect every house to be searched in the morning, and have removed some tiles in the attic. At daybreak you must creep out on the roof, replace the tiles, and remain hidden there until the search is over. Martin will be laid in the coffin. Thus, even should they lift the lid, no harm will come of it. As soon as they have gone, Cluny will bring you down, and you and he can dig the grave in the floor of the woodshed and place Martin there, then you will take his place in the coffin, which will be placed in a cart already hired. Cluny, I, Mrs. Martin, and her daughter will then set out with it."

Soon after daybreak the quick strokes of the alarm bell at the castle told the inhabitants of Berwick that a prisoner had escaped. Archie at once climbed into his place of concealment on the roof. He replaced the tiles, and Cluny carefully obliterated all signs of the place of exit from within. A great hubbub had by this time arisen in the street. Trumpets were blowing, and parties of soldiers were moving about in all directions. The gates remained unopened, orders being given that none should pass through without a special order from the governor.

The sentries on the wall were doubled, and then a house-to-house search was commenced, every possible place of concealment being rummaged from basement to attic. Presently the searchers entered the lane in which Mrs. Martin lived. The latch was ere long lifted, and a sergeant and six soldiers burst into the room. The sight which they beheld quieted their first noisy exclamations. Four women in deep mourning were kneeling by a rough coffin placed on trestles. One of them gave a faint scream as they entered, and Mary Martin, rising to her feet, said:

"What means this rough intrusion?"

"It means," the sergeant said, "that a prisoner has escaped from the castle, one Archibald Forbes, a pestilent Scottish traitor. He has been aided by friends from without, and as the sentries were watchful all night, he must be hidden somewhere in the town, and every house is to be searched."

"You can search if you will," the woman said, resuming the position on her knees. "As you see, this is a house of mourning, seeing that my husband is dead, and is today to be buried in his native village, three miles away."

"He won't be buried today," the sergeant said; "for the gates are not to be opened save by a special order from the governor. Now, lads," he went on, turning to the men, "search the place from top to bottom, examine all the cupboards and sound the floors, turn over all the wood in the shed, and leave not a single place unsearched where a mouse could be hid."

The soldiers scattered through the house, and were soon heard knocking the scanty furniture about and sounding the floors and walls. At last they returned saying that nothing was to be found.

"And now," the sergeant said, "I must have a look in that coffin. Who knows but what the traitor Scot may be hid in there!"

Mrs. Martin leaped to her feet.

"You shall not touch the coffin," she said; "I will not have the remains of my husband disturbed." The sergeant pushed her roughly aside, and with the end of his pike pried up the lid of the coffin, while Mrs. Martin and the other three mourners screamed lustily and wrung their hands in the greatest grief at this desecration of the dead.

Just as the sergeant opened the coffin and satisfied himself that a dead man really lay within, an officer, attracted by the screams, entered the room.

"What is this, sergeant?" he asked angrily. "The orders were to search the house, but none were given you to trouble the inmates."

Mrs. Martin began to complain of the conduct of the soldiers in wrenching open the coffin.

"It was a necessary duty, my good woman," the officer said, "seeing that a living man might have been carried away instead of a dead one; however, I see all is right."

"Oh, kind sir!" Mrs. Martin said, sobbing, "is it true what this man tells me, that there is no passage through the gates today? I have hired a cart to take away my husband's body; the grave is dug, and the priest will be waiting. Kind sir, I pray of you to get me a pass to sally out with it, together with my daughter, sister, and niece."

"Very well," the officer said kindly, "I will do as you wish. I shall be seeing the governor presently to make my report to him; and as I have myself seen the dead body can vouch that no ruse is intended. But assuredly no pass will be given for any man to accompany you; and the Scot, who is a head and shoulders taller than any of you, would scarcely slip out in a woman's garment. When will the cart be here?"

"At noon," the woman replied. "Very well; an hour before that time a soldier will bring out the pass. Now, sergeant, have you searched the rest of the house?"

"Yes, sir; thoroughly, and nothing suspicious has been found."

"Draw off your men, then, and proceed, with your search elsewhere."

No sooner had the officer and men departed than Cluny ran upstairs, and removing two of the tiles, whispered to Archie that all was clear. The hole was soon enlarged, and Archie re-entering, the pair descended to the woodshed which adjoined the kitchen, and there, with a spade and pick which Cluny had purchased on the preceding day, they set to work to dig a grave. In two hours it was completed. The body of John Martin was lowered into it, the earth replaced and trodden down hard, and the wood again piled onto it.

At eleven o'clock a soldier entered with the governor's pass ordering the soldier at the gate to allow a cart with the body of John Martin, accompanied by four women, to pass out from the town.

At the appointed time the cart arrived. Archie had already taken his place in the coffin. His face was whitened, and a winding-sheet wrapped round him, lest by an evil chance any should insist on again looking into the coffin. Then some neighbors came in and assisted in placing the coffin in the cart. The driver took his place beside it, and the four women, with their hoods drawn over their heads, fell in behind it weeping bitterly.

When they arrived at the gate the officer in charge carefully read the order, and then gave the order for the gate to be opened. "But stop," he said, "this pass says nothing about a driver, and though this man in no way resembles the description of the doughty Scot, yet as he is not named in the pass I cannot let him pass." There was a moment's pause of consternation, and then Cluny said:

"Sister Mary, I will lead the horse. When all is in readiness, and the priest waits, we cannot turn back on such a slight cause." As the driver of the cart knew Mary Martin, he offered no objection, and descended from his seat. Cluny took the reins, and, walking by the side of the horse's head, led him through the gates as these were opened, the others following behind. As soon as they were through, the gate closed behind them, and they were safely out of the town of Berwick.

So long as they were within sight of the walls they proceeded at a slow pace without change of position, and although Cluny then quickened the steps of his horse, no other change was made until two miles further they reached a woods. Then Cluny leapt into the cart and wrenched off the lid of the coffin. It had been but lightly nailed down, and being but roughly made there were plenty of crevices through which the air could pass.

"Quick, Sir Archie!" he said, "let us get this thing out of the cart before any soldiers happen to come along."

The coffin was lifted from the cart, and carried some short distance into the woods. A few vigorous kicks separated the planks which composed it. These were taken and thrust separately among bushes at some little distance from each other. Cluny then unrolled the bundle which he had brought from the cart, and handed to Archie a suit of clothes fitted for a farmer. These Archie quickly put on, then he returned to the cart, which he mounted, and took the reins. The others got up behind him and seated themselves on the straw in the bottom of the cart. Then Archie gave the horse a quick tap with his whip, and the cart proceeded at a steady trot along the road to the west.

Chapter 24

The Progress of the War

A mile or two after leaving Berwick the cart had left the main road running by the coast through Dunbar to Edinburgh, and had struck west by a country track. But few houses were met with, as the whole of the country within many miles of the sea had been harried and devastated by the various English armies which had advanced from Berwick. After proceeding for some miles they came to a point where the track they had been following terminated at a little hamlet among the hills. Here they left the cart, making an arrangement with one of the villagers to drive it back on the morrow into Berwick. They were now beyond all risk of pursuit, and need fear nothing further until they reached the great north roads running from Carlisle to Edinburgh and Stirling. Cluny therefore resumed male attire. They had no difficulty in purchasing a couple of swords from the peasants of the village, and armed with these they started with Marjory and the two women over the hills. It was early autumn now; the weather was magnificent, and they made the distance in quiet stages, and crossing the Pentlands came down upon Aberfilly without meeting with a single danger or obstacle.

It is difficult to describe the joy of Archie's mother at his return. The news spread like lightning among the tenantry, and in an hour after the wayfarers reached the castle men and women could be seen flocking over the hills at top speed to express their delight at their lord's return. By nightfall every tenant on the estate, except those prevented by age or illness, had assembled at the castle, and the rejoicings which had taken place at the marriage of their lord were but tame and quiet beside the boisterous enthusiasm which was now exhibited.

Although Marjory had at first been welcomed for the sake of her husband, the fact that she was a Kerr had excited a deep though hidden hostility to her in the minds both of those who had been her father's vassals at Aberfilly, and the old retainers of the Forbeses at Glen Cairn. The devotion and courage which she had shown in the defense of the castle and in the enterprise for the rescue of their lord swept away every vestige of this feeling, and henceforth Marjory ranked in their affections with Archie himself, and there was not a man upon the estate but felt that he could die for her if needs be.

After a week's stay at home Archie rode away and joined the king, taking, however, but four or five retainers with him. Bruce received him with extreme warmth. He had heard of his capture, and the news that he was condemned to die at Berwick had also reached him, and he had no doubt but Archie had shared the fate which had befallen his own brothers and so many of his bravest friends. His pleasure, therefore, equaled his surprise when his brave follower rode into his camp. Many of Archie's friends assembled as soon as it was known that he had arrived; and after the first greetings the king asked him for a recital of the means by which he had escaped from the fate decreed him by Edward. Archie related the whole story, and at its conclusion the king called to his attendants to bring goblets and wine.

"Sirs," he said, "let us drink a toast to the health of Mistress Marjory Forbes, one of the bravest and truest of Scottish women. Would to Heaven that all the men of our country were animated by as noble and courageous feelings! Our friend, Sir Archibald Forbes, has indeed won a jewel, and I take no small credit to myself that I was the first who advised him to make Mistress Kerr his wife."

"Now, Archie," the king said, when they were again alone together, "I suppose, seeing that you have come hither without your following, that you wish for a time to remain quiet at home, and seeing that you have suffered severe imprisonment and a grievous risk of death in my cause, methinks you have well earned the right to rest quiet for a while with your brave lady. At present I can dispense with the services of your retainers. Most of the low country is now in my hands, and the English garrisons dare not venture out of their strong places. The army that the King of England collected to crush us has been, I hear, much dis-organized by his death, and the barons will doubtless wring concessions and privileges from his son before they spread their banners to the wind again. From all reports the new king has but little of his father's ability and energy, and months may elapse before any serious effort is made against us. I am despatching my brother Edward to join Douglas in subduing Galloway, and during his absence I shall be content to remain here in the field with a small following, for the English governors of the towns will, methinks, stand only on the defensive, until a strong army marches north from England. When Galloway is subdued the lowlands will be all in my hands save for the English garrisons, and I shall on Edward's return set myself to punish the Comyns and the other traitor nobles of the north, who are well-nigh all hand and glove with the English. So long as Scotland has such powerful enemies in her midst she cannot hope to cope with the forces which England can send against her. Alone and united the task is one which will tax her strength to the utmost, seeing that England is in wealth and population so far her superior, and commands forces from Ireland, Wales, and Gascony. Therefore, my first task must be to root out these traitor-nobles from among us. When I move north I shall need your company and your strength; but until my brother Edward has cleared the English out of Galloway, captured the strongholds, and reduced it to obedience, you can station yourself near Aberfilly. Perhaps there will be times, when I have no enterprise on hand and can take a few days, that I will come and rest if you will give me hospitality."

So until the following spring Archie Forbes remained quietly and most happily at home. Several times the king came and stayed a few days at Aberfilly, where he was safe against surprise and treachery. Not long after Archie's return home, Father Anselm arrived, to Archie's satisfaction and the great joy of Marjory, and took up his abode there.

In the spring Archie, with his retainers, joined the king, who was gathering his army for his march into the north. During the winter Galloway had been subdued, and Douglas being left in the south as commander there, Edward Bruce joined his brother, around whom also gathered the Earl of Lennox, Sir Gilbert de la Haye, and others. The position in Scotland was now singular: the whole of the country south of the Forth was favorable to Bruce, but the English held Roxburgh, Jedburgh, Dumfries, Castle Douglas, Ayr, Bothwell, Edinburgh, Linlithgow, Stirling, and Dumb-arton. North of the Forth nearly the whole of the country was hostile to the king, and the fortresses of Perth, Dundee, Forfar, Brechin, Aberdeen, Inverness, and many smaller holds, were occupied by English garrisons.

The center of hostility to Bruce, north of the Forth, lay in the two great earls, the Comyns of Badenoch and Buchan, and their allies. Between them and Bruce a hatred existed beyond that caused by their taking opposite sides. Comyn of Badenoch was the son of the man Bruce had slain at Dumfries, while Buchan hated him even more, since his wife, the countess, had espoused the cause of Bruce and had crowned him at Scone, and was now shamefully imprisoned in the cage at Berwick. It must be sup-posed that Buchan's anger against his countess was as deep and implacable as that of Edward himself, for, as the English king's most powerful ally in Scotland, he could surely have obtained the pardon and release of his wife had he desired it. On the other hand, Bruce had a private grudge against Comyn, for upon him had been conferred Bruce's lordship of Annandale, and he had entered into possession and even occupied the family castle of Lochmaben.

The king and his army marched north, and were joined by Alexander and Simon Frazer, with their followers. They marched to Inverness, which, together with various other castles in the north, they captured. All of these castles were, when taken, destroyed, as Bruce had determined to leave no strongholds in the land for the occupation of his enemies. He himself could not spare men to hold them, and their capture was useless if upon his retirement they could again be occupied by the enemy. Returning southward they were encountered by an army under Buchan, composed of his own retainers and a party of English. This force was completely defeated.

To the consternation of his followers Bruce was now attacked by a wasting illness, which so enfeebled him that he was unable to sit on his horse; it was the result of the many hardships which he had undergone since the fight at Methven. His brother, Len-nox, the Frazers, and Archie Forbes held a council and agreed that rest for some time was absolutely necessary for the king, and that sea air might be beneficial to him. They therefore resolved to move eastward to the Castle of Slaines, on the sea-coast near Peterhead. That such a step was attended by great peril they well knew, for the Comyns would gather the whole strength of the Highlands, with accessions from the English garrisons, and besiege them there. The king's health, however, was a paramount consideration; were he to die, the blow might be fatal to Scotland, accordingly the little force marched eastward. They reached Slaines without interruption, and as they expected the castle was soon surrounded and besieged by the forces of Buchan, who had been joined by Sir John Mowbray and Sir David de Brechin, nephew of the King of England. For some time the siege went on, but the assailants gained but little advantage, and indeed trusted rather to famine than force to reduce the castle.

Weeks passed on, and although his followers thought that he was somewhat better, the king's health improved but slowly. Provisions now began to run very short. When they had come nearly to an end the Scots determined to sally out and cut their way through the vastly superior strength of the enemy. The king was placed in a litter, his mounted knights and followers surrounded him, and round these the footmen formed a close clump of pikes; the hundred men from Aberfilly formed the front rank, as these could be best relied upon to withstand the charge of the English horse. The gates were thrown open, and in close ranks the garrison sallied out, forming, as soon as they passed through, in the order arranged. So close and serried was the hedge of spears, so quiet and determined the attitude of the men, that, numerous as they were, the men of Buchan and the English lords shrank from an encounter with such adversaries, and with the banner of the king and his knights flying in their center the little band marched on through the lines of the besiegers without the latter striking a blow to hinder their way.

Without interruption the royalists proceeded to Strathbogie. The satisfaction of the king at the daring exploit by which he had been rescued from such imminent peril did more for him than medicine or change of air, and to the joy of his followers he began to recover his strength. He was then moved down to the river Don. Here Buchan and his English allies made a sudden attack upon his quarters, killing some of the outposts. This attack roused the spirit and energy of the king, and he immediately called for his war horse and armor and ordered his men to prepare for action. His followers argued with him, but he declared that this attack by his enemies had cured him more speedily than medicine could have done, and heading his troops he issued forth and came upon the enemy near Old Meldrum, where, after a desperate fight, Buchan and his confederates were defeated with great slaughter on Christmas day, 1307. Buchan and Mowbray fled into England. Brechin took refuge in his own castle of Brechin, where he was afterwards besieged and forced to surrender.

Bruce now marched into the territory of Comyn, where he took a terrible vengeance for the long adhesion of his hated enemy, to England. The whole country was wasted with fire and sword, the people well-nigh exterminated, and the very forests destroyed. So terrible was the devastation that for generations afterwards men spoke of the harrying of Buchan as a terrible and exceptional act of vengeance.

The castle of Aberdeen was the next stronghold to be attacked. The English made great efforts for its defense, but the citizens joined Bruce; and a united attack being made upon the castle, it was taken by assault and razed to the ground. The king and his forces then moved, into Angus. Here the English strongholds were all taken, the castle of Forfar being assaulted and carried by a leader who was called Phillip, a forester of Platane. With the exception of Perth, the most important fortress north of the Forth, and a few minor holds, the whole of the north of Scotland, was now in the king's hands. In the meantime Sir James Douglas, in the south, had again taken his paternal castle and had razed it to the ground. The forests of Selkirk and Jedburgh, with the numerous fortresses of the district, were brought under the king's authority, and the English were defeated several times. In the course of these adventures Sir James came across Alexander Stewart, Thomas Randolph, the king's nephew, who, after being taken prisoner at Methven, had joined the English party, and Adam O'Gordon. They advanced with a much superior force to capture him, but were signally defeated. O'Gordon escaped into England, but Stewart and Randolph were taken.

This was a fortunate capture, for Randolph afterwards became one of the king's most valiant knights and the wisest of his counselors. After this action Douglas marched north and joined the king. The latter sternly reproached Randolph for having forsworn his allegiance and joined the English. Randolph answered hotly and was committed by his uncle to solitary confinement, where he presently came to a determination to renew his allegiance to Bruce, and henceforward fought faithfully and gallantly under him.

Galloway had risen again, and Edward Bruce, with Sir Archie Forbes, was detached to reduce it. It was a hard task, for the local chiefs were supported by Sir Ingram de Umfraville and Sir John de St. John; these knights, with twelve hundred followers, met the Scots on the banks of the Cree, which separates the counties of Kirkcudbright and Wigton, and although greatly superior in numbers, were completely defeated by the Scottish pikemen, and compelled to take refuge in the castle of Butele. Edward Bruce and Archie continued the task of subjugating the country; but St. John having retired to England, returned with fifteen hundred men-at-arms, and with this strong force set out in pursuit of the small body of Scots, of whom he thought to make an easy capture. Then occurred one of the most brilliant feats of arms that took place in a war in which deeds of daring abounded. Edward Bruce having heard from the country people of the approach of his adversaries, placed his infantry in a strong position, and then, with Archie Forbes and the fifty men-at-arms who constituted his cavalry, went out to reconnoitre the approach of the English. The morning was thick and misty. Ignorant of each other's position, the two forces came close together, when the fog suddenly lifted, and Edward Bruce and Archie beheld close to them the overwhelming force of St. John, within bowshot distance. It was too late to fly. Edward Bruce exclaimed to Archie:

"There is nothing to do but to charge them."

"Let us charge them," Archie replied.

The two leaders, setting spurs to their horses, and closely followed by their fifty retainers, dashed like a thunderbolt upon the mass of the English men-at-arms, before they had time to form. They burst clean through them, overthrowing and slaying many, and causing the greatest confusion and surprise. Riding but a short distance on, the Scots turned, and again burst through the English lines. Numbers of the English were slain, and many others turned rein. A third time the Scots charged, with equally fatal effect. The English were completely routed. Many were killed and many taken prisoners, and the rest rode for England at their best speed. History scarcely recalls another instance of fifty men routing in fair fight fifteen hundred. This extraordinary success was followed by a victory over Sir Roland of Galloway and Donald of the Isles on the banks of the Dee, the Lord of the Isles being made prisoner; and eventually the whole country was reduced to obedience, with the exception of one or two garrisons, no less than thirteen castles being captured, in addition to the victories gained in the field.

Galloway being restored to order, Archie Forbes returned home, and remained for two or three months with his wife and mother. He was then summoned by the king to join him again, as he was about to march to reduce the region over which his deadly foes Alexander and John of Lorne held sway. The country into which the royal army now penetrated was extremely mountainous and difficult, but they made their way as far as the head of Loch Awe, where Alexander and John of Lorne, with two thousand men, were gathered to dispute the passage. The position was an extremely strong one, and the Lornes were confident that it could not be forced. Immediately to the north of the head of the lake rises the steep and lofty mountain Ben Cruachan. From the head of the lake flows the river Awe connecting it with Loch Etive, and the level space between the foot of the mountain and the river is only wide enough for two to ride abreast. This passage was known as the Pass of Brander, and the Lornes might well believe that their position was unassailable.

Before advancing into the pass Bruce detached Douglas, with Sir Alexander Frazer, Sir William Wiseman, and Sir Andrew Grey, with a body of lightly armed infantry and archers. These, unnoticed by the enemy, climbed the side of the mountain, and going far up it, passed along until they got behind and above the enemy. The king ordered his main body to lay aside all defensive armor so that they could more easily climb the hill and come to a hand-to-hand conflict with the enemy. Then he moved along toward the narrow pass. As they approached it the men of Lorne hurled down a torrent of rocks from the hillside above.

With a few heavily-armed men Bruce pushed forward by the water side, while Archie Forbes led the main body up the hillside. The climb was stiff and difficult, and many were swept down by the rocks hurled by the enemy; but at last they came to close quarters with the foe, and a desperate struggle ensued.

In the meantime Douglas and his party had attacked the defenders from the other side, at first showering arrows among them, and then falling upon them with sword and battle-ax. Thus attacked in front and rear, the men of Lorne lost heart and gave way. On both sides the royalists pressed them hotly, and at last they broke from the hillside and fled down to the river, intending to cross by a wooden bridge and destroy it behind them; but before many had passed, Douglas with his followers arrived upon the spot and seized the bridge, cutting off their retreat. Great numbers of the men of Lorne were slain, and the survivors made their escape up the mountain side again. The Lornes themselves were on board some galleys on Loch Awe, their intention having been to land in Bruce's rear when he was fairly entangled in the narrow pass. On witnessing the utter confusion of their followers they rowed rapidly away, and landed far down the lake. Alexander fled to England, where he ended his life.

Bruce now advanced through the country of Lorne, which, having never suffered from the English raids that had over and over again devastated the rest of Scotland, was rich and flourishing, and large quantities of booty were obtained. Dunstaffnage was besieged and captured, and having received hostages from all the minor chiefs for their good behavior the king and his army returned to Glasgow.

In the following spring a truce was negotiated by the intervention of the King of France between the belligerents; but its duration was but short; for so long as the English nobles held estates and occupied castles in Scotland, breaches of the peace would be constantly occurring. Bruce besieged the castle of Rutherglen, near Glasgow; but Edward's son despatched the Earl of Gloucester to stop the siege, and as Bruce's army was still small he was forced to retire at his approach.

In February, 1309, the clergy of Scotland assembled in a provincial council at Dundee, and issued a declaration in favor of Bruce as lawful king of Scotland. In this document they set forth that although Baliol was made king of Scotland by the King of England, Bruce, the grandfather of the king, was always recognized by the people as being nearest in right; and they said: "If any one, on the contrary, claims right to the aforesaid kingdom in virtue of letters in time passed sealed, and containing the consent of the people and the commons, know ye that all this took place in fact by force and violence, which could not at the time be resisted, and through multiplied fears, bodily tortures, and various terrors."

This document was sealed by all the bishops, as representing the clergy. A similar document was drawn up and signed by the estates of Scotland. Therefore, henceforth Bruce could claim to be the king not only as crowned and by right, but by the approval and consent of the clergy and people of Scotland. A few months afterwards James, the Steward of Scotland, whose course had ever been vacillating, died, and his son Walter, a loyal Scotsman, succeeded him. He afterwards married the king's daughter Marjory, and became the founder of the royal line of Stuart.

Chapter 25

The Capture of a Stronghold

While Bruce had by his energy and courage been liberating Scotland, step by step, from the English, no serious effort had been made by the latter to check his progress. Small bodies of troops had from time to time been sent from the north; but the king had made no great efforts, like those of his father, to reduce the country to obedience by the exercise of the whole strength of England. Edward II differed widely from his father in disposition. At times he was roused to fits of spasmodic energy, but for the most part he was sunk in sloth. He angered and irritated his barons by his fondness for unworthy favorites, and was engaged in constant arguments with them.

So-called governors of Scotland were frequently appointed and as often superseded, but no effectual aid was given them to enable them to check the ever-spreading insurrection. Perth, however, was now threatened by Bruce; and the danger of this, the strongest and most important northern fortress, roused Edward from his lethargy. A fleet was fitted out to carry men and supplies into Perth. Troops, under the Earl of Ulster, were engaged to be transported by an English fleet of forty ships, supplied by the seaports, and intended to co-operate with John of Lorne in the west. Edward himself, with a powerful army, accompanied by the Lords Gloucester, Warrenne, Percy, Clifford, and others, advanced into Scotland as far as Renfrew. Bruce could oppose no effectual resistance in the field to so large a force, but he used the tactics which Wallace had adopted with much success. The country through which the English were advancing was wasted. Flocks and herds were driven off, and all stores of grain were burned and destroyed. His adherents, each with their own retainers, hung upon the skirts of the English army, cutting off small parties, driving back bodies going out in search of provisions or forage, making sudden night attacks, and keeping the English in a state of constant watchfulness and alarm, but always retiring on the approach of any strong force, and avoiding every effort of the English to bring on an engagement.

The invaders were soon pressed by lack of provisions, and horses died from lack of forage. The great army was therefore obliged to fall back to Berwick without having struck a single effective blow. After this Edward remained inactive at Berwick for eight months, save that he once again crossed the border and advanced as far as Roxburgh, but only to retreat without having accomplished anything. The Earls of Gloucester and Warrenne reduced the forest of Selkirk and the district, and restored the English power there; while the king's favorite, Piers Gaveston, Earl of Cornwall, went by sea to Perth and tried to reduce the surrounding country; but the Scottish, as usual, fought him, and he, too, after a time, returned to Berwick. The efforts of the defenders to starve out the invading armies of England were greatly aided by the fact that at this time a great famine raged both in England and Scotland, and the people of both countries were reduced to a condition of hunger and suffering. Not only did the harvest fail, but disease swept away vast numbers of cattle and sheep, and in many places the people were forced to subsist upon the flesh of horses, dogs, and other animals.

During the years which had elapsed since the battle of Methven, Bruce had never been enabled to collect a force in any way worthy of the name of an army. His enterprises had been a succession of daring feats performed by small bodies of men. Even now, when the nobles dared no longer to openly oppose him, they remained sullenly aloof, and the captures of the English strongholds were performed either by the king or his brother Edward, with their retainers from Annandale and Carrick; by Douglas with the men of Douglasdale; or by some simple knights like Archie Forbes, the Frazers, Boyle, and a few others, each leading their own retainers in the field. The great mass of the people still held aloof, and neither town nor country sent their contingents to his aid. This was not to be wondered at, so fearfully had all suffered from the wholesale vengeance of Edward after the battle of Falkirk.

Great successes had certainly attended Bruce, but these had been rendered possible only by the absence of any great effort on the part of England; and all believed that sooner or later Edward would arouse himself, and with the whole strength of England, Ireland, and Wales again crush out the movement, and carry fire and sword through Scotland. Still the national spirit was rising.

Archie Forbes divided his time pretty equally between the field and home, never taking with him, when he joined the king, more than a third of the entire strength of his retainers; thus all had time to attend to their farms and the needs of their families, and cheerfully yielded obedience to the call to arms when the time came.

One day while the king was stopping for a few days' rest at Aberfilly, a horseman rode in.

"I have great news, sire," he said. "Linlithgow has been captured from the English."

"That were good news indeed," the king said; "but it can scarce be possible, seeing that we have no men-at-arms in the neighborhood."

"It has been done by no men-at-arms, my liege," the messenger said; "but as Forfar was taken by Phillip the Forester and his mates, so has Linlithgow been captured by a farmer and his comrades, one William Bunnock."

It was indeed true. The castle of Linlithgow, forming as it did a link between the two strongholds of Edinburgh and Stirling, was a place of great importance and was strongly garrisoned by the English. Naturally the whole country round suffered severely from the oppressions of the garrison, who supplied themselves by force with such provisions and stores, as were needful for them. Payment was of course made to some extent, as the country otherwise would speedily have been deserted and the land left untilled; but there was still much oppression and high-handedness. Bunnock, hearing of the numerous castles which had been captured by the king and his friends with mere handfuls of followers, determined at last upon an attempt to expel the garrison of Linlithgow. He went about among his friends and neighbors, and found many ready to join his enterprise. These one night placed themselves in ambush among some bushes close to the castle gate. Bunnock himself concealed eight chosen men with arms in a wagon of hay. The horses were driven by a stout peasant with a short hatchet under his belt, while Bunnock walked carelessly beside the wagon. As he was in the habit of supplying the garrison with corn and forage, the gate was readily opened on his approach. As soon as the wagon was exactly between the gateposts Bunnock gave the signal and struck down the warder at the gate; the driver with his hatchet cut the traces, the men leapt up from their concealment in the hay, and the main body lying in ambush close by rushed up, and, taken wholly by surprise, unarmed and unprepared, the garrison was speedily overpowered and the castle taken.

It was in the spring of 1311 that this important capture took place. Bruce, as usual, had the castle leveled to the ground. Bunnock was rewarded by a grant of land which still bears his name, softened into Binney. Again the English made preparations for a renewed invasion, but the barons were too much occupied by their quarrels with the king to assemble at his order, and nothing came of it. Bruce's position at home was so established that he resolved upon a counter invasion, and accordingly, having assembled a larger force than had hitherto gathered under his banner, crossed the border near the Solway, burnt and plundered the district round Gilsland, ravaged Tynedale, and after eight days' havock returned with much booty to Scotland. In the following month he again entered England, carried fire and sword through the country as far as Corbridge, swept Tynedale, ravaged Durham, and after levying contributions for fifteen days returned with much booty to Scotland.

Although the English made much outcry at this invasion, the English author of the Chronicle of Lanercost, whose monastery was occupied by the king during the raid, distinctly states that he slew none save in actual conflict; and again, that though "all the goods of the country were carried away, they did not burn houses or slay men." Thus, though Bruce's wife and daughter were still prisoners in England, though his brothers had been executed in cold blood, he conducted his warfare in England in a manner which contrasts strongly indeed with the conduct of the English in Scotland.

After this Bruce marched north again and laid siege to Perth. For six weeks he besieged the town, but without making any impression. Then he retired his forces as if abandoning the attempt. At night, however, he returned, ladders were placed in the ditches against the walls, and with his knights he led his followers on to the assault. The garrison were carousing in honor of their successful defense and the defeat of the enemy, and taken wholly by surprise were unable to oppose a vigorous resistance, and all were killed or captured. Some accounts say that the English soldiers were made prisoners, and the renegade Scots fighting with them were put to the sword; while others affirm that all who were taken prisoners were spared.

Another incursion into England followed the fall of Perth. Hexham, Corbridge, and Durham were destroyed. Douglas penetrated as far as Hartlepool and an immense spoil was carried off, until the people of the bishopric purchased a truce for the sum of £2000, and those of Northumberland, Cumberland, and Westmoreland bought off the invaders at a like price.

Carlisle was assaulted by Douglas, but unsuccessfully. He also attempted to surprise Berwick by a night attack, and had placed his scaling-ladders against the wall, when the garrison was alarmed by the barking of a dog, and the assailants were repulsed. The Scots recrossed the frontier laden with an enormous booty.

The king himself now entered Galloway and reduced the four remaining strongholds held by the English there— the castles of Butele, Dalswinton, Lochmaben, and Tibbers. He then proceeded to Dumfries, which he forced to surrender, and entered it as the victorious King of Scotland, just seven years after the time when he had commenced the war by expelling the English justiciary.

Archie Forbes did not accompany the king in this campaign. He had indeed been summoned, but just before the army started on its raid into England Bruce was lamenting, in Archie's hearing, that the continued possession of the strong castle of Dunottar on the east coast still afforded the English an opportunity for creating diversions in the north, by landing troops there.

"If you will permit me, sire," Archie said, "I will undertake its capture with my retainers. It is doubtless too strong to be captured by open assault with such a strength, but as Douglas has thrice taken Castle Douglas by stratagem, 'tis hard if I cannot find some way for capturing Dunottar."

"Be it so, Sir Archie," the king said. "If you succeed you will have done good service indeed; and as I know that though ever ready to buckle on your armor when I need you, you would yet rather live quietly at Aberfilly with your fair wife; I promise you that if you capture Dunottar, for a year and a day you and your retainers shall have rest, except if the English cross the border in such force that the arm of every Scotsman able to wield a sword is needed in its defense."

Having chosen a hundred of his most active and experienced men Archie set out for the north. Crossing the Forth above Stirling, he marched through Perth and across the Carse of Gowrie through Forfar on to Montrose. Here he left his band, and taking with him only William Orr, both being attired in peasants' dress, followed the coast till he reached Dunottar.

The castle, which was of great strength, stood in a little bay with a fishing village nestled beside it.

"'Tis a strong place, William, and, if well provisioned, might hold out against an army for months, and as supplies could be thrown in by sea it could only be captured by battering down its solid walls by machines."

"'Tis indeed a strong place, Sir Archie," William Orr replied, "and it were assuredly better to slip in by the gates than to climb over the walls; but after the captures of so many of their strongholds by sudden surprise, we may be sure that a careful watch will be kept."

"Doubtless they are shrewdly on guard against surprise," Archie said; "but as they know that the king and his host are just now crossing the border into Cumberland, they may well think that for a time they are safe from disturbance. 'Tis in that that our best chance lies."

Entering the village they purchased some fish from the fishermen, and asking a few careless questions about the garrison, found that it was composed of one hundred fifty men, and that extreme precautions were taken against surprise. The gates were never opened except to allow parties to pass in and out, when they were instantly closed and the drawbridge raised. Only ten of the garrison at a time were ever allowed to leave the castle, and these must go out and come in together, so that the gates should not be opened more than twice a day.

"They generally come out," the man said, "at eleven o'clock and go in at four; at eleven o'clock all with corn, wood, and other stores for the castle must present themselves, so that the drawbridge need only be lowered at those times. The governor, Sir John Morris, swears that he will not be caught asleep as were those of Linlithgow and Castle Douglas. I fear," he concluded, "that we of Dunottar will be the last in Scotland to be free from the English yoke."

"That is as it may be. Other castles have been captured, and maybe the lion of Scotland may float on those walls ere long."

The man looked keenly at him.

"Methinks there is meaning in your words," he said, "and your language does not accord with your attire. I ask no questions; but be sure that should an attempt be made, there are a score of strong fellows among us who will be ready to strike a blow for freedom."

"Is that so?" Archie replied; "then, man, taking you to be a true Scot, I will tell you that the attempt will be made, and that soon; and that, if you will, you can aid the enterprise. I am Sir Archibald Forbes, of whom, perhaps, you have heard."

"Assuredly," the man said in a tone of deep respect, "every Scotsman knows the name as that of one of the king's truest and bravest knights."

"My purpose is this," Archie said. "On a dark night some ninety-five of my men will march hither; I need a faithful friend to meet them outside the village to lead them in, and to hide them away in the cottages, having already arranged beforehand with their owners to receive them. I, myself, with four of my men will come hither in a fishing boat well laden with fish; we will choose a time when the wind is blowing, and will seem to have been driven here by stress of weather and disabled. Then I shall try to sell our cargo for the use of the garrison. As we carry it in we shall attack the guard; and at the signal, those hidden will rush out and cross the drawbridge."

"The plan is a good one," the fisherman said; "its difficulty mainly lies in the fact that the drawbridge will be raised the moment you have crossed it; and long before your followers could arrive it would be high in the air, and you would be cut off from all aid. It never remains down for an instant after men have passed over it."

"That adds to the difficulty," Archie said thoughtfully; "but I must think of some plan to overcome it. I suggest that you quietly go about among those you can surely trust and arrange for them to be ready to open their doors and take my men in without the slightest noise which might attract the sentries on the walls. So long as the wind is quiet and the sea smooth we shall not come, but the first day that the wind blows hard you may expect us. Then do you go out on the south road and wait for my party half a mile from the village. If they come not by midnight, return home and watch the following night."

"I understand," the fisherman said, "and will do as you bid me; and when the time comes you can rely upon twenty stout fellows here in addition to your own force."

"'Tis nigh eleven," Archie said, looking at the sun, "and we will be off at once, as the soldiers will soon be coming out; and it were best the governor did not hear that two strangers were in the village. Vigilant as he is, a small thing might excite his suspicion and add to his watchfulness."

Archie and William Orr returned to Montrose, and there the former made an arrangement with the master of a large fishing boat to keep his vessel ready to put to sea at any moment.

Three weeks passed without any change in the weather; then the wind began to rise and the aspect of the sky signaled a storm. William Orr at once set out with ninety-five men for Dunottar. Archie went down to the port and purchased a large quantity of fish which had been brought in that morning in various boats, and had it placed on board the craft that he had hired. Then he with four of his followers, the strongest and most determined of his retainers, dressed as fishermen, went on board and the boat at once put to sea, having, besides Archie and his men, the master and his two hands. The main body had started on foot at ten in the morning, but it was late in the afternoon before the boat put out, as Archie wished to arrive in broad daylight the next morning.

The wind was on the rise, and the boat was sorely tossed and buffeted. Early the next morning, showing but a rag of sail, she ran into Dunottar harbor. They had had great difficulty in keeping off the coast all night, and the play had almost turned into a tragedy; so narrow had been their escape from being cast ashore. The bulwarks were washed away, and the boat was in a sore plight as it drew alongside the little quay. Assuredly no suspicion would occur to any who saw her enter that nothing save stress of weather had driven her in.

It was twelve o'clock in the day when they reached the port. Most of the inhabitants had come down to the waterside to see the storm-beaten craft enter, and among them were some soldiers from the garrison. Archie ordered four of his men to remain below, so that the unusual number of hands should attract no attention. One of the first to come on board was the fisherman with whom Archie had spoken.

"Your men are all here," he said in a low tone to Archie, "and are stowed away in the cottages. Everything went well, and there was not the slightest noise."

Archie now went on shore and entered into conversation with one of the soldiers.

"Think you," he said, "that the governor would buy my cargo of fish. I have a great store on board, for I had good success before the storm suddenly broke upon me just as I was leaving the fishing grounds for Montrose. The gale may last for some days, and my boat will need repairs before I put to sea, therefore my fish will be spoiled before I can get them to market; and I will make a good bargain with the governor if he will take them from me."

"I should think that he will do so gladly," the soldier said, "for he can salt them down, and they make a pleasant change. How much have you got?"

"About ten baskets full," Archie replied, "of some hundred pounds each."

"I will go with you to the castle," the soldier said. "The governor will lower the drawbridge for no man, but you can speak with the warder across the moat and he will bear your message to the governor; and should he agree, you must present yourself with your men with the fish at four o'clock, at which time the drawbridge will be lowered for us to return to the castle."

Archie accompanied the soldier to the end of the drawbridge, and parleyed with the gate keeper. The latter acquainted the governor that the master of the fishing boat which had been driven in by stress of weather would like to dispose of his cargo of fish on cheap terms. A few moments later, an answer came back that the governor would give sixpence for each basket of a hundred pounds. Archie grumbled that he would receive thrice that sum at Montrose; still that as he must sell them or let them spoil, he accepted the offer, and would be there with the fish at four o'clock.

He then returned to the boat, his ally, the fisherman, taking word round to the cottages that at four o'clock all must be in readiness to sally out on the signal; and that William Orr was to dress half a dozen of his men in fishermen's clothes and saunter up carelessly close to the castle, so as to be able to rush forward on the instant.

At the appointed hour Archie, accompanied by his four followers, each of whom carried on his shoulder a great basket filled with fish, stepped on to the road and made their way to the castle. By the side of the moat facing the drawbridge the ten English soldiers who had been out on leave for the day were already assembled.

"Are you all there?" the gatekeeper asked.

"Yes," Archie said, "but I shall have to make another two trips down to the boat, seeing that I have ten baskets full and but four men to carry them."

"Then you must bring another load," the gatekeeper said, "when the drawbridge is lowered tomorrow. You will have to stop in the castle tonight, and issue out at eleven tomorrow, for the governor will not have the drawbridge lowered more than twice a day."

"I would like to return to my boat," Archie said, "as I want to be at work on the repairs; but if that be the rule I must needs submit to it."

The drawbridge was then lowered. The soldiers at once stepped on to it. The four pretended fishermen had set down their baskets, and now raised them on their shoulders again. One of them apparently found it a difficult task, for it was not until Archie and his comrades were half across the drawbridge that he raised it from the ground. As he did so he stumbled and fell, the basket and its contents rolling onto the ground.

"You must wait until the morning," the gatekeeper called; "you are too late to enter now."

The man lay for a moment where he had fallen, which was half on the drawbridge, half on the ground beyond it.

"Now, then," the gatekeeper called sharply, "make haste; I am going to raise the drawbridge."

The man rose to his feet with a shout just as the drawbridge began to rise. He had not been idle as he lay. As he fell he had drawn from underneath his fisherman's frock a stout chain with a hook at one end and a large ring at the other. This he had passed round one of the chains by which the drawbridge was raised, then under the beam on which it rested when down, and had fastened the hook in the ring.

Surprised at the shout, the gatekeeper worked the windlass with extra speed, but he had scarcely given a turn when he found a sudden resistance. The chain which the fisherman had fixed round the end prevented the bridge from rising. As the man had shouted, Archie and his three comrades were entering the gate. Simultaneously they emptied their baskets before them. Concealed among the fish were four logs of wood; two were three feet long, the full depth of the baskets; two were short wedge-shaped pieces. Before the soldiers in front had time even to turn round, the two long pieces were placed upright in the grooves which the portcullis would fall, while the two wedge-shaped pieces were thrust into the jamb of the gate so as to prevent it from closing. Then the four men drew long swords hidden beneath their garments and fell upon the soldiers.

Chapter 26

Edinburgh

So vigilant was the watch in the castle of Dunottar that the instant the cry of alarm rose almost simultaneously from the warder (gatekeeper) above and the soldiers at the gate, the portcullis came thundering down. It was caught, however, by the two upright blocks of wood, and remained suspended three feet above the sill. The armed guards at the gate instantly fell upon Archie and his companions, while others endeavored in vain to close the gates. Scarcely had the swords clashed when the man who had chained down the drawbridge joined Archie, and the five with their heavy broadswords kept at bay the soldiers who pressed upon them; but for only a minute or two did they have to bear the brunt of the attack unsupported, for William Orr and the five men who had been loitering near the moat dashed across the bridge, and passing under the portcullis joined the little band.

The alarm had now spread throughout the castle, and the governor himself, followed by many of his men, came rushing down to the spot, shouting furious orders to the gatekeeper to raise the drawbridge, being in ignorance that it was firmly fixed at the outer end.

Archie and his followers were now hotly pressed, but soon a thunder of steps was heard on the drawbridge, and the whole of the band, together with some twenty or thirty of the fishermen, passed under the portcullis and joined them. Archie now took the offensive, and bearing down all opposition burst with his men into the courtyard.

The combat was desperate but short. The governor with some of his soldiers fought stoutly, but the suddenness of the surprise and the fury and vigor with which they were attacked shook the courage of many of the soldiers. Some, instead of joining in the fray, at once threw away their arms and tried to conceal themselves, others fought feebly and half-heartedly, and the cries of "A

Forbes! A Forbes! Scotland! Scotland!" rose louder and louder as
the assailants gradually beat down all resistance. In ten minutes
from the falling of the portcullis all resistance was virtually over.
The governor himself fell by the hand of Archie Forbes, and at his
death those who had hitherto resisted threw down their arms and
called for quarter. This was given, and the following day the prisoners were marched under a strong guard down to Montrose,
there to be confined until orders for their disposal were received
from the king. For the next fortnight Archie and his retainers,
aided by the whole of the villagers, labored to dismantle the castle. The battlements were thrown down into the moat, several
wide breaches were made in the walls, and large quantities of
straw and wood piled up in the keep and turrets. These were then
fired, and the Castle of Dunottar was soon reduced to an empty
and gaping shell. Then Archie marched south, and remained quietly at home until the term of rest granted him by the king had
expired.

Two girls and a son had by this time been born to him, and the
months passed quietly and happily away until Bruce summoned
him to join, with his retainers, the force with which Randolph
had sat down before Edinburgh Castle. Randolph was delighted at
this accession of strength. Between him and Douglas a generous
rivalry in gallant actions continually went on, and Douglas had
scored the last triumph. The castle of Roxburgh had long been a
source of trouble to the Scots. Standing on a rocky eminence on
the margin of the Teviot, just at its junction with the Tweed and
within eight miles of the border, it had constituted an open door
into Scotland, and either through it or through Berwick the tides
of invasion had ever flowed. The castle was very strongly fortified, so much so that the garrison, deeming themselves perfectly
safe from assault, had grown careless. The commandant was a
Burgundian knight, Gillemin de Fienne. Douglas chose Shrove
Tuesday for his attack. Being a feast day of the church before the
long lenten fast the garrison would be sure to indulge in convivi-
ality and the watch would be less strict than usual. Douglas and
his followers, supplied with scaling-ladders, crept on all fours
towards the walls. The night was still and they could hear the
sentries' conversation. They had noticed the objects advancing,
but in the darkness mistook them for the cattle of a neighboring

farmer. Silently the ladders were fixed and mounted, and with the dreaded war cry, "A Douglas! A Douglas!" the assailants burst into the castle, slaying the sentries and pouring down upon the startled revelers. Fienne and his men fought gallantly for a time, but at length all surrendered, with the exception of the governor himself and a few of his immediate followers, who retired into a tower, where they defended themselves until the following day; then Fienne being seriously wounded, the little party also surrendered. As Douglas had no personal quarrel with the garrison of Roxburgh such as he bore with those who occupied his ancestral castle, he abstained from any unnecessary cruelties, and allowed the garrison to withdraw to England, where Fienne soon afterwards died of his wounds. The castle was as usual leveled to the ground, and as the stronghold of Carlaverock soon afterwards surrendered, the districts of Tweeddale and Galloway were now completely cleared of the English, with the exception of the Castle of Jedburgh, which they still held.

Randolph had been created Earl of Moray, and after establishing himself in his new earldom he had returned with his feudal followers and laid siege to Edinburgh, whose castle was considered all but impregnable. It had been in the possession of the English ever since it was captured by Edward I in 1296, and was strongly garrisoned and well provisioned.

Even when joined by Archie Forbes and his retainers Randolph felt that the castle could not be captured by force. The various attempts which he made were unproductive, and it was by stratagem only that he could hope to carry it. The news of the capture of Roxburgh by Douglas increased his anxiety to succeed. Accompanied by Archie he rode round the foot of the steep rock on which the castle stands, eagerly scanning its irregularities to see if by any possibility it could be scaled.

"I would give a brave reward," he said to Archie, "to any who could show us a way of climbing those rocks, which, methinks, even a goat could scarcely manage to ascend."

"I can tell you a way," a Scottish soldier who was standing a few paces off when he made the remark, said, saluting the earl. "It needs a sure foot and a stout heart, but I can lead a score of men with such qualifications to the foot of yonder walls;" and he pointed to the castle rising abruptly from the edge of the rocks.

"If you can make good your word, my brave fellow," Randolph said, "you may ask your own reward, and I pledge you my word, that if it be aught in reason it shall be granted. But who are you, and how did it come that you know of a way where none is supposed to exist?"

"My name is William Francus," the soldier said. "I was at one time, before the king took up arms, a soldier in the castle there. I had a sweetheart in the town, and as my turn to go out from the castle came but slowly, I used at night to steal away to visit her. I found after a great search that on the face of yonder wall where it looks the steepest, and where in consequence but slight watch is kept, a man with steady foot and head could make shift to climb up and down, and thus, if you please, will I guide a party to the top of the rock."

"It looks impossible," Randolph said, gazing at the precipice; "but as you tell me that you have done it others can do the same. I will myself follow your guidance."

"And I," Archie said.

"What, Sir Archie, think you is the smallest number of men with whom, having once gained footing on the wall, we may fight our way to the gates and let in our friends."

"I should think," Archie replied, "that with thirty men we might manage to do so. The confusion in the garrison will be extreme at so unexpected a surprise, and if we divide into two parties and press forward by different ways they will think rather of holding together and defending themselves than of checking our course; and one or other of the parties should surely be able to make its way to the gates."

"Thirty let it be then," Randolph said. "Do you choose fifteen active and vigilant men from among your retainers; I will pick as many from mine, and as there is no use in delaying let us carry out the enterprise this very night; of course the rest of our men must gather near the gates in readiness to rush in when we throw them open."

As soon as it was dark the little party of adventurers set out on their way. Francus acted as guide, and under his leading they climbed with vast difficulty and no little danger up the face of the precipice until they reached a comparatively easy spot, where they sat down to recover their breath before they prepared for the final effort.

They could hear the sentries above speaking to each other, and they held their breath when one of them, exclaiming suddenly, "I can see you!" threw down a stone from the battlement, which leapt, crashing down the face of the rock close beside them. Great was their relief when a loud laugh from above told them that the sentry had been in jest, and had but tried to startle his comrade; then the two sentries, conversing as they went, moved away to another part of the walls.

The ascent was now continued, and proved even more difficult than that which they had passed. They were forced continually to halt, while those in front helped those following them, or were themselves hoisted up by the men behind. At last, panting and breathless, they stood on the summit of the rock, on a narrow ledge, with the castle wall rising in front of them. They had, with enormous difficulty, brought up a light ladder with them. This was placed against the wall. Francus was the first to mount, and was followed by Sir Andrew Grey, whom Randolph had invited, by Archie Forbes, and by the earl. Just as the latter stepped on to the battlements the sentries caught sight of them and shouted:

"Treason! treason! to arms!" An instant stir was heard in the castle. Rapidly the thirty men followed each other up the ladder, and so soon as the last had gained the battlements they divided in three bodies, each headed by one of the leaders. One party descended straight into the castle and there attacked the soldiers who were hurrying to arms, while the others ran along the wall in opposite directions, cutting down the sentries and brushing aside all opposition until together they met at the gate. This was thrown open, and the Scots outside running up at the top of their speed poured into the castle. At first Randolph's party, which had descended into the courtyard, had been hotly pressed, and had with difficulty defended themselves; but the attention of the startled garrison was distracted by the shouts upon the walls, which told that other parties of their assailants had gained footing there. All sorts of contradictory orders were issued. One commanded them to cut down the little party opposed to them, another ordered them to hurry to the walls, a third to seize the gate and see that it was not opened. The confusion reached its height as the Scots poured in through the open gate. The garrison, surprised and confounded as they were at this, to them, almost magical seizure of the castle by their foes, fought bravely until the governor and many of the officers were killed. Some of the men threw down their arms, and others, taking advantage of their knowledge of the castle, made their way to the gate and escaped into the open country.

The news of the capture was immediately sent to the king, by whose orders the castle and walls were razed to the ground. Thus another of the strongholds, by whose possession the English were enabled to domineer over the whole of the surrounding country, was destroyed.

While Douglas and Randolph were thus distinguishing themselves Edward Bruce captured the castle of Rutherglen, and afterwards the town of Dundee; and now, save Stirling Castle, scarcely a hold in all Scotland remained in English hands. Thus was Scotland almost cleared of the invader, not by the efforts of the people at large, but by a series of the most daring and hazardous adventures by the king himself and three or four of his knights, aided only by their personal retainers. For nine years they had continued their career unchecked, capturing castle by castle and town by town, defeating such small bodies of troops as took the field against them.

After Edward Bruce had captured Dundee he laid siege to Stirling. As this castle had for many months resisted Edward I backed by the whole power of England, Bruce could make little impression upon it with the limited appliances at his disposal. From February till the twenty-fourth of June the siege continued, when the governor, Sir Philip Mowbray, becoming apprehensive that his provisions would not much longer hold out, induced Edward Bruce to agree to stop the siege on condition that if by the twenty-fourth of June, 1314, the castle was not effectually relieved by an English force, it should then be surrendered.

No satisfactory explanation has ever been given of the reasons which induced Edward Bruce to agree to so one-sided a bargain. He had already invested the place for four months, there was no possibility of an army being collected in England for its relief for many months to come, and long before this could arrive the garrison would have been starved into surrender. By giving England a year to relieve the place, he virtually challenged that country to put forth all its strength and held out an inducement to it to make that effort, which internal dissension had hitherto prevented. The only feasible explanation is that Edward Bruce was weary of being kept inactive so long a time before the walls of the fortress which he was unable to capture, and that he made the arrangement from sheer impatience and thoughtlessness and without consideration of the storm which he was bringing upon Scotland. Had it been otherwise he would surely have consulted the king before entering upon an agreement of such extreme importance.

Bruce, when he heard of this rash treaty, was highly displeased, but he nevertheless accepted the terms; and both parties began at once their preparations for the crowning struggle of the war. The English saw that now or never must they crush out the movement which, step by step, had wrested from them all the conquests which had been won with such vast effort under Edward I; while Bruce saw that a defeat would entail the loss of all that he had struggled for and won during so many years.

King Edward issued summonses to the whole of the barons of England and Wales to meet him at Berwick by the eleventh of June with all their feudal following, while the sheriffs of the various counties and towns were called upon to supply twenty-seven thousand foot soldiers. The English of the settlements in Ireland were also summoned, besides O'Connor, Prince of Connaught, and twenty-five other native Irish chiefs, with their following, all of whom were to be under the command of Richard de Burgh, Earl of Ulster.

The Prince Bishop of Constance was requested to furnish a body of mounted crossbow men. A royal fleet of twenty-three vessels was appointed to assemble for the purpose of operating on the east coast, while the seaports were commanded to fit out another fleet of thirty vessels. A third fleet was ordered to assemble in the west, which John of Lorne was appointed to command under the title of High admiral of the Western Fleet of England. From Aquitaine and the French possessions the vassals were called upon to attend with their men-at-arms, and many knights from France, Gascony, and Germany took part in the enterprise.

Thus, at the appointed time over one hundred thousand men assembled at Berwick, of whom forty thousand were men-at-arms, and the rest archers and pikemen. For the great armament the most ample arrangements were made in the way of warlike stores, provisions, tents, and means of transport, together with the necessary workmen, artificers, and attendants.

This army surpassed both in numbers and equipments any that Edward I had ever led into Scotland, and is considered to have been the most numerous and best equipped that ever before or since has gathered on English ground. Of the whole of the great nobles of England only four were absent —the Earls of Warrenne, Lancaster, Arundel, and Warwick—who, however, sent their feudal arrays under the charge of relations.

Among the leaders of this great army were the Earls of Gloucester, Pembroke, Hereford, and Angus, Lord Clifford, Sir John Comyn, Sir Henry Beaumont, Sir John Seagrave, Sir Edmund Morley, Sir Ingram de Umfraville, Sir Marmaduke de Twenge, and Sir Giles de Argentine, one of the most famous of the Continental knights.

While this vast army had been preparing, Bruce had made every effort to meet the storm, and all who were loyal and who were able to carry weapons were summoned to meet at Torwood, near Stirling, previous to the twenty-fourth of June. Here Edward Bruce, Sir James Douglas, Randolph, Earl of Moray, Walter the Steward, Angus of Isla, Sir Archibald Forbes, and a few other knights and barons assembled with thirty thousand fighting men, besides camp followers and servants. It was a small force indeed to meet the great army which was advancing against it, and in cavalry in particular it was extremely weak. The English army crossed the border, and marched by Linlithgow and Falkirk toward the Torwood.

Each army had stirring memories to inspire it, for the English in their march crossed over the field of Falkirk, where sixteen years before they had crushed the stubborn squares of Wallace; while from the spot which Bruce selected as his battleground could be seen the Abbey Craig, overlooking the scene of the Scottish victory of Stirling Bridge. On the approach of the English the Scottish fell back from the Torwood to some high ground near Stirling now called the New Park. The lower ground, now rich agricultural land called the Carse, was then wholly swamp. Had it not been so, the position now taken up by Bruce would have laid the road to Stirling open to the English.

The Scottish army was divided into four divisions. The center was commanded by Randolph. Edward Bruce commanded the second, which formed the right wing. Walter the Steward commanded the left wing, under the guidance of Douglas, while the king himself took command of the fourth division, which formed the reserve, and was stationed in rear of the center in readiness to move to the assistance of either of the other divisions which might be hard pressed. The camp-followers, with the baggage and provisions, were stationed behind the Gillies Hill.

The road by which the English would advance was the old Roman causeway running nearly north and south. The Bannock Burn was fordable from a spot near the Park Mill down to the village of Bannockburn. Above, the banks were too high and steep to be passed; while below, where ran the Bannock through the carse, the swamps prevented passage. The army was therefore drawn up, with its left resting on the sharp angle of the burn above the Park Mill, and extended where the villages of Easterton, Borestine, and Brachead now stand to the spot where the road crosses the river at the village of Bannockburn. In its front, between it and the river, were two bogs, known as Halberts Bog and Milton Bog, while, where unprotected by these bogs, the whole ground was studded with deep pits; in these stakes were inserted, and they were then covered with branches and grass. Randolph's center was at Borestine, Bruce's reserve a little behind, and the rock in which his flagstaff was placed during the battle is still to be seen. To Randolph, in addition to his command of the center division, was committed the trust of preventing any body of English from passing along at the edge of the carse, and so making round to the relief of Stirling.

On the morning of Sunday, the twenty-third of June, immediately after sunrise, the Scots attended mass, and confessed as men who had devoted themselves to death. The king, having surveyed the field, caused a proclamation to be made that whosoever felt himself unequal to take part in the battle was at liberty to withdraw. Then, knowing from his scouts that the enemy had passed the night at Falkirk, six or seven miles off, he sent out Sir James

Douglas and Sir Robert Keith with a party of horsemen to reconnoitre the advance.

The knights had not gone far when they saw the great army advancing, with the sun shining bright on innumerable standards and pennons, and glistening from lancehead, spear, and armor. So grand and terrible was the appearance of the army that upon receiving the report of Douglas and Keith the king thought it prudent to conceal its full extent, and caused it to be rumored that the enemy, although numerous, was approaching in a disorderly manner.

The experienced generals of King Edward now determined upon making an attempt to relieve Stirling Castle without fighting a pitched battle upon ground chosen by the enemy. Had this attempt been successful, the great army, instead of being obliged to cross a rapid stream and attack an enemy posted behind morasses, would have been free to operate as it chose, to have advanced against the strongholds which had been captured by the Scots, and to force Bruce to give battle upon ground of their choosing. Lord Clifford was therefore despatched with eight hundred picked men-at-arms to cross the Bannock beyond the left wing of the Scottish army, to make their way across the carse, and so to reach Stirling. The ground was, indeed, impassable for a large army; but the troops took with them bundles of wood and beams, by which they could make a passage across the deeper parts of the swamp, and bridge the little streams which meandered through it.

As there was no prospect of an immediate engagement, Randolph, Douglas, and the king had left their respective divisions, and had taken up their positions at the village of St. Ninians, on high ground behind the army, whence they could have a clear view of the approaching English army. Archie Forbes had accompanied Randolph, to whose division he, with his retainers, was attached. Randolph had with him five hundred pikemen, whom he had withdrawn from his division in order to carry out his appointed task of seeing that the English did not pass along the low ground at the edge of the carse behind St. Ninians to the relief of Stirling; but so absorbed were knights and men-at-arms in watching the magnificent array advancing against the Scottish position that they forgot to keep a watch over the low ground.

Suddenly one of the men, who had straggled away into the village, ran up with the startling news that a large party of English horsemen had crossed the corner of the carse, and had already reached the low ground beyond the church.

"A rose has fallen from your chaplet, Randolph," the king said angrily.

Without a moment's loss of time Randolph and Archie Forbes set off with the spearmen at a run, and succeeded in meeting the horsemen at the hamlet of Newhouse. The mail-clad horsemen, confident in their numbers, their armor, and horses, laid their lances in rest, struck spurs into their steeds, and, led by Sir William Daynecourt, charged down upon the Scottish spearmen. Two hundred of these consisted of Archie Forbes' retainers, all veterans in war, and who had more than once, shoulder to shoulder, repelled the onslaught of the mailed chivalry of England. Animated by the voices of their lord and Randolph, these, with Moray's own pikemen, threw themselves into a solid square, and, surrounded by a hedge of spears, steadily received the furious onslaught of the cavalry. Daynecourt and many of his men were at the first onslaught unhorsed and slain, and those who followed were repulsed. Again and again they charged down upon the pikemen, but the dense array of spears was more than a match for the lances of the cavalry, and as the horses were wounded and fell, or their riders were unhorsed, men rushed out from the square, and with ax and dagger completed the work. Still the English pressed them hard, and Douglas, from the distance, seeing how hotly the pikemen were pressed by the cavalry, begged the king to allow him to go to Randolph's assistance. Bruce, however, would permit no change in his position, and said that Randolph must stand or fall by himself. Douglas, however, urged that he should be allowed to go forward with the small body of retainers which he had with him. The king consented, and Douglas set off with his men.

When the English saw him approach they recoiled somewhat from the square, and Douglas, being now better able to see what was going on, commanded his followers to halt, saying that Randolph would speedily prove victorious without their help, and were they now to take part in the struggle they would only lessen the credit of those who had already all but won the victory. Seeing the enemy in some confusion from the appearance of the rein-forcement, Randolph and Archie now gave the word for their men to charge, and these, rushing on with spear and ax, completed the discomfiture of the enemy, killed many, and forced the rest to take flight. Numbers, however, were taken. Randolph is said to have had but two men killed in the struggle.

Chapter 27

Bannockburn

After the complete defeat of the party under Lord Clifford, and the failure of their attempt to relieve Stirling, Randolph and Douglas returned together to the king. The news of their success spread rapidly, and when Randolph rode down from St. Ninians to his division, loud cheers broke from the whole Scottish army, who were vastly encouraged at so fair a commencement of their struggle with the English.

The English army was still advancing slowly, and Bruce and his leaders rode down to the front of the Scottish line, seeing that all was in order and encouraging the men with cheering words. When the English army approached the stream King Edward ordered a halt to be sounded for the purpose of holding a council, whether it was best to encamp for the night or at once to advance against the enemy. The Earls of Gloucester and Hereford, who commanded the first division, were so far ahead that they did not hear the sound of the trumpet, and continuing their onward march crossed the Bannock Burn and moved on toward the enemy positions. In front of the ranks of the defenders the king was riding upon a small horse, not having as yet put on his armor for the battle. On his helmet he wore a purple cap surmounted by a crown. Seeing him thus within easy reach, Sir Henry de Bohun, cousin of the Earl of Hereford, laid his lance in rest and spurred down upon the king. Bruce could have retired within the lines of his soldiers; but confident in his own prowess, and judging how great an effect a success under such circumstances would have upon the spirits of his troops, he spurred forward to meet his assailant armed only with his ax. As the English knight came thundering down, the king touched his palfrey with his spur, and the horse, carrying but a light weight, swerved quickly aside. De Bohun's lance missed his stroke, and before he had time to draw rein or sword, the king, standing up in his stirrups, dealt him so tremendous a blow with his ax as he passed, that it cleft through helmet and brain, and the knight fell dead to the ground.

With a shout of triumph the Scots rushed forward and drove the English advance-guard back across the stream; then the Scottish leaders led their men back again to the position which they had left, and re-formed their array. Douglas, Edward Bruce, Randolph, and Archie Forbes now gathered round the king and remonstrated with him on the rashness of an act which might have proved fatal to the whole army. The king smiled at such remonstrances from four men who had, above all others, distinguished themselves for their rash and daring exploits, and shrugging his shoulders observed only that it was a pity he had broken the shaft of his favorite ax.

The English forces now withdrew to a short distance, and it became evident that the great battle would be delayed till the morrow. The Scottish army therefore broke its ranks and prepared to pass the night on the spot where it stood. The king assembled all his principal leaders round him, and after thanking God for so fair a beginning of the fight as had that day been made, he pointed out to them how great an effect the two preliminary skirmishes would have upon the spirits of both armies, and expressed his confidence in the final result. He urged upon them the necessity for keeping their followers well in hand, and meeting the charges of the enemy's horse steadily with their spears. He especially warned them, after repulsing a charge, against allowing their men to break their array, either to plunder or take prisoners, so long as the battle lasted, as the whole riches of the English camp would fall into their hands if successful. He pledged himself that the heirs of all who fell should have the succession of their estates free from the usual feudal burdens on such occasions.

The night passed quietly, and in the morning both armies formed their array for battle. Bruce, as was customary, conferred the honor of knighthood upon several of his leaders. Then all proceeded to their allotted places and awaited the onset. Beyond the stream and extending far away towards the rising ground were the English squadrons in their glittering arms, the first division in line, the others in heavy masses behind them. Now that the Scots were fairly drawn up in order of battle, the English could

Bruce Slays Sir Henry De Bohun

see how small was their number in comparison with their own, and the king in surprise exclaimed to Sir Ingram de Umfraville:

"What! will yonder Scots fight us?"

"That verily will they," the knight replied, for he had many a time been engaged in stout conflict with them, and knew how hard it was even for mail-clad knights to break through the close lines of Scottish spears. So high a respect had he for their valor, that he urged the king to pretend to retire suddenly beyond the camp, when the Scots, in spite of their leaders, would be sure to leave their ranks and flock into the camp to plunder, when they might be easily dispersed and cut to pieces. The king, however, refused to adopt the suggestion, saying, that no one must be able to accuse him of avoiding a battle or of withdrawing his army before such a rabble.

As the armies stood confronting each other in battle array a priest passed along the Scottish front, crucifix in hand, exhorting all to fight to the death for the liberty of their country. As he passed along the line each company knelt in an attitude of prayer. King Edward, seeing this, exclaimed to Sir Ingram:

"See yonder folk kneel to ask for mercy!"

"Ay, sire," the knight said, looking earnestly at the Scots, "they kneel and ask for mercy, but not of you; it is for their sins they ask mercy of God. I know these men, and have met and fought them; and I tell you that assuredly they will win or die, and not even when death looks them in the face will they turn to fly."

"Then if it must be so," said the king, "let us charge."

The trumpet sounded along the line. First the immense body of English archers crossed the burn and opened the battle by pouring clouds of arrows into the Scottish ranks. The Scottish archers, who were in advance of their spearmen, were speedily driven back to shelter beyond their line, for not only were the English vastly more numerous, but they shot much further and more accurately. And now the knights and men-at-arms, on their steel-clad horses, crossed the burn. They were aware of the existence of Milton Bog, which covered the Scottish center, and they directed their charge upon the division of Edward Bruce on the Scottish right. The crash as the mailed horses burst down upon the wood of Scottish spears was tremendous. Bruce's men held firm, and the English in vain strove to break through their serried line of spears. It was a repetition of the fight of the previous day, but on a greater scale. With lance and battle-ax the chivalry of England strove to break the ranks of the Scots, while with serried lines of spears, four deep, the Scottish held their own. Every horse which, wounded or riderless, turned and dashed through the ranks of the English, added to the confusion. This was much further increased by the deep holes into which the horses were continually falling, and breaking up all order in their ranks. Those behind pressed forward to reach the front, and their very numbers added to their difficulty.

The English were divided into ten divisions or "battles," and these one by one crossed the stream with banners flying, and still avoiding the center, followed the line taken by the first, and pressed forward to take part in the fight.

Randolph now moved with the center to the support of the hardly pressed right, and his division, as well as that of Edward Bruce, seemed to be lost among the multitude of their opponents. Stewart and Douglas moved their division to the right and threw themselves into the fight, and the three Scottish divisions were now fighting side by side, but with a much smaller front than that which they had originally occupied. For a time the battle raged furiously without superiority on either side. The Scots possessed the great advantage that, standing close together in ranks four deep, every man was engaged, while of the mounted knights and men-at-arms who pressed upon them, only the front line was doing efficient service. Not only, therefore, was the vast numerical superiority of the English useless to them, but actually a far larger number of the Scottish than of themselves were using their weapons in the front rank, while the great proportion of the English remained helplessly behind their fighting line, unable to take any part whatever in the fight. Now, however, the English archers came into play again, and firing high into the air rained their arrows almost perpendicularly down upon the Scottish ranks. Had this continued it would have been as fatal to the Scots at Bannockburn as it was at Falkirk; but happily the Scottish cavalry that was chosen to deal with this problem were not commanded by traitors, and at the critical moment the king launched Sir Robert Keith, the marshal of Scotland, against the archers with five hundred horsemen. These burst suddenly down upon the flank of the archers and literally swept them before them. Great numbers were killed, others fell back upon the lines of horsemen who were ranged behind, impatient to take their share in the battle; these tried to drive them back again, but the archers were disheartened, and retreating across the stream took no further part in the battle. The charge of the Scottish horses should have been foreseen and provided against by placing strong bodies of men-at-arms on the flanks of the archers, as these lightly armed troops were wholly unable to withstand a charge by cavalry.

The Scottish archers, now that their formidable opponents had left the field, opened a heavy fire over the heads of the pikemen upon the horsemen surrounding the squares; and when they had shot away their arrows, sallied out and mingled in the confused mass of the enemy, doing tremendous execution with their axes and knives. Hitherto the king had kept his reserve in hand; but now that the English archers were defeated and their horsemen in inextricable confusion, he moved his division down and joined in the mêlée.

Every Scottish soldier on the field was now engaged. No longer did the battle-cries of the various parties rise in the air. Men had no breath to waste in shouting, but each fought silently and desperately with spear or ax. The sound of clanging blows of weapons, of mighty crash of sword or battle-ax on steel armor, with the cries and groans of wounded men were alone heard. Over and over again the English knights drew back a little so as to gain speed and impetus, and flung themselves on the Scottish spears, but always without effect, while little by little the close ranks of the Scots pressed forward until, as the space between their front and the brook narrowed, the whole of the English divisions became pushed together, more and more incapable of using their strength to advantage. The slaughter in their front divisions had already been terrible. Again and again fresh troops had taken the places of those who had formed the front ranks, but many of their best and bravest had fallen. The confusion was too great for their leaders to be able to direct them with advantage, and seeing the failure of every effort to break the Scottish ranks, borne back by the slow advance of the hedge of spears, harassed by the archers who dived below the horses, stabbing them in their bellies, or rising suddenly between them to smite down the riders with their keen, heavy, shorthanded axes, the English began to lose heart, and as they wavered the Scots pressed forward more eagerly, shouting, "On them! on them! They give way! they give way!"

At this critical moment the servants, teamsters, and camp-followers who had been left behind Gills Hill, showed themselves. Some of their number from the eminence had watched the desperate struggle, and on hearing how their soldiers were pressed by the surrounding host of English men-at-arms they could no longer remain inactive. All men carried arms in those days. They hastily chose one of their own number as leader, and fastening some sheets to tent poles as banners, they advanced over the hill in battle array, and moved down to join their comrades.

The sight of what they deemed a fresh division advancing to the assistance of the Scottish brought to a climax the hesitation which had begun to shake the English, and ensured their defeat. Those in the rear turned bridle hastily, and crossing the Bannock Burn, galloped away. The movement so begun, spread rapidly; and although those in front still continued their desperate efforts to break the line of Scottish spears, the day was now hopelessly lost. Seeing that this was so, the Earl of Pembroke seized the king's rein and constrained him to leave the field with a bodyguard of five hundred horsemen. Sir Giles de Argentine, who had hitherto remained by the king's side, and who was esteemed the third best knight in Europe—the Emperor Henry of Luxemburg and Robert Bruce being reckoned the two best—bade farewell to the king as he rode off.

"Farewell, sire," he said, "since you must go, but I at least must return; I have never yet fled from an enemy, and will remain and die rather than fly and live in disgrace."

So saying, the knight spurred down to the conflict, and charged against the array of Edward Bruce, and there fell fighting valiantly. The flight of the king and his attendants was the signal for a general rout. Great numbers were slain, many men were drowned in the Forth, and the channel of the Bannock was so choked with the bodies of dead men and horses that one could pass over dry shod. The scattered parties of English were still so numerous that Bruce held his men well in hand until these had

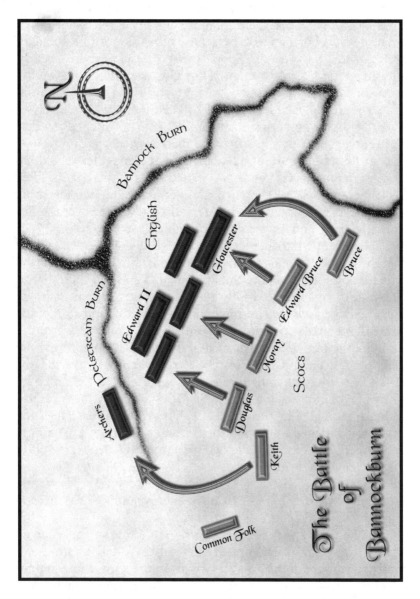

yielded themselves prisoners. Douglas was charged to pursue the king, but he could only muster sixty horsemen. A short distance from the field he met a Scottish baron, Sir Laurence Abernethy, with twenty-four men-at-arms, on his way to join the English, for even as yet but few of the Scottish nobles were on the side of the king. Upon hearing what had happened, Sir Laurence, with the easy facility which distinguished the Scottish nobles of the period, at once changed sides, swore fealty to Bruce, and joined Douglas in the pursuit of his late friends. They overtook the king's party at Linlithgow, but Pembroke kept his men well-together, and while still retiring, showed so bold an appearance that Douglas did not venture to charge. Finally the English reached the Castle of Dunbar, where the king and his immediate attendants were received by his ally, Earl Patrick of Dunbar. So cowed were the fugitives that they left their horses outside the castle gate, and these were captured by their pursuers. The main body of the king's bodyguard continued their way in good order, and reached Berwick in safety. Edward gained England in a fishing boat from Dunbar. Eighteen years had elapsed since his father had entered Scotland with an army deemed sufficient for its entire subjugation; had sacked and destroyed the rich and prosperous town of Berwick, routed the army of Baliol, marched through Scotland, and, as he believed, permanently settled his conquest. Now the son had lost all that his father had won.

Among the fugitive remains of the English army were a considerable body of Welsh, who, being lightly armed, fled at full speed toward the border, but being easily distinguished by their white dresses and the absence of defensive armor, almost all were slain by the peasantry. The Earl of Hereford, the Earl of Angus, Sir John Seagrave, Sir Anthony Lucy, Sir Ingram de Umfraville, with a great number of knights, six hundred men-at-arms, and one thousand infantry, keeping together, marched south toward Carlisle.

As they passed Bothwell Castle, which was held by the governor for England, the earls and knights entered the castle, their followers remaining without; but the governor, on hearing the result of the battle, closed the gates and took all who had entered prisoners, and, changing sides, handed them over to Bruce. Their followers continued their march south, but were for the most part slain or taken prisoners before they reached the border.

When all resistance had ceased on the field the victors collected the spoil. This consisted of the vast camp, the treasures intended for the payment of the army, the herds of cattle, and stores of provisions, wine, and forage; the rich wearing apparel and arms of the knights and nobles killed or made prisoners, many valuable horses, and the prisoners who would have to be ransomed, among whom were twenty-two barons and sixty knights. The spoil was estimated at £200,000, equal to £3,000,000 of money in these days. The king refused to take any share in this plunder, dividing it wholly among his troops. Thirty thousand English lay dead on the field, including two hundred knights and seven hundred esquires, and among the most distinguished of the dead were the Earl of Gloucester, Sir Giles de Argentine, Lord Robert Clifford, Sir Edmund Manley, Seneschal of England, Sir William de Mareschal, Sir Payne Tybtot, and Sir John Comyn. Sir Marmaduke de Twenge was among the prisoners.

Bruce's conduct to his prisoners was even more honorable to himself than was the great victory that he had won. In spite of his three brothers, his brother-in-law Seaton, his friends Athole and Frazer, having been executed by the English, and the knowledge that their mangled remains were still exposed over London Bridge and the gates of Carlisle and Newcastle—in spite of the barbarous and lengthened captivity of his wife, his sister and daughter, and his friend the Countess of Buchan—in spite of the conviction that had he himself been made prisoner he would at once have been sent to the scaffold—Bruce behaved with a magnanimity and generosity of the highest kind. Every honor was paid to the English dead, and the bodies of the chief among these were sent to their relatives in England, and the prisoners were all either ransomed or exchanged. Sir Marmaduke de Twenge was dismissed free of ransom and loaded with gifts, and even the Scottish nobles, such as Sir Philip Mowbray, who were taken fighting in the ranks of their country's enemy, were forgiven. This noble example exercised but little influence upon the English. When Edward Bruce was killed four years afterwards at Dundalk in Ireland, his body was quartered and distributed, and his head presented to the English king, who bestowed upon Bermingham—who commanded the English and sent the gift to him—the dignity of Earl of Louth.

Among the prisoners was Edward's poet-laureate, Baston, a Carmelite friar, who had accompanied the army for the purpose of writing a poem on the English victory. His ransom was fixed at a poem on the Scottish victory at Bannockburn, which the friar was forced to supply.

With Bannockburn ended all hope on the part of the English of subjugating Scotland; but the war continued fitfully for fourteen years. The Scots frequently invaded England and levied heavy contributions from the northern counties and towns, and the English occasionally retaliated by the same process; but at length peace was signed at Northampton.

In 1315, a parliament assembled at Ayr for the purpose of regulating the succession to the throne. It was then agreed that in case of the king's death without male issue his brother Edward should succeed to it; and that if Edward left no heirs, the children of Marjory, the king's daughter, should succeed. Shortly afterwards Marjory was married to Walter the Steward. Edward Bruce was killed unmarried. A son was afterwards born to the king, who reigned as David II, but having died without issue, the son of Marjory and the Steward became king. The hereditary title of Steward was used as the surname for the family, and thus from them descended the royal line of Stewart or Stuart, through which Queen Victoria reigned over Great Britain, Ireland, and their vast dependencies.

After Bannockburn Archie Forbes went no more to the wars. He was raised to the dignity of Baron Forbes by the king, and was ever rewarded by him as one of his most trusty counselors, and his descendants played a prominent part in the changing and eventful history of Scotland; but the proudest tradition of the family was that their ancestor had fought as a patriot by the side of Bruce and Wallace when scarce a noble of Scotland but was leagued with the English oppressors of their country.

As for the valiant Robert Bruce, King of Scotland, he seemed only to wait for the final deliverance of his country to close his heroic career. He retired to his castle called Cardross near Dumberton. There he lived in princely retirement, entertaining nobles and distributing to the needs of the poor. As the years passed, Robert Bruce's health continued to decline, in part because of a disease similar in many respects to leprosy.

In 1329, when Scotland was in the midst of a truce with England and at relative peace with its neighbors, King Robert was attacked by so severe an illness that he knew his end was near.

Robert Bruce, therefore, summoned together all the chiefs and barons in whom he most confided, and informed them of his terminal illness and his earnest desire that his son David be crowned king when he came to a proper age. King Robert then called to his bedside the gallant Lord James Douglas, and said to him, in the presence of the others:

"My dear friend, Lord James Douglas, you know that I have had much to do, and I have suffered many troubles, during the time I have lived, to support the rights of my crown: at the time that I was most occupied, I made a vow, the non-accomplishment of which gives me much uneasiness—I vowed that if I could finish my wars in such a manner that I might have quiet to govern peaceably, I would go and make war against the enemies of our Lord Jesus Christ, and the adversaries of the Christian faith. To this point my heart has always leaned; but our Lord was not willing, and gave me so much to do in my lifetime, and has now laid such a heavy sickness upon me, that, since my body cannot accomplish what my heart wishes, I will send my heart in the stead of my body to fulfill my vow. And, as I do not know any one knight so gallant or enterprising, or better formed to complete my intentions than yourself, I beg and entreat of you, dear and special friend, as earnestly as I can, that you would have the goodness to undertake this expedition for the love of me, and to acquit my soul to our Lord and Savior; for I have that opinion of your nobleness, and loyalty, that, if you undertake it, it cannot fail of success—and I shall die more contented; but it must be executed as follows:

"I will, that as soon as I shall be dead, you take my heart from my body and have it well embalmed; that you will also take as much money from my treasury as will appear to you sufficient to perform your journey, as well as for all those whom you may choose to take with you in your train. You will then deposit your charge at the Holy Sepulcher of our Lord, where he was buried, since my body cannot go there. You will not be sparing of expense—and provide yourself with such company and such things as may be suitable to your rank—and wherever you pass, you will let it be known that you bear the heart of King Robert of Scotland, which you are carrying beyond seas by his command, since his body cannot go thither."

All those present began bewailing bitterly; and when the Lord James could speak, he gave his promise upon his knighthood.

The king said: "Thanks be to God! for I shall now die in peace, since I know that the most valiant and accomplished knight of my kingdom will perform that for me which I am unable to do for myself."

Soon afterwards the valiant Robert Bruce, king of Scotland, departed this life on the seventh of June, 1329. His heart was embalmed, and his body buried in the monastery of Dunfermline.

Robert the Bruce's Dying Prayer

Good King Robert is near to death,
That great heart is beating so slow,
Around his bed in tears all stand,
Dreading and fearing he has to go.

Good King Robert with trembling voice:
"No need to weep, no need of tears.
My life is aye in Christ's saving hands,
About me and Scotland have no fears.

"You'll have no tears, if united you stay,
All foes will break on unity's rock.
Be just and kind and strong and brave,
And at your foes you'll always mock."

Good King Robert puts hand on heart,
"This heart aye beat for God and Scotland.
When things were blackest, I vowed to go,
And fight for God against His foe.

"My vow, alas, I could not keep,
For care of Scotland drove me full hard.
But now when body in death doth sleep,
My heart must go to where Christ made
peace."

"We'll do, good King, all that you've said,
And lay your heart where Christ made
peace."
Thankful and tearful the great king prayed,
"Now dismiss Thy servant, O Lord, in Peace.
Amen."